THE SECOND CHARLEY SCOTT MYSTERY

VANESSA WESTERMANN

For Janis—
Enjoy your escape to the lake!
Vanessa Westermann

Copyright © 2025 Vanessa Westermann
This edition copyright © 2025 Cormorant Books Inc.
This is a first edition.

No part of this publication may be reproduced, stored in a retrieval system or transmitted, in any form or by any means, without the prior written consent of the publisher or a licence from The Canadian Copyright Licensing Agency (Access Copyright). For an Access Copyright licence, visit www.accesscopyright.ca or call toll free 1.800.893.5777.

The publisher and the author expressly forbid the use of this book in any manner for the purpose of training so-called artificial intelligence systems or technologies, and reserve this title from the text and data mining exception in accordance with the European Parliament directive.

 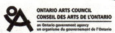

We acknowledge financial support for our publishing activities: the Government of Canada, through the Canada Book Fund and The Canada Council for the Arts; the Government of Ontario, through the Ontario Arts Council, Ontario Creates, and the Ontario Book Publishing Tax Credit.

LIBRARY AND ARCHIVES CANADA CATALOGUING IN PUBLICATION

Title: Shudder pulp / Vanessa Westermann.
Names: Westermann, Vanessa, author
Series: Westermann, Vanessa. Charley Scott mystery.
Description: Series statement: A Charley Scott mystery
Identifiers: Canadiana (print) 20250101807 | Canadiana (ebook) 20250101815 | ISBN 9781770867741 (softcover) | ISBN 9781770867918 (EPUB)
Subjects: LCGFT: Detective and mystery fiction. | LCGFT: Novels.
Classification: LCC PS8645.E7975 S58 2025 | DDC C813/.6—dc23

United States Library of Congress Control Number: 2024951788

Cover art and design: Nick Craine
Interior text design: Marijke Friesen
Manufactured by Copywell in Woodbridge,
Ontario in March 2025.

Printed using paper from a responsible and sustainable resource, including a mix of virgin fibres and recycled materials.

Printed and bound in Canada.

EU RP   eucomply OÜ
Pärnu mnt 139b-14, 11317 Tallinn, Estonia
hello@eucompliancepartner.com, +3375690241

CORMORANT BOOKS INC.
260 ISHPADINAA (SPADINA) AVENUE, SUITE 502,
TKARONTO (TORONTO), ON M5T 2E4
SUITE 110, 7068 PORTAL WAY, FERNDALE, WA 98248, USA
info@cormorantbooks.com / www.cormorantbooks.com

*For my brother Lucas,
who carves pumpkins with precision,
probably has a search engine for a brain,
and can tell a joke like a stand-up comedian.*

ONE

WHEN CHARLEY SCOTT needed a theme for her exhibit, it swam to the surface. Almost forgotten, the lake monster had been lurking in the depths of her mind for years. Now the giant serpent writhed across the thick coat of Naphthol Red. The base for acrylic waves she had yet to paint.

That local legend — a cautionary tale Grandpa had loved to recite — had stopped her from swimming out too far during summer visits to the cottage, but she'd use it now. Extract every last drop of fear. Luckily, she could walk out the gallery door and soak in the bright autumn sunshine on Main Street whenever she wanted. The equivalent of hitting pause on a horror flick for a breather and more M&Ms.

"*The Pool Where Horror Dwelt*," Charley murmured. "*Hands That Kill*." Just saying the Shudder Pulp titles out loud sent a spine-tingling buzz of adrenaline surging through her. And she'd capture that thrill, transform a chilling mystery-terror novel into an immersive art exhibit that appealed to the senses. Touch, sight, and sound.

It had to. The entry tickets to the temporary exhibit had to cover the cost of renovating the building. Structural engineers weren't cheap. If the monster didn't raise chills, her stint as curator would be over faster than she could say buckets of blood.

Oakcrest's permanent gallery would be nothing more than an unfulfilled wish, and she'd have to pack her bags.

Portable speakers amplified the slow *drip, drip, drip* of water. The groans and screeches. Tracks of recorded creature sounds set to repeat on an endless loop.

Underneath it all, the projector hummed. The shadow on the wall flicked its tail, sinuous and larger than life.

Plywood boards creaked beneath her sneakers as she stepped around Cocoa. The chocolate Labrador retriever didn't budge, her attention fixed on the door, in watchdog mode. But the door was locked, brown paper taped over the glass to stop people from peering inside.

They were safe.

As safe as could be in an empty building that, by Halloween, would be a place of terror.

Charley wiped a clammy palm down the side of her jeans, smearing Light Sap Green paint on denim.

The twisted vegetation, the disordered growth of dead spruce and maple trees, was now so dense that the blank spaces in between looked like ragged holes.

The galvanized steel tub she'd set up in the centre of the room would dare visitors to run their fingers through lake water. The light angled just right to cast reflections on the ceiling. On the walls, in the bold colours of a pulp fiction cover, the autumn glory of the Kawartha countryside blazed along the rocky shoreline of Blue Heron Lake, hinting that the things that go bump in the night lurked right here in cottage country.

But was the projected shadow terrifying enough?

Charley rubbed a finger over the tattoo on the inside of her right wrist. A dandelion, blowing in the wind. All delicate lines in pastel shades, soft as a watercolour painting.

A growl, low and humming, raised the hairs on her arms.

Cocoa faced the door, muscles tensed. A shadow loomed behind brown paper, backlit by the sun.

Passersby shouldn't be unexpected; the gallery was in a building on Main Street, in the Mews. The wooden deck formed a courtyard between the cluster of brick storefronts, in a prime spot for foot traffic. Tourists driving through town on a fall colour road trip came just to admire the gazebo and outdoor fireplace. Even in October, cottagers still made the trip to Oakcrest from Toronto on weekends to catch those last warm days of golden leaves, apples, and wood stove smoke.

Charley stretched her aching back. "It's" — she checked her watch — "four o'clock on a Saturday afternoon, people are going to be walking past —"

The door handle jiggled. One sharp, impatient twist. Cocoa's snarl dropped an octave lower.

It was probably just an after-effect of faux horror, but Charley's heart started pounding faster than before. In a voice not nearly as steady as she wanted, she called out, "Who's there?"

A fist banged against the glass. Not a polite knock. A hard rap of knuckles.

She glanced at Cocoa. "Sit."

With a warning bark, the dog lowered her rump to the hardwood floor.

Imagination working on overdrive, Charley fought back the vision of a curved blade stained with blood. She flipped the deadbolt, yanked open the door.

Laura Bouchard stood on the deck. Water dripped from the ends of her grey hair, from the sleeves of her white cotton sweater. Her red designer jeans sagged at the hem, the pricey denim smeared with dirt. Or sand? Splotches of water spread on the wooden slats around her leather boots.

"Are you all right?" Charley held on to Cocoa's collar. "What happened?"

She'd last seen Laura at the town council meeting. Newly appointed to the power generation company's board of directors, the financial advisor had stood behind the podium and faced the crowded room to present her proposal to upgrade the dam from water control to hydroelectric. The benefits and the profit. Ignoring the restless murmurs of protest. And fear.

"What" — Laura forced the word through clenched teeth — "does it look like?"

An image flashed through Charley's mind: John Everett Millais's *Ophelia*. Ophelia's face glowed with life and showed no hint of panic and despair, despite the pools of water at her stomach. The looming leaves and brush. The forget-me-nots floating around her, painted with forensic precision *en plein air*, capturing the moment just after her fall into the weeping brook. Before her muddy death. "Like you were half drowned."

"You would know." Laura shouldered her way inside, ignoring Cocoa. Water splattered the rosin paper, covering the plywood floorboards. "This is your fault."

"I'm not sure —"

"Spare me the lies." Laura stepped up to the drop cloth pinned to the wall. Too close. Her gaze flicked over the painted white pines, skimming over the high canopy of upturned branches. A wild glint in her eyes. Her face could have been painted in lead white. Her eyebrows, pencil strokes of anger. She grabbed the drop cloth. Fabric bunched.

Shock froze Charley for one pounding heartbeat. "What do you think you're doing?"

Cocoa barked, a vicious sound.

Laura's fingers twisted the fabric, staining it vermilion.

No, not a pigment. Blood.

Charley's stomach tightened. Was it Laura's blood or did it belong to someone else?

The cloth tore from the wall. A thumbtack pinged onto the floor.

Heart hammering against her ribs, she stepped between Laura and the painting, shielding her work with her body. Maybe, for once, her five-foot-four frame would be imposing. "You need to leave."

Laura glanced over her shoulder to the shadow of the monster swimming across the wall. "What you're doing here is naive."

As far as bad reviews went, that was a first. "My art?"

"Bringing the legend to everyone's attention." Laura faced her. "Raising the monster." The woman's chin trembled. But with fear or fury?

A chill slid down Charley's spine, cold as a drop of lake water. "It's inspiration."

Laura's lip curled. "It's assault."

And yet Charley felt like the one under attack. "What are you talking about?"

"The evidence is right here," Laura hissed. "I'm tougher than I look. You don't want to underestimate me. If you so much as breathe a word of this to anyone else, I will make your life a living hell."

Charley fisted her hands on her hips, anger surging. "What goes around comes around. And if you think I'm going to hide the fact that you barged in here, damaged a painting, and spewed accusations about my art, you can forget it."

"You were hoping I'd go to the cops, weren't you?"

A blast of triumphant fury aimed at her and Charley had no idea why. "Laura, whatever you think —"

"You and your sister, that journalist" — she spat the word — "can't strip away my credibility. Or drown me. Only" — she gasped — "the weak resort to violence." The words dissolved into a cough.

Laura was soaked and pale with shock. The cut on her palm was raw. Still oozing. Despite slinging accusations, she needed a doctor. Or a shot of brandy. "Look, I have a first aid kit and a towel in the —"

"Disinfectant and a Band-Aid? I'll pass." Laura clenched her fist, hiding the wound, but she couldn't hide the tremble. She'd started to shiver, the kind of teeth-chattering shake that was more than cold. "The area needs to be sealed off."

The leap from topic to topic had Charley's head swimming. "What area?"

"This." She waved a hand around the space, like the walls were covered in filth, not hours of painstaking brushwork. "All of *this*, was a scheme. A set-up." She sagged. Her back pressed against grey acrylic rocks. "Change your theme." On a wheezing breath that looked too much like Ophelia's mouth parted in mad song, Laura charged for the door. Her steps were laboured, uneven. Cocoa followed on her heels.

Laura braced a hand on the door jamb, stopping there. Another cough racked her shoulders. "Stick to flowers. Portraits."

Safe subjects? But portraits weren't safe. Not when you had to look into the deepest, darkest depths of another person's soul. "You don't want your expression immortalized in oil paint," Charley said.

Laura stepped out onto the deck, leaving the door swinging wide open. Cocoa dashed for it.

Charley's heart jumped. "Wait, watch the —"

Cocoa dashed over the deck, barking at Laura, intent on defending the gallery, maybe even the whole street.

Panic clawed at Charley. She dug in her pocket for a bribe. Anything that might get Cocoa's attention. Found only crumbs.

Not even a piece of day-old Milk-Bone.

Cocoa jumped off the deck and into the road. She barked, backing Laura toward the blue Ford Mustang parked in front of the Old General Store.

An SUV turned down Main Street, hurtling toward them at a speed way past the limit.

Adrenaline surging, Charley held up her hand to stop the car and cut in front of it. She grabbed Cocoa's collar. Closed her eyes and braced for impact.

Brakes squealed. A gust of engine fumes hit her face.

Not metal.

Charley opened one eye and saw yellow paint, a dented bumper. Bug corpses. A dragonfly's wing.

The driver leaned out the window. "Watch where you're going, eh?" He honked twice and cruised around them.

Charley stood on unsteady legs. She felt eyes watching her. Not Laura's or the irritated driver's. Someone else.

It took her a second to spot the movement in the bay window above the Old General Store. The president of the Cottage Association, Shannon Sinclair, came to the window and stared down. A witness to the near accident.

Blowing a stray curl of hair out of her eyes, heart thundering, Charley guided Cocoa back to the sidewalk.

The Mustang roared to life and crawled closer.

Laura rolled down her passenger side window. "Attack of the lake monster." Her voice, laced with sarcasm, echoed through the Mews. "You made a mistake. You have no idea who you're up against."

"Neither do you!" Charley glanced down at Cocoa. "This was not how I saw today going."

The Shudder Pulp exhibit was supposed to be immersive, but not like this.

TWO

IF THE MAYAN cocoa god required blood sacrifices, Matt had paid his debt. He had the scars to prove he'd spilled enough blood in the kitchen.

In his workroom at the back of Chocoholic's, Matt scrubbed at the chocolate that had dripped onto the counter with a cloth soaked in hot water. Hot enough to scald his fingertips. The rich, earthy scent and sweeter undertone of marshmallow filling laced the air and caught in the back of his throat.

He went through the motions, replenished stock. The selection of artisan bars had dwindled, but he'd managed to move the display around to hide that fact. The chocolate sold. The shop turned a profit. Customers came back. But there were fewer comments afterward, fewer rave reviews.

Even Charley had shot him a glance the last time she'd sampled a piece from the bowl. She hadn't said it, but he could tell what she was thinking.

The chocolate wasn't the same.

How could it be? The man who taught him how to cook — and most of life's lessons — had shown his true nature. Jeffrey had all but raised him when his dad couldn't cope, the local handyman repairing one more broken thing with kindness and recipes. Some role model he turned out to be.

Matt balled the cloth in his fist. Cocoa-stained water pooled between his knuckles and dripped onto the marble cutting board like blood.

He tossed the cloth into the sink with a splash that had the suds sloshing dangerously close to the edge.

What the hell was he going to do if he didn't get that magic back?

The sound of tempered chocolate shrinking in the molds used to be the heartbeat of the workshop, steady as a pulse. Now the chorus of crackling sounded like broken glass.

Time heals all wounds was a cliché that gave false hope. Too much time could turn the best ingredients rancid. At room temperature, chocolate confections only had a shelf life of one to two weeks. There was such a thing as waiting too long. At some point, he'd have to admit that he no longer had what it takes. And figure out who he was without it.

But not yet.

Matt released the drain, watched the water swirl away. He gave the sink one last rinse, washing away any remaining soap suds, then carefully wrung out the cloth and draped it over the tap to dry.

He grimaced at his reflection in the gleaming chrome fridge. Practiced a grin. Not great. Tried again. Better. Passable, at least.

He took his car keys from his pocket, grabbed his Ray-Ban sunglasses from the table, and pushed through the PVC strip curtains, into the shop.

The CLOSED sign already dangled in the window. The cash register slammed shut, the sound music to his ears. Hiring Beverley Callahan for part-time help was the best decision he could have made. When others were thinking of retirement and taking life at a slower pace, Beverley showed up here day after day, full of energy and fresh ideas. Yeah, he had to fight some of them, but thanks to her, he could do what he did best.

Used to do best.

He glanced over her shoulder at the End of Day tally. "How's it look today?"

She pressed her lips together, the move draining the glow from her cheeks and letting the exhaustion show through. And suddenly she looked her age. "We need to restock the burnt caramel truffles."

Right now, that was a disaster waiting to happen. "We've still got enough butterscotch truffle." How long could he keep cheating, compensating?

She jiggled her pencil, rubber eraser bouncing off the counter. "It doesn't sell as well."

But a subpar version of a popular flavour would do more harm than good.

Matt turned the cash drawer key in the lock and powered down the computer, letting the comment slide. "Ready to hit the road?"

He could drive Beverley home to the marina and still have a good thirty minutes to shower and change before Charley rang his doorbell. Hopefully the bottle of Cabernet Sauvignon would be enough to distract her when he served croque monsieurs for dinner. But it was hard to go wrong with country-style ham and aged cheddar, especially if he followed it up with breakfast in bed. And a couple other distractions that involved lingering between the sheets.

Beverley tucked the yellow pencil stub in the front pocket of her purse, then pinned him with a glance that reminded him of the way she'd studied the display case before rearranging the truffles. "Your poker face needs work."

His stomach lurched but he slid his sunglasses on and shot her a crooked grin, the dark shades a shield. "I'll stick to low-stakes games, then." He opened the door, held it for her.

She slung her beat-up purse over her shoulder. "I'm going to give you some advice. Take it or leave it."

As if he had a choice. "Okay." She didn't normally mince her words. When Beverley had something to say, she said it.

She patted his arm. "Take a vacation."

He laughed, knew it sounded forced, but there wasn't much he could do about that. Christ, maybe he didn't have a poker face. "Admit it," he kept his tone light, "you just want the shop to yourself."

"There is that." She stepped outside, onto the sidewalk. "I still think we should move the marshmallow ghosts up front."

"Replace the toffee and potato chip milk chocolates?" No way. Matt pulled the door shut, locked it. The air was dry and warm still, the kind of heat you got after the first killing frost.

"Take a few days off. It can't hurt." She led the way to his truck and swung herself up onto the passenger seat in one nimble move. Placing her purse on her lap, she folded her hands on the handle. Prim and proper as a queen. Plotting an invasion.

"I'd come back and need a map to find my way through my own shop. No, thanks." Waste his days out on the water, waiting for a fish to bite? The only solution was to get elbow deep in melted chocolate.

Matt turned on the ignition. Cracking open the window, he let the wind whip through. Maybe the breeze would kill the small talk. That or the classic rock he turned up two more notches for good measure.

The autumn sun blazed low in the sky, ricocheting off brick facades and wrought-iron railings. The quaint arts and heritage charm tourism brochures boasted about and shopkeepers happily played up with hand-lettered signs and pine cone arrangements in their windows. Overflowing baskets of chrysanthemums, colour-coded from yellow to bronze and back again.

Beverley leaned forward and, with a quick twist of her fingers, turned the volume on the radio down low. "Laura's grand plans" — it sounded closer to *schemes* — "have got me worried. Furious, even."

Matt fought the urge to reach for the volume knob. He'd lend an ear. "The marina doing all right?"

Even with the extra income Beverley earned at Chocoholic's, she and Roy scraped by in the off-season, sinking funds into maintenance and upkeep. So far, they'd kept Callahan's Blue Heron Lake Marina going, but it was a fight for survival. Not against Mother Nature but against the electronic sensors mounted on the privately owned dam. And they were losing.

"Roy worries," Beverley admitted. "I keep reminding myself, the same woman gave birth to both of them, though you wouldn't know it, the way Laura's been acting." Her fingers clenched on the purse, white knuckling. "Roy always had a soft spot for Laura, but this has gotten under his skin. Like a bad splinter."

"That you can't help worrying at." That sounded familiar. "Guess you can't choose family."

Didn't help that RBG Power Generation Company started drawdown already this fall, lowering the lake's water levels to make room for snowmelt. Roy and Beverley would have to take the dock out early, hope to get by on winter boat storage alone.

If the fall drawdown was a bare-knuckle punch, a hydroelectric dam that diverted water flow would be the bullet that killed the business.

"It's a wonder, they've stayed in each other's lives." The bitter note in her tone sounded a lot like regret. "Laura hasn't made it easy. Some years there's just a card, others, well. She always has a reason to show up again. And it's never good."

A repeating pattern? Yeah, he got that. Get let down one too many times and there was no point in hoping. Or forgiving.

Matt turned off the paved street, onto the gravel road. Past the boat launch, the sun licked flames over the surface of the lake. Fire on glass. The leaves just as hot. "You think she'll back down? After that quote from Roy in the paper —"

"Ha!" The laugh was hard and nothing like the warm chuckle Beverley normally broke into. "Not a chance. That article was a nice try but about as effective as fishing with a cork on the hook. And she'll make him pay for it. Use it to guilt-trip him into getting what she wants."

Four-ways flashed up ahead, on the opposite side of the road, heading back into town.

Beverley leaned forward and peered through the windshield. "Is that Thomas's car?"

A tan sedan. Pulled over to the side. "Looks like it." Both right wheels, front and back, sunk in the ditch. A flat tire or something worse? Cell reception could be spotty here, between the trees. "I've got a jack in the trunk." Matt pulled over. "If he has a spare tire, I can get him on the road again in no time."

"Do you need any help?"

This was why he kept having to stop her from hoisting boxes in the shop. What was it, maybe half a year since her knee surgery? Not that he'd bring that up. "I'll let you know."

Matt got out of the truck. His boots crunched over gravel and leaves, kicking up the smell of rot and dampness buried beneath all that toffee apple red.

The sun, low now, sparked off the car's roof, skating off the windows. The hazard lights blinked, a steady pulse. All four doors sealed.

No movement from inside the car.

He raised his fist to knock on the driver's side window. Knuckles an inch away from the glass, he froze.

The seat was empty.

But, on the passenger side, a prone frame hunched, slumped forward. Shit. Was he unconscious?

Only a few months ago, Thomas had a heart attack that put him in the hospital. Minor, but enough to scare the man into cutting back on the chocolate, curbing the drink. Not enough though to stop him from putting in labour on his own house. Heavy lifting, wielding a hammer, you name it, he did it. There was a word for that and stubborn wasn't it.

The guy seemed to have a death wish.

The air out here was cool, but hit with the direct sunlight, the inside of the car would heat up. He didn't even have a window cracked to let fresh air in.

Matt knocked on the glass. Hot already. He tried the door handle, gave it a tug. "Thomas, can you unlock the door?"

Somewhere nearby an animal scurried through the brush, into the trees, the rustle loud in the quiet. Probably a squirrel or a chipmunk, but it sounded four times the size.

From across the road, a steady beep signalled his truck door was ajar. Any second now, Beverley would come see for herself what had happened.

Why the hell was Thomas in the passenger seat? Was someone else driving? If so, he — or she — had vanished into thin air, without leaving a scuff mark in the gravel.

The soles of his boots skidding on loose pebbles and dirt, Matt climbed down into the ditch. The channel for winter snowmelt was deep and filled with leaves.

Beverley called, "Everything all right?"

"We'll find out."

Matt slogged through the leaves to the passenger side door, the window lower here, the car sloped at an angle. If the man didn't react, he'd call 911.

He bent and looked inside, cupping his hand to shield against the glare. Was that paper on the dash?

The man's head snapped his way. Steely, alert blue eyes met Matt's. The lock clicked down with a thud.

The door swung open, forcing him to stumble back. Branches jabbed his back.

An oversized sketchpad was rammed between Thomas's belt buckle and the glove compartment.

Blood on the paper, on his hands.

But dust red, not wet.

Pastel. That's what it was. The same colour as the leaves piled at Matt's feet. The stubby, pigmented stick clamped in Thomas's gaunt fingers, almost hidden in his awkward grip.

The man was sketching. A birch tree. A thick stump growing tubelike pores of wild crab-of-the-woods mushrooms. Moss. And animal bones, from the looks of it.

A carcass.

Thomas had switched seats to get more space to draw, using the driver's seat to rest an open box of seventy-two fine art pastel pencils, within easy reach for the detail work.

Dating Charley, Matt had gotten used to artist's ways, but this was something else.

Thomas scowled at him, the neatly trimmed white beard doing nothing to hide the sunken cheeks, thinner now than a few months ago. "What are you trying to do, scare me into another heart attack?"

"Terrify you to death? Nah. This is a rescue mission."

"Take it or leave it?"

Pretty much. The footwell around Thomas's boots was wet and streaked with mud and grit, though it looked more like sand. Silt? "Looks like you've got a flat."

"You want a medal for that observation?"

Beverley walked toward them. "Don't harp on the boy, you ungrateful old fool."

Red splotches spread up his neck. "Old?"

Thick waterproof hip waders rested on the back seat, beads of moisture still clinging to the Gore-Tex fabric. A pair of wading boots lay crumpled on the floor, heavy-duty goat-head spikes jutting out of the soles for traction on slippery rocks and algae. "Fly fishing?"

Thomas twisted around in his seat to eye Beverley's approach. "Stalking autumn."

Matt glanced at the sketch. Clawed beech trees. Bones. Still partially covered with tattered fur. Detailed enough for him to recognize the triangular face and pointed ears of a fox. "Ah — right."

"Sketching the wild requires more stealth than any fishing expedition." Thomas added another smudge of pastel, the colour of dried blood.

It was a far cry from the polished Williams Sonoma copper cookware gleam of the red foxes Matt had seen prowling through sunbeams around Charley's cottage. "Yeah, well, it's hunting season. You might want to add some orange to that outfit, to avoid getting shot." There was a reason why the hardware store, hell even the dollar store, sold orange toques and baseball caps.

He snorted. "I'd like to see the day I get mistaken for a deer."

"It might be the last thing you see," Matt murmured. Right before the bullet hit between his eyes.

"What's that?"

"Nothing."

Bev peered in the opposite window at Thomas. "Is he being stubborn?"

Thomas rolled his eyes. "I'll answer that one. Yes. With good reason."

Matt put a hand on the door frame. "Have you got a spare in the trunk?"

"CAA is on its way."

Leaves brushed Matt's shoulders as the wind shook the branches above with a bone-dry rattle.

Beverley glanced up the empty road. "Could be a while."

Thomas said, "I'm keeping busy."

Matt figured that was about all the answer they were going to get. "So that's a no, then."

Yellow incisors flashed on a smile that spread lines around the man's eyes. "No, thank you. Shut the door."

Matt shrugged. "Have it your way."

Beverley shook her head. "A few more hours out here, sealed up in that car, and he'll need a coffin, not a tow."

THREE

COCOA JUMPED OUT of the Jeep and bounded ahead of Charley, up the fieldstone path toward the cottage, straight for the corpse stretched out on their front lawn.

Charley watched her sister tug the stiff's flannel-clad arm, making it look like he was sprawling face-down in the maple leaves. Beside Meghan, a garden trowel rested on a stack of newspapers. Based on the amount of mud scuffed on Meghan's jeans and the twig tangled in her short red hair, she'd been at it a while.

"You know it's still two weeks until Halloween, right?" Charley called.

Meghan staked a Styrofoam tombstone into the ground, with a *thud* of plastic plunged into damp earth. "It's never too early to shock the neighbours."

Which were few and far between on their Fire Route now that summer was over.

Sneakers brushing through a blanket of leaves, Charley walked closer and read the inscription on the grave marker, handwritten in black permanent marker: YUL B. NEXT. "Subtle."

"That's nothing. Just wait." Hands moving as she talked, Meghan set the scene. "I'm going to dig a hole and bury a pair of rubber gloves so it looks like hands are trying to grab this guy's soccer ball head and drag him under. Then" — she brought the garden trowel's pointed blade down with a sharp move that sunk the tip in the grass — "stab him in the back. Add a splash of red paint and it'll be a graveyard smash."

Turning the 1950s lakeside cabin with its gabled roof, cherry-red shutters, and screen door into a murder scene. "Hands off my Carmine Red. I need every last drop." Run low and her Shudder Pulp exhibit would be more Kawartha countryside than *Terror Tales*.

Closer to flowers and portraits than a pulp vision of madness unleashed. And no way was she going there.

"October is not the time to skimp on gore," Meghan said. "But fine. Hoard it for your art." She reached for one of the newspapers, scrunched the front page, and shoved it down the back of the corpse's trousers.

"At least you're putting the written word to good use," Charley teased.

Meghan gave her victim's — now shapely — bottom a friendly pat. "It's my right as editor to use the print as I see fit."

"Shoving it down — Wait." Those jeans looked familiar. "Are those Alex's Levi's?"

Meghan shrugged. "He'll never notice."

"Maybe not right away." Meghan's boyfriend had other things on his mind right now. Charley glanced over at Alex's Honda, parked in the driveway. Was he buying time? Or had nerves hit, again? Maybe things would stay the same, just a little longer. "He'll piece together the clues eventually." As a cop, that skill came with the badge.

Leaves crunching, Cocoa roamed along the white picket fence, prowling closer with mischief in her eyes.

Meghan popped the corpse's flannel collar. "I found these jeans balled at the back of his closet. I doubt he even remembers owning — No!"

Canine teeth squeaked on rubber boot.

Meghan leapt to her feet. "That's not a toy!"

Cocoa yanked the Wellington off the denim leg, leaving behind a trail of newspaper stuffing.

Charley grinned. "Hey, she saw you playing with it."

Prize clamped in her mouth, Cocoa pranced a victory lap around the tombstone.

Meghan lunged, grabbed the heel, and wrestled the boot away from her. "That's mine. Bad dog."

Cocoa flung herself into a pile of leaves and rolled, paws kicked into the air, looking far from guilty.

"No messing with my crime scene," Meghan warned her.

The cottage lawn might never be the same again.

Charley picked up a wad of paper. The headline — only a week old — shot a flick of shock down her spine. "Oakcrest Doesn't Give a Dam" — Meghan's opinion piece about the damage water turbines would do to their lake, the danger the current posed to swimmers and boaters. She'd wielded her pen like a sword.

But it was the quote from Roy Callahan that drew first blood. The statement from Laura's half-brother, the owner of Callahan's marina, was indented. Dead centre of that column.

Charley had barely glanced at the article before, but now the words leaped off the page at her.

It's up to the community to take a stand against the proposed upgrade. We don't need to generate more energy than we can consume, but we do have a responsibility to protect our shorelines, and the waterfront businesses that make cottage life possible.

A call to action against his sister. And it seemed like someone had taken a stand.

Charley crumpled the newspaper. "How big of a hole are you planning to dig?"

Mischief flashed over Meghan's face, zapping the years away, so she looked closer to the edge of twelve than thirty-four. "More zombie uprising than exhumation."

Grandma Reilly would have loved it. Even sacrificed her garden for it. Then harangued them into replanting after the fun was done. "Hand over the trowel."

Brows raised, she passed it to her. "Everything okay?"

"Couldn't be better." Charley dug the blade into the dirt, churning up the earthy scent of wet soil. Dampness seeped through the knees of her jeans, but the fog was still just mist on her skin, not yet thick enough to see. "Has anything ... exciting happened?" she asked, keeping her tone casual.

"Other than Headless Nick here?" Meghan picked up the soccer ball and spun it on her finger, a blur of black and white. "All quiet." Her reporter gaze prickled hot between Charley's shoulder blades. "But it seems like your nerves are shot, sis. You're as jumpy as Alex."

Of course she'd noticed. "He hasn't been that bad." She said it as casually as she could and kept her head down.

"I'm thinking of sneaking him some of those Rescue Remedy drops."

Charley bit back a grin. "No drugging a cop, even with homeopathic remedies."

"Camomile tea?"

She pointed the trowel at Meghan. "I noticed the lavender essential oil." Not just a few drops in the closets to keep away the moths but everywhere. An aromatherapy blitz.

"I thought it couldn't hurt."

"It's a little intense." And that was putting it mildly.

Meghan grinned. "But very soothing. So, what's bothering him?"

"Beats me." Time to deflect. "We got accused of raising the lake monster today."

Meghan's focus shifted from the soccer ball, to her. "Isn't that fact, not opinion?"

"Metaphorically. But I'm talking living, breathing" — bloodthirsty — "monster." She dug deeper. The hole was probably big enough by now. A worm wriggled away, into the leaves. "Right here in Oakcrest."

"A sighting?"

Laura's voice hissed in her head. *Spare me the lies.* "Attack."

"Holy hell!" Meghan fumbled the ball. It rolled toward Cocoa, who pounced on it. "If that's true, it'll trump the 1829 sighting of Kingstie in *The Kingston Gazette* and the Belleville *Intelligencer's* 1867 article about the monster in the bay. Give me a name and contact information and I'll —"

"Get yelled at." Threatened.

Meghan propped her elbows on her knees. All sharp angles and curiosity. "Spill."

An image of a knocked-over water glass flashed through her mind. Spilled water running off the table to pool on the floor. "Laura Bouchard came by the gallery this afternoon. Soaked to the bone. She said something" — or someone — "attacked her on the water. And blamed us."

"Had she been —" Meghan mimed tipping a bottle to her mouth.

"She seemed sober." Shocked, furious, but sober.

A beat went by. Meghan shot her a glance. "You didn't —"

"No!" Charley put the trowel down. But it was worth a question. She stared her sister down. "Did you?"

"I thought about it," Meghan admitted with a shrug. "But I didn't come up with that scenario."

Who would? "Laura was furious. Told me to change the theme of the exhibit." Or else.

"As if you'd even consider that." No hesitation. Just faith, her whole heart behind it, like always.

"Exactly." The question was, who did attack Laura?

Sunlight, deepening from gold to rust, glinted off the cottage windows. "I should get cleaned up."

"For another date with the dishy chocolatier?" Meghan wriggled her eyebrows. "Things are getting serious."

A knot of tension tightened her shoulders. "Not that serious." If their relationship was a pot of melted chocolate, it was heating up on the back burner.

All because of a secret Charley chose to keep. It was one simple sentence. *Jeffrey is your father*. She just couldn't tell Matt. And every day that went by, it got harder to say.

"I'm imagining chocolate-covered strawberries." Meghan clasped her hands and fluttered her lashes. "Long, soulful gazes. Maybe even ... the *L* word?"

It didn't happen that fast. Not after just a few months. So maybe her heart flipped over at the thought. But love was dangerous. It changed everything, and made the truth that much riskier to reveal. "I'll leave you to play in the dirt."

"News flash," Meghan said. "You love him, and you know it. You're just in denial."

Nerves danced through her stomach. Charley headed up the fieldstone path. "I'm going to go say hi to your better half." She held the screen door open for Cocoa. "Tell him you stole his pants."

Meghan leapt to her feet and jammed her fists on her hips. "You wouldn't dare."

Nope. But she said, "Wanna bet?" She let the screen door slap shut on Meghan's muffled oath.

FOUR

TIRES SINKING INTO mud, Matt pulled up in front of Blue Heron Lake Marina. The grey wood siding and white trim of the dock store was well-cared for as ever. The letters spelling out *Callahan's Boat Storage and Docking*, bright as the day they'd been painted. So white, it took a while before anyone noticed the sun-faded sign for Kawartha Dairy and its four-foot pink and blue ice cream cone, sold by the scoop inside.

Canadian flags snapped on the red railing bordering the gas dock. Even on glorious days like this, the autumn lake was darker than in the summer, edging toward dangerous, and the waves steeper, churned up by a wind that had a reckless kick to it. Still, there was nothing like gunning a boat over the crests, feeling that heave, the slap as the hull hit the surface.

Of the fourteen slips, five were in use, the boats sitting low. No great white sailboats like the kind you'd find at the marina in Cobourg but fishing pontoons and towboats. The hot-rod speedboat he'd eyed back in July was already gone, along with the summer staff.

Even the unpaved parking lot was close to empty — just a blue Mustang and Roy's pickup truck, more rust than chrome now.

"Speak of the devil," Beverley said, unbuckling her seat belt. "Laura's here."

At the tone, that underlying note of worry, Matt shot her a glance. "Too late to turn back now, make a run for it. I've got a date."

"And you wouldn't want to keep Charley waiting. Just pull up here, that's fine." Face settling in grim lines, she reached for the door handle.

"Looks slippery here." All the rain in the past few days had turned the area in front of the marina, and the driveway leading up to the main house, into a mudslide. "I'll walk you to the door."

Beverley shot him a look he'd seen too many times to count. "And if you trek through the mud, the inside of your truck will be as dirty as Thomas's. I manage just fine every other day. You sit tight."

"There was a time when you used to humour me." Probably just before he stopped calling her Mrs. Callahan and switched to a first-name basis.

"I only did it for the job security." She slammed the truck door and waved at him. Shouldering her bag, she dodged a puddle, her foot skidding on sludge.

He had his hand on the door when she held up a finger in warning. "Don't you dare," she called.

Matt stayed where he was but rolled down his window. He'd leave, as soon as he heard the front door close. Hit the shower at home, then spend time with Charley. End the evening on the up side.

Waves lapped at the wooden dock, at aluminum hulls. Quiet. Peaceful.

The scream sliced through that tranquil moment like a hot knife through chocolate.

FIVE

JUST ENOUGH JUMP scares to get the adrenaline going. That was the kind of classic horror movie Charley wanted to find for tonight. Cheesy, spooky fun. If she got changed fast enough, she'd still have time to browse streaming platforms to find the perfect flick. Add some chocolate, some popcorn. Matt's arm wrapped tight around her, tensing as he tried not to jolt. Though he always did. All the makings of a perfect evening.

Charley breathed in the cottage scent of stacked logs and paperback books. Reached to hit the wall switch, to flood the room with light.

No. She stopped herself. Tightened her fingers into a fist. And took a breath.

The sunlight splashing over the exposed wood walls was fading fast, but the living room wasn't dark yet. The lamps — one on the end table and one standing by the wood stove — marked out a glowing path to the sliding doors. Even though the view of the lake through the glass seemed primed in the brown of a Tom Thomson painting, it was still visible, right down to the vivid reflections of maple and pine on white-shot waves.

It was the vase of clipped branches on the coffee table that slowed her step. A reminder of Thanksgiving and how well that family visit had gone. The bruises were still fresh from the barrage of questions she hadn't fielded well. *How long will this last?* She still didn't have an answer to that one.

Hopefully forever.

Mom's stories of the struggling artists who'd paid her accounting fees with paintings instead of cash didn't help. Meant as cautionary tales, but those "payments" Mom used as a warning had turned their dining room into a gallery wall Charley had loved.

For now, doom and gloom could wait.

Charley's phone buzzed in her pocket. She checked the screen. A new message from Matt. Her heart leapt. Already smiling, she opened the app.

Got a situation. Rain check on dinner? I'll make it up to you xxx

She'd wanted to see him, talk over what happened in the gallery, get his take on it. But it had to be bad for him to cancel at the last minute.

She typed back, *Tempering machines misbehaving?*

Cocoa stood in the entrance, wagging her tail, waiting for the promised car ride. Charley would have to break the news to her, then deal with a sulky dog for the rest of the night.

But her phone didn't buzz with a reply. No quick response to make her laugh. Just a blank screen without even three dots to show he was typing.

She wrote, *If you need a taste tester or an extra pair of hands, let me know.*

Hopefully Matt just got held up, trying out a new recipe. Absorbed by chocolate, not his own demons.

Charley backtracked to the kitchen. She pushed open the door. The yelp of shock stopped her short.

"Not yet!" Alex had his back to the fridge, fist clenched around something in his hand. Then he saw her, and his shoulders sagged. "Oh, it's you."

Who knew a proposal could make a man so nervous? At this point, Alex was looking rough around the edges. Less squeaky-clean cop and more street thug who'd earned his crooked nose in a bare-knuckle fight. The five o'clock shadow could have been prep for undercover work, not overtime put in at a desk. "Meghan's still outside, arranging the dead body." The setting sun turned the view of the lake out the window into a picture-perfect backdrop for a romantic scene.

"Good." Alex rubbed a hand over the back of his neck. His T-shirt caught on a bulge at his waistband.

Charley smiled. "You might want to lose the Glock before you pop the question."

He glanced down at the firearm and frowned. "You think?"

"It's an idea." A paper bag from the LCBO rested on the table. She snuck a peak. Champagne. Veuve Clicquot. "Nice choice."

"You know Megs. She's going to want a story with a capital S. I'm still not sure this is it." Alex scanned the kitchen, as if he might find inspiration in the Hoosier cabinets, instead of Pyrex bowls and Depression-era glass. Or maybe he was just considering stress eating the bag of all-dressed chips still lying open on the counter.

And no wonder. The pressure was on. Meghan collected stories like keepsakes. "What's the plan?"

Alex jerked a thumb at the fridge.

The old fridge magnets? Faded and worse for wear. No. In between the grinning Granny Smith apple, the dancing bacon and eggs, were strips of text, black on white.

WILL MARRY ME.

She smiled. "I think you missed a word."

He opened his hand, peeled the magnet off his palm. His skin looked clammy. "Four words." He stuck the YOU on the fridge, pushed the tiles around so that they formed a complete sentence.

"The Charter rights are longer, and I can recite those, while snapping on cuffs."

"You're proposing to her, not arresting her." Although he would be detaining her for life. But that wasn't fair. Think like that and Charley would never be able to celebrate when the moment came. "You're going to have to drag Meghan away from that tombstone, to get her in here."

Alex stared at the magnets, looking pale around the gills. "Or you could just ask her for me."

She opened the fridge and scrounged for the Tupperware container of leftover turkey slices and cranberry sauce. Cocoa sat at her feet, eyeing the food not with hope but certainty. Oh, who was Charley kidding? She'd probably give Cocoa two. But the sandwich, that was off limits. "You can't call in backup for a proposal."

"A tactical squad might —" A ringtone sounded. The Batman theme song. "Shit." Alex dug his phone out of his pocket and answered. "Yeah?" His brows shot up as he listened. "Callahan's Marina?" He frowned. "Who found her?"

A chill spread through Charley. *Found her*. That could only mean one thing.

Alex turned to the fridge, pocketed the text magnets, one by one. "I'll be there in fifteen." He hung up the call. "Hide the champagne for me?"

"What happened?" Charley slid the bottle into the bottom cupboard, behind Alex's whole wheat granola and Cocoa's bag of dog food. Safe as a vault. She closed the door and straightened.

Meghan strolled into the kitchen. "Our cottage is officially haunt-worthy." She stopped short and shot them both a look. "What's going on? Did you eat the last of the pumpkin pie?"

Charley held up the Tupperware. "Turkey."

Meghan narrowed her eyes at Alex. "Why do you look so guilty?"

He squared his shoulders. A defensive move, better suited to a confrontation with an armed suspect. "I'm going to have to miss dinner. A case came up."

Meghan cocked her head. "Petty crime? Theft?"

Charley scanned Alex's face. She'd seen that grim expression before, just once. "Murder?"

A muscle jumped in his jaw. He shot a glance at Meghan and away. "I don't know anything yet."

Meghan took Alex's car key off the hook on the wall, held it out to him. "Who died?"

He cautiously took the key dangling from her fingers. "Laura Bouchard."

The steady *drip, drip, drip* of water echoed in Charley's mind, along with Laura's words. *Only the weak resort to violence.* "At the marina?" Had she left the gallery and gone straight there?

Meghan grabbed the spiral-bound notebook she'd left lying on the counter. "I call shotgun."

Alex's frown bordered between frustration and exasperation. "This isn't a group event."

Meghan crossed her arms, her stance the same as when they'd bickered about who left the wet towels lying on the bathroom floor. And she'd won that round. "You've got a badge, but so do I."

Alex pushed the kitchen door open with the flat of his hand. "Mine says *police*."

And all that meant was that he had handcuffs and backup when things went wrong. Charley gritted her teeth and followed. "Hold on —"

Alex shrugged into his leather jacket. "I don't have time to discuss this."

She caught the screen door before it slammed shut behind him. "Just listen for one —"

He unlocked his Honda. "I'll fill you in when I get back."

"But —"

He slammed the car door and gunned the engine.

Meghan came to stand on the front step and watched him back out onto the road. "So, the marina?"

Something happened to Laura. Something Charley could have prevented. Should have acted on, if she'd just listened. "I'm driving."

"Fine by me."

Laura's voice rang through Charley's mind, clear as a bell. *You made a mistake.*

It sounded like a threat.

But maybe it was a warning.

SIX

THE JEEP'S ENGINE rumbled with a low-level roar. Clouds hung heavy in a starless sky. The gathering dusk closed in around the headlights. Fog, thicker now, slithered over gravel.

"Laura got attacked," Charley said. "And now she's dead." Adrenaline and guilt spiked her pulse.

The last time she drove to a crime scene with Meghan, they ended up knee-deep in questions and secrets. And come out on the other side scarred.

Meghan opened her notebook to a fresh page, pen scratching as she scribbled a title in between potholes. "I get the cause-and-effect theory, but you missed one minor detail. Laura survived. Seems to me that fail once and try, try again is a risky approach to murder."

Risky to some was a challenge to others. "Depends on how determined the killer is."

The Jeep bounced off the road, juddering over uneven ground, toward the marina. The headlights picked up a driveway, glinted off corrugated metal — the limbs of a Tin Man, pieced together from recycled cans and strung from a tree. More swung from the branches. A hobby turned cottage industry and a recognizable landmark, even in the dark. They were close.

Charley slowed, fingers tightening on the wheel. There. The sign appeared ahead. *Callahan's Boat Storage and Docking*. She turned into the unpaved lot.

Alex's Honda was parked out front. Beside Matt's truck.

Got a situation now seemed like an understatement.

Meghan leaned forward. "What's Matt doing here?"

"Your guess is as good as mine." The cryptic message wasn't much to go on. Worry settled in the pit of her stomach.

Meghan clicked her ballpoint pen, locking the ink cartridge into the barrel the same way others released the safety on a gun. "Let's go collect some facts."

Charley parked her Jeep in a space pitted and pockmarked and nearly buried beneath the leaves. "Don't slam" — the sound ricocheted before she finished the sentence — "the door."

So much for a subtle entrance.

Meghan grimaced. "Oops."

A breeze whipped off the lake, chasing chills over Charley's skin, bringing with it the kind of damp that seeped through flesh straight to bone. The faint smell of motor oil. Her sneakers sunk in the mud, like the earth itself was trying to slow them down. Or drag them under.

Meghan hunched into her jacket as they walked around the dock store, toward the water. "I always loved coming here with Grandpa to buy worms."

Five-inch night crawlers, a wriggling mass in opaque plastic containers. Stocked close enough to the wire rack of twenty-five cent Nancy Drew mysteries for her to slip away and browse. "I remember the waffle cones and chocolate ice cream. Double scoops."

"Callahan scoops," they said at the same time.

Scoops so big, the ice cream dripped down her arm before her teeth could scrape the cone.

Since then, the Callahans had renovated the dock store. Added windows and sills for boaters to pay their fees at. Safeguarded the siding with stain. The name above the door bright and white and hopeful.

In the distance, up the dirt path, the Callahans' stone-blue clapboard house loomed, the colour of water, right before a storm.

Matt stood to the side of the track, near the oak trees. Back to them, hands dug in his pockets. Alex was beside him, taking notes. And then there was Roy. In his late sixties, windburn and UV rays had given him a rugged hardiness, despite the receding hairline and salt and pepper moustache. But grief had drained his tan to a sallow pallor.

The three men stood over a tangle of clothes.

The body. Laura.

But there was no flash of burgundy red or white. Instead, denim and brown wool blended with the dirt, the long grass. The fog blanketing her feet. At rest, but maybe not at peace.

Pebbles crunched as they walked closer.

Alex glanced over his shoulder toward them. Not so much as a blink of surprise to show they'd caught him off guard. "There's probably no point in asking you to wait in the car."

Charley shrugged. "You can ask."

Matt met her gaze and that quick connection chased away some of the cold. "Be a waste of time, if you ask me."

Meghan nodded. "And every minute counts in the early stages of an investigation, right?"

Alex opened his mouth. Seemed to think better of it and closed it again. On a long exhale, he said, "Right." He turned back to the woman, lying on the ground. "Did anyone move or touch her?"

"I —" Roy blinked, looked around as though searching for the answer in the fog. "I don't know."

Matt shook his head. "Beverley checked her pulse. That's it." The shock of the find was still easy to read in his eyes.

Laura lay on her back, one arm flung out, palm up. A bandage carefully taped over the cut. Her face was turned to the sky. She stared up in surprise. Dirt stained her side, but her makeup was pristine. Freshly applied. Carefully blended and showing none of the signs that she'd rushed over it or smudged it on with her fingers. Her hair was dry, not wet. The ends curled, blow-dried over a brush.

There was no blood.

Not on the ground. Not on her.

No bruises. No obvious injuries. Only shock. And dirt.

Laura went home, got changed, fixed her makeup, and — what? Came here?

To die.

Goosebumps prickled over Charley's skin. "I saw Laura today."

Roy jerked as though the words carried an electric current.

Alex shot her a look. "You kept that to yourself?"

Charley frowned. "I tried to tell you."

Meghan said, "You didn't listen."

"Next time, try harder." Alex thumbed to the next blank page of his notebook. "Where?"

The realization that her exhibit was about to become a footnote in a police report settled between Charley's ribs. "She came to the gallery. Around four o'clock."

Roy frowned. "Why?"

To blame. Argue. Accuse. "She wasn't happy with the exhibit." And that was an understatement.

Roy shifted his weight as though land had turned to water under his feet. "That doesn't sound like Laura. She couldn't care less about art."

That much was obvious. "She said someone tried to scare her into leaving." And she'd sent the woman away. All but kicked her out.

Roy shook his head. "Nothing scares Laura." Regret moved across his face. "Scared her."

But there had been fear in Laura's eyes, in her voice. "This did. She was attacked. In the water."

"And she didn't have a run-in with a pike," Meghan added.

Matt glanced toward the docked boats. "You don't mean the —"

"Lake monster?" Charley asked. She couldn't believe she was saying the words out loud. "Yeah, I do." She wished she didn't.

A beat of silence went by, filled with the crash of waves.

"Yours?" Matt asked.

Hers. As if she'd staked a claim on the monster. And caused this. Maybe she had. "Laura's clothes were soaked. She was wearing red jeans and a white sweater. And her hair was wet."

"So," Alex said slowly, "Laura went home. Then came here."

At the end of the gas dock, the Petro-Canada sign rattled on its metal pole. The shadow ghosted over the pump and the white wrought-iron bench, settling in the cracks riddling the concrete dock, deepening them, like the concrete might break apart at any second.

Roy bristled. "What does that have to do with her —" He swallowed. "With this?" He gestured at Laura.

Maybe everything. The marina looked scraped and worn, but loved with the kind of ferocious, cling-to-it-for-all-you're-worth intensity you gave to something precious as it was slipping through your fingers. "She said someone — or something — tried to drown her."

"Yeah, well," Roy said, "right now she's on dry land."

Alex asked, "Did she have any heart trouble?"

Roy shrugged, a helpless, frustrated lift of his shoulders. "You think she'd tell me, if she had health problems?"

Shutting him out or just standing on her own?

Matt said, "She's been under a lot of stress lately."

The woman Charley saw in the gallery had been pushed to her

limits, but not by stress.

Roy's mouth tightened. "She didn't run herself into the grave. She had family to lean on."

Family who gave a statement to the local paper condemning her actions. Charley asked, "How did you feel about Laura moving to Oakcrest?"

Roy stepped back. One small move away from the body. A wary expression crossed his face. "Wasn't none of my business."

"But you were worried," Meghan said in a casual tone, "about Laura's proposal for the dam."

Roy's head snapped up at that. "I gave my quote to the paper, had my say. Blood counts."

Matt went still, a guarded look in his eyes. "Did Laura know that?"

"'Course she did." That was a little bit too fast. Too urgent.

Alex tapped his pen on his notebook. "Those scratches on Laura's hands. Could be she cut herself on a rock or a mussel."

Nestled under layers of sand and sharp enough to slice bare feet. Or a hand reaching out, searching for a hold. Charley said, "The wound was fresh when I saw her." Bleeding. Red on green paint.

Alex said, "We won't know anything for sure until the coroner examines her."

Roy flexed calloused fingers. "Is that necessary?"

"To determine the cause of death, yes." Alex stepped forward, toward the body sprawled at the edge of the dirt track.

Roy moved into his path, blocking him from Laura. "So, pull her medical records."

A wave slapped against aluminum, hollow and empty.

"I know it's difficult," Alex said, his voice calm. Reasonable. "But I need you to move aside."

Roy tightened one weathered hand into a fist.

More than a shield. The first line of defence.

How would she feel if it was Meghan? Protective, still. More now than ever before. "It's the only way to get answers."

Roy's shoulders stiffened. He looked about to argue, but fell back instead. "She'd want to be treated right, with respect."

Was it just brotherly instinct? Or was there a reason why Roy didn't want her body examined?

"We'll take care of her. You have my word on that." Alex squatted beside the woman, leaning down as though to listen. For a secret, whispered by the dead. "Was she coming or going?"

Roy glanced up the path. "I reckon" — voice gone rough, he cleared his throat — "she was heading toward the house."

To family. For help? Charley asked, "Did you see her or talk to her?"

A flicker of guilt crossed the man's face. "No."

"Any idea why she came here tonight?" Alex's tone was casual. But Charley had heard him use that same technique before. Play it down. Ease back.

"To visit." On the defensive now, Roy asked, "Why else?"

To search for safety, which she hadn't found. "Did Laura do that often, drop by like this, unannounced?"

"Once in a while." Roy's gaze evaded hers, dropped to the ground, and settled on his boot.

Matt studied him. "When did you last talk to her?"

"Thanksgiving."

A few days ago. And they hadn't spoken since. Why?

A beam of fading light caught on the rose-gold mesh of Laura's watch, the band too wide, too large for her wrist. A statement piece. Expensive. The watch face was foggy. "There's moisture inside her watch."

"What does that matter?" Roy sounded close to losing his patience.

"It means," Charley said, "she was deep enough in the water to submerge it." More proof Laura hadn't gone willingly into the lake. "Wouldn't she wear something waterproof, if she was going canoeing?"

Roy dug his hands in his pockets. "She didn't get dragged off the dock by some prehistoric sturgeon, if that's what you're thinking. There is no monster."

"Maybe not one with scales." Even if the creature didn't exist, the story lived and breathed. "There've been sightings, rumours for years —"

"Twenty-five or twenty-six of 'em." Roy nodded. "But those rumours started with a prank."

Shock whipped through her. She'd done her research. She should have heard a whisper of that. And she hadn't. "A practical joke?"

Alex straightened. "Go on."

Roy shrugged. "There's not much to tell. Way back then, I rented a cabin here on Blue Heron Lake for Thanksgiving weekend. I invited Laura to join us, get her involved in my family."

His family. Not hers. "She came to Oakcrest?"

"Just the one weekend. She and the other cousins were in their twenties." Roy ran a hand over his moustache. "Probably shoulda kept my eye on them better. One of 'em had a CD with Halloween sound effects. You know the kind. Creaks and groans. Screams to make your hair stand on end. Laura stuck strips of green garbage bag on a wetsuit, made tentacles. Late one night, they took a boom box down to the water's edge. Laura hid behind a rock."

"Where was this?" Alex asked.

"Couldn't say. Close enough to shore to terrify the living daylights out of some kid. Mind you, I didn't know it at the time," Roy said. "I only found out when talk of the exhibit got out. Laura was pleased as punch, she started a local legend."

But she was furious about the exhibit's theme today, weeks after the posters first went up. Why did Laura wait, only come to her now? "But she accused me of raising the monster." When she'd brought it into Oakcrest, all along. It didn't make sense. None of it did.

Meghan tugged her jacket closer around her. "Fear always evolves from a lie."

"Practical joke," Roy corrected. "And she grew out of those, 'bout the same time she realized she could make a living from numbers and a good one at that. She liked things that add up, make sense. Monsters don't. She didn't believe in them. Never did."

"Who was the kid?" Meghan asked.

A cottager, here one summer and gone the next?

Roy shrugged. "I tried to find that out. Grilled those fools good too, once I heard what they got up to under my watch. But a quarter century on, the best I got out of them was that the kid ran like the devil himself was after him. Hightailed it out of there."

"Never to be seen again?"

Charley lifted a brow, knowing what Meghan was getting at. "You think he took revenge?"

Matt didn't tense but she sensed the shift in him, the uneasiness.

Alex held his hands up. "No one said anything about revenge. Or murder." The word dropped into the silence like a pebble down a deep well.

"But someone attacked her," Charley said. He couldn't argue that.

Sirens sounded in the distance.

Beverley came toward them from the house. She'd pulled a windbreaker on, one of Roy's from the size of it. Her good-humoured face was lined and drawn. Her eyes, dry. "Coffee's hot," she said. "Mugs are on the counter. If you're done watching

Alex work, you can come inside, warm yourself up with a cup of java. And fill me in."

Charley waited for Alex to shoot a glance at her or at Meghan, for the silent exchange, the nod to collect intel. But Alex's focus stayed on Laura.

"We'd love a cup," Charley said.

Matt shifted. His face in profile was hard to read. "So long as it's not too much trouble."

"Trouble?" Beverley repeated. "Leave without telling me what you've been talking about here and you'll know what trouble is." She touched her husband's arm. "Let the man do his job. There's nothing else we can do for her."

But that wasn't true. They could find out what happened.

SEVEN

WALKING INTO THE Callahans' kitchen, Charley caught the scent of stew, of beef and rosemary and orange peel, and a burned undertone of boiled and blackened tomatoes, even though the pot was off the gas burner and the ceiling fan whirred.

The pine trestle dining table in the centre of the room was set for two. They hadn't been expecting company.

Roy went to the window and looked out, over the wooden boards of the deck, toward the closed dock store. The darkness swallowed the wavering beams of light where Laura lay. "I let her down."

Beverley passed a blue enamel mug to Matt and one to Meghan. She filled a third to the brim and took it to Roy. "Stuff and nonsense. You know how Laura was. She always handled her own problems."

Roy held his cup absently, the handle dwarfed by his weathered hand. "Always has, since she was old enough to tie her own shoelaces."

Meghan took a chair at the table and dropped her purse on the floor. A red notebook popped between the teeth of the zipper. "Determined and independent at the age of five?"

"And stubborn long before that."

Driven by a need to prove herself, or by the fact that she didn't have anyone else to turn to? Charley asked, "She never came to you for help?"

"Once." No hesitation. No pause to think about the answer. Roy settled in the chair beside Beverley's but shot another restless glance out the window. "And even then, I was just the chauffeur."

One mug rested on the counter. Charley reached for the pot, lighter now, and poured a quarter cup. The last drops splashed in. Empty. She'd just add extra cream, make it look like more.

Beverley cleared the placemats, porcelain clinking as she stacked the plates, one on the other. Matt moved to help. She shot him an impatient glance.

He backed down with a sigh, sat instead. "What happened?"

"She wanted me to take her trick-or-treating. Begged." Roy smiled. At the memory? Or the fact that his half-sister had begged for help? "Our mother waitressed long hours that drained her time and energy. I offered to drive out, take Laura. When I got there, she was running a fever of a hundred and one. Burning up. She wanted to go anyway. I couldn't talk her out of walking that block. She wouldn't even let me carry the damn bag of candy for her."

Matt paused, coffee cup halfway to his mouth, and grinned. "She did it for the chocolate."

An emotion flickered across Roy's face. Something bitter and hard and gone in a flash.

"For the Mars bars and Tootsie Rolls." Beverley reached for the porcelain bowl in the centre of the table, took off the lid. "Sugar's here. Help yourselves."

Charley perched on a stool at the corner of the table. A seam ran down the centre of the pine surface. Extendable. If family came by, all Roy and Beverley had to do was add a leaf, pull up more chairs. But that required planning. It didn't allow for unannounced guests, not for dinner. To be welcomed into that kitchen, you had to be invited. "What did Laura want to be? For Halloween?"

"Some superhero." Roy shrugged.

Matt set his cup down on the placemat. "Out to save the world?"

Roy shook his head. "Invincible. That's all she ever wanted to be."

Too powerful to defeat? Or just safe from harm? "A masked crusader?" Charley asked. "Or a supernatural goddess?"

"Nothing copped from a comic book. She did things her own way."

Beverley closed her hand over her husband's and squeezed. "A trailblazer through and through." The sentence was bitter, but the tone wasn't.

Roy turned his hand over to twine his fingers through hers. "Never afraid of anything or anyone."

But you didn't wish to become invincible, if you had nothing to fear. Charley asked, "Did Laura keep a boat here?"

Roy shook his head. "She had a canoe she kept at her own dock."

Meghan glanced down at her notebook but didn't reach for it. "Was she a strong swimmer?"

Roy's gaze turned distant, inward. "Yeah, she could swim." He blinked, shook his head. "But in these temperatures, she wouldn't dip a toe in the water."

Not by choice. Not willingly. A shiver ran down Charley's spine. "It took guts, to push that proposal for the dam." Even when she found out how unpopular the idea was.

"Stubborn," Roy said, "that was her all right."

Beverley gave a wry smile. "Like someone else I know."

Roy shook his head. "No. Once Laura got something into her

head, she wouldn't let it go. No matter what. That's a different kind of stubborn." Unbridled judgment in his tone.

Matt shifted in his seat. "Some people can't back down from a challenge."

Roy nodded. "Nothing was worth doing, if it didn't earn her a couple enemies along the way."

Meghan raised a brow. "So, the town council meeting was successful then."

Beverley stirred her coffee, spreading ripples. "Wildly."

The meeting room had been packed. Even with the extra folding chairs, people had stood in the back, arms crossed and staring. Laura had gotten up and faced them.

Roy's mouth tightened in a hard line. "David could have saved his breath. A threat or two weren't going to stop her."

For a normally level-headed teacher, David had lost his cool, but he hadn't threatened her. He'd quoted facts, statistics, used persuasive techniques, and manipulated the room like his audience had been just another class of antsy second graders. The urgency built as he hit his main point: *Profit can turn maximum power production into a higher priority than water conservation or even public safety. There have already been six deaths in the past twenty-five years linked to the dam. That's not a coincidence. That's a warning that's been ignored long enough. Add water turbines to the mix and someone else will die.* "He wasn't threatening Laura, when he said someone would die."

"Not then," Roy said. "After. He cornered her as we were leaving. Took it further."

A cold wave washed over Charley. How well did Kayla know the man she'd started dating? During childhood summers at the cottage, she and Kayla had been the closest of friends, through thick and thin, but that was a long time ago. Back then, Charley could have asked her about David without worrying the questions might be seen as a sign of betrayal. But things had changed. Kayla was finding her identity as a widow and as the town's community events coordinator. Even though she was using her maiden name, Siku, and advocating for the arts, parts of the past hadn't yet found a place in her new life — like the trust they'd once shared.

Matt leaned forward. "David cornered Laura, intentionally?"

"Seemed like it."

"Maybe you misunderstood," Charley said. A tone could be misinterpreted, twisted.

Beverley raised one brow. "He told Laura that pushing the upgrade to the dam was a mistake."

Roy shook his head. "A risk. That's what he called it. And not just to the community. But to her personally, if she continued."

It was still too vague, too open to interpretation. "Do you remember what he said? How he said it?"

Roy's mouth twisted. He spoke the words, loud and clear, "That Laura's death would be a small loss, if it meant saving the life of a child."

A cold comment. But something David might say. And mean. "He'll regret that now."

"I hope so. Either way, he got his wish." Roy looked at Beverley. "Knowing when to quit, that was one thing Laura never learned."

Charley shivered. An inability to let things go — it sounded too much like a fatal flaw.

EIGHT

LOOKING AT CORPSES, talking about monsters, it wasn't how Matt imagined they'd spend the evening. Some discussion about supernatural creatures, he would have bet on, but facing death, that hadn't been on the plan. Not again.

Matt braced himself against the gust of cold wind as he followed Charley and Meghan out of the house. He ducked under the antique maritime bell hanging by the door — the Callahans' version of a doorbell. What had Beverley told him? *The ship's bell was maintained by the cook. The passing of time measured by the trickle of sand through a half hourglass, marked by the sounding of the bell. A signal and a warning, to guide vessels through the fog. Eight bells meant all's well.*

Or that a sailor had died.

In the distance, in the stark bright crime scene lights, a flicker of yellow caught Matt's eye. Caution tape, recognizable even from here. Beverley and Roy had one hell of a night ahead of them.

Charley stopped on the path, like she was sketching that picture in her mind. "It's like a Shudder Pulp cover." It took him a second to recognize the undertone to her voice. Fear.

"We've even got the monster." Meghan slid her ballpoint pen in her jacket pocket. "I'll have to post an update to *The Oakcrest Courier*'s social media page ASAP."

Soon as the news broke, Roy and Beverley would be fielding questions left, right, and centre. Hell, if anyone found out that they had been here, they would be, too. "It can't wait?" Matt asked.

Meghan said, "Not with this location."

She was right. Even in October, people would come by the marina, take their boats out for early fishing, catch the autumn sunrise in all its glory. And that damned yellow tape would be visible from the water.

He'd have to be ready for the customers coming into Chocoholic's, browsing the chocolates as an excuse to pry for intel. And shield the Callahans from it, best he could. "At least, we'll get ahead of the rumours."

"With these facts?" Meghan said. "Good luck with that."

"Facts?" Charley asked. "All we've got so far are questions."

Meghan grinned, a flash of white teeth in the dark. "But everyone loves a good mystery." She trudged ahead.

Matt slowed, putting a couple steps between them and her. He murmured to Charley, "You don't think this was an accident."

She glanced up at him, worry and more in her eyes. "Do you?" Her voice was tight with tension.

The right answer, the safe answer, would be *yes*. But he'd be lying. "No."

Somewhere a hull squeaked on a rubber dock fender. Water crashed against wood.

Charley's shoulders stiffened. "Accidents don't normally come with motives."

It might just be coincidence. But she was right. His instinct told him there was more to it than that.

Meghan half turned back and looked at them over her shoulder. "You two can keep spinning your wheels on what-ifs, but I'm going home. Wait for Alex to get back with more info."

Charley fished her car keys out of her pocket. "I should let Cocoa out."

Matt gave it a beat. "Guess I'll just drive home. Alone." He heaved a sigh, playing it up. "Wait to read about it in the paper."

Charley stopped by her Jeep, a smile chasing away some of the guilt from her eyes. "Matt, would you like to come wait with us?"

He pretended to mull it over. "Well, I don't know. I'm kind of busy."

"Okay, then." Charley yanked open the driver's side door with a creak of rusted hinges.

Shit. "Yes." He caught the door fast before it closed. "I want to come."

"Couldn't tell." The teasing was a front, he knew. A tough facade, but he took it as a good sign.

Meghan climbed into the passenger seat, buckled her seat belt with a snap. "Not so fast. You don't get in on the intel for free. I'm thinking, hot chocolate."

Charley quirked a brow. "Now that's an idea."

He'd exchanged chocolate for information before. He could do it again. "I think I can manage that. I'll follow behind you."

Meghan leaned over the console. "This time, try to be quiet when you leave at that godawful hour in the morning. Wake me up, and you're dead meat."

"Noted." Only a fool would face off with Meghan before her first cup of coffee.

Charley started the engine. "A-splishing and a-splashing" burst from the radio. A recorded gurgle of water. Fast, she reached over, twisted the volume down.

Bobby Darin whispered, "Good golly."

Not a bad reaction to what went down today.

Matt kept his hand on the car door, waited for Charley to meet his eyes. "You didn't attack her."

Her gaze slid away from his. She looked out the windshield, toward the red railing lining the waterway. "Whatever happened to Laura, she was convinced I had something to do with it."

And now Charley was, too. "That's not on you." But it would take more than that to chase away the haunted look in her eyes.

Meghan turned the volume up again, catching Darin reeling with a feeling. "Don't kid yourself. Prank or not, that lake monster was already here."

NINE

"I'm not making hot chocolate with that." Matt eyed the value-sized tin of quick mix on the kitchen counter. At his feet, Cocoa twitched her ears.

"It's all we've got." Charley rummaged in the hanging cupboard above the sink, pulled down a twenty-four-ounce glass mason jar.

"But —" Matt opened the fridge, checked the shelf on the door. A container of cream cheese. Strawberry jam, green relish. Aerosol cream. Not exactly fresh whipping cream but better than nothing. He grabbed the spray can. "Where's that bar of bittersweet chocolate I gave you the other day?"

Charley reached past him for the carton of two percent Kawartha Dairy milk, arm brushing his. "You're kidding, right? That's long gone."

The cottage kitchen hit the sweet spot between being functional and preserving the past. Full of memories of meals cooked with love. But the pantry shelves, the fridge, could be better stocked. Although who was he to judge? His own shelves were looking just as bare and he hadn't hit the farmer's market in weeks. "What about cocoa powder?" He could work with that, at least.

"Only if you want to go to the grocery store." Charley poured milk into the glass jar. "Zap this in the microwave and shake it until it's frothy."

"I can't even —" Matt shook his head, then muttered, "You're supposed to heat milk in a saucepan, on the stove."

"Next time."

Resigned, he spooned powder into the jar and set the timer on the microwave. "This never leaves the cottage."

She smiled. "It'll be our secret."

"I trust you. I'm not so sure about Meghan."

"She won't print it in the paper."

But laptop keys clicking at high speed in the living room had become a familiar sound by now. He'd believe it when he saw it.

Charley leaned back against the counter, wearing that same far-off look as when she'd been planning the exhibit. Only this time, it was more brooding than daydreaming, and no wonder.

They had sixty seconds before the microwave stopped humming. Going on impulse, needing the contact, he took her hand in his, tugged her closer. Not for that flash fire burn of desire but just to touch. Run his hands up and down her back. Hold her and drive away the memory of a woman, lying dead and alone in the fog.

Charley laid her head on his chest. "Do you think Laura had any regrets?"

He breathed in the familiar honey and cassis scent that was all her and tried to imagine anyone going through life without one mistake. Something they wished they'd done differently. "Death and regret go hand in hand. Unless you don't care what kind of memory you leave behind." Some didn't. Sacrificed that in a misguided attempt to get ahead.

"I think Laura cared, a lot."

That put a twist on things. Then again, Charley saw more than others. Curiosity caught at him. That familiar tug he'd felt once before. And look where that got him. "How do you figure that?" Laura didn't try to win anyone over.

"The designer clothes. The way she spoke, loud and commanding. The way she walked into a room. It was all about making an impression. Claiming power."

Laura had tried it on him, too, when she'd shelled out a cool hundred bucks for chocolate bars he doubted she'd even planned on eating, right before the town council meeting. But — "You only have power if others bow to it."

The rhythm of Charley's heart kicked up. He felt the change a second before she pulled away and looked at him with a glint in her eye he recognized. "She was in the process of getting the whole town to bow to her."

He knew what she was getting at. "Someone fought back."

"And won."

Another murder. How the hell did he feel about that?

The microwave beeped. Cocoa stood and wagged her tail. Way too eager.

The microwave meant food. That figured.

Matt pulled back. "Your pal there just outed your cooking skills."

Charley squatted and rubbed Cocoa's ears. "The B&B lounge makes a mean takeout. And we like to support local."

"Uh-huh."

Matt took the milk out. Flecks floated on the surface. They'd have to stir. A lot.

He poured the chocolate-flavoured milk into the thick mugs Charley had set out. The scent rising with the steam didn't have the same roasted intensity of chocolate but just enough of it to trigger a memory. Of snow days and Lego skyscrapers built in the basement.

Life was short. Why waste a minute of it? "If we could figure out what happened to Laura before she came to the gallery —"

"We'd know what she saw in the water. We'd solve one mystery."

It was a stretch to think they might be able to do that. But it was hard to argue, when that smile lit her face. Finally, true and straight from the heart. The kind he regularly counted as the highlight of his day.

Charley sprayed a thick swirl of whipped cream on each drink.

Too bad they couldn't top it with curls of bittersweet chocolate. Or at least a dusting of cocoa powder. "We'd have to collect evidence," Matt said.

"Hunt down clues." Charley opened a drawer and took out three meat skewers. "Chase a monster."

Matt fought the urge to step back, away from the dangerous ends. "And skewer it?"

"No." Charley gripped the handles, light sparking off the tips. "These are for roasting marshmallows over the fire."

And why the hell that comment made his heart turn over, he had no idea.

CHARLEY HELD THE bag of marshmallows high as Cocoa danced around her legs. In the living room, flames crackled in the wood stove. Reflected in the glass sliding doors, the fire seemed to burn through the room, licking over the old sofa and armchair.

Meghan pounded a final key on her laptop. She glanced up from her screen. "Took you two long enough."

Matt handed Meghan a mug. "Any faster and you'd be drinking a skin of congealed milk proteins."

Meghan flashed a grin. "Yum."

"Watch it or he'll scald yours on purpose." Charley made room on the coffee table for the skewers. She shifted the autumn issue of *Watershed* magazine to the side and reached for her sketchbook. Opened to her last drawing, to her research notes that should have been limited to the gallery, not studied for clues.

A sweep of charcoal, heavy and dark on the cream paper, outlined the serpentine shape. An animal, strange and terrifying. A deformity. A freak of nature. The deviant made monstrous.

And make-believe.

Charley closed the spiral-bound book with a snap and glanced over Meghan's shoulder at the photo filling her laptop screen. Uploaded and already pulling in reactions and likes.

The image showed the marina: a dark glimpse of the sign, a fragment of the dock store, and yellow crime scene tape. The perspective was angled, revealing just enough to raise curiosity.

Charley read the caption out loud: "'Breaking News —'"

Meghan hummed. She blew on the steam rising from her cup. "Gotta love those words."

With the power to destroy. Charley read on, "'A fifty-year-old local woman was found dead near the gas dock of Callahan's Marina at six p.m. tonight. The cause of death is under investigation. The marina will remain closed until further notice as the police document the scene. Check back for more information as it becomes available.'" Keeping Laura's identity hidden for now. "'Follow @OakcrestCourier for updates.'" Using tragedy to expand the reach of the paper. She glanced at Meghan. "Nice plug."

She shrugged. "You do what you gotta do."

Matt opened the fireplace door, letting out a blast of heat. The snap of red-hot birch bark. "A lot of people will be able to read between those lines and figure out who died."

Meghan shrugged. "One way or another, word always gets out. And the more people talk, the more we find out."

Hopefully, who attacked Laura and where. And why she thought she'd seen — wrestled with — the lake monster.

If they figured out the most likely locations, maybe they'd be able to spot an area along the shoreline that looked disturbed.

Charley sat cross-legged on the rug in front of the fire and tore open the plastic bag of marshmallows on a waft of powdery sugar. "We need to create a timeline of Laura's movements."

Meghan dropped a sofa cushion on the floor. Reached for the bag and pulled out a fistful of marshmallows. She speared them on her skewer, three in a row. "Figure out how she ended up in the water."

Matt dropped down in the little space that was left between them. His shoulder pressed against Charley's and the contact spread more warmth through her than the fire, crackling in the grate.

He took the bag, dug out two marshmallows for himself. "Easier said than done." Matt's voice turned thoughtful. "Unless someone saw her. When I drove Beverley home —" Cocoa squeezed in the middle, nosing her way under his arm. "Give a guy a little space, will you?"

But there was a familiar, hungry gleam in her brown eyes. Charley said, "Careful —" Too late.

Cocoa snatched the marshmallow from Matt's hand and wolfed it.

Matt stared at the dog, more resigned than anything else. "I should have seen that coming."

Yup. "You can't let your guard down around her." When she saw an opportunity, she seized it.

The same way someone else had. Means, motive, and opportunity. That was what it came down to.

Cocoa settled her head on the corner of the rug, paws flat out in front of her. Pleased and ready to pounce again.

Charley thrust her marshmallow into the fire. Orange flames flared, turning the sugar golden, blackening the edges.

"You're holding it too close to the flame," Matt warned. "It'll —"

"Catch fire?" Sugar bubbled, blistered.

Meghan held the tip of her skewer in the blaze. "Isn't that kind of the point? The burned ones taste the best."

"Charbroiled?" Matt raised a brow. "You're supposed to caramelize the sugar, not torch it." At their expressions, he held up his hands. "Fine, fine."

"No one likes a back-seat marshmallow toaster," Charley warned him.

He grinned at her. "I wouldn't want to risk getting uninvited."

"Wise," Meghan agreed.

Charley carefully pulled the hot and melted marshmallow off the end of the skewer. Sparks flew in the grate. "If Laura couldn't see what was happening, if it was dark enough and she felt threatened, do you think she might really believe she was being attacked by a monster?"

Imagination taking over in the darkness, feeding off fear.

Matt shifted, his arm brushing hers as he reached behind them for something on the coffee table. Her sketchbook. He pulled it closer and shot her a questioning glance, waiting for her permission to open it.

Nerves fluttered through her. Her notes. Her unfinished, unpolished sketches. But every final piece started with an idea and evolved from there. She took a breath and nodded.

The spine creaked. Matt flipped the pages, thick with mixed media, flashing past swatches of scale patterns. Snake and crocodile. Pencil shaded callused skin, the texture of cracked earth. Rough copies of ancient rock face petroglyphs she'd done in thick scratches of charcoal. A taped-at-the-corners printout of Norval Morrisseau's *Water Spirit*. The horned water lynx in earth-toned acrylic and brown kraft paper, representing the dualities of good and evil.

Grandpa's voice echoed through her mind. *The monster exists. This story really did happen and I can show you where.*

But he never had. Each time he told the tale, the location shifted, changing like the dimensions of a fish in dockside boasts about the biggest catch of the year.

Matt asked, "Is this what most lake monsters look like?"

"Most lake monsters." Meghan shot him an amused glance. "That's something I never thought I'd hear anyone say."

One foot in diameter. Thirty foot in length. Lines of text from century-old explorers she'd read while researching. The words repeated through different accounts. *A living fossil.* "The descriptions are similar," Charley said. Even though they were recorded in different times and places, over the course of thousands of years on rock faces and birchbark, in whispers and books published and catalogued as non-fiction. "A sinuous dark blue and brown scaled body. A great, shaggy head like a lion or a bulldog. The antlers of a deer. A tail that swishes when it moves. A growl like a buzz saw."

The descriptions were active, not static. A living account of habits and movements.

Meghan held up her arm. The fine hairs stood on end. "Yup. Chills and thrills."

Not just wonder tales, but warnings that were passed down from generation to generation, the same way Grandpa's story was. "Canadian folklore is teeming with lake monsters."

"That makes sense," Matt said. "We live in lakeland."

The monsters were a part of their collective unconscious, because fresh water was everywhere. Charley nodded. "Oral tradition filled those waters with mythical creatures."

"Including Blue Heron Lake." A horror movie echo to Meghan's voice, pitched to resonate just right.

Charley wrapped her fingers, sticky with caramelized sugar, around her mug, the comforting scent of cocoa and milk rising with the steam. "The Anishinaabe people told stories of Micipijiu, who had to be placated to get safe passage through the lakes of the Canadian shield." The horned water lynx with the power to conjure a storm with the flick of its tail. "The Inuit spoke of Qalupalik, the mythical half-human sea creatures who lured children into their icy underwater lairs." Far beneath the depths of the water.

Meghan leaned forward, face lit by the flames. "In Kingston, kids towed logs through the water with ropes, to trick people into thinking they were seeing a lake monster."

The way Roy said Laura had.

"Did it work?" Matt asked.

"For a while. Long enough to spread fear. Until people tried to find a different solution."

An explanation that would turn terror into science. The kind of explanation Dad looked for in an autopsy. But a legend couldn't be x-rayed or cut open. "Some accounts try to explain the serpent away as a subterranean sturgeon."

Matt frowned. "Without river access?"

Meghan shrugged. "Stories that last always have a vein of truth running through them."

Bang! The slam of the front door jolted through Charley.

Meghan laughed. A breathless, nervy laughter that could echo through haunted houses. "That's a cop, not a cat burglar," she said, but her voice wasn't steady.

Alex entered the room, rubbing his eyes. He walked to Meghan, kissed the top of her head, and swiped the skewer from her hand. He dropped onto the sofa and pulled off the sticky marshmallow.

None of the caffeine high of a fresh case or the blood rush of the hunt in his movements.

"Was Laura murdered?" Charley asked.

Alex shot her a look. "Hello to you, too." He sank deeper into the sofa cushions. "The doc thinks it's possible she respirated water."

Of course she did. She fell in the lake. "I could have told you that, too."

Alex shook his head. "He thinks she had a near-drowning experience. That water irritated her lungs so that they filled up with liquid. Leading to fatal breathing difficulties." He turned the skewer over in his hands. "If the doc finds traces of sand or silt in her airways, we'll know whatever happened to Laura in the lake killed her."

Guilt tightened in Charley's chest. The cough. She'd heard it, seen it wrack the woman's shoulders. "But she spoke to me. You're saying, she stood in the gallery and she was" — what? — "drowning?" Dying.

Alex said, "Symptoms can start up to seventy-two hours after the event, making them hard to diagnose."

Meghan sat up, hugged her arms around her knees. "Dry-drowning. The catchy non-medical term that freaked parents out last summer. A fad story that spread warnings through local papers during cottage season. 'The Hidden Risk of Summertime Swims.' 'Water Play Kills.'"

An innocent moment of joy linked to death in a single, catchy headline.

Alex said, "Apparently, it takes less than half a glass of inhaled water to drown."

It was a terrifying thought. Charley set down her cup. "Laura must have thought she was safe." On dry land. In the gallery.

"All she'd notice was a cough," Alex said. "Some chest pains. A change in mental state or mood from oxygen depletion."

Had her behaviour been out of character? It was hard to say without knowing Laura better.

Matt reached for the poker. He stirred the embers, sending sparks flying. "Why did she go to the marina?"

There was one logical reason. "To borrow a boat?" Thinking she'd try to hunt down the lake monster?

"She owned a canoe," Alex said, "but it's still tied to her dock."

Which only meant she hadn't chosen that option. "A motorboat would be safer, sturdier, and faster than a canoe."

"You think she'd go back out on the water, after nearly drowning?" Matt asked.

It seemed unlikely. But Roy had said Laura had been fearless. "To take photos?"

Alex shook his head. "Her phone wasn't on her. It wasn't in her car either."

That caught Charley. "Laura never went anywhere without her phone." She was always on call. Maybe it was another power play, a way to look important, but she had it on her at all times. Scrolling through emails in the checkout line at the grocery store. Holding up the queue at the ATM in the bank, just to fire off another text message.

"Maybe it's in the water," Matt suggested.

"Or on the shoreline." Which would help pinpoint where she'd been. "Laura said, 'The area needs to be sealed off.'"

Alex shrugged. "There are places on the lake that should be marked with buoys but aren't."

That less than thrilled tone, so far from exhilarated it could have been on the opposite end of the spectrum. Charley rested her elbows on her knees and took a closer look at Alex. Normally, there was nothing he liked better than bringing a criminal to justice. "You're not really going to write this off as an accident, are you?"

Alex sat up straight, leaning forward, on the edge of the sofa. The sudden intensity blasted away fatigue. "It's the most realistic option we've got. Even if the evidence shows she died as a result of near-drowning, there's no reason to think it might have been foul play. Maybe she was out on the lake and fell into the water. It happens. Oxygen depletion can do strange things to the mind. Her imagination filled in the blanks."

Laura said she'd been lured into a trap. Set up. "Or," Charley suggested, "she really was attacked. Taken by surprise. If something or someone dragged me underwater, my first thought would be a horror movie scenario."

"I wonder why," Meghan said, deadpan.

Matt stood and paced away to the bookshelves, gaze on eye level with her copies of *The Concise Gray's Anatomy* and *The Native Trees of Canada*. The worn reference books were shelved in between paperback PI novels. Grandpa's collection of hard-boiled romantics. Detectives who heard voices crying in the night and couldn't help going to see what was the matter.

Charley said, "We need to narrow down a suspect list."

Alex shook his head. "Not this time."

Meghan glanced at him. "Come on. You've got a list. In case this turns into a homicide investigation."

Alex's jaw tensed. "And if it does, it'll be my investigation."

Matt turned to face them, hands jammed in his pockets. "Good luck with that."

What did Alex think they'd do? "If we find a clue, we should, what, ignore it?" Charley asked.

Alex rested his elbows on his knees, levelled his gaze at them. "You leave it exactly where you found it. Then tell me. No stealing."

"That was once and —"

Alex talked over her. "No asking follow-up questions."

"But —"

"It's going to come out," he said, "that Laura saw you before she died. That she spoke to you."

Matt tensed. "And if someone attacked her —"

"I'm a threat," Charley finished his sentence.

"And a threat is a target," Meghan said grimly.

But Charley had had a gun pointed at her before and she'd survived. This was different. This was her monster, her research. Her fault.

Alex pointed a finger at her. "Better safe than sorry. Stay out of it this time. I mean it. No sleuthing. No" — he dug in the bag for another marshmallow — "capturing monsters."

"Tough luck with that one," Charley said. "That's all I'm doing right now." Following up on a history of man-made monsters.

"Myths and legends are fine." Alex leaned back, stretched out his legs, getting comfortable because, to him, the conversation was over. "Just don't go looking for them in human form."

They set out, hoping for a glimpse of the beast. The line surfaced in Charley's mind, though where she'd read it, she couldn't remember. *Into the frightening unknown.*

But fear lurked even in the still waters of everyday life. Eventually, it reared its head. You had to face it or drown.

TEN

"YOU'RE DOING IT again."

Charley glanced at Matt. He drove down Main Street, his concentration focused on the dark road ahead. From the back seat of the truck, Cocoa snored, snuffling in her sleep, making it loud and clear she would have preferred another hour to snooze. "Doing what?"

"Going over the clues in your mind."

As if there were that many. "Maybe I was thinking about paint." If she'd already had a second cup of coffee by now, she could have come up with a better lie. But Matt was right. She couldn't help wondering why Laura came back to the marina, if the reason was connected to her attack.

"Sure, you were." Matt nodded. "Along with suspects and motives."

Shades of night hung over Main Street. It would still be another three hours before the Coffee Nook put their chalkboard sign out on the sidewalk, advertising homemade pumpkin-spiced lattes. Polyester cobwebs stretched over balconies and railings. A mannequin in the Blast from the Past Boutique window posed in a tattered evening gown and black feather mask. Zombies and vampires peered out of shop windows, along with four-dollar rubber faces that could turn anyone into a creature with gills.

"You might be close with that guess," Charley admitted.

"I'd say I hit a home run." Matt pulled up at the curb and parked. The silence was sudden after the lick of guitars from the speakers, the low-level rumble of the engine. "You could leave the sleuthing to Alex."

Wait it out, as if the answers didn't matter? Somehow, she'd set all this in motion. Charley shifted in her seat to face Matt. "I can handle it."

"Yeah, I know." A smile crooked the corner of his mouth. He looked out the windshield. "I'm not so sure I can."

Her heart did a somersault. "Are you worried about me, Thorn?"

He shrugged, but his smile shifted into a full-blown grin. "Couldn't care less."

For a guy who'd used a proposal as a pickup line on the first day they met, he'd dodged any attempt to talk about feelings. And she hadn't pushed. Even though she wanted to. "It almost sounds like you might be getting attached."

His eyes flashed over her face. "Are you sharpening your detective skills on me?"

Close but still miles away from *I love you*. "I might as well put them to good use."

"It's safer than the alternative."

There it was again. Another warning. But exposing the truth — any truth — always came at a risk. Broken bones or a broken heart.

Morning sun glanced off the gallery's gabled roof, the glass windowpanes. Charley bit her lip. "Roy has motive." The most to gain. And a damning quote in the paper.

A muscle jumped in Matt's jaw. "I know what you're thinking. But the incident that led to Laura's death —"

Incident? "Attack."

He raked his hand through his hair. "Whatever it was, it happened earlier."

But maybe Laura came back to confront her half-brother.

Accuse him. "Who would you put at the top of your suspect list?"

"A hypothetical list? David, for one."

Nerves tightened in her stomach. There was no getting around it. If it was murder, the killer was one of them. "I don't think he attacked Laura."

Matt shrugged. "But he threatened her. And judging from his speech, I'd say his motive was personal."

"When it comes to protecting kids, it's always personal for David." If only they knew if he had an alibi. Where was he on Saturday afternoon?

"Be careful," Matt said. "Don't go down —"

"These mean streets?" Sunlit and draped in fake cobwebs.

"Not alone, anyway. Even Philip Marlowe knew this wasn't a game for knights."

Of course, he'd quote Chandler at her. A desperate move and one she could counter. "Marlowe fought for what's right anyway."

"Dodging bullets along the way." Matt cupped his hand around the back of her neck. "Seems to me, chasing monsters is even more dangerous."

Charley pressed a kiss to his lips, felt the familiar rush, the spike in her pulse. "All I'm going to do is paint them on the walls." She got out of the truck, opened the back door. Cocoa leapt out and made a dash for a candy wrapper, tumbling toward the gutter. Charley grabbed the leash, held on tight.

Matt rolled down his window and said, "A solo show doesn't give you licence to go rogue."

But it did put her in charge. "Are you offering backup for painting or sleuthing?"

"Both."

The promise so quick and true, her heart leapt. Walking backwards, Cocoa already pulling toward the gallery, Charley grinned. "Easy for you to say now. Wait until I hand you a paintbrush."

ELEVEN

MATT UNLOCKED THE door to Chocoholic's. The sense of unease caught him at the back of his throat, like something burning. And it wasn't just the familiar gut punch of breathing in the bitter aroma of chocolate. Not guilt, but the sense that something was wrong, the feeling as real as rotten fruit or cream gone sour.

Then he heard it.

A rustle in the kitchen. A scrape of sound where there should have been silence.

The PVC strip curtains hanging in front of the door to the workshop were dull, no light within. The door behind was sealed. Same way he'd left it.

Warning bells going off in his head anyway, Matt pushed through into the workroom.

It wasn't empty.

Of course, he probably should have figured that. Matt dragged in a breath, kicked himself for being surprised. "Do I have to remind you that this is your day off?"

Even on the days Beverley worked, she was never here this early. And not dressed in an old sweatshirt and flannel pants — possibly pyjama bottoms — without a hint of pink lipstick to add colour to her face.

She carefully nestled a chocolate praline in the black box. Halloween themed, the kind covered in silver bats, not skulls. "I was up early and had to get out. I kept going over every conversation we had with Laura in my mind. Wondering what we missed."

Matt knew what that was like. That need to get answers. And the price you paid when you got them. He leaned a shoulder against the doorjamb. "How's Roy?"

"Coping." She paused over the next chocolate, then set it aside in a separate bowl.

Chocolates with cracks, chips, scratches, or any other flaws were sorted out. But Matt knew that all of those mocha chocolates were flawed. The balance was off, just a hint sweeter than they should be.

He reached for the tin of coffee and a filter, flipped the top of the coffee maker open, and stopped short. The pot was already half full and still hot. And, from the looks of it, Beverley was two cups ahead of him.

He'd have to be careful. She was sharp at the best of times and even more so when fuelled with caffeine. "Have you had breakfast?"

The pause was a beat too long. "I was thinking about it."

No, then.

Matt scrounged for two bowls, grabbed the box of Special K cereal from the cupboard, and poured two portions. He dug out the chocolate chips and ignored the raised brow he got.

"Is this how you eat breakfast?" A high-potency infusion of judgment in that single question.

"Sometimes," Matt said, but often enough for that casual comment to be a lie. He added a generous handful of dark chocolate chips to his, milk chocolate to Beverley's. Poured milk on top and carried both to the scarred wooden table. "Sit."

She pulled up a stool with a scrape of wood over floor tiles. Sat and picked up her spoon. Then looked at him. "It wasn't an accident."

It could have been a question, but it wasn't. And the statement chilled him. It was too close to a confession. "You're not saying —"

"Of course not." She brushed away the idea with a sniff. "Don't be silly. What I have is a keen sense of intuition I happen to trust. And it's telling me that Laura was murdered."

He wished he'd at least managed a sip of coffee first. Maybe then he'd come up with a better reply, but there was no easy answer. No platitudes or greeting card slogans to fall back on. "You didn't want to give yourself another hour before digging for the truth?"

She raised her chin, a stubborn set to it he'd learned not to underestimate. "Laura and Roy didn't always see eye to eye. That's a fact. But I won't let her death destroy everything I hold dear. The faster the killer is identified, the easier it will be. The less of a mark it will leave."

He'd thought that, at one point. "That's not how it works." Sometimes, you couldn't avoid the scar. And it took a hell of a long time to heal over. If it ever did.

"I won't sit by and wait and watch." The crisp snap to her tone was sharp, not brittle. "It isn't in my nature. I need to be doing. Collecting the facts. If something is broken, you fix it. You mend the hole in the boat, you don't let it sink. It's that simple."

Matt took the stool across from her, propped his heel on the rung. "You can't fix the boat when you're sitting in it." The irony was not lost on him that he was sitting here in his workshop, the copper pots hanging over their heads slowly oxidizing as they spoke, losing the lustre he'd always worked hard to maintain, the scent of chocolate fading like a bittersweet memory.

Beverley leaned forward, waited for him to meet her eyes. "You can bail it out and hope you stay afloat long enough to save yourself."

Advice for him or her? "You could let Alex do his job."

"The way you did?" She took a breath before he could react, do anything more than absorb the blow. "I'm sorry. But the more people ask questions, the faster we'll uncover the truth."

And sometimes the truth hurt. "Whatever you find out, even if we prove it was an accident, it will be linked to Roy. You can't get around that. He was her closest contact here. You both were."

Her smile twisted. "And look how that turned out."

But she'd be looking at everything through a haze of guilt. "There's no way you'll be able to see clearly."

"Or I'll see clearer than most."

The ego at work. *I can do it. I can fix it.* He'd fallen for that one, too. "What are you going to do if it turns out that Roy somehow was involved in this?" It could happen. The people you trust the most often had the most to hide.

Beverley straightened in the stool. Steel through her spine. "I'm well aware that something we did, or said, led to this." She laid her hand on the table, palm flat, as though the stain of death was right here, in the room with them. "It's why she died at the marina. We ignored the warning signs."

"So did she."

"But we shut her out." The confession, the way she said it, reminded him of chopping chocolate on marble, the cut not clean but splintered off under the force of the blade.

"If you start asking questions, you'll question everything." *Why* was a hell of a dangerous word. "You'll keep pushing until something breaks. Let someone else do that."

"That's not a bad idea." Beverley leaned forward. "Are you volunteering?"

Cereal flakes lodged in his throat like drywall plaster. He swallowed hard. "What?" That's not what he'd meant.

"You know the lake," Beverley mused, light returning to her

eyes, some colour to her cheeks. "You know us."

Matt put his spoon down on the table. "True, but —"

"You'll come for dinner, report new findings." Hope and relief brightened her expression.

What had he gotten himself into? But there was enough curiosity there to stop him from arguing.

He'd just gotten the go-ahead to follow up on the questions he'd already been turning over in his mind, that Charley wanted to look into anyway.

What else was he doing? Adding notes to a cookbook that might never see the light of day? Making another batch of chocolate, only to throw it away? "If we find anything out, sure."

"We?" Beverley frowned. "I don't want Charley involved in this."

Leave her out of it? Unease settled over Matt. "Why?"

She took a spoonful of her cereal, studded through with milky chocolate. Gaze lowered, expression iced over. "I trust you. You'll do what's right."

Unshakable faith. He had that at one point. "Charley notices things others miss."

"So do you. And we need a friend on our side."

Not a stranger? The implication was clear, and it riled him. But he knew how it felt when the odds were stacked against you and you no longer knew who to trust. "Two friends are better than one."

"On some occasions."

And this was one of them. But he let it go, for now.

If they went about it right, they might be able to spare Beverley and Roy some of the shock, some of the guilt, the investigation was bound to dredge up.

TWELVE

GUT INSTINCT, FLOW state, or magic — whatever you wanted to call it — this was it. Charley washed Ultramarine Blue acrylic shadows over the chalk outline she'd already traced on the gallery wall. The rough sketch should have been a guide. She ignored it, working instead on intuition as the face appeared.

Finding the dark first. Then the light.

Using values and tones to shape the cheeks, the forehead, she drew the features up out of the drop cloth, feeling for the face.

The form that wanted to be found.

Charley dipped her brush in the paint, blue drops splashing onto rosin paper. Too bright, too bold for lake water. But still the memory flashed through her mind. Of water on wood. Vanished without a trace.

She'd read enough detective novels to know to document everything, but what had she done? "Erased the evidence, that's what." The blood.

Cocoa lifted her head. The breeze blew in through the door — propped open with a folding chair — and ruffled her fur. She looked as disappointed as a dog could.

And with good reason. "Maybe the projection influenced Laura."

But the lake monster — *her* lake monster — was just a dare. To look the beast in the eye.

It was a mistake to think the lake monster was the source of fear. The people lurking in the shadows of the walls were.

The source of menace was a grasping hand, reaching out into the room. A hungry gleam in an eye. The figure, taller than it should be, looming.

The threat came from people.

"So, this is the lake monster," a voice drawled behind her.

The paintbrush slipped from Charley's fingers, hit the floor.

Cocoa leapt to her feet, her ears flicking as the chair holding the door open scraped over the floor.

Eric strolled in. The owner of the Blast from the Past Boutique wore stonewashed blue jeans and a white dress shirt. A blue silk paisley-patterned pocket square — the same electric shade as his eyes — pooled out of the breast pocket of his waistcoat. "Congratulations. It's a nightmare come true." His tone was bright, but his expression was guarded.

"That was the goal."

"Turning our lake into a place of terror? You pulled it off." His hand went to cover his heart.

No, his breast pocket, as though covering a treasure, not an accessory. She'd seen that move before. "Let me guess. Another charm to ward off evil influences?"

Cocoa's tail wagged hard against her leg.

He shrugged. "A little extra protection against the devils and demons. Especially the fiendishly handsome ones." The self-deprecating tone was stylish and charming and just as much an accessory.

Eric had a superstition for every occasion. "And fabric wards off evil, how?"

"Elegance intimidates." He drew the silk square from his pocket, running the fabric through his fingers. "Devils and demons are drawn to the cunning complexity of the knotted handkerchief — not unlike the way some of us are drawn to cunningly complex men — and become so distracted by trying to untie it that they forget about whatever evil they were planning to inflict."

"Confusing the devil with a knot." An unsolvable puzzle that became an obsession. That sounded familiar.

He stepped forward, tucked the handkerchief in the pocket of her jeans. "Here. A gift for the artist who chooses to surround herself with monsters."

And it had been her choice. Maybe the wrong one. "Thanks," Charley said dryly.

"Just don't use it as a rag." Eric strolled along the wall, pausing in front of the winterberry shrubs. Bony and leafless and bright with toxic berries. "Dior collected talismans. Chanel believed in the magic of numbers. Fashion is rife with superstition."

Not just fashion. Salvador Dalí carried around a little piece of Spanish driftwood to help ward off evil spirits. If it worked, she had no idea. "So is art."

"Which is why I think you need it more than I do." Eric turned on his heel, to face her. "You've been keeping secrets from me." Frost-bitten branches framed his face, but it was the ice in his voice that chilled her.

Of course a mysterious death would catch his attention. "You know I can only tell you what's been printed in the paper."

Disbelief and shock shifted across his face in minute changes. Like a burst of close-up photographs in a shoot for an autumn editorial, the range of emotions flickered across his features. Over in a fraction of a second. "It's been announced?"

Announced? "What are you talking about?"

"Vintage jewels, darling." Eric waved his left hand in the air, flashing an invisible ring. "I risked life and limb to smuggle that heirloom piece into Oakcrest. That proposal had better have been solid gold to match."

"Alex didn't give Meghan the ring."

Eric dragged his hands through his hair. "He changed his mind and opted for Tiffany's. I told him not to. That 1920s gold *Toi et Moi* twist ring with cream-peach-toned pearl and diamond was perfect. But no, he had to go and —"

"Eric." Charley cut him off. "Alex didn't propose."

He lowered his hands. "Why not?"

"Because —" Charley hesitated. But the news would be all over town soon, if it wasn't already. It wasn't hard to figure out who was missing. "He got called to investigate."

"At the marina. I saw Meghan's post." Eric settled into one of the folding chairs in a lithe move. "So much for the boys in blue, brave and true."

Charley picked up the paintbrush. "You're still talking about the proposal."

"I'd like to move on to veils and trains. But at the rate this is going, I'll be retired and living in the tropics with a closet full of linen by the time Alex pops the question." Eric rolled up his shirt sleeves, revealing the VOGUE tattoo on his forearm. "Since there's no hope of romance, yes, by all means, let's discuss tragedy." He glanced up. His eyes locked on the space on the wall she'd been working on. He sucked in a breath through his teeth in a hiss. "That image is enough to chill your bones."

Exactly the reaction she'd hoped for. And the projector wasn't even on. "Thank you." Charley glanced over her shoulder to see which part of the exhibit caught his eye.

A flick of shock shot down her spine.

"You cast the perfect villain," he said. "The likeness is spot-on. Maybe too good."

That imperious lift to the chin. The face long and lean, peering out from the tangle of twisted vegetation. Haggard lines etched around the woman's mouth. Lips stretched tight. Strands of wet hair clinging to her cheek. Her face turned, not in the direction of the projected image of the lake monster, but into the room. At them.

She'd drawn Laura on the wall.

But she hadn't filled in the woman's eyes. Not yet. No pupils. No irises. No windows into the soul. Just deep wells of empty space between lids and lashes. Bottomless voids.

And still, Laura stared. An unseeing gaze you couldn't hold, couldn't break.

Legs unsteady, Charley sank into the other chair. "It does look like her."

"Only more bedraggled."

Her subconscious had taken over. Of course she'd been thinking about Laura. And she'd brought the woman back to life.

She'd have to change it. Paint over it.

The empty gaze burned into her. It was just dabs of colour, but in a combination that tingled cold fingers of fear up her spine. "Did Laura shop at the boutique?"

He rolled his eyes. "Did those accessories look like they came from my shop? She never spent a dime. She waltzed into the boutique her first week here and asked" — he lifted his chin, sucked in his cheeks — "'Do you sell thrift or vintage?'" The tone was clipped, haughty, and impatient. He shrugged, flicked a speck of imaginary dust off his pant leg. "So long as it had the right label, she didn't care what it was."

"Were you rude?"

"Very." He grinned. "There's a word that rhymes with witch that I'm not going to say in front of Cocoa." Eric leaned forward and patted the dog's head. The half-hearted tail wag implied she knew exactly what he meant and was still deciding whether or not to be offended. "Laura came to my shop for one reason and one reason only."

"Clothes?"

Eric raised one brow. "To buy a vintage crown that would transform her into lake royalty."

Looking for a little bit of magic? As well as the upper hand. "She wanted to impress everyone." Or one person in particular.

"Don't we all? But it's not that simple. Some people can wear a paper tiara and make it look like gold. Others wear the real thing and turn it gaudy. Even draped head-to-toe in couture, she'd always be playing dress-up." Eric narrowed his eyes. "Why the sudden interest in — Wait." He glanced at the portrait. A muscle jumped in his jaw. "You asked, 'Did she shop at the boutique?' Past tense. What happened at the marina?"

To say Laura died was true but not quite right. The feel of damp lake-soaked air, the clank of boat chains flashed through her mind. "Let's just say, it wasn't boat theft."

"That's a relief," Eric drawled. "I was worried I might have to install extra security on the Breton striped shirts." His smile slipped. "Was it an accident?" He looked toward the portrait of Laura. "Or murder?"

It was interesting that murder was his first guess. "Why do you think that?"

"I met the woman. Abrasive would be too kind." He sketched a cross in the air in front of his chest. "Rest her soul."

Rest? The woman she'd painted on the wall seemed wide awake. The unfinished portrait was a heartbeat and a few brush strokes away from breathing. "We don't know what happened yet. It's" — she paused for a second, searching for the right word — "mysterious." In so many ways.

"Is that why you painted her on the wall?" Denim-clad legs stretched out in front of him, Eric's pose was more waiting-room anxious than relaxed. "She looks a second away from taking on that lake monster of yours."

Yours. There it was again. That claim she hadn't realized she'd staked. "She did."

"Did what?"

Eric lived for gossip. Maybe he knew something. "Just hours before Laura died, she came here. She'd been attacked by something in the water."

He stared at her, his features an unreadable mask. Something about it was just as scarred as the rubber faces sold in the stores. "The creature supposedly lurking in the bottom of the lake?"

"Or something that looked like it." Whether the monster was human or supernatural was still up for debate.

Lines creased around his mouth. "Pareidolia."

It could have been a spell, an incantation. Or a curse. "What?"

"The human tendency to spot patterns in random sensory information. Faces. Our brains are wired to see monsters."

Palms gone clammy, Charley met Laura's gaze. That same intimidating glare she'd seen in person. Too much like an ultimatum from the afterlife. "What do you mean?"

The metal chair frame creaked as Eric shifted in his seat. "It's a warning device. The amygdala responds faster to emotionally charged characteristics. To trigger a fight or flight response, the faces have to be bizarre. Threatening. Monstrous." His tone was firm. "It's a false perception."

"Deceived by our senses?" Laura had been. But she hadn't known how to see the lines, how to look for the shadows and shades and see the truth.

Maple and birch trees cast acrylic shadows, leaning forward, closing in, tricking the eye because Charley wanted them to. She'd drawn from observation and used colours, textures, and edges for her own purposes. Created three-dimensional shapes from a flat surface.

Eric said, "It's the brain's 'gestalt' tendency to make a perception whole, fill in gaps." He could have been telling a ghost story around a campfire. "Seeing the occasional monster is the price we pay for creativity."

A toll fee. Another sacrifice. Charley touched the handkerchief Eric had tucked into her pocket, feeling for the knot. "Are you quoting the myth of the mad artist at me?"

"Genius and madness? No, this is sanity, at its base form." A flush that could have been passion or anger heated his cheeks. "A psychological tool to reason children out of night terrors. Stop them from crying wolf."

So that they'd be believed when danger really did strike, when the monster in the dark was real. "For now, this is strictly need to know. You can't breathe a word of this to anyone."

"Your secret is safe with me," Eric promised, humour brightening his blue eyes like a carefully placed white highlight. "I'll guard it the way a designer guards the preliminary sketches of a Met Gala ball gown."

Not the best analogy, if he wanted to spark confidence. "Doesn't that intel normally leak?"

"Only as an intentional PR ploy. Have a little faith. I've kept Alex's secret — so far." Eric smoothed his waistcoat. His fingers trembled. "If April is the cruellest month, what does that make October?" His tone lightened but the lines around his mouth looked carved. "The boys of summer are gone, and evil is afoot."

From the wall, Laura stared.

Not pleading. Not accusing.

Demanding to be believed.

The evidence is right here. That was what Laura had said. And maybe it was here, on the walls. In the fallen tree with the exposed roots. The sheared-away granite rock face. The clear, shallow water running over rocks.

Wherever Laura had been, she would have left traces behind — disturbed leaves, scuffed footprints in gravel. It was easy enough to check, to compare. Charley had a document of what the setting looked like before taped in her sketchbook. Research photos for art, not murder, but somehow the two were now linked.

It couldn't hurt to take one look.

And she wouldn't let her senses deceive her.

THIRTEEN

MATT HAD FISHED Blue Heron Lake often enough to know there were blind spots. Pockets of water shielded by pines. Rocky shallows motorboats steered clear of, but a canoe glided across.

But there were also three times as many vantage points. Someone sketching outdoors would know that.

And that thought wouldn't let him go, which was why he'd closed Chocoholic's early and driven here.

Thomas's house was starting to take shape, even though the fresh mud scraped on the camper trailer's steps implied it wasn't livable yet. Stained cedar lap siding and stone accents blended the sprawling building into the surroundings. The landscaping was finished, but not by anyone local. There were too many neat lines for that, too little imagination. Everything under control, as much as possible, this close to the water.

Put your heart and soul into it. That's the only way to do a job right. Jeffrey's voice echoed through his mind. Not bad advice for a general contractor or a chocolatier.

But this was nature in a straitjacket.

Wide windows reflected the red and gold trees, the lake. Too much glass for Matt's taste, but you'd have one hell of a view of the fall colours.

A clean line of sight.

Matt turned to face the water. Against the glare of the sun, a dark silhouette stood at the end of the dock. A man, balanced precariously on the metal frame of the dock, bending to heft the boards out. Ass backwards.

It might be easier to lift the boards that way, but one slip of his heel, and Thomas would be swimming with the fishes. He could have been standing on solid boards, working his way back on steadier ground. But he'd chosen to do it this way. Faster, only if it all went right.

What was he planning to do, take the dock out on his own?

Waves lapped around a rock farther out in the water. On the flat surface, a water snake basked in the sun. Coiled like that, it was hard to tell if it was three feet or four and a half feet long. Keeled scales splotched dark brown. Not quite up to Charley's lake monster, but close enough to wonder if maybe that was what had people fooled. A reptile, less wary of humans than other snakes, bold enough to approach a swimmer.

Matt headed Thomas's way, scuffing his boots over the ground, making sure he heard him coming. Startling the man would guarantee he ended up drenched. And Matt really didn't want to have to jump in after him.

Thomas hefted the boards with a grunt, forearms straining under the load. "I hope you're not here to check up on me. I could have saved you the trip. Told you to mind your own business." He lugged the boards down the length of the dock and dropped them under the tree with a thud.

The best way to counter acidity when cooking was to neutralize it. The same technique probably applied here. "Thought I'd see if you made it home."

"I did." Thomas dragged his arm across his forehead, wiping away the sweat beading in his thinning grey hair.

"You could have had help with this, if you'd asked."

"Figure yourself lucky I didn't. Besides, I didn't want to wait." Push faster. Rush the job.

Matt dug his hands in his pockets. "Wouldn't have mattered much, give or take a day to avoid an injury."

"Has to be done." Thomas squinted up at the clouds, as though reading the shades of grey for signs of snow. "It needs maintenance. I want to get the sanding done and fix the loose bolts, while I can still feel my fingers."

The boards did look rough. Rough enough to leave splinters in bare feet, though it was hard to say how much use the dock even got. The lake was deep enough for swimming here, but clogged with yellow pond lilies and cattails, the dark brown cigar-shaped flowers shooting up in boggy areas and spreading out. And Thomas didn't own a boat. Not that Matt knew of. Besides, he didn't take Thomas for the fishing type. Not enough patience.

Matt stripped off his denim jacket. With any luck, there wouldn't be any dock spiders. "Well, I'm here now. Might as well accept a helping hand."

"Don't need one." Thomas headed back out, wood creaking under his weight. He breathed hard through his nose, out of breath and trying to fight it.

Matt waited.

It didn't take long before Thomas jerked a shoulder, skin translucent. "Fine. Get the next ones."

Matt walked through a mud pie of wet soil and fallen leaves, only noticing the slope of the dock when he took Thomas's place. He bent but couldn't get a good grip on the boards. He shifted his hold, the grain rough against his palm, but there wasn't enough room to yank the board out. The strips of metal behind him looked more like the frame of the guitar cutter he used to slice ganache than support beams. "Got anything to pry these up with?"

"It'd take me more time to hunt for a crowbar than finish the job myself."

Shit. Matt stepped out onto the frame. Waves lapped beneath him. The water was dark and deep. He really didn't want to get wet.

He bent, grabbed a board. Lifted it, boots braced. The board was heavier than it looked. Fall in and he'd never live it down.

Matt carried it to the end of the dock and waited.

Thomas looked back at him.

Jeffrey would have grabbed the boards from him, taken them to the tree, without needing to say anything. They'd worked as a team too many times to count, in the workshop and in the kitchen.

Thomas didn't pick up on the hint.

Matt gritted his teeth and carried the board the rest of the way, then went back for more. A trickle of sweat ran down his back. "Did you see anyone yesterday, by the water?"

"I make a point to avoid people, when I can," Thomas said dryly. "Unfortunately, that doesn't always work out."

Matt ignored that one. Hopefully he'd get more for his effort than snide comments. "You said you were" — he lifted the last board — "hunting the season."

The pause was like a missed beat in a busy kitchen. The silence of a cut finger. "Stalking autumn."

"From the water?" There'd been beech trees in the sketch Thomas was finishing in the car. Not a water setting, although the hip waders had been covered in mud and still wet.

Thomas had caught his breath now and was watching him warily. "Occasionally."

"Wouldn't think you'd want to run the risk of dropping your sketchbook in the lake."

"Can't do justice to a subject without getting a good look at it."

Matt gave it a second, partially so he could lift out the last board, hoping Thomas would fill the pause with more. He didn't. "So which part of the lake has the best view?"

"Depends on the sun's rotation."

No straight answers here. He should have figured that.

Matt jumped off the dock frame onto land. "Let's wheel this thing in."

They both got a handle on it.

"On three. One, two —" The yank on the frame almost knocked Matt off his feet. "What the hell happened to three?"

"It's your own fault for taking a breath just then." Wiry hands gripped metal. Paint embedded in the creases of the man's knuckles. The skin on his arms was stretched as thin as phyllo pastry over tendons and bone.

But, yeah, Thomas was going to pull the dock out on his own.

Water ran off the wheels, cutting ruts into the grass, slicing into soft soil. "Where do you want it?" Hopefully not all the way by the bunkie.

"Here's fine," Thomas grunted.

Far enough from the water, some protection from the wind. It wasn't a bad spot. Just behind the RV, Thomas might not even see it from his window.

Matt said casually, "You can't beat the view near the marina."

"So that's why —" Thomas bit off on a gasp, close to a snarl. His face went dead white, one hand shooting to the small of his back. He hadn't yet fully straightened up.

Matt recognized the move. "Spasm?"

A battle to hide the truth, despite the hand braced on the aluminum end rail. "This wouldn't have happened" — he managed through gritted teeth — "if I'd been going at my own damn pace."

Yeah, sure. It was his fault. How Charley managed to work with this guy beat Matt. "I'll help you to the RV. Got some painkillers?"

"It's fine."

The guy could hardly move. What was he going to do, lie prone on the ground and wait it out, count the clouds? "Okay then. Good luck." Matt turned, made to head to his truck.

It took two steps before Thomas spoke up. Just loud enough to be heard. "Hold on. Maybe I could use a hand, getting up those steps." The tone was grudging as all hell.

Matt got his arm around Thomas's waist, took on some of his weight. Not that it was much. The man could use a three-course meal, heavy on the gravy and cream. "Ready?" He smelled coffee, mud, and sweat.

Thomas grimaced. "I'm not waiting until you count to three again. Just move."

"Got it." Slow and halting, they made their way over exposed roots and rocks to the RV.

Thomas eyed the three steps up. With a grunt of pain, he lifted his foot up onto the first one. It had to hurt like hell. And the steps were hardly wide enough for the two of them.

"Almost there. Just one more." Matt got his hand on the door. Bad enough that it opened out. He pulled, swung it open on a waft of burned popcorn. No, roasted nuts. The smell of food was bound to linger in the small space, but the strong scent of hazelnuts caught him off guard. Or was it almonds? An undertone of sweetness too, like dried fruit. Maybe cranberries or cherries.

He helped Thomas through the door, stepped in after him. And blinked at the acorns. A whole cookie sheet full, resting on the stovetop. Some blackened, burned at the edges. Oven roasted.

Thomas yanked a pillow off the sofa and dropped heavily down onto it with a squeak of worn springs. Judging from the pillows and the quilt, he'd been sleeping here, rather than in the narrow loft bunkbed. And the view from there looked right onto the house.

Thomas gestured. "There should be some painkillers in that drawer over there."

The dark cabinets and fixtures made the compact kitchen seem smaller, more claustrophobic than it actually was. Matt pulled the drawer out, moved a cardboard box of pastels and a six-pack of Double-A batteries, and found the bottle. Expired a month ago. "What's with the acorns?"

"Art project."

He should be used to it by now. Charley always seemed to have something on the go, too, but baked acorns was new. Matt took the empty Scotch glass from beside the sink and grabbed the green plastic bottle from the counter. He checked the label — lime-infused Perrier. Water fizzed into the glass. He filled it halfway — less likely to spill. "So, how do you stalk autumn?"

"By catching it unawares. At its most natural. Most wild."

He handed over the glass and the meds. "Like that fox carcass you were sketching?"

Thomas swallowed a pill and shot him a look that might have been haughty, if he wasn't laid up flat on his back. "A graphite and pastel study."

Of bones. It took a certain type of personality to see beauty in that.

An open sketchbook lay on the table. The spiral binding jutted up like exposed spine or cartilage. The cream paper was covered with a soft-smudged composition of orange and brown. Another pastel study: crab apples on fallen leaves. Now that, he could understand, although the apples looked bruised and riddled with worm holes.

"Apples and caramel," Thomas said, a smile in his voice now. "A match made in heaven. I could finish it with a wash of watercolour and frame it. We could negotiate a consignment deal."

On his terms? "Rotten food won't go over well in Chocoholic's. I like to remind customers that I work with fresh ingredients."

"The devil's in the details," Thomas scoffed.

Mixing art and sin. But he was right — the details mattered. "The fox carcass though, that one I'd take."

Thomas held the glass in his hand, head resting on the pillow. He looked anything but trapped. "You turn down rotting fruit for a dead animal?"

Matt shrugged. "Why not?" He mentally racked up how much he'd be willing to shell out for a picture that, frankly, creeped him out.

"It's not for sale."

Matt's brows rose. The man was mercenary when it came to selling his paintings and normally never missed out on the chance to sell his artwork. "I'm willing to buy it, as is, right now."

"No deal." He added, "I don't sell unfinished work. Period."

It sounded like an excuse. "Worried it'll tarnish your reputation?"

Thomas snorted. "That'll be the day. Did you know that a group of foxes is called a skulk? They're solitary. Tend to avoid other animals and people, except for their own. But" — Thomas flicked his gaze toward Matt — "if someone threatens their young, they'll attack." He left a beat. "Stealing 'one more chance, or other life.' Margaret Atwood," he attributed what Matt hadn't even realized was a quote.

"Didn't take you for a poetry man."

"Some people say it in words. Some paint. The subject's the same. The fox pins his victim between his paws," Thomas clenched one fist, chapped knuckles gleaming white as bone, "then delivers the killing bite."

A butcher shop image flashed through Matt's mind. Red meat

and silvery gristle. "Looked like the one you were sketching met with a worse fate."

"A coyote got to it. You're only cunning until the end. And there's always someone higher up on the food chain."

"Didn't you say you were hunting the season?"

Grey brows drew together in a scowl meant to intimidate, and were closer to succeeding than Matt cared to admit. "With pencil lead, not a bullet. I was preserving the wily scoundrel before his bones got picked clean."

A moment of grace? Matt fought the urge to glance at the open RV door, the narrow swatch of light outside. "We're trying to trace Laura's steps that afternoon."

"Looking for a scapegoat? Or a witness?"

A suspect.

"Judging from your art," Matt said, "it seems like you notice details." It couldn't hurt to play to the man's ego. "I thought, if anyone saw something, it would be you."

"I didn't see her." It sounded like a half-truth. Thomas closed his eyes. A wafer paper–thin lid flicked open, the one-eyed stare far from drowsy. "Be nice, if you vanished, too."

FOURTEEN

CHARLEY STOOD ON the gravel road leading to the crest of the dam. Water roared like something alive, barely trapped by the man-made structure that changed the river's course. The water flowed from Algonquin Provincial Park — the source of inspiration for the Group of Seven's landscape paintings — into an artificial lake. Their lake.

She tightened her hold on Cocoa's leash. Just four steps ahead of her, the reservoir gleamed, still and calm. The surface was smooth as glass. Deep and inviting.

Bordered by trees, a weed-free stretch of shore led down to the water, wide enough to back a boat trailer into. An apple juice box lay on the ground, crushed and empty, as out of place as Warhol's soup can in an exhibit of Monet's water lilies.

Behind her, water crashed down the spillway, tumbling past sheared-away granite over rocky ridges.

On the wooden walkway of the crest, low concrete walls protected pedestrians, but the metal fence only blocked off the reservoir. On the other side, posts and wooden rails formed a cross-hatch pattern with wide spaces between and a dizzying view of the downstream slope, the rocky embankment. Wide enough for someone to crawl through. Or fall through. A steep drop no one could survive.

This wasn't where Laura was attacked. It was too open. Not

enough places to hide, not on the walkway, or along the shore.

But the narrow trail cutting a twisting path through the dark tangle of growth, down to the riverbed, offered plenty of opportunity for cover. The shrubs, pine, and maple formed a rugged forest thick enough to hide in. The rushing water was loud enough to drown out the crash of leaves. Or cries for help.

It had felt different here before. Yes, there'd been an edge of danger even then, but also inspiration. Possibilities. But that was before the monster took shape in her imagination. Began to live and breathe.

Leaves almost hid the white metal sign. The splash of graffiti and red letters.

Blue Heron Lake Dam. In Case of Emergency Call 911.

Cocoa stopped short. Hackles rising, she eyed the path downhill. But why? It might be just the crash and roar of the water. The blinding streak of a sunbeam. The shadows pooling between the trees, thick as blood.

"Come on." Charley dug in her jeans pocket for a biscuit. Pumpkin and cranberry flavoured, Cocoa's favourite.

Cocoa ignored the treat and that, more than anything else, was a warning sign. She sat down with a whine.

"You'll have to wait in the car," Charley warned her.

That normally got a reaction, but Cocoa just flicked her ears. She didn't move but sat there and panted, eyes wide with fear. Even though they'd been here before together, explored, and taken photos.

It was either go alone or coax her all the way. Then spend more time focusing on keeping her calm than on the surroundings. And risk missing out on a clue.

Bringing Cocoa back to the Jeep went against every instinct, but Charley did it. She rolled down the windows and patted Cocoa on the head. "I'll be back soon."

Cocoa's anxious gaze burned into her back as Charley walked away, doing nothing to set her mind at ease. But the sun was shining and there wasn't another car in sight. So long as she didn't slip, she'd be fine.

Charley checked her cellphone. One bar of reception. And she'd lose even that, the farther she went into the trees.

She set off down the path alone, stepping carefully over loose stones. The view was different now. Splashes of flickering colour and wavering light. Papery birch trees. Grey rocks. A whirl of leaf reflections.

The trail curved, levelling out to the plateau she'd stood on just weeks ago. But the burned logs were new. Remains of a bonfire, mildewed from rain. The smell of mouldering newspaper rose from the pile but the paper in the ashes looked glossy.

Charley squatted down. Photographs as kindling? She tugged a half-burned corner from the cinders.

The paper was thin. Not a photograph, but an image cut — or ripped — from a magazine.

A middle-aged woman in a snug floor-length dress leaned against a Ford Model T, typing on a cellphone, the device anachronistic and her grin rebellious. On another singed fragment, a young male actor wore a 1920s getup, complete with a perfectly lived-in brown trilby, yanked down low over a smouldering gaze. A mic dropped into the frame, revealing the technique behind the magic. Another crisp and curling fragment showed a wall dividing two sets.

Broken illusions. But what did they mean?

Probably nothing. Still, Charley slipped one of the torn images in her pocket.

If Laura came this far, had stood here by the burned-out fire, would she have walked farther? All the way to the river's edge? To that quiet pool of water below, where a giant serpent might swim.

A sacred water spirit. A living fossil.

Or where a person might wait.

Some patience, that was all it would take. Hide in the trees and they could track Laura's path, every step of the way. Then slip into the stream. And, at the last moment, attack.

Ripples spread on the surface of the water.

Heart racing, Charley moved forward. Pebbles skidded under her sneakers. Dry leaves crunched. Water rushed and gurgled.

A hand closed over her arm.

Fear slamming into her, Charley spun.

And looked into David's face. Normally his clean-cut features were bright with boyish curiosity and intelligence. But fury had tightened his face into something unrecognizable. "What the hell do you think you're doing?" he demanded.

Anger warred with fear and won. "I could ask you the same thing."

He glanced down the gravel path. "Go any farther and you'll become a live sacrifice for your lake monster."

A blood sacrifice. A hand cut on a rock. Her heart thudded.

Maybe it was a joke. It sounded like it and she wanted to give him the benefit of the doubt, but his eyes were as hard as the fingers clamped on her arm.

"I'm doing research." It was close to the truth. "Let go."

He blinked and released his hold, flexing his hand as though checking it belonged to him. "It isn't safe here."

"You're telling me." Kayla trusted him. But the anger in his tone, the narrow gravel path, the isolated setting all set off warning bells in Charley's head.

David didn't pick up on her discomfort, didn't make a move to back down or step away. "That current's strong and unpredictable. There are eddies here that you can't see but can drag you under."

"Why are you here?" Compelled to return to the scene of the crime? She blocked the thought out.

"Washing graffiti off the signs."

A good Samaritan through and through. "You do that often?"

"Every few weeks."

A routine. Did Kayla know? But where were his supplies? "Without soap?"

David smiled, the patient smile of a man used to answering children's questions. "I left it on the walkway."

She hadn't heard his car pull up. "How long have you been here?"

"Five minutes, maybe. I'll walk you back up. Make sure you don't hurt yourself."

Why did that sound threatening?

David stepped aside to let her pass. She'd wanted to go down further, but he wasn't going to leave without her, that much was obvious. "Thanks."

He followed behind her. A presence at her back that sent panic scrabbling through her.

If only he'd gone ahead.

Normally outgoing and talkative, David was silent now. His runners crunched over gravel and dry leaves, lanky legs eating up the ground.

She reached the top. A firm hand at her back nudged her toward the walkway. Away from her Jeep.

"See?" David pointed to the walkway. "Soap, brush, and bucket."

The bucket was full. Suds floated on the surface.

Neon letters bled down red metal. Any warning hidden under wildstyle graffiti.

Proof he hadn't lied? About that, at least.

The breeze snatched her breath away. This was a mistake.

In between the steel posts, there was nothing but air. Below, water churned. "This is how you're spending your Sunday afternoon?"

He shrugged, his expression whitewashed by the sun. "Danger signs don't do much if you can't read them."

She planted her feet on wooden boards that creaked. "Seems like you had a busy weekend."

He frowned. Body tensed in jagged lines, a mass of wary shock. "Why do you say that?"

"Yesterday Kayla came by the gallery on her own."

He picked up the brush. Water splashed onto dry wood. "You know how it is." He shook the excess off, splattering drops. "She's busy organizing the Haunted Carnival. I had prep to do. Though I could have saved myself the effort, now that Monday's field trip to the marina has been cancelled. Goes to show, you can't plan for everything."

A comment that applied to life or death. If the attack on Laura had been carefully planned, the rest had spiralled out of control. "Did you do your lesson planning in the Coffee Nook?" He sometimes did.

"In my apartment." Stiff bristles scraped over metal. "I don't have an alibi, if that's what you're asking."

The casual remark jolted through her. "For what?"

"Laura's murder."

"No one said anything about murder." Yet.

"No?" He eyed her with a sharp blue-grey gaze. "She should have been more careful around the water."

Charley kept her expression neutral. Who was interrogating who? "What did you hear?"

"Not much. But I can put two and two together. A woman in her fifties dies at the marina. No one's too upset by it. Who else is it going to be?"

The clue he'd relied on to piece it together was emotion, not fact. "You didn't like her."

"Like and dislike don't have anything to do with it." His fingers tightened on the brush. He scrubbed the same surface again, his gaze on the sign but his attention elsewhere. "When she bribed Shannon to back down, I stepped up."

The president of the Cottage Association? An honorary member of the not-for-profit volunteer organization since she opened the Old General Store, Shannon didn't own a cottage or lakefront property. But she'd beat out her competitor for president by a landslide vote anyway. It helped that she handled drama with the ease of a former costume designer turned shopkeeper, used to sweet-talking actors and customers. She knew the ins and outs of the cottage community. "Bribe is a strong word."

David jerked a shoulder. "I always think it's best to call it what it is. Laura paid her membership dues to find out who to influence and who to avoid. Everyone knows, if you want the waterfront scoop, you join the club. And once she was in, she silenced the president with a cheque made out to" — David scrubbed harder — "the Aquatic Invasive Species Prevention Fund."

Pointing the finger at Shannon. But Charley had seen the woman in her apartment at a time when Laura's clothes were still dripping wet. There was no way Shannon could have been in two places at once. "If she did take a cash donation, she probably assumed there was enough opposition to sink Laura's proposal."

"Then she had insider intel, because it felt like a one-man show to me."

The roar became louder, deafening. Waves crashed in the river.

"Releasing," David shouted, his words snatched away. "Flash flooding dry ground. Downstream."

Sweeping away any evidence there might have been.

Below them, the roar died off to a rumble.

"Water levels can change fast," he said, "swamp everything in sight." Paint-muddied drops ran down his arm. "You taught an art club, right? Do you think my seven-year-olds could draw what the world would look like if air was water?"

A chill ran through her. The reference was too close to Laura's cause of death. "What are they learning?"

David shoved the bucket closer to the edge of the walkway. "The ways in which living things, including humans, depend on air and water."

And how that could be used against them? "I'm sure you'll get some creative sketches."

"That's what I'm hoping for." He grinned. "Yeah, we'll get through Monday just fine." Confidence warmed up his voice like a glaze of cadmium yellow.

"I'd wish you luck, but I don't think you'll need it."

He scoured away the wildstyle curves and arrows, the intricate shapes, revealing the red letters beneath. N — G — E. "Here's a fun fact for you: Sixteen percent of British Columbians believe in Ogopogo."

The legendary serpent of Okanagan Lake was well-documented in the media. Had even become the smiling mascot of a local hockey team. But statistics could be manipulated. "Monsters are great for tourism."

"I'll bet Oakcrest's stats will shoot through the roof when your exhibit is over." The boyish enthusiasm was a forgery of the real thing, and nowhere near a perfect fake. "But you might want to look for inspiration somewhere else. This isn't the place for it."

David stepped back, read the sign with a satisfied nod.

DANGER

FIFTEEN

HAD SHANNON REALLY taken a bribe? She was about to find out.

Charley pulled open the door of the Old General Store. Cocoa nosed in ahead of her, on the scent of the maple syrup candles, hand poured into recycled sugar shack tins.

The dark wooden shelving, Benjamin Moore Blue walls, and cast-iron hooks echoed the feel of the hardware store that once occupied the building. From the digital jukebox in the corner, Ella Fitzgerald crooned about a paper moon sailing over a cardboard sea. Hudson's Bay blankets hung draped over the rungs of a wall ladder. Blue Heron Cottage Association T-shirts dangled from a metal rack, the slogan promising wearers they'd be "Living on Lake Time."

Out of sight, the cash register chimed, barely interrupting the flow of chatter. "— right outside the gallery."

Charley stopped short beside a table of ceramics. Not eavesdropping. She didn't have to. The conversation was loud enough as it was.

"On the street," the woman continued, "arguing in plain sight."

Two guesses who they were talking about.

Annoyance simmering, Charley tugged Cocoa away from the tins of hard candies and headed around the shelf of small-batch bitters and Tyrrell's chips.

The woman standing at the counter had her back turned to Charley, her jeans and navy jacket a subdued contrast to Shannon's brick-red wool shirt-dress and brown pumps. The woman didn't look familiar, but Charley had gotten used to being recognized by strangers. Less so to being gossiped about.

Over the woman's shoulder, Shannon's gaze met Charley's. She winked, crow's feet deepening on a flash of black liner, more like brush-stroke calligraphy than kohl.

Shannon packaged up a brightly patterned wool shawl, one of the Ojibway Star Quilt designs, symbolizing honour and protection. The ghost of a dimple creased her cheek as she tied a turquoise ribbon to the handles. "If you're leaving this at the cottage through the winter, store it somewhere clean and dry. Safe from moisture and" — the dimple deepened — "pests."

The woman took the bag from her with a crunch of paper. "Can't seem to get rid of 'em, no matter what I do."

Shannon nodded. "I know *just* what you mean. I'd say Charley does too."

The woman pivoted on her heel. A flush darkened her skin when she saw Charley.

So much for being subtle. But, given the opening ... Charley bit back a grin. "I've had some in the gallery."

"Well, I —" the woman stuttered. "I should get going."

Shannon waggled her fingers after her. "Take care now."

The customer fled the shop with a crash of door chimes.

Shannon's laugh gave every joke an x-rated edge. She rested her palms on the counter — just an old door balanced on wooden legs, topped by a sheet of glass. "You put on a good show on Saturday, but you could get people really talking. Change that sketch you did for the Cottage Association newsletter to the monster, attacking."

Not much worse than the sketch she'd originally done for Shannon. White pines, ripples tinged with blood, and a floating paddle. More of a premonition now than promotion for the exhibit. "That might just make the rumours worse."

Shannon shrugged. "Live a little. Fan the fire. Watch the flames dance."

"Or let it burn itself out." Like the charred remains at the dam.

"How boring." Shannon smiled, nose wrinkling. "But safer. Monsters are like wild horses. Some take longer to break than others." She circled around the counter and rubbed Cocoa's ears. "But you're already broke to death, aren't you?"

The turn of phrase sent a prickle of unease through Charley. A tamed monster too close to why she was here. "You know how my Saturday afternoon went." Casual. Careful. "How was yours?"

"Productive." Shannon gave Cocoa one last pat and straightened. She touched a hand to her belt and twirled. "My latest creation. A vintage Butterick pattern, completed on Saturday afternoon, by six p.m. sharp. A shirt-dress with collar, contrasting cuffs, and flounced skirt. Worn with" — she pointed a toe — "seamed stockings and" — she twitched her hem up, flashing white fabric beneath — "a crinoline."

A hand-stitched alibi. "It's gorgeous."

Shannon nodded. "Bravo would have been better, or wild applause, but I'll take what I can get."

The dress was detailed. But had anyone actually seen Shannon earlier that day? Had she really been in her apartment the entire afternoon? "Did Jenny mind the shop for you again?" Thomas's daughter occasionally did, on Saturdays.

"From ten a.m. on. She's doing such a fantastic job tending the cash, if I were more trusting, I'd give her a set of keys and steal the whole day for myself."

Jenny would be able to confirm the time. And that scratched the president of the Cottage Association off the suspect list, which left David at the top. So much for getting the waterfront scoop.

Cocoa wandered to the end of the lead, nose sniffing dangerously close to the candle flame.

"Mint tea?" Shannon asked.

Share a cup and she might get some intel. "Sure, thanks."

Shannon turned to the shelves, secured in the drywall beside a hand-drawn lake map. Old but new to the store. Detailed as a medieval map, down to the great blue heron flying across the lake. Not exactly a mythical animal but too menacing to be anything but a reference to the bizarre terrestrial-aquatic hybrid animals sixteenth-century map-makers added to suggest a world full of danger.

Hadn't there been photos on that wall before? Personal shots. Smoky club scenes. A kiss in front of the limestone arches of the St. Lawrence Market. The lip-lock between Shannon and a mystery man was candid but the hues too saturated to be an amateur shot. Postcards. Close-ups of textiles. All replaced now by a pen and ink arial view of their lake, framed in reclaimed wood.

Shannon reached past the retro kettle for a jar of thick gold liquid and a vintage Lipton soup tin. She popped the metal lid with a waft of spearmint. "Loose leaf. What's the point of beating the flavour out of a tea bag, when you can let it unfold naturally?" From the display table, she chose two cups, painted with white pines. "I'll just wash these. Chip the pottery and you'll pay for it. Literally."

Charley leaned against the counter. "Cash or debit?"

"I take both." Shannon disappeared into the backroom.

A tap ran, water splashing.

It had been a few weeks since Charley had last been in the store, but other than the wall of pictures, nothing had changed. The hand-painted wooden stand shaped like a loon still perched beside the register, straining under the weight of spiral-bound Blue Heron Lake cookbooks. Edited and printed by the Cottage Association.

The vintage metal recipe box on the cover could have been a replica of Grandma Reilly's. Although she'd stored 2 oz. bottles of J. Herbin's scented fountain pen ink in hers, not index cards. Lavender and rose — her favourite shades for nature studies.

Charley picked a copy up, flipped to the first page. A line of text ran under the black-and-white photo of the library, which doubled as the community centre. *A book about what we cook and eat together at the lake and the relationships that keep us inviting friends and family to our cottages. Thanks to our lake association and cottagers for sharing their recipes.*

Shannon returned, drying the cups with a tea towel. "All proceeds go to protect the lake experience and preserving the natural landscape."

"I'll take one." Matt would love it.

"We'll call it payment for the sketch you did."

But she couldn't let Shannon print that drawing in the newsletter, not now. "I was thinking of changing it. Submitting something else."

"Then the cookbook is an advance. To ensure you deliver."

It could have been a bribe. "What did you think of Laura?"

"I've known enough character actresses in my time to recognize a persona when I see one." Shannon measured out tea leaves into sieves, spooned sticky liquid from the jar. "Honey. Better than a throat lozenge. In the theatre and in the shop, you lose your voice at your own peril. Forget persuading a shy starlet to drop her clothes. Try convincing a cottager to open her wallet on the way to the lake."

Charley grinned. "Honey's the secret?"

"To catching more flies? You bet." Shannon pitched her voice over the rush of boiling water. "Shame Laura didn't try that strategy. She might have made more friends."

And fewer enemies? "Was she close to anyone in Oakcrest?"

"Soul sisters and confidantes? She didn't go in for heart-to-hearts. Not that that made her heartless." Shannon drained the sieves with a dark swirl of tannins, slid a cup in front of Charley.

"You didn't argue against her proposal."

The pause was brief, a single frozen moment the length of a breath. Then Shannon smiled. "I had a better plan for her. With that head for numbers, she would have made the perfect treasurer."

"Volunteer to protect the lake?" Somehow, she couldn't imagine it. "It seems like Laura was generous with the Association." Too generous?

Shannon shrugged. "You have to give to receive."

And claim a debt? "Donating money or time?"

"You mean, when her minutes were counted?"

Charley winced. "Not that she realized it."

"Barely fifty." Shannon tutted. "How lucky we are, to believe we still have half our lives ahead of us. You don't imagine it'll end one night at a marina. After a tangle with a freshwater serpent."

Charley swallowed a honey-laced sip, nearly choked.

Eric. He hadn't even held out twenty-four hours. So much for keeping secrets. The news was out now.

Charley wrapped her hands around her mug, felt the heat against her palms. "The lake monster is just a story. A cautionary tale, to keep kids away from danger." It had worked on her. But — "It's a fantasy creature."

Shannon levelled an amused glance at her over the rim of her cup. And said nothing.

"You don't really believe there's a monster swimming in our lake."

A wry expression crossed Shannon's face. "Skin and bones and heart and all?" Her careful diction sliced through the smoke-sweetened air. "I don't have to believe it. I've seen it."

Charley jolted. Hot tea sloshed over her fingers onto the counter. "Seen what?"

"Your monster." The woman's voice was soft as ripples on water. "Three years ago. Black and snake-like, with a ring of brown around her neck. Her head rose, four or five feet above the surface."

Shannon's description could have been a quote from *Shipwrecks, Monsters, and Mysteries of the Great Lakes*. Charley's heart raced. "Where?"

"Right here." Bronze nail polish glittering, Shannon placed a finger on the map. On the space between two small circles, near Fire Route 36A and the library.

Cursive-italic script arched above the markings. *Knights Nightmare. Table Rocks.* An undeveloped island and a flat slab of exposed Precambrian rock that jutted above the water. Far away from the dam. But close to Laura's house.

"Did you get a photo?"

Shannon laughed. "Sweetheart, you can't always trust a camera." She leaned closer and whispered, "They lie."

But a reflection on the lake could create an optical illusion too.

Charley looked at the map, at the terracotta ink on off-white paper. More art than science. "Medieval cartographers filled blank spaces with sea monsters, because they were afraid of leaving empty spaces in their work." Filling gaps in perspective. A warning for travellers. *Here there be tygers.* "The same way this artist filled in the centre of the lake with a sketch of a blue heron in flight."

"You'll have to take that up with Thomas."

Caught off guard, Charley fought the urge to move closer, to study the details. "This is his work?" She should have guessed it. Normally a painter, he didn't have much practice in hand lettering. The script labelling the boat launch had bled on loose paper fibres, the pencil too heavily erased before the ink work, not after.

"I spotted him pouring over an old lake map and wrangled him into the job." Shannon drained her cup. "The copy turned out better than the original. Good thing too, considering what he charged me for it."

A wavy line traced the shore. *Her head rose, four or five feet above the surface.* "You think the lake monster is female?"

"Don't you?"

Charley shivered.

Horror vacui. The art history term was no longer a dusty fragment from a half-forgotten textbook, but advice for the here and now.

The need to fill voids in maps with imaginary monsters. Out of fear.

Until the land, the water, was explored. And the truth revealed.

SIXTEEN

MATT SAT AT the desk, well aware he was leaning over it, the same way his dad had for years. The chair one notch higher, but the similarities were getting harder to ignore, even when he was thinking about chocolate splatter instead of blood splatter, or working on a cookbook that might never see the light of day. And more so now, when his thoughts kept turning back to murder.

Matt glanced up at the sheet of paper he'd left tacked into the drywall above the typewriter.

Write your way to the truth. A note to self with yellowed corners and a missing splice through the heart of the *t*. And Dad got there in the end.

Matt swivelled the chair around and stared at the PI novels lined up in a row on the bookshelf. The pseudonym on the spines. The paperbacks that might not have his dad's name on them but were filled with the plots he'd spun right here. Brainstorming mysteries for his fictional hero to crack. Shutting everything else out for black marks on a page. Choosing to escape into a world of murder and solitary detectives.

What did it take to turn a good man bad? The answer wasn't in fiction. Matt leaned back in the chair, laced his hands behind his head.

No matter the method, it boiled down to the same ingredients.

A dark and bitter seed of emotion. Hatred, resentment. Anger and betrayal.

Matt reached for the envelope on the desk he hadn't yet sealed, even though he'd found a sheet of stamps in the drawer that covered the postage and more.

He took the photo out and felt the familiar stab of anger hit between his ribs. Slice straight through, whetstone sharp.

Sepia-hued and faded, Jeffrey laughed up at him from the helm of a motorboat. A moment in time captured decades ago. Before he'd taken on the father role his own dad had been more than happy to pass on. The photograph was a storage-box find Matt had meant to give to Jeffrey, but that was before. Now he was stuck with a keepsake he didn't want, in a workspace cluttered with memories and a handful of typed-up recipes.

Cooking, at its most basic, was a chemical reaction. Remove one element and the reaction failed. All you had to do was kill the heat. Or add a new flavour that changed the recipe.

But to do that, you had to know what the ingredients were.

Any recipe can be changed, if you know how it works. Jeffrey's voice shot through his mind. Advice from the past. A memory almost as faded as the photograph. What had he said?

"Recipes can be adapted," Matt murmured. "Turned into something new. If you've got the skills." Always that little challenge, that push to aim higher.

He'd had the skills, once. Maybe, if he solved this mystery for Beverley, he'd get them back.

The doorbell rang, jerking him back to the here and now.

Matt was halfway to the front door before he realized he was still holding the photograph in his hand. He paused, took out his wallet, slid it in between a ten and a twenty. He could figure out what to do with it later.

When he opened the door, Charley aimed a smile at him that swept thoughts of lies and deception clean out of his mind. Cocoa stood at her feet, fun glinting in both their eyes.

Charley said, "You were looking for inspiration."

Either she'd read his mind, or it was just that obvious. Matt leaned a shoulder against the door jamb, kept the shock off his face with a grin. "I think I just found it."

"Nope. I beat you to it. Here." It took him a second to realize she held a spiral-bound book out to him.

Glossy cover, paperback-weight paper. "A Cottage Association cookbook?"

"I thought you might like it." She stepped past him, into the house, all but bouncing in her sneakers. But it wasn't all excitement. Or even anticipation. Not with that edgy undertone of nerves. Cocoa pranced circles around his feet, just as hyped up.

He flipped the pages and recognized the names, the roads in titles. Recipes, passed down through generations, shared neighbour to neighbour. *Nan's Coffee Cake. Mr. R's Ultimate* BBQ *Ribs. Venison Spaghetti Sauce (Carol's).* A story to go with each one. Simple dishes seasoned with memories and emotions, packing a flavour punch you couldn't buy in a shop, or at any farmer's market.

Charley sat on the wooden bench to yank her shoes off. "Chocoholic's was closed early."

He'd locked the door to chase info and come back empty-handed. Because it felt like she'd caught him playing hooky, he shrugged. "I had an errand to run."

"Groceries?"

He thought of his empty fridge. Probably should have. "Are you hungry?" Cocoa nudged past him. A second later a collar tag jangled on metal. Nose in the water bowl he'd bought for her. But the best thing he had to offer Charley was an open bottle of red wine.

"Starving, but we don't have time to eat."

He led the way to the kitchen anyway, remembering too late that he'd left dishes stacked in the drying rack. He winced at the Nutella-stained knife lying in the sink, the box of crackers and jar of chocolate-hazelnut spread on the counter. Too late to hide now. "Got plans?"

She grinned at him. "Are you up for an adventure?"

The memory of laughter in the half-light of candles and lace under his fingertips had his blood leaping. He slid his hands around her waist and ran them up her back. "Depends on what you had in mind."

"A boat ride."

It took a beat for him to refocus, catch up. "What?"

"To search along the shore."

It would only take a minute or two to hook up the johnboat's trailer to his truck. But — Matt glanced out the window at the haze of pink on the horizon. "It'll be dark soon." Hard to see the rocks lurking beneath the surface of the water. And whatever the hell else was out there.

Drawing her closer, he nibbled a line down her neck, teeth scraping lightly, and felt her pulse scramble.

"We'll be fine" — she said, voice catching as his fingers tangled in her hair — "if we leave now." She pulled away.

Matt sighed. Might as well give it one last shot. "And miss dinner?"

"That's what snacks are for." She reached for the box of crackers and passed a Triscuit to Cocoa in a seasoned move. "We've got that covered."

Matt scrubbed a hand over his jaw. "Do you want a plate?"

"Just a knife." Charley reached for the cutlery drawer, slid it open before he could move to stop her.

Matt fought the urge to grab the handle and slam it closed, hiding the stack of envelopes he didn't want her to see.

It was his own fault; he'd set the table with that cutlery early on in their relationship, trying to make an impression with antique silverware.

"Don't tell me," Charley said. "Blackmail letters?"

The address was written in Jeffrey's half-legible scrawl, same as Matt's favourite recipes. Pencil scratches on pages torn from yellow legal pads, gritty with sawdust. The basis of the best chocolates in his shop.

Maybe it had always taken two minds to come up with those flavours.

Matt had two options. He could answer. Confess to hiding those letters was the easiest fix. Or he could dodge the topic, like Jeffrey always had. "Being the only chocolatier in town, I'm an easy target." He nudged the drawer closed, sealing it with a click. Those blue eyes looked at him like she saw straight through him.

"That would explain why you haven't bought any groceries."

"Because I'm being bled dry." The line echoed with a note of déjà vu he tried hard to ignore.

"Makes sense then, that you'd keep the letters with the knives." Too much empathy there. An offer to take the conversation any way he wanted.

He ignored it. "Safest place for them," Matt said.

"A weapon on hand. Easy to grab."

"Only as a last resort." He opened the drawer by the coffee maker. Took out a stainless-steel butter knife and handed it to her. "Whatever Jeffrey has to say, it doesn't matter, not in the long run."

She reached for the jar he'd left on the counter, unscrewed the lid on a scent of hazelnuts and cocoa butter, shot a glance at him in a way that had his nerves jangling. "Are you sure about that?"

You're only cunning until the end. Thomas's words came back to him. "I'll read them, when I'm ready." Eventually he would be. But not yet.

"Out of sight, out of mind?" Charley took a cracker from the box. "How's that working out for you?"

"Pretty well." Up until right now.

"Uh-huh." Charley spread a thick layer of chocolate cream on a cracker.

To lighten the mood, he took it from her. "Thanks." He grinned and popped it in his mouth.

She rolled her eyes and dug out another cracker. "You're as bad as Cocoa."

The dog wagged her tail.

The taste on his tongue more salt than sweet, Matt grabbed a glass from the dish rack, filled it with tap water, took a swig. Let the clean taste fill his mouth, wash away the chocolate. "How about fish for dinner?"

She sealed the bag on the crackers. "The grocery store had some on sale."

"We can do better than that. A fresh catch. Fry it in some butter and herbs." He glanced at the parsley on his windowsill. The plant looked like it needed saving. Or its last rites. "Maybe lemon and garlic." He opened the fridge, grabbed the one item he still stocked on a weekly basis.

Charley peered over his shoulder. "Bacon?"

"Bait." Dad's tip. One of the few family traditions Matt had kept up.

"What are you trying to catch?"

"Smallmouth bass." Or a lake monster.

Two hours left until dusk. Not enough time to pinpoint an exact location — not without a lot of luck — but they might be able to narrow the options down.

He didn't have Thomas's drawing, but he'd recognize the place, if he saw it. A sketch was as good as a map.

THE PROW OF the boat rose and crashed down hard. Cold mist sprayed Charley's skin. An icy splash, too much like when Meghan had shouted, "The water's fine!" And lied.

Charley had spent hours floating starfish-like in the lake, buoyed up from below, sunspots dancing over her toes. But today the peaks and tree-lined shores seemed less familiar. The lake bigger. Deeper. The sandy bottom a long way down.

Where dark things stirred and swam. Just like Grandpa said.

"Laura could have been standing on a dock." Matt navigated around an orange buoy. "Maybe someone hid underneath. Grabbed her ankles and yanked her in. Held her under."

Dark water closing over her. Charley shook off the image. "You'd need a wetsuit for that, this time of year."

Cocoa hung her head over the side of the boat. Prickly tentacles of seaweed broke through the surface, brushing at the hull.

Laura's house was around the next peak. Or it should be. The fog settling in the pines made it harder to tell where they were. The cottages were just flashes of coloured siding between the trees. Even with the islands as markers, the brown ink lines of Thomas's map were hard to trace.

The boat rocked on the swell of a wave. A gust of wind whipped Charley's hair into her eyes, a mean streak to it. The bite of winter frost. "Alex said Laura's canoe was still tied to her dock."

Matt scanned the shoreline, the outcroppings of rock. "If she was out on the lake, got dragged into the water by something she thought was a lake monster, she'd have to get in her canoe, then paddle all the way back."

The dam made more sense as a point of attack. Laura could have driven there and back again. But. Charley looked at the slate-grey lake, a tingle pricking at the back of her neck. "If Laura got attacked on shore, it had to be somewhere with easy water access."

The boat rocked on the swells.

The next wave broke on granite rock.

Matt swore. "Hold on!"

The boat jerked. Cocoa bumped against her knees. Rock scraped the aluminum hull with a scream of metal that vibrated through Charley's bones.

Matt's face was grim, knuckles white on the tiller steer. "Are you okay?"

"Great." The next wave washed over the hull of the boat, soaking her jeans. Cocoa lapped at the puddle in the bottom of the boat.

Matt pitched his voice over the engine, the crash of water. "We're going to have to go slower."

"I won't argue. I'd rather not get stranded on a rock." Not with the sun going down.

"It's not the worst thing." Matt flashed his crooked grin, his eyes on the horizon ahead of them. "Dad hit a rock once, when we went fishing."

From the warmth filling his voice, it was a good memory. One that had seeped into the cracks. "How old were you?"

"Maybe six. It sounded like the boat was being torn in half. I flew off the seat, scraped my knees on the bottom of the boat."

The after-effect of adrenaline still spiking her blood, Charley said, "You're right. It sounds like a blast."

"All Dad had was bacon, a hook, and some cheap fishing rods. And suddenly, we were stuck out there, on the lake. Just the two of us, the engine high and dry." A pirate gleam lit Matt's eyes. The thrill was contagious.

"So, the bacon worked?"

"Nope." He grinned. "Didn't catch a thing. Eventually, we got a tow back. Mom skinned him alive. But it was her idea to open a can of tuna."

More than just a quick fix for dinner, but a part of the adventure. "You had fish for supper anyway."

"Tuna melt sandwiches, grilled under the broiler with a side of dill pickles and chips. Best sandwich I ever had."

Made better by the memory. By then, Lizzie must have ended the affair she'd been having with Jeffrey. Put her family first.

Charley should tell him. The truth pressed at her chest. But she couldn't. Matt still hadn't gotten his love for chocolate back. The joy was missing. And if she told him what she knew, it would only become worse. So, she said instead, "I like that story."

"Me too." The smile hitched a corner of his mouth.

Between the trees, silvery siding loomed. Charley straightened. "That must be it."

Matt steered toward the property.

The copper roof bled green stains down the pale siding from snow melt and rainwater runoff. The metal spokes of the dock rose into the air, uneven. The dock listed to the left.

A canoe rocked against the dock bumpers.

Charley leaned forward, a fizz of excitement building inside her.

Matt idled close to the dock, let them drift. The johnboat swayed, rising on the next swell. The lake was a living, breathing creature beneath them.

The canoe was long and wide. Probably sixteen feet long. The hull formed from red cedar, aged and darkened. Brass tacks flashed, catching the dying light. "Doesn't look like it would tip easily."

Matt shook his head. "You'd have to be experienced to handle that canoe. See the shallow arch bottom? If Laura paddled Canadian style, she'd be kneeling low, close to the water. And that depth would catch the wind. But just look at those decks." His tone was reverent. "That mahogany trim and hand-caned seats. Heartwood."

The water was darker, rougher now, and taking on a shade close to black. Opaque as ink.

Nailed to a tree was a yellow sign. *No Trespassing.* Charley shot a glance at Matt. "That sign makes a pretty clear statement."

He nodded. "It's kind of hard to spot, though."

She grinned. "It is faded."

"Hardly readable." Brown eyes locked on hers.

Charley said, "We should take a closer look."

"Just to be sure." Matt eased the boat alongside the dock.

She caught hold of the metal pole and passed the wet nylon rope around it and through the loop. Her fingers remembered the half hitch knot Grandpa had taught her, even though it had been years since he'd shown it to her. "The water is too shallow for anyone to hide under the dock. Laura would have seen them right away."

Matt dug his hands in his jacket pockets. "But if she walked up to the house from here, we might still be able to spot traces."

Scuffed leaves. "Footprints. Alex's anyway."

"A good couple shoe sizes bigger than Laura's."

Cocoa would have to wait in the boat. Even if she could scout out evidence for them, she'd trample any prints. Charley rubbed her ears. "You're going to have to stay here. We'll be right back."

Cocoa glanced up at Matt.

He shook his head. "I'm with Charley on this one."

Grudgingly, Cocoa sat down in the boat.

Matt knelt to check out the canoe, but a flash of colour caught Charley's eye. There, between the brown tree trunks, a metre above the thick layer of rust-coloured leaves, a line of red floated in the air.

String? Too high to keep geese off the property.

She moved closer, touched a finger to it.

Wire.

Strung taut between the oak trees, straight across the open expanse of lawn that led to the water. Some kind of makeshift alarm system?

Matt came up behind her and whistled through his teeth. "That's nasty."

"To stop people from trespassing?"

He nodded, his expression grim. "But not on foot. She's got a bolt snap hook on this end, so she can open it, walk through. But, in the winter, snowmobiles come up off the lake, use properties, especially empty cottages, to cut back up to the road. Most people put up a snow fence. Bright enough to see and a decent barricade. This" — he nodded at the wire — "is closer to a booby trap. See the height of it? Hit that wire at high speed, sitting on a snow-mobile, and it can take your head off."

A shiver ran through her that had nothing to do with the wind gusting off the water. "Isn't that illegal?"

"Only if it's concealed. The wire is red, and she's got it flagged with a warning sign at one end." Tucked nearly out of sight, close to the tree. "She could argue her case, if anything happened."

"We did say she was ruthless." Charley ducked underneath, Matt right behind her.

Behind them, something splashed into the water.

Charley whirled around.

The boat was empty.

Where was Cocoa? Fear hit. Charley shielded her eyes from the setting sun, scanning the choppy water for a dark head. "Do you see her?"

Matt searched. "There." He pointed.

Ripples spread, rings spiralling out.

"Cocoa, come here!" No reaction. Either her ears were water-logged, or she was fixated on chasing ... what? There wasn't a bird in sight. Had she spotted a fish?

Or something bigger.

Matt asked, "If she wears herself out, will she turn back?"

"Not a chance." Charley headed for Matt's boat. "Labrador retrievers are bred for swimming." In the icy waters of Newfoundland. "Her thick undercoat will protect her from the cold. We're going to have to go after her." Act, now, before Cocoa was out of earshot. Or out of sight.

Charley yanked the trailing end of rope out of the water, working to loosen the knots she'd just tied. Too tight. Her numb fingers couldn't get a good grip on it. She flexed them, tried again. "If Cocoa gets disoriented in the water or goes up on land somewhere, we'll lose her." She fought to keep her voice calm, but fear clutched at her heart.

How would they get Cocoa back into the boat? Sixty pounds of slippery fur.

Motorboats wouldn't be on the lookout for a Labrador retriever. How much daylight did they have left? They couldn't lose her, not in the dark.

"Keep your eye on her." Matt climbed in the boat and revved the engine.

Cocoa was now halfway to the island. The one marked on Shannon's map. *Knights Nightmare.*

"How fast can she swim?" he asked.

"Faster than you'd think." Charley scanned, searching.

There, a gleam of brown fur.

Closer. They were gaining on her.

Cocoa glanced back and started paddling harder away from them. What was she doing?

"Can you cut the engine for a second?" In the silence, Charley called for her again. "Cocoa!"

A wave swept over the dog's head. Charley's heart leapt into her throat.

A dark brown head bobbed to the surface in the shallows.

"There's nowhere to dock," Matt said, his tone worried.

"Just get me close enough." Charley yanked off her sneakers, grabbed the leash she should have kept Cocoa on. On impulse, she reached for the cooler, shoved the Ziploc bag of cured meat in her pocket.

Grim, Matt said, "Told you, bacon's the perfect bait."

"Let's hope Cocoa's the biggest catch of the day." Charley climbed out of the boat. Her feet hit cold water and she sucked in a sharp breath.

Cocoa plunged through the shallows, heading toward sand. The cluster of wind-shaped pines and bare rock.

Charley's socks dug into silt, sucked down into ooze. "Cocoa, get back here."

Cocoa stopped moving. Intent on something on the ground. A fish? Or something worse?

The painting of Ophelia flashed through Charley's mind, water-soaked hair fanning out.

Charley sped up. "Got you." She caught hold of Cocoa's collar, clipped the leash on with shaking hands. Cocoa nosed at the thing on the sand. Something copper and white.

Charley's skin crawled. Her reaction was physical, even as her brain processed what she saw.

Burnished fur. Bone and flesh. An animal head.

Her stomach twisted. She glanced back over her shoulder.

Long marks she hadn't noticed before but saw now trailed through the sand. Leading to — no, from — the water.

"Matt." She cleared her throat, tried again, louder. "Cocoa found something."

In the boat, he shielded his eyes with one hand. "Good girl. Evidence?"

Yes. But not the kind they'd been looking for. "A fox." What was left of it.

Our brains are wired to see monsters.

Monsters that weren't there. That didn't exist. But here, right now, she was looking at proof.

A deep groove, clearly visible even where loose sand rolled into the imprint. A sinuous trail, like the track of a snake, only bigger. Much bigger.

SEVENTEEN

AN HOUR LATER, in the glow of Charley and Meghan's kitchen, Matt still couldn't shake the line snapping at the heels of his thoughts. *The killing bite.*

Why would Thomas sketch the carcass, then move it? Draw attention to it? And not the whole thing. Just the skull.

But if he didn't move it, who — or what — did?

"Are you done with that?" Charley reached past him for the Dijon mustard.

"Sure." He'd barely finished buttering his sourdough toast, but he was lucky he'd scored a corner of the counter to make his sandwich. Nearby, Alex spooned coffee grounds into the filter. Meghan had staked her claim on the kitchen table. Even the floor space was at a premium, most of it occupied by a wet chocolate Lab, sprawled full length and twitching in her sleep.

Alex flipped the switch on the coffee maker. "The beach gets the brunt of the wind. The carcass could have washed to shore from somewhere else."

Charley raised a brow. "Just the head?"

And that was a visual Matt wouldn't be able to shake for a long time.

"Look, between us, I have no idea what this is." Alex swiped a bread and butter pickle off Meghan's plate. "I've documented the facts — if we can call them that — but you're asking me to submit a report connecting a fox skull on a beach to a death at the marina the day before."

Charley pointed her knife at Alex. "Caused by a near-drowning."

"All we know is that Laura inhaled enough water for her lungs to fill with pulmonary oedema fluid, leading to asphyxiation. Not that someone tried to drown her."

That stopped Matt halfway through slicing off a hunk of cheddar. Maybe the cop was just playing devil's advocate. Or maybe he really believed there hadn't been any foul play, that Laura's death was an accident and nothing more.

Meghan squeezed ketchup onto a slice of Wonder Bread from a height. Then mayo, squirting a white line down the centre of the pool of red. "Don't you normally say there's no such thing as coincidence in an investigation?"

Alex lined up colourful Fiesta Ware mugs on the counter, the scent of fresh coffee adding a caffeine kick to the air. "Nothing about this is normal."

At least he had that right. Matt watched Meghan load up three slices of ham and winced. "Same as that sandwich."

Meghan squished the second slice of bread on top, leaving behind four finger imprints. "Do you put tomatoes on your ham sandwich?"

"Yeah, but —"

Meghan licked ketchup off her thumb. "I rest my case."

Alex reached for the pot, not yet full, the coffee still running through. Drops hissed on the burner, scorching. He filled the cups, steam rising. "Those tracks — or whatever you want to call them — were made after the last rain, which means they could be anywhere from three to four hours old to forty-eight." He hesitated, one beat. "The doc said, if Laura had gone to the hospital, they might have been able to regulate her breathing."

The blood drained from Charley's face. "I let her leave the gallery."

As if she could have stopped her. "What were you going to do?" Matt asked. "Force her to stay?"

Alex spooned sugar in his cup, enough to turn the coffee to syrup. "That's called taking a hostage. I'd have to arrest you for that."

Charley looked out the window, blue just visible in the dark and nothing more. "But she'd still be alive."

Meghan shook her head. "Whoever or whatever attacked her is the one to blame. Not you."

Alex took the creamer from the fridge, slamming the door with enough force to rattle jars and plastic bottles. "Seems like that's one thing we've got more than enough of in this case. Questions."

"Luckily" — Meghan sliced her sandwich in half — "I happen to love questions."

"Here's another one for you." Charley carried her plate to the table. "Why a fox?"

Matt's shoulders tensed. Time to confess, he'd been hoarding intel. If that was what you could call it.

Charley leaned forward. "A fish — a muskie — would make more sense. Something a lake monster would eat." The tone was too similar to how she might talk about Cocoa's taste in kibble. "But of course," she said slowly, "a fish, no matter how big, wouldn't raise the same questions. Not at the beach, so close to the water. This is unsettling and I think that was the point."

"Unsettling is right," Alex muttered. "Where the hell are the footprints?"

There weren't any. The sand was undisturbed except for those side-looping tracks. A fast slither into the water.

Meghan shrugged, a gleam in her eye. "No footprints, no ... feet." She let that thought hang there.

Charley shook her head. "Smudged away, I'll bet. Hidden by the tracks."

It was possible. Matt carried his ham sandwich to the table, sat beside Charley. "Whoever put that carcass there could have escaped through the shallows."

Alex leaned against the counter, the only one still standing. The closest he could come to a uniform and badge? Or to stay in control? "It doesn't have to be human," he said. "Bears drag their prey, too."

To shelter, sure, but to a beach? Matt picked up his sandwich. "I've never heard of a bear taking food to an open space. And we didn't see any paw prints." He bit into the sourdough crust, tasted spicy mustard, cheddar, and maple-glazed ham.

"The meat is opening its eyes," Charley murmured.

Matt swallowed hard.

Meghan shuddered. "Now you're just creeping me out."

Charley tore the crust off her bread, scattering crumbs across her plate. "It's from one of Kayla's legends."

Those Inuit legends were not just a part of Kayla's childhood but Charley's too, the equivalent of a melting pot of friendship and life lessons that kept threatening to boil over.

Alex sighed. "Sure, let's add another story to the mix."

Charley reached for a paper napkin, pinned beneath Jadeite salt and pepper shakers. "Pen?"

Meghan magicked a ballpoint out of her pocket and passed it to Charley.

Matt shifted his chair closer to Charley's, watched her sketch out lines that had a rough edge to them. An urgency that was all tamped-down emotion.

In a storyteller's tone that sounded like someone else's, she said, "A grizzly bear living in human form stole away dead bodies from the nearest village to feed on." The short strokes turned to fur. Then eyes, nearly human. "One day, a man pretended to be dead. He lay down in a grave. The bear carried him to his home." Thick curved lines. Claws digging into the ground. No. Into sand. "The bear's children shouted, 'The meat is opening its eyes!' The man sprang up, took an axe, and killed the bear." Waves flowed up from the bottom edge of the napkin, ink bleeding on the absorbent paper. "The bear's wife chased after him, but the man drew a line on the ground with his finger. A great rushing river sprang from the ground. The bear's wife saw the river and asked how he got over it." Ripples spread around the female bear. "The man lied and said that he swallowed it down and emptied it. So, she lay down and drank and drank until" — Charley glanced up — "she burst. All the water she drank rose up in a mist over the earth and became fog."

A beat went by.

"Lies and deception," Matt said. That sounded about right.

Charley laid the pen down, straight across the centre of the drawing, dividing it into two halves. A plastic borderline. "In the legend, a human drew the line on the ground, not a bear."

Meghan reached for the napkin. Her thumb smudged ketchup over the bear's face, a red stain. "Life imitates art?"

And that was an opening if he'd ever heard one. It was now or never. Matt braced himself. "I've seen that carcass before. In a sketch."

They rounded on him as one. But Charley's gaze cut through him.

"Where?" Meghan asked.

"Whose sketch?" The snap to Alex's voice could have put him on track for an RCMP task force.

Matt held Charley's eyes. "Thomas's."

It was shock more than betrayal that flashed across her face. "Why didn't you say something before?"

Because he hadn't known enough. Because he'd wanted to get answers. Chase the truth. Unearth it, before it crawled out. But how the hell could he admit that with everyone staring at him? "When I drove Beverley back to the marina, we passed Thomas on the road. He had hip waders in his car, wet with lake water. And he was sketching that fox carcass."

Alex reached for the notebook he'd left lying open on the counter, the page already half filled with notes and a few question marks. "What makes you think it's the same one?"

"How rough was the sketch?" Charley asked. "What medium was he using?"

Matt shifted in his seat and figured he should have seen this coming, but that didn't help ease the regret or the guilt now. At least, he could answer that one. "Pastel pencil and chalk."

"Thick lines," Charley said.

"With enough details."

"But his work is abstract, more shapes than —"

"Not this one." It was hyperreal. Nearly identical.

"It would be better if we had the sketch, to compare," Alex said.

Meghan shook her head. "If that sketch can tie Thomas to the crime scene, I doubt he has it anymore."

Especially after he'd let slip that it was important. Matt kicked himself. And now he was about to make things worse. But he had to say it. "He told me he didn't see Laura."

Charley pinned him with a glance that had all of Alex's intimidation tactics beat. "He told you that?"

Alex looked pained. "Thomas was furious about the effect the hydroelectric dam could have on his shoreline. If someone attacked Laura, he's a viable suspect. And now it seems like he knows it."

Charley picked up the pen again, working designs into the corners. A whirlpool pattern spiralled out, flash flooding the bear. "Why would he draw attention to the carcass he was sketching?"

Meghan said slowly, "As an attempt to divert attention to the lake monster? Another victim attacked by something in the water."

Charley shook her head. "Thomas is smarter than that. He wouldn't have used the same animal."

"Maybe he didn't have much choice," Meghan suggested. "Roadkill would never work."

Alex raised a brow. "Too messy?"

Meghan polished off the last corner of ketchup-soaked toast. "The tire marks would be a dead giveaway. And with the coyotes and the wolves roaming around, intact carcasses are hard to find."

Alex straddled the chair across from Matt's. "Did Thomas tell you what he was doing there?"

Matt shrugged, raised his cup. He needed more caffeine in his system, if this was about to turn into an interrogation. "'Stalking autumn,' whatever that means."

Charley said slowly, "Artists study behaviour in people and animals. Catching those moments, those poses and gestures in the wild — it's like stalking prey."

Alex went still. "An artist as predator?" He leaned forward, elbows braced on the top rail of the wooden chair. "Here's a thought for you. Someone is trying to make it look like a lake monster actually exists. Not many people would want to do that." He looked at them each in turn. "Except if you're trying to raise interest in an exhibit with a lake monster theme."

Matt set his mug down, worried he'd snap the handle between his fingers. "What are you getting at?"

"Murder for profit and gain?" Charley asked, voice too dry. Not nearly enough nerves in it, though it seemed like the right time to worry.

Alex said, "If this turns into a homicide case, you should be my prime suspect, Charley."

Should be? Or would be? Nails biting into his palm, Matt realized he'd curled his hand into a fist, fought the urge to defend. Charley didn't need anyone to step in to battle for her.

She laid her fork and knife on her plate with a clink of steel on china. "Look for a better one."

They already had another lead to chase. "What about Thomas?"

Alex sighed. "The force isn't a one-man show. If this turns official, I have to go through the motions. Charley, you argued with Laura before she died. You were the last person to see her alive. You have motive —"

"A lot of people do," Meghan cut in. Waves of impatience radiated from her.

Alex held his ground. "There are too many similarities to Charley's research to ignore the connection."

Matt said, "It's still a local legend." Most people had heard of it at one point or another.

Alex nodded. "But Charley brought it back to everyone's attention."

Raising it from the dead?

Charley twisted the pen between her fingers. "I found most of my research material in the library. The books about lake monsters are shelved with shipwrecks on the Great Lakes and unfinished voyages. Anyone else could have read them too."

And checked them out, which might give them something to work with. "All Alex has to do is go over the circulation records."

Charley shook her head. "That won't help us. Deb set up a special display weeks ago. Lake monster themed. In-library use only."

Shit.

Meghan leaned forward, the ceiling light flaring off her red hair. "There's only one person who might have more info than all of us combined." She paused. "The original source. The kid who first saw the monster. Laura's victim."

Of a prank that happened years ago. "We have no idea who that is," Matt pointed out, "or if they're even local."

Meghan waved her hand. "Had to be. A cottager couldn't have spread the word that fast. I'm thinking born and raised in Oakcrest. All we need to do is find someone with a good memory."

But this was about the present, not the past. Matt said, "You're assuming this kid found out it *was* a prank. All we know is that he or she got taken in by a DIY costume, then told everyone who'd listen about the monster in the lake."

Alex nodded. "People kill to get something they want. Escape abuse. Claim an inheritance. Eliminate an obstacle. How would attacking Laura benefit the prank victim now?"

Meghan shrugged. A smile, close to bloodthirsty, played over her face. "I'd have to do an interview to find out."

"Focus on the past." Alex stood and pushed in his chair, the effect dampened by the felt feet whispering over linoleum tiles. "Because it'd make my life a lot easier, Charley, if you'd stop turning up at my crime scenes."

She tilted her head to the side. "So, you admit it's a crime scene."

Alex downed the last of his coffee, probably just as aware as Matt was that she hadn't made any promises.

EIGHTEEN

CHARLEY CUT THROUGH the farmer's market in the Mews toward the gallery. Even on a short leash, Cocoa pulled to sniff at a basket of acorn squash.

The only danger here was the combination of hungry canine and bushels of farm-fresh apples, displayed at nose level. Not an imaginary lake monster.

A shadow who could slip under a locked gallery door.

Even now, Charley could almost see the shape of it, slithering around the gleaming display of Honeycrisps, feel the scales brush her arm as it slipped right by her to wreak havoc.

She took a breath and blocked out the image. All she had to do this morning was complete the finishing touches on the exhibit.

But that final brushwork, those last few highlights, could add realism or destroy it. The trick was knowing when to step away from the painting and call it done.

Whoever attacked Laura didn't know when to stop, each element building, one on the other. Eventually, the details would clash, the mistake glaring enough even for Alex to see.

But wouldn't it be smarter to look for an error in the work in progress? Act instead of wait?

In the moving rush of early morning shoppers there was a sudden stillness. A woman stood, not in the centre, but on the fringe of activity, watching, eating chocolates from a Cellophane bag cupped in her hand.

Sarah Felles. She ran the Blue Heron B&B and owned the building the gallery was in.

Nerves shot through Charley. She steeled her spine and headed toward the woman. "Shopping for more wreaths?" she asked. And hoped. But chances were good that Sarah was actually here to check up on the exhibit.

As a retired romance editor, there was nothing Sarah loved more than correcting lives, giving people their happily ever afters. And what had Charley done with the one she'd been given? She'd welcomed in death. Possibly inspired a murder.

"I'm not shopping." Sarah sniffed. "I'm browsing. Collecting, I should say."

Probably not decorative gourds. Sarah wore a black cardigan with an open weave and deep pockets. The wide-brimmed purple hat was tugged low to hide the wrinkles lining her eyes. She gazed at the people exchanging greetings. And those that weren't.

"And observing?" Charley asked.

"Taking a few mental notes." A smile curved the woman's lips. "What do you know about the Exquisite Corpse?"

Shock tightened Charley's fingers on the leather leash. Did she mean Laura? "Not enough."

Cocoa sat on Charley's feet, eyes fixed on the display of maple walnut fudge.

Sarah said, "Then it's lucky you've got time before Thursday to do your research."

A deadline? As if Laura's life was an open book. Unless they were talking about two different things. Cautious now, Charley asked, "Research what?"

Sarah rooted in her bag of chocolates with a rustle of plastic. "The parlour game."

Not murder in the dark, but a different kind of corpse entirely, Charley realized. "The collaborative drawing approach?" Invented by Surrealist artists. Each member of a group drew a part of a body on a piece of paper and folded it to hide the image. The end result was a body made up of pieced-together composite parts. No stitches or grave robbing required. "I'm surprised you know it."

"I didn't until yesterday. Kayla sent me the info."

After Laura died. A ball of fear tightened inside Charley's chest. It might just be a clever idea, something to add to her list of successes as community events coordinator, but if Kayla wanted to distract her from investigating, this was the perfect way to do it. Charley took a steadying breath. "We'd need supplies."

"Pens and paper? Yes, I know." Sarah studied a creamy Belgian truffle with a frown. "Bring Matt. I enjoy seeing you two together. You'll introduce the Shudder Pulp exhibit, explain the fundraiser, and lead guests in creating their own" — her teeth cracked through the chocolate coating — "Exquisite Corpse."

Were there even any current examples she could show? Charley flashed on a vision of creatures, multi-limbed and many-headed. The comic-horror imagery of the Chapman brothers and their series of Exquisite Corpse etchings displayed in the Tate gallery. Grotesque animal heads, blood dripping and spurting from wounds, writhing intestines. Spiders hanging from threads. Insect wings and branching roots in the place of limbs. She could work with that. "You want participants to make their own monsters."

A canny gleam lit Sarah's green eyes, dangerous as the flick of a lighter in a mid-summer forest. "Did you know that the picture game evolved from a word game called Consequences? While playing, the sentence emerged, 'The exquisite corpse will drink the new wine.' There is always a cause and effect involved in any game of chance. When we create, we open the door into the unknown. You never know what will enter. Or walk out."

Creaking sound effects and all. "To drink the wine?"

Sarah looked toward the gallery, which was only partially hidden behind market stands. "Or take to the water and swim."

That line wasn't a coincidence. Not some casual reference to the Shudder Pulp exhibit, but to Laura's death. And how she had gotten attacked. "Who first started the legend of Oakcrest's lake monster?"

Sarah turned that keen gaze on her. "That legend was just an organ donor. The heart is beating inside your creation."

Thud, thud, thud. Cocoa scratched her ear with her front paw, hind leg thumping on the ground. Not quite a tell-tale heart but close.

Charley licked dry lips. "Laura's death might have something to do with the past."

Sarah stepped back to let a woman by with a stroller and an armful of sunflowers Van Gogh could have painted with three shades of yellow and nothing else. "Only insofar as anyone is influenced by their own past. Laura was good at finding other people's weaknesses. Targeting those with the most to lose and using them for her own gain."

The sunshine, and the market itself, seemed too bright for a conversation better suited to shadows and fog. "Who did she have a hold over?"

"The better question is, who wanted to break that hold?" Sarah let that linger, the words ringing out like a death knell. "It's a shame some people feel they need to forge relationships through coercion. They become soldered together like sheets of metal and are weaker for it. It's so much better to patch things up, which is exactly what I told Jenny."

The flash of insight felt like the shift in perspective that transformed dabs of paint into a field of wildflowers or stacks of hay. "Thomas's daughter?"

"I recommended a family outing to the pumpkin patch. Convinced her it was worth letting Allison skip school to spend the morning outdoors with her mother and grandfather." Sarah smiled, flashing sharp white teeth. "Sometimes, all it takes is a change in setting. I'll find out soon, if it worked."

"They went this morning?" Alex wouldn't be able to question him, not until later in the day when Thomas was back at his trailer or working on a painting. In his comfort zone.

"I just saw Thomas's car turn off at the intersection, heading out of town."

Which was why Sarah was here, not browsing the produce or waiting to talk to her about the exhibit, but watching the road. "Lucky you were here to see him drive by," Charley said dryly.

"Luck had nothing to do with it." Sarah dismissed the idea. "In forty-five minutes, that family will be sipping hot apple cider at Grovewood Farm. Making new memories, and about time, too." She flicked a glance at Charley that made her nervous. "Chocolate?" She held out the bag, emptier now. "Cardamom nougat and cassis ganache. Take one of each." She shook the contents enticingly. The sticker shone like tempered chocolate. *Chocoholic's*.

"Thanks." Charley reached into the bag. The chocolate melted in her fingers, on her tongue. The texture was perfect, but. But.

The cassis gel was too sweet. The ganache, not bitter enough. The magic was missing.

With a sinking feeling, Charley took another. Cardamom this time. A milk chocolate square with a pattern Jackson Pollock would have appreciated. She bit into it.

But instead of rich, spicy, roasted notes, she tasted a bitter undertone. Something unbalanced. The cardamom was overpowering. Too harsh, too strong. She dragged in a breath.

The chocolates looked perfect, but appearances could be misleading.

Sarah was watching her closely. "Ambitious, as always."

"But not the same. Something is —"

"Wrong. Yes."

Her heart tightened. "I wouldn't use the word 'wrong.'"

"I would." Sarah slid her hands in her pockets. "Fear kills inspiration. There's a reason why the root word of monster is linked to the Latin *demonstrare*, meaning to show or demonstrate. Monsters reveal what we really fear."

But this mystery felt like one folded piece of paper, each section hiding the next clue. It was a game of Consequences Charley was about to lose if she didn't get answers soon.

She should focus on the exhibit. She had more than enough to do. But it felt too much like hiding away. Adding white acrylic highlights to a painting of Blue Heron Lake wouldn't fix what was happening right now outside the gallery walls.

But finding out what Thomas saw on the lake just might. If they knew where the fox carcass was before it ended up on the beach, they'd have one more clue to work with.

And the cottage could use a pumpkin. Freshly picked.

NINETEEN

FLIES CIRCLED THE caved-in hollow of a pumpkin the size and shape of a human head. Fleshy pulp and seeds spilled into the dirt. Charley stepped around the remains. The mud at Grovewood Farms sucked at the soles of her sneakers as she walked between ghost pumpkins. Drained of colour, they rose from the earth. White, not orange. Brown veins etched through ribbed skin in a pattern like cracks in fire-glazed pottery.

People strolled through the pumpkin patch. More than she'd expected. But only one had his head bowed over a sketchbook. Thomas.

Four steps away from him, Jenny pushed a rusty wheelbarrow. Her yellow jacket was Crayola bright in a field that looked like a forgotten page in a colouring book. A dark-haired girl skipped ahead, hopscotching over vines. That must be Allison. But Thomas held the A6 hard-bound sketchbook between him and them like a barrier.

Splash. Charley's right foot landed in a puddle. A slurry of cold muck soaked through her canvas sneaker to her sock. Ugh. Sneakers were great for a day in the gallery, not a smart move for a trip to a farm. She shook her foot out and kept going.

Closer now, she caught a glimpse of Thomas's sketch. Not a landscape this time, or not entirely. The field could have been the focus or even the ribbed skins of the pumpkins. The broad expanse of sky split by a swooping V of wild geese. But he'd centred the image around a portrait. Of mother and daughter. An open smile. A coat winging out on a light-footed step. Hands and faces soft-toned as clouds, not a hard edge in sight.

He'd cushioned love and laughter in blurred charcoal pencil.

And captured a moment he wasn't a part of.

Adding a cheerful note to her voice, hoping it didn't sound as forced as it felt, Charley called out, "I hear you've been stalking autumn."

Thomas's pencil lifted off the page, the only sign of surprise. "Is that what you call pillow talk these days? Vantage points and art supplies?"

She tucked her hands in her jacket pockets, touched dog-biscuit crumbs. A pencil stub. "Sometimes murder."

Thomas squinted at tangled vines. "If that's your idea of a segue, you can forget it."

She shrugged. "I'm just here to pick a pumpkin."

He snorted. "Sure." He watched his granddaughter bend down to look at a pumpkin.

Sizing it up with a scalpel-sharp gaze, Allison said, "It would be so cool to watch a pumpkin rot. We could get this one, carve it, and dissect it. Then videotape it as it goes mouldy. Play it back slow-mo."

Amused, Thomas shook his head. "Not that one. It's already bruised."

Jenny's smile slipped. "It's not perfect. Grandpa won't want it in his house."

Allison glanced up, a stubborn set to her chin. "But it looks like it's already got a face." Her finger traced the white skin, forming the shape of eyes. A nose. A mouth. Misshapen in a leer.

"We want a blank canvas," Thomas said.

Allison nodded, quick to agree. "Got it." She wandered ahead, inspecting each pumpkin closely.

To find that perfect blank canvas?

But most artists started with an idea first. With research. Drawing from life was the key to a good understanding of people and animals. Thomas would have had to work out the anatomy and form of the fox. From reference photos, but also life sketches — a form of visual note-taking he could refer back to in the studio.

His sketchbook would be a treasure trove of research — if she could just get a closer look at it. Pulse kicking up a notch, Charley said, "You could smudge in the underlying shape of the hair with your fingertip. Then build on it by rubbing out strands with a putty eraser. Add a deeper smudge on top and go over the details with fine strokes of a 2B pencil."

"You see a 2B pencil?" The growl in his tone nearly had her backing up. "This is what I've got."

Charley pulled the blacklead pencil from her pocket, worn down to the jousting knights of the Faber-Castell logo. She held it out to him. "It'll add contrast to the soft rendered areas."

He raised a brow. "Some much-needed contrast?" The tone was sharp as a lance.

She stared right back. "If you pinch that rubber into a point, you'll get a finer highlight."

He snorted and took the pencil from her. Angling the sketchbook away from her, he scratched the lead over paper, his attention on Jenny and Allison as they walked ahead.

Nerves scrambling, Charley moved closer. "I'd add lines at the temple. Shorter strokes. Then another sweep of the eraser to add detail to the facial features."

He scowled. But it seemed more like a reflex. She had his attention.

He passed her the sketchbook and the pencil. "Fine. Show me."

Fingers tingling, Charley held his sketchbook in her hands. The bound cover was stained with oil paint, smudged with pastel, the cartridge paper thick and warped with taped-in leaves and mixed media. Off-white to eliminate reflections — perfect for outdoor sketching.

Her heart pounded.

Allison hefted a pumpkin in her arms, a determined set to her chin. Sunlight gleamed off ivory beads. She was wearing a necklace, the strand tucked under the neckline of her sweater. The beads were round, irregular shapes, the warm colour of yellow ochre, raw sienna, and titanium white. "This one. It's perfect."

Jenny flinched. "Which doesn't matter because —"

"Let me see." Thomas bent down, hands on his knees. A slow, careful move. A wince of pain he hid but not fast enough.

Pulse racing, Charley flipped through the sketchbook's pages. Back four, then five.

Allison glanced up at Thomas. "You could come trick-or-treating with us."

His gruff features softened. "That's an idea."

Jenny said, sharp, "Grandpa would only want to look at the houses. You'd never make it around the block. He prefers architecture to candy."

Thomas straightened. "I've got a sweet tooth." He sounded defensive.

Jenny yanked the zipper of her jacket higher as though chilled. "Only since you discovered Chocoholic's."

Charley turned the next page and saw it. The fox. In graphite and red pastel. Rough drawings and scrawled notes. Observations. She skimmed them, as quickly as she could, knowing she had seconds at most.

The element of speed is key to their overall survival. Chasing young in games of tug-of-war.

The handwriting was all spikes and sloped lines. *Sharp teeth to kill. Rip into chunks.* A box caged in the word, "kill".

The drawings showed detailed variations of the long nose and pointed ears. Too close, too fragmented, to tell if it was the remains they'd seen on the beach.

She would have labelled the sighting. He hadn't.

The sketchbook got yanked from her hands.

Anger darkened Thomas's face. He gripped the book. "That's a violation of trust."

Allison held on tight to her pumpkin. "Like breaking a rule?"

"Exactly." Thomas snapped the book closed.

Jenny met Charley's eyes. Frustration sharpened her face. "You can't control everything and everyone, Dad."

Allison's cheeks flushed. "He's not trying to. Why are you always picking on him?"

Jenny looked stricken. "I'm just —"

"This was supposed to be fun, but it sucks!" Allison dropped the pumpkin on the ground, splashing drops of mud. "I wish I was at school." She stomped between the vines. Sitting on the biggest pumpkin, she jammed her chin on her fists.

Jenny's lips tightened as she turned on her father. "You couldn't put the sketchbook aside for one hour?"

Thomas's shoulders hunched. "You two were getting on fine without me."

"So, you thought this was the right moment to work on the fox again?"

A zip of adrenaline shot down Charley's spine. "I might be interested in the final piece for the gallery."

Thomas's fingers tightened on the book. His attention shifted from Jenny to her. "That gallery still needs to be renovated before you can think about curating a collection. Don't make promises you can't keep."

Allison shot a glance over her shoulder. Just a flash of profile. The corner of a brow, a cheek. The catch of a breath being held. Charley wondered why.

She said, "I'd find a way to display it." She'd have to, now.

Thomas opened the book to the roughest sketch. A close-up study of bone and fur. "And turn me into the next Chaïm Soutine? With a fox instead of a slab of beef?"

And just as polarizing. "I can't say until I've seen it."

He tilted his head, studying her in the same way he probably studied the animals in the wild. "If I'd known a damn carcass would get me this much attention, I'd have gone looking for dead animals sooner."

"You must have picked the right spot."

"I just found the right composition."

But where? "How long do you think it'll take you to finish the piece?"

On what might have been regret, he said, "I've scrapped it."

Destroyed it or set it aside? "It sounded like the piece had promise."

Jenny rolled her eyes. "Dad likes to catastrophize about his failures. If he's written the piece off, you'll never convince him to give it another go."

But there were so many techniques, so many ways to revise a piece. He'd said it himself when they'd set up the Cover Art exhibit together. *Unfortunately, revisions are all part of the creative process.* "Mistakes can be fixed."

"Layered over?" The dismissive tone didn't allow room for argument. "The error's still there, underneath. Tainting the colours. Bleeding through, no matter what."

"And sometimes those first attempts add dimension." But she

wasn't here to convince him to redo the piece. It was the original she needed to know more about. "Where did you find the fox?"

Thomas's shoulders stiffened. "I didn't see her," he snapped.

Jenny's gaze bounced from one to the other. "See who?"

"It doesn't matter." Thomas stepped toward the pumpkin, stared at it as though weighing it. "We've got a pumpkin. Let's go."

Jenny didn't move. "Is this about the woman who died?"

Allison stood, a figure at the outskirts, still as a deer in the headlights.

"No," Thomas said.

"Yes," Charley said.

Jenny crossed her arms. "I'll tell you where he was." Exasperation stripped away the patience from her voice. "The dam. That's his favourite spot at the moment. Am I right, Dad?"

Shock wiped his features clean. "How do you know that?"

"I listen."

Unlike you. The accusation hung in the air.

Cold flicked down Charley's spine. Close enough to the reservoir, the carcass might have washed into the lake. But they'd found only the skull on the beach. "Was that where the fox was?"

A muscle jumped in Thomas's jaw. "No. I spotted it on my way back. In the trees at the top of Sugarbush Road." He held her eye contact, without a flicker of guilt or the hint of a lie.

Drive to the dam and you passed the turnoff for Sugarbush Road. Someone severed the fox's head from the body and moved it. Intentionally. "Did you see a car drive by?"

"There wasn't another living soul around."

The turn of phrase sent a shiver running through her.

Thomas glanced over his shoulder. "Where's Allison?" Panic pitched his voice.

Jenny gestured toward the corn maze. "Over at the entrance."

"Shit." He lunged forward, boots sinking in earth.

Jenny stayed where she was.

He stopped short, turned back, impatient. "That maze is one acre large. It takes twenty to thirty minutes to get through it."

"She knows she can't go in without an adult." Jenny hefted the pumpkin into the wheelbarrow. "This was a bad idea."

"I agree."

"That's what you agree with me about? Wonderful." Jenny trudged past him, rusted wheels screaming. "Allison was right. This was a blast. Now I get to cheer up a disappointed eight-year-old. Thanks for the day, Dad."

Thomas rounded on Charley, the hurt as raw and open as a wound. He jabbed the spine of the book at her, stabbing the air with one dented corner. "Watch yourself. You go around asking questions like this and you'll end up like that fox."

Fear prickled at the back of her neck. "Dead?"

"Guess we'll find out." He thrust the pencil at her. Turned and followed his daughter at a slower pace, close to a limp.

Charley dragged in a breath. She gripped the pencil tight in a hand that trembled. She wouldn't be able to draw a straight line right now, with or without coffee. But she'd known Thomas long enough to be certain — or almost certain — that his parting remark was nothing more than a gruff warning.

Sugarbush Road. David drove to the dam the day after Laura had died. The day after Thomas had sketched the fox. Charley stood with him on the crest, his car parked beside her Jeep. Had he stashed a skull in his trunk?

She had to talk to Kayla, find out more about him without letting slip that David might be a suspect. But drop by unannounced and Kayla would wonder why, no matter how focused she was on turning Oakcrest into an autumn harvest tourist attraction, wrapped in caution tape and lit with grinning jack-o'-lanterns.

That was it. Charley stopped short beside a burlap scarecrow, pointing the way to the corn maze and the exit.

She needed a distraction. Something seasonal that checked a box on Kayla's to-do list. An invitation she'd never be able to resist.

But she couldn't invite Kayla to the cottage, where Alex might wander through at any second. Maybe at Matt's? No.

Chocoholic's. After closing. All she had to do was convince Matt to let them use his counter space.

She'd bring the knives. And the pumpkins.

TWENTY

CONDENSATION IN THE polycarbonate molds and Matt had missed it. Grey dull marks stained the coffin-shaped shells he'd already started filling with truffles.

Sugar bloom. Just a few drops of water but the damage was done.

Some of the shells had turned out fine. Enough of them anyway. The dark milk chocolate — forty-eight percent cocoa solids — had a nice sheen and sharp edges. If he filled them with milk chocolate and dried strawberries, brown-butter ganache, chocolate-crusted cocoa nibs, they'd sell.

But mess up again like that and he might as well just tape an apology to the door of Chocoholic's and be done with it, use the workshop for pumpkin carvings and interrogations instead.

As soon as Chocoholic's was empty, he would take the chocolate shells out to the Dumpster and bin his mistake, pretend it never happened.

Only one customer browsing — he'd get his chance soon. The eight-year-old girl was a sure thing for the marshmallow ghosts anyway. The kid was already prepped for Halloween with a costume jewellery necklace falling in three strands over her fleece sweater, although those pearls almost looked like the real thing.

Something about the way she walked, planting the heels down

first, jogged Matt's memory. New boots, only a few scuff marks on the toe. The kind you got from kicking around a soccer ball. Or maybe it was the eyebrows, straight lines drawn over a sharp gaze.

Aimed at his whiskey-laced pralines. The Scotch pairing sampler.

Matt left the coffins scattered across the glass counter like a mass funeral and headed her way. "If you're looking for the marshmallow chocolates, they're right at the front."

She shook her head. "Have you got anything that goes well with an evening bourbon?"

"Ah." Matt blinked. He paused, to regroup. "As a ... gift?" He hoped.

"My grandpa loves chocolate." She scanned the shelves of the refurbished antique cupboard at the front of the store, gaze flicking over and past the milk chocolates shaped like animals, the hot chocolate bombs, and the jars of honey. "He had a rough day and I doubt he's going trick-or-treating, so I thought I'd get him some. It's a surprise."

In other words, don't spoil it. Yeah, he got the message, loud and clear. "Do I know your Grandpa?"

"If you don't, you're the only one in town. Grandpa Kelley knows everyone."

Thomas Kelley? Yeah, she had his walk all right. And that fierce take-no-prisoners stare.

Matt hesitated, one second. But kids listened, noticed things. Maybe she overheard something that could take the heat off Charley. And convince Alex to get a move on with the investigation. "I visited your grandpa the other day." He wouldn't mention he'd all but gotten kicked out in the end.

Her eyes went big and round, shock and awe in them. "You got to see his house?"

Reverence there like he'd gotten a tour of a magic castle. "From the outside," he admitted.

"Mom and I haven't been yet." She played with the cuff of her jacket, rubbing at specks of mud but just working it deeper into the cloth. "Were you in the trailer?"

"Yup."

"Did you see our acorns?"

Surprise shot through him. Thomas's art project. "Yeah, I did."

"We're going to paint them." Her defiant tone didn't seem to suit the statement.

Matt said seriously, "I can't take on any more consignment pieces right now."

She laughed, the sound echoing around the shop. "They're not for sale."

"Maybe one day." Matt searched his memory for the girl's name. Jenny's daughter. Something with an *A*.

She shrugged. "I'm going to be a scientist, not an artist. You get to ask questions, figure out how things work."

"Artists ask questions too. A good portrait captures personality. Who the person is, inside and out. And to do that, you have to know them." At least that was what Charley had said, last time she dug out her sketchbook to draw him. Looked at him and through him. And he still hadn't seen the results.

"But scientists get to blow things up." The girl moved to the counter where he'd been working just a minute ago. "What are those?"

Allison. That was it. "Coffins." He fought the urge to slide the tray away. "Shells. I'm filling them with chocolates."

She peered into the glass display case at the truffles. "Can I put together my own?"

"Sure."

She walked the length of the case, hand trailing along the glass, almost touching but not quite, fingers coasting through the air. "Do you have taste testers?"

"For some." He reached beneath the counter, pulled out the small sample selection of pralines he kept out front, cracked the lid on the airtight container, releasing the earthy aroma of bitter chocolate and spice.

But she didn't reach in right away, the way he figured she would. Instead, she said, "I don't like to gift anything I haven't tried myself."

"Booze-free, then."

"Duh." She twirled the pearls around her finger as she studied the chocolates.

Curiosity got the better of him. "That's a classy necklace."

"It was my grandma's. She had exquisite taste." It was lucky she picked a chocolate then, her attention off him, so he could hide the grin. "Mom wasn't happy Grandpa gave it to me. But it's magic."

A simple statement, without any frills. "Yeah? How's that?" Matt thought of the stories Jeffrey used to spin. Tall tales that grew, filling the workshop with power and secrets.

She took a bite, let the chocolate melt almost completely before she chewed, reminding him too much of a food critic. "When you wear them, you can be any character, from any story."

So, she really was a kid, not a grown-up scaled down to size. "You can be whoever you want to be?"

"For as long as you need to be braver." She wiped her fingers on her jeans. "Or stronger. Or smarter."

Pretend to be someone else. That wasn't a bad idea. But the past was so damn hard to let go of. Maybe it was easier when you only had eight years behind you. The future was still bigger, brighter. "Where can I get one?"

She rolled her eyes. "It's not that easy."

You're telling me. "I figured that." She seemed too confident, too gutsy, for a kid who wanted to be braver. "Which character are you right now?"

She nibbled at a chocolate-crusted cocoa nib. "Someone who really likes coffins, actually. And tombstones." She glanced at him and sighed with something close to pity. "She befriends a boy in a graveyard. They play hide and seek with ghosts." At his expression, she sighed again. "It's a book for kids."

In other words, he was way past it. "Try me."

She tilted her head to the side. "Do you know what a ghoul gate is?"

He wracked his brain. "Not a clue."

"See?"

That was it. He'd proved her point. And damned if he wouldn't go home and Google it later. "So, what do you think of the chocolate?"

"It's not bad. Can I try that one too?" She eyed the brown-butter ganache.

Resigned, Matt held the container out to her again. "Sure."

She turned the praline over in her fingers. "Do you think Ms. Bouchard is a ghost?"

Oh, man. Matt shot a glance over his shoulder toward the workshop. It was probably too late to signal Beverley for help. How the hell was he supposed to answer that? "I figure, people live on in our memories." Good or bad.

"So that's a yes." She frowned down at her reflection in the glass countertop. "She was nice to me. Ms. Bouchard."

And that wasn't something he'd expected to hear, not after what others had said. "I'm sure Mrs. Callahan would like to know that. I could let her know you're here, ask her to come talk to you." Have some backup.

"I can't." She crunched the chocolate between her teeth. "Grown-ups don't keep their promises. Doesn't seem fair, that kids have to."

When really adults were just holding out hope that someone could. "We try our best."

"And then life happens, right?" She propped her chin on her hand, elbow on the counter. "Do you think we have to keep someone's secrets, even when they're dead?"

Now that had his attention. "That depends."

Allison nodded. "Sometimes to do the right thing, you have to do the wrong thing, right? The girl in the book does that too. She's not supposed to go to the graveyard, but she does."

He was so far over his head here. "Don't go to graveyards on your own."

She squinted an eye at him. "Do I look stupid?"

"No." Far from it. Even though she seemed to think she needed to be braver and smarter to solve her moral dilemma. "In my experience, secrets tend to make things worse."

"But the truth hurts too." She gnawed at her thumbnail. "I think Grandpa is plagued by a guilty conscience."

Matt turned a laugh into a cough. Holy hell. Guilty about what? Murder? "Did he break a promise?"

"He's been getting better at keeping them."

Better than before. And she'd picked up on the change. "Confessing sometimes helps with a guilty conscience."

"People only say that so you 'fess up. And then you get punished. Right?"

It was hard to argue that one. "Sometimes."

"That's what I thought. What are those marks?" Allison leaned closer, studying the chocolate shells.

Matt felt himself tense. Trust the kid to spot it. "Sugar bloom."

"Like flowers?"

That put a positive spin on it. "More like watercolour." A bleed effect. He'd learned that one from Charley. "You know, like when colour spreads on wet paper."

"So, it's a mistake."

Was this what Jeffrey had to put up with when he watched him cook at this age? "Yeah. It's a mistake." If he wasn't careful, she'd be talking him into giving her twenty-five percent off. And eat half his stock while she was at it.

Allison straightened, her gaze on the wall behind him, on Charley's painting of the femme fatale lounging in a hammock, gun resting on her stomach as she ate chocolates straight from the box. *Choosing the Sweet Life*. "Did you know that water can change from one form to another?"

That, he did know. "From solid to liquid and gas."

"Right." She nodded, leaving him feeling like he'd just earned a gold star.

Allison was holding on to a secret for Laura. But what? Something big enough to have her worried she'd be haunted by a ghost if she didn't keep quiet. "Do you have a hypothesis about what happened to Ms. Bouchard?"

"Sure." Allison glanced around, checking the store was still empty, and lowered her voice. "If water can make things move, it can stop things from moving, too."

Matt placed his elbows on the counter, lowered his voice too, wondered where this was going. "Uh-huh."

"Solids and liquids can change from one form to another. We know that. It's been proven." The words came fast and thick, like she'd spent time thinking it through, had the reasoning down pat and ready to deliver to anyone who'd listen. "I think Ms. Bouchard breathed in fog. And it turned solid in her lungs."

That was a grisly thought. Fog solidifying in Laura's lungs, clogging her throat. Goosebumps crawled over Matt's skin. "I don't think that's how it works."

She shrugged. "Scientists make new discoveries all the time. You have to question what you think you know. The first step is admitting you don't know everything."

"Yeah, but —"

"I'll take the coffin." She pointed. "That one."

TWENTY-ONE

CHARLEY SHOULDN'T HAVE walked this far down the dead-end road. But Cocoa needed a decent walk before she left her to go to Chocoholic's and she hadn't noticed how far they'd walked.

Boulders and white birch trees lined the road. Gravel skidded under her boots, pebbles sliding away and down the slope. Cocoa wagged her tail, leading the way toward the slate-grey water churning below. The air smelled of frost.

There were no cars in the driveways here. Bird feeders stood empty over earth, bare without seeds. Metal docks were laid up on land like skeletons of beached metal creatures, waiting for summer. Above an outhouse, the bone-white skull and antlers of a buck hung like a warning.

The names on handmade wooden signs, nailed to the oak tree, were the only evidence that this road came to life in the summer.

Cocoa swerved and sniffed. Charley's steps slowed. An uneasy feeling tugged at her. There was no dry crunch of leaves, no scuff of pebbles, but still the feeling caught at her. They weren't alone.

At the end of the road, between birch trees and the foam-green siding of an old boathouse, waves crashed toward shore, breaking on the rocks. On the left, a white one-level cottage perched at the top of a rocky incline. The windows were boarded up with plywood. The driveway, empty. Yellowed newspapers poked out of the mailbox. But — Charley looked closer. The front door was open. Just a crack.

But it couldn't be. Probably just a trick of the light, bruising shadows in recessed corners.

A narrow deck wrapped around the deserted boathouse. Tattered lace curtains hung in the windows.

What better spot to get a clear view of the lake?

Tempted, Charley checked over her shoulder. There was no one in sight.

Cocoa leapt onto the narrow deck first, paws scrabbling over wooden slats, waves breaking underneath.

Charley jumped after her.

Boards groaned and creaked under their weight. Cocoa's ears flicked. Somewhere, wood snapped. And held.

Charley looked out at bristling cedar trees. Edgings of granite rock. The light filtered by storm-grey clouds. The lake cast in lead, molten and not yet hardened, churning with life.

The wind took her breath away, but the birch trees sheltered them from the worst of its force. The triangle of earth was held together by exposed roots, like reaching limbs.

Cocoa nosed under the railing, peering down, tail wagging, searching for fish in the waterweeds.

Charley imagined the snake-like head rising, streaming water. She reached in her back pocket, pulled out her Field Notes journal and the pencil stub.

She flipped past filled pages. Rough sketches of Matt. Just ideas, compositions that looked like textbook studies on how to use the rule of thirds. Not yet what she wanted, even though she had that take-your-breath-away grin down. But capturing his portrait, or even one of those perfect moments, felt like trying to catch a summer firefly in a mason jar.

She flattened the next blank page against the railing — posts swaying. *Sketch what you see, not what you think you see. Really look.* Grandma Reilly's advice echoed in her mind. So, what did she see?

The autumn shore exploding in red and yellow and darker evergreen hues. The wind-tossed lake.

The details took shape. But, as she drew, a void formed in the centre of the page. A vanishing point but not on the horizon line.

A door banged. A bone-dry snap of wood on wood.

Charley jumped. The notebook fell from her grip and splashed into the water. "No!"

Cocoa barked.

The book floated on the crest of a wave. Water stained the edges, spreading fast. Could she fish it out? Maybe, if she could grab a branch to help her reach and lean out far enough. Farther, if she rested her weight on the railing.

Charley looped Cocoa's leash twice around the post. Checked to make sure it held and tried to ignore the dry cracks, the rot.

Charley crouched, stretching for the branch trapped in the rocks. Her fingers brushed wood, almost touched it. Just a little farther.

The sketchbook drifted, caught on the backwash of a wave. Still close enough, but barely.

Her fingers closed over the branch. Boots slipping on damp slats, she yanked it free.

Charley braced her hips against the rough-worn railing and stretched as far as she could, reaching with the stick. The posts creaked.

Water frothed, rushing in, washing the sketchbook onto the forked ends of the branch. Yes! She lifted the notebook.

Cocoa barked, a warning sound, but Charley was so close.

Crack. Something splintered. The railing gave way. Broke.

Charley grabbed for the post. Touched air.

Something yanked the back of Charley's sweatshirt and pulled her backwards.

Heart pounding hard, Charley sagged against the siding of the boathouse. The wall solid against her back. The notebook in her hands, dripping.

"You're trespassing," Shannon said, letting go of Charley's sweater. She wore leather boat shoes, which explained why Charley hadn't heard her.

She fought to catch her breath. "So are you."

"To save you from taking a nosedive." Shannon glanced at the splintered wood, sharp as a stake now. She leaned a shoulder against the peeling siding. The wind whipped a flush into her cheeks. Her burnt orange jacket was the same shade as the leaves. Perfectly tailored camouflage. Silver earrings swung from her earlobes. Celtic spiral knots. The triple interlocking pattern symbolized creation, protection, and destruction. Life, death, and rebirth.

Charley untied Cocoa's leash from the remains of the railing. Her fingers not quite steady, jittery panic still coursing through her. "I didn't notice your car." She would have, on this road.

"Too many rocks and fences." Shannon waved a hand. "I've already got one scratch on the fender. I don't need another. I parked at the top of the lane and walked."

"Here?" To a boat house and a boarded-up cottage.

"Just because it's a dead end doesn't mean there's nothing worth visiting." Shannon rooted in her jacket pocket. "Come on. I'll walk back with you, after I lock up."

"The cottage." That was it. The open door. Not just a shadow but gaping.

Shannon pulled out a leather ring, jangling with keys of different shapes and sizes. "I check the place once a week for the

Taylors, in exchange for apricot anise bread and custard Danishes. But, for me, the real treat is being here." Shannon stomped her boot on the deck, something formal about the move, a ritual like the opening of a dance. Or a knock on hallowed ground. "I unlock the door, step inside, and pretend I've come home."

A memory flashed through Charley's mind. Of melted Aero bars. Aerated milk chocolate warm from coat pockets. Grass-stained jeans. Exercise books full of clues and sketches. Made up mysteries. "Every game Meghan and I played at the cottage started with 'let's pretend that.'"

Shannon smiled. "An incantation, if ever there was one. With the right costume, 'let's pretend that' becomes real. Lets you slip into someone else's skin."

And shed your own? Like a snake. "Do you miss designing costumes?"

"Imagination on a budget?" Shannon's expression twisted. "No. I got tired of bringing other people's visions to life. Always at the mercy of the director's whims and starlet's weight. The worst was when the actors starved themselves into a rack of bones. If I wanted to dress a coat hanger, I'd do it. Now I get to create my own world in my shop." A ring of power to her tone Charley wondered if she even noticed. "We wanted to retire in a place like this, my husband and I. With the property prices being what they are, I can't afford it. But a fantasy, that doesn't cost a thing."

So that explained it. "That's why you run the Cottage Association."

"And take care of other people's slices of heaven." Shannon swung the keys so they caught the light. "Normally my job as caretaker is easy. You're the first trespasser I've caught. Besides the mice."

The image of a metal trap, snapping shut, flashed through Charley's mind. "Sorry. I saw the view and —"

"You were powerless to resist?" Shannon patted her hand. "It happens to the best of us. I'm here for the same reason. I just got permission first to steal a moment of cottage life." She winked, then her smile faded. "When we pretend, we open the Possible World Box, come what may."

Like snakes, slithering out. Serpents. Had someone slipped into the lake monster's skin? "How could someone turn themselves into a lake monster?"

"Are we talking for real or —"

"A costume."

"Ah. I thought we were about to discuss magic potions and curses." Shannon looked out at the water, as though searching the depths. "Greasepaint. By buying a *Creature from the Black Lagoon* mask from the Dollar Store. They've been selling like hot cakes this year."

It was true. All it would take was a cheap mask and a dark night to make even a human form seem monstrous. "Hard to believe a 1954 horror movie is still so popular."

Shannon arched a brow. "Build a story on truth and it'll stand the test of time."

The chill that started in her cold, damp hands spread out and through her. "What truth?"

"You don't know? Oh, you'll love this." Shannon's tone shifted to that of a seasoned storyteller. Of someone who knew the weight of words and of silence. "It started at a dinner party. A South American cinematographer told the tale of an amphibious humanoid monster who'd emerge from the Amazon jungle once a year to snatch a young woman from the local village and then disappear again. The story, he said, was true. He could prove it with photographs."

Goosebumps tingled over Charley's skin. "Did they take him up on it?"

"No one knows. But that's not important, because they brought the creature to life on the screen. In 3-D." Shannon's eyes glowed. "Can you imagine? That scaly, webbed claw reaching out to the audience for the first time, from a black-and-white underwater world. The Gill-Man costume was the real star of the show: a seamless sci-fi invention, created by a team of artists and sculptors." She held out her hand, palm up. "May I?"

"Sure." Curiosity hooked, Charley handed over the damp sketchbook and her pencil.

Shannon found a dry page and sketched as she spoke, keys still clutched in her left hand. "Audiences had never seen a full-body monster costume like it before. The gaping, gasping fish mouth." She illustrated the image. "The frilled scales." The details were sharp and crisp, the pencil lines confident. "The long fin running down his back, adding depth. And, still, you can see the yearning in his expression, his movements." The amphibian face appeared on paper, full of human longing. "The costume was elaborate. Detailed and believable. Even the gills moved when he breathed. There was no man behind the makeup. This was a perfect, evolutionary melding of man and fish. Underwater, the Gill-Man glided through the seaweed. Julia Adams's stark-white bathing suit was designed simply to draw attention to the alien nature of the creature in the darkness of the lagoon."

Both victim and tool. "So, they created the perfect illusion."

"No." Shannon held up the pencil. "They created a living, breathing monster that survived through three films and haunts imaginations still. The same way your exhibit will."

And didn't that just twist the knife, a little deeper? "Hopefully without the trail of destruction." Although it had already begun.

Shannon shook her head. "You're immortalizing a monster — bringing it to life through the tricks and tools of the trade."

Acrylic paint and a projector. "But the filmmakers didn't just bring the creature to life. They asked the viewer to empathize with him. They made him close to human."

Shannon handed the sketchbook back to her, the page open to the monster, with eyes that shone — not with a glint of menace or even hate but with hope. "There's always a reason behind the worst of deeds."

It didn't take much of a twist in perspective to watch that film play out from the monster's point of view, to see the scientists as villains.

"That's what a good detective does," said Charley. "She figures out the hidden story, the motive behind the crime."

Shannon twisted the keys in her fingers, thumb rubbing over the teeth, like worry beads. "You can't go on a hunt and still see your prey as human. It's a dangerous thing, to get too close. To swim in the water, in that black-and-white world." She looked at her now. "Like when Julia Adams takes her dip. She has no idea that the Gill-Man is just feet below her, mimicking her movements, reaching closer and closer." She moved forward, one step, then two. Charley backed away, the gap in the railing a hole at her back. "Until he brushes her leg." Shannon stood still, smiled at Cocoa. "But instead of screaming, she dives below the surface to investigate, completely unaware what a mistake that is." With a snap of metal, she clutched the keys tight in her hand. "Of course, Julia gets kidnapped. And, in the end, the monster lives."

Charley's pulse pounded. She wanted to get off the deck, away from the water. "If he hadn't survived, there wouldn't be a trilogy."

The grin winged Shannon's black eyeliner out at the corners. "Sometimes a monster is seamless, not because the costume is so well-stitched, but because there aren't any seams. No zipper. No man of flesh and blood, sweating within. No heart concealed and beating. Not human, anyway. And you've risked it all, to look the monster in the eye, searching for seams you'll never find."

Charley touched a hand to Cocoa's warm fur and fought to keep the nerves out of her voice. "The only way to defeat a monster is to approach it. Get close enough to see it for what it is."

"But it's so much more fun to enjoy the illusion from the audience. And safer." Shannon turned, started heading back toward the ground covered in wet leaves. "Snack on the popcorn. Let the big-screen hero take the punches."

Charley stood on the deck. "You mean, sit back and watch from the cheap seats?"

"The cheap seats?" Shannon laughed. A blue jay startled from its perch in the birch tree, feathers flashing bright between the branches. "Honey, it seems to me someone's given you a ticket to a private screening. Might as well enjoy it. From a safe distance."

TWENTY-TWO

"A SPECIAL WEATHER statement is in effect." Charley paused, her fingers on the key in the ignition. Instead of turning off the Jeep's engine, she reached over, cranked up the volume on the radio. "A Colorado low has Ontario in its grasp. Hot and cold air are colliding to create wind gusts raging up to eighty kilometres an hour. Drive safe folks."

So much for staying safe. Wind buffeted the car. She'd had to park a few spaces down from Chocoholic's, all of the closer spots already taken when she got here.

How heavy were the ghost pumpkins? Probably fourteen pounds each, at least. Just like the turkey they'd roasted for Thanksgiving to feed eight people.

She'd carry one in, then ask Matt to help her with the others.

Outside, the wind tore at the trunk door that creaked on rusted hinges. Charley hefted the pumpkin out.

The heavy door swung toward her. Arms full, she stepped back fast. The door rushed past her face and slammed shut.

Awnings snapped. Sharp-taloned shapes shifted over the sidewalk. Balconies and street signs cast shadows. There was an underlying flicker to it all like a black-and-white movie.

The CLOSED sign dangled in the window of Chocoholic's. Fifteen minutes from now, Kayla would show up. And Charley still didn't know how to broach the topic of murder.

She shifted the pumpkin's weight in her arms.

"Need help getting into the slaughterhouse?" a voice shouted behind her.

Charley whirled around and saw a flash of teeth as David grinned.

He clutched a hand to his heart. "'If I have any more fun today, I don't think I can take it.'"

A few steps behind him, Kayla rolled her eyes. "He's been quoting *Texas Chain Saw Massacre* since I told him about the pumpkin-carving plan."

David cut in front of Charley and opened the door with a gallant flourish. "I invited myself. I hope that's all right." Wind-blown and clean-shaven, he looked anything but dangerous.

He looked relaxed. Too much like he'd won.

Nerves twisted in Charley's stomach. Forget the plan, the casual questions she'd wanted to ask Kayla about David. It was all improv now. And she'd just have to hope Matt followed her cue. "That depends." She walked past David into the shop, which was empty of customers but filled with the scent of dark chocolate, orange, and an earthy spice, like ground black pepper. "How are your pumpkin-carving skills?"

"Not too shabby." Not even close to modest.

Kayla held up a cloth tote bag — one of the tourist souvenirs, stencilled with Oakcrest's postal code. "I brought the clay-modelling tools."

Wind rustled over the display of Cellophane-wrapped ghost chocolates.

David kept the door propped open with one shoulder. "Are there more pumpkins?"

"In my trunk."

"We'll get them," Kayla said as Charley handed her the keys. "Be right back."

That would give her a minute, maybe two, to warn Matt. She'd take every second she could get. "Take your time."

The door blew shut behind them.

Charley followed the muffled wail of guitars to the back of the store. There was her painting, framed and hanging right behind the display counter. The femme fatale looked so at ease, probably because she had a gun — and chocolate — within easy reach. Charley pushed through the plastic curtain strips and into the workroom.

Matt stood at the sink, wiping out a chocolate mold. He'd tied a colourful bandana over his tousled hair and tapped his foot to an '80s rock song, his shoulders moving to the beat.

"Nice moves," Charley said.

Matt whipped around, ears flushing pink. He cleared his throat. "How long have you been standing there?"

"Long enough to enjoy the show." She hoisted the pumpkin onto the table, beside the black-handled knives Matt had already laid out. Not his perfectly balanced chef's knives but the big-box-store set of utilitarian kitchen knives. The ones that could stand up to rough use. The blades — six inch to nine — shiny and sharp as all the rest.

Matt set the mold down and glanced over his shoulder. A crinkly-eyed grin lit up his face and the finished portrait flashed through her mind. This was it. The composition she'd been looking for. And it was all him. Excitement zipped through her, straight to her fingertips. The chocolatier in his workshop. Appliances gleaming behind him. The tempering machine and the guitar cutter he used for slicing ganache. The room dim at the end of the day. Broken pieces of chocolate still strewn across the marble cutting board.

"You look cheerful," she said, although hopeful might have been the better word. And so much more like himself. "Things go well at the shop today?"

"You could say that."

But she didn't see any fresh batches of chocolate. Just a paper towel, pinned under a coffee mug and covered in a scrawl of black marker. Measurements. Tablespoons. A slash, underscoring the last ingredient, heavy and dark. And that question mark that took up more space than it should have, overwhelming everything else. "There might be trouble tonight. David's here."

Matt raised a brow. "This turned into a double date, fast."

"Change of plans." They'd done other things together — Lord, had they done other things — but a tag-team interrogation, without any prep, was a first. "I call bad cop."

Matt frowned. "Isn't that a change of heart, not plan?"

Charley thought of Shannon's advice. Let the big-screen hero take the hit for her? As if that was even an option. "You have to roll with the punches."

He moved closer and put a hand to her cheek, brushing his thumb over her cheekbone. The intensity in his eyes sent her insides quivering. "Or dodge them."

She couldn't argue. He caught her mouth in a kiss thorough enough to weaken her knees. "Not fair," she murmured against his lips. She felt him smile.

He pulled back. "Sometimes you have to fight dirty."

She glanced at the knives, the glinting blades. Sarah's words echoed through her mind. *Monsters reveal what we really fear. And fear kills inspiration.*

Matt grabbed another stool still pushed against the wall, dragged it up to the table. "Do you think David knows Thomas's granddaughter?"

Allison? But she hadn't told Matt yet that she'd seen the girl at Grovewood Farm. "Probably." But this wasn't about Thomas, not tonight. "No hijacking the conversation."

"I found out —"

The plastic curtain strips rustled, and Kayla stepped in, entering ahead of David. Both carried ghost pumpkins in their arms.

Matt muttered, "The unexpected guest, take two." Before Charley could ask what he meant by that, he said, "Aprons are on the counter. Help yourselves."

Kayla picked one up and dropped it over her head. Her features had a china-doll fragility that people often underestimated, and she used it to her advantage, closing off her expression so no one could spot any cracks in the surface. But tonight, there was joy on her face she didn't try to hide. "How much of a mess are we going to get in?" She tied her apron strings behind her back in a neat bow that could have finished off an evening gown.

Matt grinned. "Let's just say, you're all on clean-up duty afterwards."

David inspected the knives gleaming on the work table. "I thought we'd be using those plastic saws."

Probably a better plan than handing whetstone-sharpened weapons to a suspect.

"And spend hours sawing?" Matt asked. "I could do better than that. But what you see is what you get," he warned. "Don't even think of touching anything else in this kitchen."

"Yes, chef." David grinned easily. "Mind if I scalp them?"

This was a bad idea. Charley said, "Actually —"

"Go ahead," Kayla cut in. "Charley never gets the first cut perfect anyway."

"The pressure's on then." David's hand closed over the handle of the longest knife.

The overhead lights flickered. Panic gripped Charley's chest, a hard fist.

If the power went out, the generator would kick in. They wouldn't be left in the dark. With knives all around. But that didn't help reason away the fear.

The lights held, even as another gust of wind rattled the windowpanes. All she had to do was focus on the conversation.

But that thought didn't ease the tightness in her throat.

Charley took the bar stool beside Matt's, across from David. Rolling up her sleeve, she reached her bare hand into the first pumpkin and pulled out a fistful of cold slimy threads. "Gotta love the goo."

Orange tops lined up on the table — sliced off at high speed with annoyingly even zigzags — David scraped a flat-edged spoon along the inside walls of his pumpkin. "I figured you'd be more into the design process. The shading and sculpting."

"That's Kayla's specialty." Precision work that turned pumpkin flesh lantern thin.

"Don't jinx it." Kayla uncapped a Sharpie, sketched out a design on blank paper. "The trickster raven. Before he turned black."

"In his argument with a loon," Charley remembered. After a deal gone wrong.

David scooped pumpkin into a plastic mixing bowl. "Nothing beats a paradoxical hero."

Kayla studied her drawing with a critical eye. "The Raven breaks the rules, plays tricks, but it's normally for the good in the end. He schemes and is seemingly only out for himself, but he's also the mastermind who made the world. And brought light."

Charley fought the urge to glance at the windows, the black sky. She reached for a marker. "And then Edgar Allen Poe banished him into darkness."

"Which I still can't forgive him for," Kayla said. "Leaving the Raven with just one word."

"'Nevermore,'" Matt quoted. The syllables echoed off the red floor tiles.

David reached past Charley, chose a long, narrow knife.

"Peering deep into the darkness. Filled with a terror he'd never felt before."

It wasn't a threat, aimed at her. Just a reference to the poem. But it felt like one. A cut to the soul. "That's the power of art," Charley said. "To create and destroy." Even the art they were creating now had a half-life. The pumpkins would decompose within a week or two, depending on how cold the nights were. And their designs would shrivel and rot with them.

David made a careful incision, the blade slick and wet as he drew it out. "There's been a lot of speculation from my students about what happened to Laura. The guesswork is giving my water unit a whole new twist. I never thought I'd be fielding questions about lake monsters."

A class full of kids was the perfect way to spread a story through town. A supernatural scapegoat for murder. Charley fought the urge to glance at Kayla. "What did you tell them?"

"I distracted them with a question. How do we explain the world we see?" David let that linger. "I stole inspiration from the 500s of the Dewey Decimal system. Natural science."

Where the books had been shelved before Deb moved them to the new display.

Thunk, thunk. Kayla punctured raven's wings into her pumpkin. "There's always been a market for monstrosity."

The satisfaction in her voice had Charley looking at her more closely. It was the same tone she'd used when she swam first to the floating dock and knocked her fist on the plastic owl, with a breathless shout of "I won!" "The lake monster attack is just a rumour. But it spread fast." Had Eric mentioned it to Kayla?

She stepped back, studied the holes riddling her pumpkin, wiped the awl on her apron. "It's an immersive exhibit. Why not play on it? Look on the bright side. There's normally some good that comes from death."

Even murder. That was what Kayla meant.

David said, "It's not a bad idea to play to your audience. Give them what they want."

"Like the parlour game?" Charley pushed.

Kayla flashed a grin. "You're welcome."

And maybe it had just been a favour. An opportunity. "It's going to be time-consuming."

"Don't get hung up on prep," David advised.

"Wing it?"

"I do it all the time." He grinned. "I'll be there, so you'll have support."

A kindness from a seasoned teacher or a hint that she might need backup?

Kayla rolled her eyes. "He just wants to steal your ideas."

David shrugged. "I like to call it research."

Matt pried a chunk of white flesh out of his carving. "Teaching is a performance, isn't it?"

"Sure." David drew jagged teeth with a screech of black Sharpie. "You do what you can to make learning fun. Make the classroom a happy space, by whatever means necessary. Try to create a family."

A unit against the world? Or ties that bind. "But they're not family," Charley said. "They're students."

Matt rested his elbows on the table, focus on David. His pose was relaxed, like it was just small talk. "Do you know Allison, Thomas Kelley's granddaughter?"

Why was that so important to Matt? She'd missed a step.

"I taught her last year." If David was just as surprised as she was by the turn the conversation had taken, he didn't show it.

Matt watched him. "She seems like a smart kid."

David sawed a hole in the pumpkin. The eye. Blade winking. "You'll get whiplash from a conversation with her, if you're not careful."

"Seems like she's got a strong code of honour."

Charley straightened. How would he know that?

David nodded. "She's quick to help others, too. Always showed a lot of empathy."

Charley turned to Matt. "You spoke to Allison?"

"She came by the shop earlier today."

After Grovewood Farm. Why?

Matt held a wooden-handled clay-fettling tool, the tip hovering over the final letter in the hollowed-out word. TRICK. "She seems close to her grandfather."

David said, "Close as can be when her mother tries to keep them apart. Jenny doesn't think he's a good influence."

His responses came so quick, it sounded like he'd prepped for a parent-teacher conference. Charley said, "Seems like Allison made an impression on you when you taught her."

David cut out sharp edges, twisting the knife at the corners. "I've never been an Etch A Sketch teacher." He caught her quizzical expression. "Shake and erase at the end of the school year. If you don't let it matter, if you stop caring, what good are you?"

Matt worked the tool into the letters. "But you can't fix what goes on outside of school."

"That's not true." Pride lifted Kayla's voice. "David had a student who spent recesses playing in snowbanks in his worn-out sneakers. Then one day, the kid's mom actually dropped off a pair of new boots for her son at lunch. The same mom who bribed her neighbour to walk her kid to school, because she was too hungover to do it herself."

The subtext was there, hinting at a lack of choice. Pressure from someone else. Charley said, "She did it because David called her."

David scraped fibres from his jack-o'-lantern's leer. "I pushed the right buttons."

Threatened?

Matt's knee brushed hers as he shifted to look at David. "Not many teachers go above and beyond like that."

He shrugged. "Some do and that's what counts."

Kayla touched David's hand. "If there were more like you —"

"The world would be a better place?" Charley asked, testing.

Kayla frowned at her tone, but it was David's reaction she watched for.

He sat back on the stool, his face closed off. "I'm just trying to minimize the damage."

"Trap people in a room together long enough, they're bound to —"

"Kill each other?" David kept his gaze on the pumpkin, slid the knife in, shaping the guileless triangle eyes. The goblin grin.

The lights flickered. An eerie glow pulsed through the room. Her heart jumped in her throat, hammered there. "Fight, I was going to say."

The upgrade to the dam was a safety hazard, a threat for kids. If David's actions at school were anything to go by, would he really leave it at one speech? Or would he take matters into his own hands and offer a more permanent solution, to make sure the kids were safe?

She was suddenly very aware of the knife glinting in his hand.

David shrugged. "And that's why I don't sleep at night. Still figuring out how to keep the chaos to a minimum."

She had to push, now, before the conversation shifted again. "You must be sleeping better, now that the upgrade to the dam isn't happening."

The handle of a blade hit pumpkin with a *thunk*. Kayla yanked the knife out, kept it clenched in her fist, knuckles white.

The lights went out.

Dark. That was all Charley could see. Black all around.

But it wasn't completely dark in the workroom. Not with the green glow of the emergency LED lights, pooling in the cut-out shapes of the jack-o'-lanterns, etching shadows on their faces.

Bright light flooded the room, burning away the unfamiliar expressions. Charley let out the breath she hadn't realized she'd been holding, fingers still shaking.

David stood, the knife clenched in his fist, his gaze aimed at her. "Are you accusing me of something?"

Matt pushed his chair back, palms flat on the table.

"No," Kayla snapped. "She's not. Friends don't accuse each other."

Kindred spirits, through thick and thin.

Charley wanted to trust her. But how far would Kayla go to protect David? "Didn't you say, the Raven lied to bring about something good? But he paid a price." There always was one. "He lost his magic power. And had to flutter over the tundra, just like other birds."

Kayla trimmed the silhouette of the beak, scouring away slivers of pumpkin, sharpening the outline. "Only because the Raven married a human. Found love. And that was the most important thing."

David dropped his knife on the table. He went to the sink, ran the water, and soaped his hands, drops splashing into the basin. Hands dripping, he reached for the towel lying on the countertop. "Instead of wasting time with accusations you can't prove, maybe you should take another look at the victim. When kids act out, they're normally trying to get attention from someone." He folded the towel, squaring the damp corners. "If they've done things right and gotten ignored, or don't get the praise they were hoping for, the alternative is to do everything they can to piss that person off. Get a rise out of them. Anything to show that they matter. Just so that they finally see them for who they are. Seems to me that upgrade to the dam was a shout for attention after a lifetime of being ignored."

By a sibling. That was what he meant.

She didn't trust David. But he was right. They didn't have proof he'd attacked Laura and they wouldn't get it like this.

Alex had said it before. *Find out how the victim lived, and you'll find out how they died.*

Charley glanced at Matt. She murmured, "Maybe we should take a trip to the marina tomorrow."

A beat went by. A second of hesitation. He nodded. "We have a standing invitation. Might as well use it."

TWENTY-THREE

MATT PARKED THE truck in front of the marina. "I thought it would take the cops longer to clear the scene." His Ray-Bans rested in the cup holder, but the world still had a light brown gradient to it, orange leaves filtering the late-afternoon sun. The dock store looked deserted. The ice cream cone sign was more faded than ever. Everything was open, business as usual.

Charley unbuckled her seat belt. "Alex said they collected all the evidence they could."

Which just meant the clues were somewhere else. Wherever that "somewhere else" might be, they weren't here. "David sent us on a wild goose chase." When they should be following up on Thomas.

"Could be." She got out of the car, opened the door for Cocoa. "But at least we're getting dinner out of it. And you never know. Roy might be able to tell us what the connection is between Laura and Allison. Why she's keeping a secret for the woman."

Maybe. Matt reached into the back seat and grabbed the paper-wrapped bottle of bourbon he'd picked up at the LCBO. He figured Roy could use a stiff drink, probably more than another plate of food. "Just hold back on the interrogations tonight."

Charley let the leash go slack, giving Cocoa free rein to nose over the ground, the gravel raked through by tires. "I thought we came here to ask questions."

But it was easy to push too hard when the answers mattered. "To get info, not to put people on the defensive."

"People?" She waited for him to lock the truck, meet her eyes. "Or one person, in particular?"

She'd picked up on the tension. Of course she had. Probably sooner than he had. But there was one thing Charley didn't know yet. "Beverley asked me to investigate."

"Ha!" Charley pumped a fist in the air. "Wait until I tell Alex —"

"Me." He cut her off. "Not us."

"Oh." Charley blinked, but he caught the stunned hurt before she hid it. "That makes sense. You've known them longer."

He caught her hand in his, laced his fingers through hers. "Let me take the lead."

She glanced toward the track leading up to the Callahans' house. "Fine. I'll follow your cue."

Not exactly what he'd meant, but it was probably the best he'd get.

They walked over mud and rocks and rotting leaves. Laura's body hadn't left a mark, just a half-moon impression of a heel and even that might have been his imagination.

Charley paused at the edge of the ground no longer marked by caution tape. It still felt like an invisible force field, a boundary even Cocoa seemed to sense. They crossed it.

A crank of metal. The sound of a boat hitch being lowered. A truck had been backed up to the boat ramp, the red Princecraft Starfish almost hidden behind it.

Roy stood nearby, hands tucked in his pockets, looking anything but happy. "You sure you don't want to store that boat here for the season?"

"Nah." The man straightened. Nodding at them, he lifted and resettled his hunting cap, revealing a glimpse of receding hairline under the camouflage. "We've got the space on our property now. We'll be back in the summer to dock it. Besides, we don't want to trouble you. You've got enough going on." Meaty hands worked the latch on the trailer. "It's amazing how much paperwork a death in the family makes, am I right? Hardly leaves time to grieve. Though that's probably a curse and a blessing."

"That's not a word I'd use to describe what happened." Roy's dry tone didn't hide the heat underneath.

Cocoa's ears flicked. Matt checked his step, shot a glance at Charley. The conversation was on the borderline between small talk and insult.

The man slid the safety pin in place. "Seems like there's more work involved when the death is unexpected. Not much the deceased could do to prepare. I know, I've spent ages with our lawyer, setting up my passwords, so Miranda has access to it all."

Empathy took the edge off Roy's expression. "You sick, Henry?"

"Just being smart about it. Death's coming for us all, one of these days." He crossed rusted safety chains, latched them on. A smart man would have ended the conversation there. Or shifted it to fishing tales. "Might as well take away some of the burden, while the mind's still sharp."

"Laura was a planner through and through." Roy's voice had gone calm. Same way the lake did, right before a storm moved in. "She still didn't see this coming."

"No?"

Hard to tell if that surprised tone was honest or put on. But the guy had to know it would hurt. Matt felt Charley tense beside him.

Roy said, "You want to put that into words for me?"

The man bent down to check the hitch. "What I'm saying is, she must have known she was pushing all the wrong buttons.

Now, I don't want to speak ill of the dead, and I know she's your sister, but coming here with that big-city swagger was a mistake. We don't need that sort around here. No good ever comes of putting on airs, trying to force change where it's not needed or wanted." He rose, wiped his hands on his jeans.

Roy's punch was a solid right hook. Blood spurted from the man's nose.

"Shit." He stumbled back, hand flying to his nose. "What the fuck, Callahan?"

Cocoa barked, lunging forward, body blocking Charley from danger, even as she braced to hold the dog.

Matt moved, no clear thoughts as to what he'd do other than step in and keep one from the other, when Roy backed off.

He shook out his hand. "Get your boat off my property. And don't bother coming back next season."

"Screw you, Roy." The man cupped his palm, catching the blood dripping off his chin. He dug a tattered Kleenex out of his pocket. "This'll sink your marina. You won't be able to keep it afloat after this." Head tipped back, he climbed into his truck. Still cursing beneath his breath, he slammed the door.

Roy looked at his knuckles. Blood-smeared. "Jesus, he has a hard head. Shoulda figured he would. But I haven't done that in years."

"Hurts, doesn't it?" Matt asked.

Roy flexed his fingers. "I shouldn't have done that."

Charley studied him a moment, as though trying to read him. Or look for more signs of violence. "The guy was a class A jerk."

"But he paid upfront, in cash."

Matt said, "Didn't sound like he was going to be doing that in the next while."

"Saving me the trouble, my ass," Roy muttered. "Saving me

the trouble of what? Paying my phone bill on time? Yeah, that's a real pain."

Shock flashed over Charley's face. Same way it probably had over his own.

Was that what riled Roy? Not the comment about his sister? These days, it was harder to trust — to take it all on blind faith and hope for the best.

And it ticked Matt off that his thoughts went there, that he'd lost that optimism. Because there was a good part of guilt in the mix, he held the bottle out to Roy. "We brought you this."

Roy slid the paper down, checked the label. "Good old-fashioned bourbon."

"For medicinal purposes."

"Nothing like it to heal the soul." Roy tucked the bottle under his arm and patted Cocoa's head. "We'll go to the garage. It'll give me the chance to stash the bottle, before Bev catches a glimpse of it."

Turning a gift into what felt like aiding and abetting. "Hiding the liquor?"

"Sometimes, you gotta live on the edge." Roy winked, but the jaunty glint didn't meet his eyes. "I've got something to show you two."

TAPED TO THE glass door pane was a scrap of paper, *Poppa's Oasis* written in big, careful crayon letters. Matt noticed it as he stepped into the garage behind Charley and Cocoa.

The space inside was spotless and smelled faintly of beeswax and wood glue. There was a nice workbench up against the window and a sawhorse in another corner. No film of sawdust, though. Every surface was swept clean. An old tube TV sat on a wooden bench in one corner.

"Is that a VCR?" Matt asked.

Roy aimed a finger at him. "Still the best way to record a hockey game, I'll have you know. No scheduling, no five-step button combinations. Just stick in a tape, rewind, and hit record."

"Picture quality?"

"You can follow the puck."

But you'd probably have a shoddy view of a home run.

Off the leash now, Cocoa roamed the room. Stuck her nose in a plastic bowl on the floor the right size for a mastiff. Looked surprised to find it empty, the bottom dry and cracked.

Three mismatched folding chairs formed a semicircle facing the garage door. Open the door on a warm day and those seats would offer a clear view of the water, sheltered from the wind.

Matt's brows rose at the framed poster on the back wall. Not a classic pin-up art poster, but the illustration had that same 1960s come-hither vibe. A nearly naked redhead stood knee-deep in lake water. Glancing back over her shoulder, she dragged her blouse up over her shoulders — the last piece of clothing she still wore. The expression in her eyes was an invitation and a challenge. More for skinny dipping than sex. A flower power dare. Rocks and green trees in the background, with enough details to turn a poster of a leggy temptress into art.

Matt focused his gaze on the sawhorse. Hell if he'd let Charley catch him staring at another woman's bare backside, no matter how well drawn it might be. Even if it reminded him of Charley's.

"Is that a McGinnis print?" Charley asked, zeroing right in on the one thing in that garage Matt was trying his best not to stare at.

Roy shrugged. "Could be." He put the bottle on the shelf, already filled with empty, unlabelled glass bottles. "I found it at a flea market, frame and all."

"I prefer his paperback covers." Used to art gallery etiquette,

Charley kept a careful distance to the picture. "But just look at the details on those ferns, the texture of the rocks. The floral pattern on her blouse."

Matt took a deep breath and looked up at the ceiling. "Yup."

"You can instantly recognize the McGinnis Woman," Charley said. "Impossibly tall, mysterious. Dangerous and powerful. And always in the foreground, the spy or gumshoe behind her."

Probably happy and willing to follow her to the ends of the earth. Especially if she aimed one of those glances his way.

If that hot, challenging gaze belonged to the McGinnis Woman, then Charley had stolen it from the front cover of a book and made it her own.

Matt tugged at the collar of his sweater. He needed more oxygen. They had to get off this topic and fast.

How did Beverley feel about the McGinnis Woman hanging framed on her husband's wall? Although the idea that there might be jealousy also implied there might occasionally be sex, and he really didn't want to go there.

Matt zeroed in on a little red paper boat perched on the work table. Not a sailboat, or some boxy replica of a rowboat. A red origami speedboat. The gunwales were all sleek lines, complete with a paper windshield. It looked like the boat would fly over imaginary waves. Matt squatted down to get a better look, afraid to touch it in case he dented it or bent one of those crisp corners.

Roy joined him. "I'll get the grandkids to name it. All it needs is a light coat of beeswax, before its christening. Best way to waterproof the hull."

"It'll float?" Charley asked.

"Might even win the race. The kayak shoulda surfed more readily, but never got great hull speed." From the tone of voice, Roy could have been describing one of the boats docked at the marina.

"You ever build anything bigger?" Matt asked.

"Not enough time or space." Roy gave a wry smile. "These old fingers don't do so well with the detail work anymore, but I prefer to tackle them miniature sized." He gestured at the dark blue bookshelf on the far wall, and the row of bottles with ships inside.

The shelf must have been built without a level; so sloped, it made you feel like you were at sea, just looking at them. Small-sized versions of the wooden skiffs that drifted on the lake, mid-summer. Balsa wood hulls. Yellow-, red-, and blue-striped cotton sails. Masts and rigging lines made of white string.

"It would make a nice still life," Charley mused, that far-off look in her eye — not daydreaming, but taking in more than others saw, capturing those details in tonal shades, colours he'd never know were part of that glass until she put them on paper and it somehow all made sense.

Roy picked up the x-acto knife lying on the work table, precision sharp and missing its safety cap. "You know what other name those ships go by? Impossible Bottles." And that was the tone of a man who could happily talk about his hobby all day.

"It's a good name," Charley said. "It does seem impossible."

"It just takes skill. A couple tricks, the right tools." He opened the portable steel tool box, tossed the blade inside on top of wire cutters and tweezers.

Charley had been studying the shelf closely, walking the length. "Minor distortions and soft-tinted glass, to hide the hinges on the masts, right?" She turned to look at Roy now.

The way she watched Roy, it was like she was waiting to catch him in a mistake. Something twisted in Matt's gut. Something that felt too familiar. What were they doing here? They weren't here for Roy. They were here for intel on Laura, not to trap the man.

Roy scratched his jaw, his gaze suddenly a little more wary, like he'd picked up on it too. "Right. Not on all of them though."

"Like fitting a monster into a lake," Charley murmured. "Why did Laura move here, to Oakcrest?"

"You mean, because of that big-city swagger?" Roy's tone had an edge sharp enough to cut through thin metal. He caught himself, heaved a sigh. "She packed that back-off attitude in her luggage, along with her high heels and all her defences. I told her she wouldn't need them here, but she didn't listen. Never did. That could have been me."

Matt grinned. "Packing your high heels, Roy?"

The man frowned. "Building defences. She was tough. Didn't let anything hurt her, and there was a lot that could have. And she did all right for it. Better than I would have."

Matt wondered about that. Seemed like a hard shell kept out as much as it protected. "Thomas's granddaughter, Allison, seems to have been impressed by her."

"Really?" The surprise was too honest to be anything but real. "Well, that's something. Kids are a good judge of character. See right through you."

And Allison thought Laura was nice. Nice enough to protect, even after death. Or just determined to keep a promise when other people in her life had disappointed her by breaking theirs.

"Laura must have been happy, being closer to family," Charley said.

A beat went by, filled only with the pad of Cocoa's paws on concrete. Roy looked at the row of Impossible Bottles. "She was. Even that first Thanksgiving weekend, she had fun while she was here. I've got video footage to prove it." Defiant. Like he'd spent the past few days convincing people and finally found some evidence to back it up.

Which was probably exactly how that scenario had played out.

Charley's eyes glinted. "A home video?"

"We don't have much of Laura, but this VCR tape is better than any Polaroid. Keep in mind, I'm no Scorsese." Roy rubbed at the back of his head. "But you'll see what Laura was like, before —" He let that hang. "Ah, what am I going on about? Pull up those chairs and see for yourself."

Matt scooped up a stack of *Classic Boat* magazines off one seat and moved it closer. Metal chair legs shrieked over concrete as the VCR whined to life, the tape slowly whirring back to the start.

Matt sat carefully. The folding chair didn't look too sturdy, but it held his weight. He shot Charley a glance. She leaned forward in her seat, elbows on her knees, her gaze fixed on the grey snow flickering over the screen. Cocoa lay on the floor beside her, stretched out flat. Nowhere near as relaxed as when Charley had watched a film noir, even with the gunshots and wisecracks flying on TV.

"There." Roy came and joined them. Hit play. He sank back in the seat, watching the TV intently.

The opening image framed a close-up of leaves, curling and black at the edges. The camera zoomed in and out, refocusing, and there was a jolting motion of the cameraperson walking.

The view angled up, aimed at the lake. Bright kayaks — two of them — floated in the foreground. A boy and a girl in their early twenties paddled in one, smooth and in tandem, gliding along the shore. The other, solo paddler could have been a younger version of Beverley. All three wore water-resistant jackets, probably some fleece underneath, too.

In the distance, a canoe teetered in the water. It wasn't slick or expensive like the one tied to Laura's dock, and it didn't glide easily. It rocked, zigzagging a slow path through a beam of sunlight that whitewashed the camera's viewfinder. The girl reached ahead of her with the paddle blade and dug it into the water. At the wrong angle. She struggled, pulling it back toward herself, shoulders bearing the bulk of the work.

"Keep that paddle vertical!" Roy's voice thundered from the TV.

Beside Matt, Charley jumped. On the water, the shouted instruction would have carried across the lake.

"Straighten those arms!" A beat went by, the camera following the kayaks, paddling lazily. But Roy's attention was still on Laura. "Use your core to paddle, not your arm muscles. Rotate that torso. You hear me?"

The woman in the kayak closest to them said mildly, "Everyone can hear you, Roy."

Yeah, that was Beverley, all right.

The camera panned away to focus on the others. Laughter carried over the water.

Until it was broken by a splash.

The camera shot up, further out, to where Laura waded through the water, dragging the canoe behind her, teeth chattering.

She wore a life vest, straps pulled tight, and a zippered hoodie over what looked like black leggings. No water-resistant jacket, no fancy gear for her. Her bangs stuck to her forehead. Youth didn't soften her face. If anything, it hardened her features. Silently, she knelt and tied the boat to the dock.

Then she walked toward the camera, stopped right in front of it, face filling the frame. Young and determined. "I'll figure it out myself."

"Atta girl. Have fun?" Roy sounded hopeful.

She turned away and stopped short, shoulders stiff. "A blast."

It took wishful thinking for Roy to mistake that tone for anything but sarcasm.

"Don't go far," he called after her, already turning the camera back to the kayaks. "We're having s'mores later."

"Can't wait."

The camera held on a view of the lake, recording proof of a harmonious family reunion. A picture Laura had walked away from. Or had been left out of.

What had Charley said? The McGinnis Woman was always in the foreground? If that was the case, Laura was in the background, and it looked like she had been there for a long time. It was hard to make assumptions from one video clip, but it sure as hell looked like she was used to playing a supporting role. Maybe not even that. Part of the scenery, and blending right in.

Roy said, "That canoe could have fit another person, but she wanted to try it alone. Sometime later on, she went out, bought a book on canoeing. Phoned me up to tell me about it. Though how the hell anyone learns how to boat from a book, beats me. She did it, though." Pride there. "Got her own gear, too. She loved being on the water." His expression sobered.

Charley glanced at him. "The same as you."

Common ground? Or was Laura just trying to prove that she could do it on her own?

"Beverley will be wondering where we've gotten to." Roy stood. "We've got a buffet spread for dinner, thanks to the neighbours. Tuna noodle casserole, beef stew, mac and cheese. Pretty much anything that comes in a Crock-Pot. You name it, we've got it."

Cocoa wagged her tail, pink tongue flashing as she licked her chops.

"Sounds great," Charley said.

Matt was less sure how well this would go.

TWENTY-FOUR

CHARLEY HEARD THE brass bell peal across the water, loud enough to cut through a heavy blanket of fog on an open ocean.

Beverley waited for them on the front step, the door cracked open behind her. "Thought I'd sound the dinner bell." She chuckled. "Once Roy gets started, he can talk the socks off the moon."

Charley saw the illustration in her head: a whimsical collage of pen and ink figures. The man was in silhouette, his face turned up to the tissue paper sky, bathed in moonlight, arms stretched out wide. "Or talk the moon into an Impossible Bottle?"

"You'd think she'd be hard to trap," Matt said.

Roy walked up the steps behind them. "Just takes some quick thinking, is all."

And a silver tongue? A lie that could spread through an entire town? Roy saved up his words like Spanish doubloons, made them count when he used them.

"Come on in." In the entrance, Beverley opened the cupboard and took out three wooden hangers. "Here, give me your jackets."

Roy knocked the dirt off his boots before stepping inside. "You fuss too much, Bev."

"It's not every day we get company. Table's set."

"Hope you brought an appetite." Roy headed to the kitchen, to the sink. Water splashed into the metal tub as he soaped up his hands. "Plan is, you'll help us clear some space in the fridge."

Four place settings were laid out on the big wooden farm table, extended to full length. Melamine plates, white paper napkins. A candle spluttered, dripping thick globs of wax onto a round metal circle that looked like a canning lid. A slab of butter sat in a glass dish, a knife stabbed into it.

Dishes were lined up on the island and the kitchen counter, buffet style, evidence of a lot of love a couple of days past their best-by date. Shepherd's pie topped with a thick layer of mashed potatoes and cheddar cheese, dried at the edges. Tuna noodle casserole, the crunchy edges now gummy. A bowl of green beans, streaked white with hardened butter and bacon grease. Beef stew, a layer of congealed fat jiggling on top. Down at the far end, some kind of dessert squares with a graham cracker base and chocolate chips.

Matt rubbed a hand over the back of his neck. "Looks great," he said.

An orange enamel floral cooking pot with a matching lid sat in the centre, not nearly as full as the others. Even cold, the scent of lime and coconut rose from the dish. "Shannon's vegan sweet potato curry?" Charley guessed.

Beverley nodded. "With enough heat to burn your tongue. That girl always shows us up at potlucks. If it weren't for her wild sense of humour, we'd have stopped inviting her."

Those potlucks were an Oakcrest tradition, hosted by locals in the off-season. No one was ever uninvited. And if anyone dared turned down an invitation, they'd better have a damn good reason for doing so.

Beverley reached for a serving spoon, took Matt's plate from him, and began serving. Large portions.

Matt made a strangled sound. "That's enough, thanks. That's loads."

Beverley added one more heaping spoonful of tuna noodle

casserole to his plate before handing it over. "Just nuke that, hon."

Matt put his plate in the microwave, studied the buttons for a second, before setting a time and hitting start. He turned and caught Charley's eye and sent her a wink.

Roy loaded up his own plate, taking only from the shepherd's pie and beef stew. The gravy seeped into the potatoes. "I showed them that video of Laura."

Beverley paused, spoon poised over the casserole. "Did you?"

Charley had spotted the bone structure in the video. The features were softer and the hair different, but the eyes were the same. "You were there that day too, weren't you?"

Beverley nodded. "For the whole visit. Separate bedrooms though."

A surprisingly boyish expression lit Roy's gruff features. "Technically."

Matt held up his hand. "We don't need the details."

Roy knocked potato off the spoon, back into the bowl. "I don't normally like rehashing days gone by, but I wanted to add my two cents after Bev harangued you into investigating."

It didn't sound like Roy agreed with what she'd done.

Beverley raised a brow. "Harangued is a strong word."

"What would you call it then?"

"A polite request." Beverley scraped a spoon through the shepherd's pie.

"Did it feel like you had a choice?" Roy asked dryly.

The microwave beeped. Matt took his plate out. "We're happy to help."

Roy's gaze turned cold. "Fish for secrets? You must have caught a few by now."

The sharp tone, the edge of combat to it, sent a jangle of nerves through Charley. "We haven't discovered anything that Alex hasn't already dug up."

"Except for the video," Roy said. "Put that in your casebook. She was loved."

By everyone? She glanced at Beverley. "What did you think of Laura? The first time you met her."

Beverley frowned at the plate she held, filled mostly now with mashed potatoes. "I saw a girl desperate to fit in." She paused. "No, that's not right. Desperate to stand out. Who made do with what she had, but was full of want."

"For what?" Charley asked.

"Everything she didn't have. Everything she couldn't have." Beverley sighed. "She painted her fingernails with white-out but wanted the sparkle nail polish the other girls wore. You'd see it in her eyes. She'd never ask to borrow any. Just looked and hungered. If there's one word I would have used to describe that girl, it was starved. For attention. For things."

Roy scraped a chair over the ground, sat at the table. "No harm in wanting more than the lot you're given."

"You know that girl was unhappy."

"Of course she was happy." Roy slammed the ketchup bottle on the table. A blob spurted out, landed on the table. He wiped it away with a finger, then he ground it into the scarred surface of the table. There was guilt there, whether or not he realized it. "She just played to win, that's all."

Of course, she hadn't won, in the end. The thought settled over the room.

"At least," Roy said, "she made a killing when that slick real estate agent sold her house in Toronto."

"And then she went and spent a good portion of it on waterfront property here." Beverley handed Charley her plate. "Careful, it's hot." She replaced the lid on the casserole dish with a heavy ceramic clink. "It's hard separating that first impression from the person you've gotten to know later on, isn't it? It's like trying to peel aluminum foil off a frozen chicken. A little bit always sticks. Laura wanted to be able to provide for herself. She didn't accept gifts or help well. Maybe that was her need for independence. That need to be self-reliant."

"Damn stubborn about it, too," Roy added.

Charley sat beside Matt. She picked up her fork. "You and Laura were half-siblings."

"Same mother, different fathers." Roy cut a line down the centre of his mashed potatoes, gravy rushing to fill it. "Mom did her best, but she had me at seventeen. She was relieved, and no wonder, when my dad came to take me in, five years down the road. He pulled his life together, got that head start without being shackled with a kid. Got the stability she never had. By the time Laura came along, she'd made a go of things and gotten her feet back under her, best she could anyway."

Beverley said, "She was tough on Laura, though."

Matt pushed the green beans around on his plate. His attention was on Roy, not the food.

Roy chewed, swallowed. "She didn't want Laura making the same mistakes. Mom waitressed," he explained. "I added what I could, but anything I gave them went to necessities. I don't think there was much to spare for anything close to what you'd call a luxury item."

For wishes. Charley touched the pastel lines of the dandelion tattoo on her wrist. Wishes mattered.

"I always got the feeling," Beverley said, "Laura was ashamed of how little they had."

Roy's knife lowered to his plate. "You've never said that before."

"I didn't think it needed to be said."

"Why do you think that?" Matt asked.

"Laura tried her best to hide worn seams. Fixed the soles of her boots herself. Used a Sharpie to colour in the cracks in her purse, though it worked better for Julia Roberts in *Pretty Woman* than it did for Laura. She cinched dresses with belts to make them fit better. And she poured over those old fashion magazines left in the cottage. Same way I read through the weekly grocery flyers. She might as well have been circling items in red. Soon as she was on her own, she bought every fancy, frivolous item faster than the time it took to punch in the pin code for her credit card. The steeper the price tag, the better."

"I guess so." Roy looked like he was rethinking the past.

"Laura learned too early on that love hurts."

Charley fought the urge to flick a glance Matt's way.

Roy took his wife's hand. "But it also heals."

Beverley squeezed his fingers. "And those who shut that out never get the chance."

It looked like a moment of perfect harmony between husband and wife. Maybe it was. But it was too easy to use love to cover a darker emotion.

"Laura shut me out." Roy's mouth tightened. "Never even gave me a spare key while she was alive. I tried to talk her into it, said it was safer if someone else in town had one, and that someone shoulda been me. Seems ironic I've got one, now that a cop handed it to me."

"It takes a while to work up the trust to give someone a key to your home," Matt said.

A bitter undertone to his voice probably no one else picked up on except Charley.

"Home is where the heart is," Beverley said, "where we keep the things most important to us. I'm sure Laura would have given you a key. It was only a matter of time."

Time that Laura didn't have. "Have you been inside, since she —" Charley paused.

Roy nodded. "I had a walk-through after Alex gave me the all-clear. Made sure the doors and windows were locked, that sort of thing."

"Did you notice anything that might tell us where she went?" Charley watched him carefully, but it was Beverley who answered.

"Unless it was marked by a buoy, he wouldn't have." Her tone was dry.

"When it comes to noticing details like that, I'm out of my depth," Roy admitted.

Beverley patted his hand. "We all have our strengths."

A warmth there, of reassurance. As if he needed to be reminded. And Charley wondered why.

But Roy was wrong. The video wasn't a show of affection. It was a battle of wills. A battle Laura had won. Once, at least.

TWENTY-FIVE

IF HOME WAS where the heart was, Charley was getting into tricky territory. Ending the day with Matt, at his place, was starting to feel normal. Cocoa was asleep downstairs in the dog bed he'd bought for her. The post and beam house creaked as the temperature outside dropped — a sound she was now familiar with.

Charley took off her earrings and dropped them into the small indigo blue cardboard box on the bookshelf — the same type of box customers got when they purchased a gift set of pralines at Chocoholic's. The open bookshelf was a contrast to the closed cabinets in the rest of the house, filled with crime fiction — old and new — and a worn French-English dictionary, the ragged edges stained with butter and coffee.

Of course, there was no view of the lake from this window. No woodsmoke scent of the cottage. No cry of a loon echoing in the distance. But there was Matt.

And she got to climb between the sheets and warm her cold toes on his.

Charley scurried over the chilly floor and slid under the covers, pulled the quilt up to her chin. The mattress cover felt cool on her skin still, but she stretched out one foot, touched it to his.

Matt sucked in a breath with a flinch. But he didn't shift away. "Keep those ice cubes to yourself."

She wriggled them against the arch of his foot. "They'll thaw in a second."

"Guess I'll just suffer through until then." He propped himself up on one elbow and brushed a curl away from her cheek.

The simple touch sent a flutter through her stomach. *Is that what you call pillow talk these days?* Thomas's words shot through her mind. But wasn't that one of the perks of sharing a pillow with someone? The opportunity to discuss murder. "Dinner was interesting."

"You could say that." A guarded note entered Matt's voice.

But they had to talk about what they'd discovered. "Especially that video." Giving them a glimpse into the past, exactly what they'd been looking for. Matt might not want to admit it, but they had gotten info at the marina. "When Laura said she'd figure out how to paddle a canoe on her own, her tone was tough." Full of gritty resolve. "It sounded like a declaration of power." Aimed at Roy.

Matt shook his head. "We know she did the same thing with Thomas."

"And Shannon."

He raised a brow. "You got intel you haven't shared?"

She turned on her side to face him. The light from the landing — a dusk to dawn LED bulb plugged into the socket — was only one watt but bright enough to see his expression, curious and wary at the same time. "According to David, Laura bribed her with a donation to the Aquatic Invasive Species Prevention Fund. But, before you start thinking Shannon did it, she has an alibi. I saw her in her apartment." Standing clear as anything in her window, looking down on the street below. And there was no way she could have been in two places at once. "But —" She hesitated, and nearly kept the rest of it to herself, but knew that if she didn't say it, Alex would. "Roy could have taken a boat from the marina."

If his expression was guarded before, now it was a shield. "Without being noticed?"

If the dock hand was busy with a customer, helping with winter boat storage, it was possible. "It was a quiet afternoon. And it's not unusual for him to take a boat out." She thought of Roy's tone, the annoyance in it, when he said Beverley harangued them into investigating.

Matt's jaw tensed. "Innocent until proven guilty. And we're not going to figure it out tonight." He stretched an arm past her, reaching for the nightstand. For the block of yellow Post-it notes? Already covered with crooked block letters, scribbled during some other sleepless night. DRIED MULBERRIES? DARK CHOCOLATE.

Matt reached right over the paper, grabbed the alarm clock instead, set a time. "I have to be out of here by five tomorrow."

Charley bit back a wince and flopped back on the pillow. "I'll leave before you." Somehow, she'd make it out the door. Even though the earliest she had ever set her own alarm was six. Who was she kidding? Six thirty.

He shot her an amused glance. "So you can get to the cottage and have a nap before leaving for the gallery?"

She'd get in a decent snooze, at least. But she said, "Or go for a long walk."

Matt chuckled. "The coffee maker's programmed and ready to go. Half-and-half cream's in the fridge. And there are toaster waffles in the freezer."

Exactly the energy boost she'd need. She wriggled her toes against his again. "I like you."

"Yeah?" The mattress dipped as he shifted. He grinned down at her. "How much?" A serious note had slipped into his tone.

What would Matt do if she told him exactly how she felt?

Words rose from her heart to her lips, clumsy and awkward and nothing close to the emotions that quickened her pulse whenever she saw him. That drew her to him, whether she liked it or not. Edward Hopper had a point. *If you could say it in words, there would be no reason to paint.* So she said instead, lightly, "Enough to get up at the crack of dawn for you." She'd expected to see disappointment, maybe even relief, on his face. Not patience.

"For the promise of caffeine," he teased.

"Yup." She closed her eyes, snuggled under the covers.

"You wanna say that again?" His fingers slipped under her T-shirt and tickled her ribs.

His hands sent sensations buzzing through her. Breathless with laughter, she gasped, "Not fair!"

"I know all of your weaknesses." His brown eyes locked with hers and his expression heated, warming her from the inside out.

But he didn't know all of them. Not nearly.

Matt cupped her chin and pulled her in, the kiss far from teasing and hot enough to sear straight through her. Laughter faded until it was just a quiver inside her. His hands zeroed in on all the right spots, sending the rhythm of her heart leaping.

Joy and need were enough for now, until she found the right words.

TWENTY-SIX

THERE WAS NOTHING like starting the day in a good mood. Matt breathed in the fresh air, a grin still on his face. He stood on his front step and fit his key in the lock. Even though it was still dark out and the fog hadn't burned off yet, there was that pre-dawn hum of potential, clear as birdsong.

Or the low rumble of tires over gravel.

The heat of headlights hit between his shoulder blades. Matt turned, back to the door, and shielded his eyes with his hand, but a glare of bright light flashed spots across his vision.

An unannounced visitor, now? This early, just a couple minutes after Charley left? The warning bells went off in his head, along with a quick rush of adrenaline he normally felt at the stove.

The slam of the driver's door echoed.

Matt might as well be a sitting duck. He'd left himself wide open. And why the hell that was his first thought, he had no idea. Maybe too many PI novels were inscribed on his DNA.

The engine hummed. Footsteps came closer. The heavy crunch of boots. A grind and twist of a heel, like one leg was being favoured. Or a bad back.

The silhouette took form. Six foot tall, maybe. The wiry build and broad shoulders of a man.

"Thomas," Matt said.

"Figured I'd visit you at your place of residence." The tone had a gravel grind to it, sharp as the cut of those boots. "Return the favour. You came to my home, I come to yours."

An eye for an eye? "I guess that makes us even, then."

"Depends on how you're counting." Thomas stood in the light, arms hanging loose at his sides, hands open.

But a man could do enough damage with bare knuckles. Matt had seen Thomas swing a hammer, following the blow through with force and sheer stubborn determination.

The hard expanse of the door at his back, Matt asked, "Something on your mind, Thomas?" Shoulders squared up, straightening. A fall-back move he couldn't shake, even as he felt the echo of the past. That same level calm Jeffrey had used that had pissed him off seeped into him. It felt like a tool now, or even a weapon. Although that easy familiarity, that quick slide and shift of his character, picking up on those traits so easily, had him wondering — worrying — what else he'd picked up from Jeffrey.

How far he'd go, if pushed. How much it would take for that calm control to snap.

Thomas stepped closer, boots rocking on the loose fieldstone slab. "Oh, there's something on my mind, all right."

"I'd invite you in, but I take it this isn't that kind of conversation." Not with that tone and the engine still running.

"Look at you, picking up on the clues." Sarcasm sharpened each word to a knife-edge.

But Thomas would have to work harder than that before he felt the sting. Matt said, "Go ahead and get it off your chest before you kill your battery."

He didn't move. "You sent the cops after me."

So that was it. "Alex talked to you?"

"Yesterday. Checking up on my alibi." Same distaste as if "alibi" had been "blood work." "He asked why I was on Sugarbush Road on Saturday afternoon and why I sketched a fox carcass." As if the question was a personal attack. "You brought my art into this and turned it into evidence for the cops to confiscate."

Good to know Alex was following up on leads. "Did he?"

Further down the street, a screen door banged. A dog yapped and didn't let up, startled by something in the yard, a squirrel or a fox, and working hard to chase it off.

Thomas snorted. "Alex was more than welcome to help himself to the ashes."

"You burned it?" Shit.

"Paper makes for good kindling. And I wasn't happy with the way I captured the look of surprise on what was left of that fox's face."

Matt's stomach twisted. He still couldn't read Thomas's expression, not with the headlights glaring at him. And the scuff marks on the man's Blundstone boots didn't give anything away, other than the fact that for now Thomas was keeping his distance. "You often take time to study the dead?"

"Only when I come across the right subject. I'll do better with the next one." Like it was a point of pride, to master the subject. "It's always best when they're fresh. You still get those tattered pieces of flesh on bone. Makes for interesting texture."

A casual tone that was meant to get under his skin. "If you're trying to threaten me, you might want to just come out and say it. 'Cause you're leaving a lot up to subtext here." And the damn headlights aimed at him didn't help.

Thomas laughed. "You've been spending the past few days reading subtext into everything, drawing your own conclusions and taking them to the police. Why should I spell it out for you now?"

"I asked you why you were there, and you dodged the question."

"Because it was none of your goddamn business. Still isn't. And it was not" — Thomas stabbed a calloused finger toward him — "your place to accuse."

Matt held his hands up, palms out. Things were escalating here, and he needed to tone it down. Thomas was angry — pissed the hell off — but not defensive. If Matt was going to get dressed down on his own doorstep, he might as well try to get some intel out of it. "You're right. So, give me the facts now."

"No badge, no answers. I don't owe you anything."

"But you owe Charley." The man had a soft spot for her, that much Matt knew. "She admires your work. You clear things up for me, I can put her mind at ease." She'd take him to task for that one, but he'd have to deal with that later.

Thomas laughed, a short, dry bark of sound. "She's got a better handle on what's what than you do right now. The only reason you feel like you have to put anyone's mind at ease is because you misinterpreted what you saw and meddled in affairs that don't concern you."

If it put Charley in danger, it sure as hell concerned him. "What was I supposed to do, lie to save your ass? That's a lot of blind faith you're asking for, from someone you barely know."

"A little common courtesy would be nice."

Tact and discretion didn't have much to do with murder. "How about showing a little courtesy to the victim?" Matt asked. "That's all anyone is trying to do here."

"Laura Bouchard was a cold, conniving bitch. She doesn't deserve courtesy." Spittle flew on the snarl.

That touched a nerve. "You're going to have to talk me through that logic."

"Bare my soul?" Thomas sneered.

Matt shifted his weight from one leg to the other. He was in this far. "Might as well turn your car off. You're burning fuel."

"Wouldn't want the fumes clouding your judgment." But Thomas turned. Favouring one leg, he stomped back to his car. He switched off the headlights and Matt let out a sigh of relief.

Though he still held on to the tension, couldn't let go of it. The silence was sudden and complete.

He wanted answers but he didn't want to ask the man in. That was a boundary he wasn't about to cross.

Thomas walked back, but instead of heading to the door, he lowered himself slowly onto the front step with a grunt. The action was cautious and stiff, like his joints weren't what they used to be. "Go ahead. Ask me."

Wary, Matt sat down beside him, hands hanging between his knees. He caught the spearmint, slightly medicinal scent of an anti-inflammatory cream rubbed into the man's skin. "Did you kill her?"

Thomas's lip twitched, a wry tug that fell short of a grin. "No. But I'd say that even if I did, wouldn't I?"

"Yeah."

"So that doesn't help us much. Do you really think I waited for her in the lake? That's a younger man's move."

"You hurt your back somehow." Maybe out in the water.

"You were there when it happened. Actually, I'd say you played a pretty big part in that injury."

But it could have been an older injury, flaring up again. A weakness triggered. "Are you going to sue me?"

"Thinking about it."

Thomas had hip waders in his car. He wouldn't have had to be submerged in the lake, not completely.

But Thomas was right. Matt couldn't see him planning the attack ahead, choosing this method. Though the man had the quick imagination to seize an opportunity. If he'd already been in the lake when Laura showed up, at the right spot, the right distance away. With the right players, this could be a crime of passion. "So, what'd Laura do to you?" It was more personal than the dam for Thomas.

He shook his head. "That's a loaded question. You're asking me to hand you my motive. And I'm thinking you'll turn that little piece of intel over to the cops too, signed, sealed, and delivered."

If Matt wanted to get anything out of him, he'd have to push. Use the one thing he hadn't wanted to bring into this conversation. But he hadn't exactly had time to prepare for it. No way to line up intel on the counter like herbs and spices. So, he'd use what he had on hand. "Allison knows."

The man turned to stone beside him. Hard and grey and still. "You spoke to my granddaughter? That's crossing a line you don't even want to toe."

"She came to Chocoholic's. Said you had a guilty conscience about something." How far should he push? Harder. He needed a reaction, a rise. And hopefully, he wouldn't end up with a broken nose. "Said she made a promise to Laura."

A sound came from deep in Thomas's throat. It took Matt a full second to realize it was laughter. Shoulders shaking, the man rested his weight on his elbows and laughed into his chest. "Well, that's done it then. Get out the cuffs."

"You want to share with the crowd?"

"Okay." Thomas swiped a hand down his face, sobering. "I lost Allison."

The phrasing threw Matt. "You lost her, how?"

"We went to collect acorns for an art project. I lost sight of her for a second — No." Thomas cut himself off, started again, like he was pushing himself to confess, practicing for another audience. For a confession that wouldn't take place on a dark front step. "I got distracted. The light hit the leaves just right. The kind of gold rays you don't see every day. I stopped to sketch. And then she was gone."

Enough paths, tangled trees, and brush to spend hours searching. "You were by the water?"

"Scared the living daylights out of me. The fear hit like you wouldn't believe." He fisted a hand on his gut. "Jenny — it's taken a while to earn my daughter's trust. But Allison's a smart kid. She followed the trail back to town while I was still wondering where the hell she'd gotten to, imagining all sorts of scenarios. Injuries. Tears. She ran into Laura."

"Ah-ha." So that was it.

"The girl told her the whole thing. Laura took her to the Coffee Nook. When I finally showed up, Laura knew all the details. Got them from my granddaughter for the price of an apple cider. I ran the gamut with Allison about not wandering off on her own. Laura cut my lecture short with one line. 'Maybe that little girl needed you to pay more attention to her.' Laura spotted other people's weaknesses like bull's eyes and aimed straight for them."

"Yeah, I noticed that." Hard not to.

"I sat at the table with them and ordered a damned coffee. What else was I going to do? I said to Allison, 'Your mother is going to have my hide for this.' Didn't think that was such a mistake, not then. Not until Laura said, 'Maybe she doesn't have to know.' Turned to Allison — to *my* granddaughter — and asked the girl if she liked keeping secrets. What eight-year-old girl doesn't like keeping secrets? She drew that girl into a lie, fast as a snake charmer."

Put her under her spell? "Allison thinks Laura was a nice person."

"And that nice woman held my granddaughter's promise over my head. She didn't miss a chance to remind me that I owed her. Did it subtle enough so she could mention it in front of others. Made us seem like allies, like I was on her side. She twisted it to suit her. Said it never hurt to have a friend in town." Sarcasm there and a hell of a lot of it.

"So, you killed her."

"Ha." Thomas wagged a finger at him, amusement and exasperation warring in his expression. "Someone else took care of that for me." The creases around his mouth deepened. "If Laura was willing to get an eight-year-old girl in on a plot to pressure me, what did she do to others?"

It was a good point. Laura seemed to do whatever she thought she needed to, to get her way. No-holds-barred. "Probably more."

"Worse." Thomas rose slowly, carefully, dusting off the seat of his pants. "That's the truth, whatever you want to make of it."

"Let's say I believe you." And, despite himself, he did.

Thomas's eyebrows rose. "Let's."

"Who do you think did it?" Might as well ask.

A beat went by. A pause, as if Thomas hadn't given it much thought before then. And maybe he hadn't. "Someone who had a lot more to lose than I did."

"More than love?" Family and trust. Hard to imagine anyone with more to lose than that.

"I've lost it before." Thomas shrugged, his expression hidden in the shadows. "You learn to live with it."

Maybe. But Matt would rather wake up with a smile on his face than a hollow ache between his ribs.

Thomas headed toward his car, said over his shoulder, "Now, would you stop sending the cops after me?"

"You've got nothing to worry about." Matt couldn't resist. "If you're innocent."

That broke Thomas's stride, for one second, but he didn't turn back.

There was something they were missing in all of this. Some detail that had slipped them by. Or gone unnoticed.

Alex went through Laura's house, but he'd been distracted lately, to say the least. Roy had searched it too but admitted he wouldn't notice anything that didn't have CLUE stamped on it in red ink.

It might be worth talking to Beverley this morning, see if she could convince Roy to unlock Laura's door for them. A fresh perspective couldn't hurt.

TWENTY-SEVEN

EVEN WITH THE Jeep's high beams on, the boulders lining the Fire Route were hard to see. The lake was a wall of white between the cottages, like some other world of monsters and murder. Pass a hand through and you'd never return.

The light bounced off the red reflector Charley had staked into the ground so she could spot the driveway, even in the dark. Cocoa sat up straight and pressed her nose to the back window — not with her usual excitement, but with the kind of edgy nervousness she'd radiate when they'd pull up outside the vet's. Then again, maybe she'd just picked up on Charley's tension. The cold dread she hadn't been able to shake since they'd found Laura's body. The dread she wouldn't be able to get rid of until they figured out what happened to Laura.

Charley opened the door for Cocoa, leaned over her to unhook the seat belt from her harness. Normally Cocoa used the opportunity to lean in, maybe lick her face. A thank you for the car ride Cocoa loved. But as soon as Charley unhooked the seat belt from the harness, Cocoa leapt to the ground, not on her leash yet and raced across the driveway.

Not again.

She was heading toward the cottage, not into the trees. Charley slammed the Jeep's door.

The bark jolted through her. The next just as sharp, no breath between.

Charley stumbled over gravel, onto the dry crunch of leaves. Her eyes adjusted, picking out shapes. Branches. The air smelled of earth. The Fire Route not nearly as quiet as she'd expected it to be before dawn but rustling instead with unseen creatures. The plaintive *whoo-whoo-whooo-who* of a great horned owl, somewhere in the hollow of a tree.

Each bark Cocoa gave shot through her bones. Charley's breath shortened. Her heart beat jackhammer fast.

The picket fence ahead caught the first pale beams of sunlight. An eerie, white perimeter. A broken line in the dark.

Cocoa stood in front of it, hackles rising. Staring.

Charley put her hand on warm fur, felt taut muscles. She snapped the leash onto her collar.

What was Cocoa looking at? Charley scanned for eyes.

But the dog's gaze was fixed lower, between the fence posts.

Charley squatted down. "What is it?"

Cocoa moved forward, nosed at something hanging from the vertical board, dangling in the evenly spaced gap between white-painted wood.

Charley dug out her phone, turned on the flashlight app. The beam — bright, but narrow — picked up something red. An artificial deep brown-red. Not nylon cord or even kitchen twine or string but something more delicate.

Thread, the colour of dried blood.

Knotted into a rope. Small, tight knots, too many for her to count on the spot. Black feathers, floated, horizontal to the earth, spaced equal distances apart.

The rope spun in a current of air, like a mobile. Or a silent wind chime.

Something to attract the birds? But why hang it here?

Another Halloween decoration? But it wouldn't have Cocoa this on edge.

Charley snapped a photo of it. Somehow, framed on the screen, the contrast sharpened, the carefully tied thread and black feathers looked more ominous. Otherworldly.

The Wi-Fi was strong enough here. She opened an image search, uploaded the picture. The screen glared blue.

Results appeared. *Cord magic. Knot spells.*

A shiver ran through Charley. In the distance, the owl hooted again. Branches shook.

A *witch's ladder.*

Was that what this was?

Cocoa sat and growled, low in her throat.

Heart pounding, Charley skimmed through the article. The article that emphasized mankind's sense of wonder when faced with strange events and experiences. But it didn't feel like wonder. Not now.

Pieces of string or rope made from natural fibres like cotton, hemp, or human hair into which forty-three knots are tied, sometimes accompanied by feathers. Used in the practice of black magic, to inflict pain or loss on another person.

To *cast death spells.*

Someone hung it at their cottage. But when?

Alex would be up soon. She'd show it to him then.

And tell him ... what? That someone cursed their house?

The knots could be a downscaled version of boating knots. They were close to double overhand knots pulled tight and repeated down the length.

They'd had dinner with Roy, been with him from five p.m. on.

Could he have driven here late that night, without Beverley noticing? Parked at the top of the road. Tied the string to the fence.

She dives below the surface to investigate, completely unaware what a mistake that is. Shannon's words came back to her. Fear prickled over Charley's skin.

The cottage was safe. Or it had been. The picket fence was enough to keep out the wolves.

But what about the monsters in human form?

OUTSIDE THE KITCHEN window, the sun burned away the mist still hanging over the lake. On the counter lay the witch's ladder, sealed in a Ziploc bag.

Alex stared at it with a frown. "It could be a Halloween decoration."

"That a friendly neighbour tied to our fence in the dark?" Charley drew a feather in her sketchbook. The nib of the pen scratched over the paper, fine black lines. Cocoa snored at her feet, warm chin resting on her toes. "It's either a curse or a red herring. And it smells fishy to me."

"All I smell is lavender," Alex said dryly.

He was right. Even in the kitchen, the herbal scent was faint but unmistakable. And not as calming as it should have been. She took a sip of her coffee. She should have added more cream. It was way too strong, but she'd needed the boost to deal with witchcraft this early in the day. "It's not black magic." Or a death spell.

Alex took a bowl from the cupboard and dug out the box of granola. "But you picked up on the meaning behind it and that might have been the whole point."

"As far as threats go, it's cryptic."

He poured a carefully measured amount of unsweetened oats, flaxseeds, and raisins into the dish. The sound of clusters of oats hitting the stoneware was not interesting enough to get Cocoa's attention. "Less risky than a note. Porous, rough surfaces like textiles are hard to lift prints from."

As if disposable gloves weren't easy to pick up in the nearest drugstore. "But —".

The kitchen door swung open. Meghan stopped short, a newspaper tucked under her arm, ready to edit copy in an oversized cropped sweater and jeans. "You're up early."

Talk about stating the obvious. "There's coffee, if you want some."

"Only in an IV." Meghan reached for a cup, poured a mug, wrapped both her hands around it, and took a long sip. Without adding cream or sugar. "Mmm, that's the stuff. Finally, you made a decent cup."

Of course Meghan would appreciate it. "That's only because you live off caffeine."

"That's not the worst thing in the world."

Cocoa snuggled closer, her head nestled right on Charley's foot now. "Could you pass me the half-and-half cream?"

"Can't handle it, huh?" Meghan opened the fridge and took out the carton.

Sure, she could drink it, if she had to. "I like drawing in straight lines. I don't need my hand shaking."

"It wears off after about an hour." Meghan grinned. Then her smile faded. "What's that?" She nodded at the makeshift evidence bag.

Alex reached for a banana from the fruit bowl and sighed. "We're not sure."

"Yet," Charley said.

Meghan frowned. "It's in an evidence bag."

"Yeah." Alex didn't look happy about it. "It is." He took a paring knife from the drawer. Then set it down, spooned more sugar in his coffee instead, and drank like a man in need of a fast energy boost.

Meghan watched him for a second, then turned to face Charley. "You missed dinner last night."

A statement of fact Meghan would use as a starting point for an all-out interrogation. "I gave you a heads-up. Saved you from cracking open that second box of Kraft Dinner."

Meghan pulled a face. "Funny. We had a very nutritious meal, thank you very much. What was it, the third date this week with the dishy chocolatier?"

"Actually," Charley said, "we had dinner at the Callahans'." She added another feather to the drawing, now spanning both pages. And another. Spaces formed between them. Pointed ovals.

Eyes.

A half mask. Like a Venetian carnival mask. Or something peering out of the dark corner of a nightmare.

Alex paused, the knife poised to slice the top off the banana. "At the marina?"

"The scene of the crime?" Meghan planted her hands on the table. "I'm chasing dead-end trails to find some kid who saw a fake lake monster years ago while you got a hot lead on the mystery?"

"It wasn't a hot lead."

Meghan crossed her arms. "Did you find out more about the vic?"

Police slang. Quick and concise and impersonal. "You mean, Laura? Yes."

"First-name basis." Meghan pointed a finger at her. "You did find out more. And you got dinner out of it, too."

Reheated shepherd's pie. "Leftovers."

Meghan waved a hand. "Potato, potahto."

Cocoa suddenly sat up, scenting the air.

Alex cut the banana into neat rounds. "What did you find out?"

How much a few simple actions could hurt. "That Laura wanted to be a part of a family she felt she didn't belong to. I don't think Roy noticed it, but that hunger was obvious even in the short video we saw."

Meghan straightened like Cocoa had when Alex peeled the fruit. "Video footage?"

Alex spooned thick Greek yoghurt into his bowl, ignoring Cocoa's stare, even though it must have been burning into his back. "Roy shared that with you willingly?"

As if it somehow proved his innocence. "We didn't hold a gun on him."

He shot her a wry look. "That's a relief."

"We need details," Meghan said. "The full plot summary."

Charley still held her pen. And there was more than enough room left on the page. "How about a sketch?"

Alex swallowed a mouthful of granola. "Of the young Laura?"

"A picture's worth a thousand words." Charley grinned. She knew the saying bugged the hell out of Meghan.

"Yeah, yeah." Meghan waved her coffee cup in the air. "Now's your chance to prove it."

"Challenge accepted." She'd sketch the Laura who had stood straight and tall in front of the camera and said she'd learn how to do it herself.

But as the ink spread over the paper, the posture changed. The shoulders hunched. The gaze turned hungry.

Lake water flowed around Laura's legs. The orange life vest too large. A small tear in the black leggings Charley had forgotten she'd noticed until now. There was no room left to draw the kayaks. The other, laughing friends. The carefree family.

The shard of pain in Laura's expression, Charley stole from the grown woman who had come to see her in the gallery.

She turned the sketchbook around for Meghan and Alex to see and hoped she'd done Laura justice.

Silence fell. Not the hush of an art gallery but the heavier silence of a funeral parlour.

"Poor kid," Alex said, his voice low.

"An origin story that started in the lake," Meghan murmured.

"And ended there." The girl in the video had no idea what lay ahead of her.

Alex frowned. "I've been looking into the deaths linked to the dam."

Six deaths in the past twenty-five years. "The ones David mentioned in his speech?" Charley asked.

Alex nodded. "Accidents and none of them led to a case of criminal negligence."

She glanced at him. "It might still be a motive." For murder.

"Maybe," Alex agreed. "But none of the victims were local. Two cottagers, sunbathing below the dam, got caught off guard, swept away by the water. Similar thing happened to two fishermen, one sixteen-year-old boy and a thirty-year-old man. A fifty-five-year-old woman who used the dam as a shortcut from one side of the waterway to another. And a boy, age seven." Alex sighed, rubbed the bridge of his nose. "Chris. He got caught in the back current while swimming."

A child. The same age as the students David taught. Was it a coincidence? A shiver ran through Charley. "How many years ago was that?"

"Twenty-four."

How old was David now? Probably thirty-four or thirty-five. Was there a connection?

Meghan said, "I've been looking up stats. The Trent-Severn Waterway has more than 130 dams and not all of them are fenced."

And warning signs didn't do much if they couldn't be read.

Charley thought of the intensity with which David had scrubbed at the letters, the paint-streaked water dripping down his arm.

Meghan narrowed her eyes at the sketchbook, put a finger on the left-hand page, on the edges of the mask. "Are you thinking of changing your Halloween costume?"

Still absorbed by the lake monster, the inky ripples spreading out, it took a second for Charley to pick up on the change in topic. "What do you mean?"

Meghan held the sketchbook up. "Isn't that the mask from Eric's window display?"

Charley jolted. Lukewarm coffee splashed over her fingers, splattering the table and the folded newspaper. She snatched the sketchbook from Meghan. Was it that simple?

Meghan grabbed a napkin, dabbed at the liquid spreading on newsprint. "I was about to read that."

Alex held his bowl out of the way but didn't back up. He glanced over Charley's shoulder. "Did you put a creative spin on that or are those really the same feathers?"

"My imagination must have pieced the two images together." Did the boutique sell those feathers individually?

Meghan straightened suddenly. "There's an ad in the newspaper that I didn't approve."

Alex spluttered. Milk ran down his chin. He swiped at it with the back of his hand. "What?"

"It reads like a personal ad. Or a death trap. Aimed at me, I think." Meghan folded back the paper — the page full of black-and-white blocks of local ads. She read, "'M, remember this?' Then there's a colour photo of, well, I don't know what. It looks like a close-up of caramel or something. Under the photo it says, 'Clue 1 of 4. Use those reporter skills. No bribing, stealing, or forming sibling alliances.'" She shot a glance at Alex. "Did you do this?"

"No. Can't be." He'd gone a worrying shade of pale. "Do what?"

"Set up a scavenger hunt."

Was this Alex's new plan for his proposal?

"That's — it could be mine." It sounded like a confession dragged out after a lengthy interrogation in a black ops cell.

"Sibling alliances?" Charley asked.

Meghan gave him the side-eye. "He means us."

"You can't start today." Alex put his bowl in the sink.

Meghan frowned. "Why not?"

"You can't track down the first clue for twenty-four hours."

Meghan flipped the paper against her palm. "You just made up that rule."

"I can do whatever I want. It's my game." But the desperation in his voice hinted that maybe he wasn't so sure who was in control.

"Sounds rigged to me." Meghan stood, took her empty cup to the sink. "But I'll play. What's my prize?"

Alex looked queasy. "Nope. No spoilers."

Meghan rolled up the newspaper. "I'm taking this to work with me. I'll figure it out in no time, just you wait." She whacked him on the shoulder with the paper and shot a grin at Charley. "Lavender oil."

Alex looked dazed. "What?"

"Gotta go." She kissed him on the cheek and left, holding on to the newspaper like it might just be the best gift ever.

Which it probably was. "You made her day."

He downed the rest of his coffee and grimaced. "That ad was supposed to be postponed. I scheduled it for today, then bumped it when the case came up. I got an email, confirming the change. I think. Maybe not. Shit." He raked both hands through his hair. "How fast do you think Megs will crack that first clue?"

It only took Meghan half an hour to solve *The Globe and Mail*'s cryptic crossword on Saturday mornings, and this was a photo clue, not a riddle. Her code-cracking skills got a regular workout. "I'd say, that depends on how many questions she has to field at work. All she'll need is twenty minutes to concentrate on the clue." Maybe less.

He paced, spun. "Sarah got me into this mess."

"Felles?" A word clue seemed like something she'd suggest, but it was awfully specific, even for her.

"'At the heart of every romance is a quest.' That's what she said." Alex stalked past the window and back again. "But it's only a quest if Megs has clues to follow. That first one is supposed to take her to the next, but guess where those envelopes are."

"Not where they're supposed to be?" Charley hedged.

"Stashed in the glove compartment of my car."

Oh boy. "Are you sure Sarah meant a literal quest?"

"What else?" Alex headed for the door. "Chocoholic's first," he muttered as he snatched the witch's ladder off the counter. The feathers sealed in plastic.

Maybe he'd turn them in to the lab first. But it sounded like Alex had a list of stops on the way.

"A scavenger hunt proposal." Charley rubbed Cocoa's ears. "Let's hope that goes well."

But someone had to investigate the curse. Spell. Whatever you wanted to call it, the knotted thread was a threat.

Eric showcased the feather mask in the boutique's window. Maybe he had posted a picture of it on the store's social media account. If she could zoom in close enough, she'd be able to see if the feathers were the same.

Charley headed to her bedroom and grabbed her laptop. Sitting cross-legged on the quilt Grandma Reilly had stitched years ago, she logged in.

A grid of images appeared, mostly people posing in front of the backdrop she'd done for Eric. A pulp fiction trope painted fast and rough on plywood board. Oversized, looming green hands, curved nails dripping blood, framing whoever stood in front of them in the monster's grasp.

Scrolling, she saw faces she recognized and many she didn't. The styles ranged from baroque-print silk head scarves worn á la Grace Kelley and elbow-length opera gloves to vintage high-waist wranglers and crocheted tops.

The next photo, though, had her freezing.

David and Kayla, posing in a shot together. The view wide and low, like they'd set the camera app on self-timer. David was on his knees and Kayla had her hands around his throat, a bowler hat with a black feather tipped low over her eyes.

Only one feather, but was it the same? She double-clicked the screen to enlarge the image. The view shot to the side, framing a face in the background.

Shock flashed through Charley.

She'd drawn those features, shaped the same lines, sketched the woman's face on the gallery wall.

Laura.

Eyebrows arched with shock. Lips tight and thin. Gaze aimed at —

Charley moved the frame. Her pulse hammered in her throat.

Eric. Staring back at Laura, his eyes narrowed. Lips pulled back over clenched teeth. His palm raised in Laura's face. Not violent but close to it. A gesture meant to shut down a conversation. Or an argument.

When was the post uploaded?

Charley checked and swallowed hard, her mouth suddenly dry. Friday. The day before Laura died.

Maybe Kayla didn't upload the picture right away. It could have been earlier than that. Not necessarily right before the attack.

But the photo looked unedited, the angle too wide to have been cropped. The colours weren't vibrant, didn't have that vintage cast to them, to imply a filter had been added. No, Kayla took the photo and shared it. Instantly?

The shop had decent cell reception. It would have been easy to take the shot — a fun pose Kayla captured just right — and post it straight to social media from the phone's camera roll.

Laura waltzed into the boutique her first week here, Eric had said. And hadn't been back since? That was what he'd implied.

Unsettled, Charley stared at the image filling her screen. According to that photo, he'd lied.

TWENTY-EIGHT

MATT STOOD ON Laura's porch and waited. The sun glared bright, blasting away the last of the fog, but there was no heat to it. Just high UV rays and a cold breeze. Matt dug his hands in his pockets. Probably could have used gloves today.

The view wasn't half bad from here. Sure, it was of the road, not the water, but it would be a nice spot to have a drink on a quiet night, watch for deer. The sunbeams played over the clusters of purple aster lining the ditches. The leaves piled up against the tumble-down farm fence on the other side. You could spend a couple hours out here. Although, the porch needed maintenance. The eavestroughs were clogged. A steady drip from the overflow had rotted some of the boards, leaving behind wood damage.

The roar of an engine with a failing muffler gave Matt enough time to brace before Roy's truck came into view, driving at a country pace. He didn't pull into the driveway but stopped in front of the mailbox. To collect the mail? The red flag was up.

No. The man parked but didn't so much as shoot a glance that way. So why stop on the side of the road instead of driving right up to the house?

To make a quicker getaway. That must be it.

Roy could peel the vehicle back out into traffic at a moment's notice. But it also meant he had to walk down that driveway, toward the house. Dragging out the inevitable? Buying another moment's grace?

Beverley had pushed Roy into coming out here, in the middle of the day. So here he was. But he wasn't happy about it.

The man stopped a few paces away, keeping distance between himself and the glass-panelled front door of his sister's house. "I'm here to let you off the hook. You don't have to do this."

Help search Laura's house? Seemed like that would be something her brother would want to do. Take matters into his own hands. Solve the case, by any means necessary. Even if it meant letting someone else into her home. "And miss the chance to help get justice?"

Roy flipped a key ring in his fingers, the metal chinking when it hit his palm. Then swung again, jagged teeth glinting. "Bev watches too many crime shows. She's got high opinions about what an amateur sleuth can do." Heavy emphasis on amateur.

More than he'd think. Matt knew that from experience and wished he didn't. "We'll find out soon enough." Sometimes, all it took was one object to trigger a memory.

"Bev's got herself worked up over this." The frown darkened his face, draining away some of that easy-going kindness. "You're making it worse."

The animosity there took Matt by surprise. "I've spent a lot of hours now, working with Beverley, and she's got a mind of her own."

A flicker of bitterness. A snap and clench of the keys in his hand. "When it comes to fixing problems, yeah, she does. Especially mine. But some things can't be fixed, no matter how hard you try." Roy shook his head, a muscle tightening in his jaw. "You can't save a dying business by working yourself to the bone doing two jobs. And you can't fix death by figuring out whodunnit. The dead stay dead, either way. It's the living I'm worried about. I don't want Bev thinking she can solve this case herself."

"I agree." That was why he was here.

"But I don't think you're listening."

"I hear you." Loud and clear.

Roy stepped forward now, boots almost knocking against that first stone step leading up to the porch. On lower ground but the hard stare made Matt feel like he was the one at a disadvantage. "You share something with Bev you think is a clue, do you really think she's just going to sit back and wait for the police to do their job?"

An uneasy feeling crept over Matt. "That's why I offered to look into this. So she didn't have to."

"If you believe that, you're living in a fool's paradise," Roy snapped. He dragged in a breath, the same expression on his face a man might have when sailing a boat caught in a squall, fighting for control. "My wife has a good head on her shoulders — she's smarter than me by a long shot, and I'll be the first to admit it. She's not afraid to roll up her sleeves and get her hands dirty. Takes on more challenges than I would want to. She's capable of a lot of things, but she is not a cop."

"I get it, but —"

"Doesn't seem like you do." Lash of emotion, breaking out.

"If you think Beverley's going to go rushing off, put herself in danger, then you're underestimating her." For one second, Matt thought Roy was going to climb the steps and punch him. He'd take it, if he had to. But hell if he wasn't relieved when Roy didn't budge.

A muscle jumped in the man's jaw. "I want you to stop passing information on to her. The cops will do their job."

Alex would appreciate the show of faith, but it was hard to believe the man who had stepped in front of Laura's body to protect her from an investigation really felt that way. "We're here now. We might as well have a look inside. Even if you don't want Beverley involved, I figured you would want to help, as much as you can." It was a low blow, but Matt figured it had to be said.

Anger flushed Roy's cheeks, a dark shade that showed through the leathery skin and the windburn. "Fine. One walk-through, and we'll make it fast." He climbed the steps now, stomped to the door, scuffed his soles on a bristly welcome mat that looked cleaner than any Matt had seen in the fall on front steps around the lake. "If I die before Bev, and God knows I likely will, I hope she won't invite strangers to rummage through my personal effects."

Still protecting his sister? Or was there an undertone of fear? "I guess it depends on how worried you are about what people will find."

"We've all got dirty laundry."

Sure, maybe that was it. Just worried about keeping his family's personal affairs private. Matt wanted to believe it, but it seemed like finding out how your sister died should overrule that instinct.

Matt followed Roy inside. The walls were the colour of earth, the dark tones narrowing the small space. On a paint swatch, in the fluorescent lighting of the hardware store, the colour probably looked warm and rich, but on the walls, it had taken on a sickly shade. The entrance was a lot less welcoming than the doormat.

No beach-inspired furniture here, unlike in the Callahans' home. Everything was traditional, bordering on being forced into the straitjacket of convention. The heavy mahogany furniture looked like Laura had been trying to anchor down the corners of the room, to ground the house, battening down the hatches to withstand a storm. Though, in the end, it hadn't worked.

The sofa looked hard and uncomfortable and uninviting. You'd end up perching on it, no matter how you sat or slouched. Laura had suffered through discomfort, just to prove she could afford it.

What would Charley think of the art on the walls? It looked like Laura had picked anything gilded, so long as it flashed and sparkled.

Matt watched Roy as they made their way through the room. Light poured through large windows, but he had a feeling it wasn't the glare or dry eyes that had Roy blinking rapidly. It was stress or nerves or a bit of both.

"Spot anything?" Roy asked, an edge to his tone.

Matt rubbed the back of his neck. "I'm better with kitchens." What had he expected? That he'd spot the evidence as soon as he walked through the door? A murder weapon, maybe, already flagged and marked for evidence. Proof the Callahans had nothing to do with Laura's death.

"Not sure what you'll find, besides the takeout containers I still need to take to the dump." Roy strode past the next open doorway, fast, angling his shoulders to block a good portion of the view inside the room.

Matt said he'd wanted to check out the kitchen, but this seemed evasive. "What's through there?"

"TV room. Nothin' in it but the telly."

Somehow, Matt doubted that. He made for the door.

Roy's grip landed on his shoulder, hard and strong. "There's nothing there to see."

The doorway was a bad spot for any kind of evasive move. No chance for distance. And Roy had more practice throwing a punch than he did. The raw knuckles were evidence of that. Matt reached for the man's wrist, clamped his hand on it. "You worried about something, Roy?"

He blinked. It took a full second, but then he released his hold, stepped back, resignation on his face. "No."

And that was a lie if Matt ever heard one. What was the man hiding? Roy hadn't been this worried before. Nervous, yeah, but not like this.

A muscle worked in Roy's jaw. "Remember, you're here on good grace."

"Can't really say I've seen the house though, if we stick to the entrance." Matt turned to look at the room.

"Didn't take you for a stickler for honesty." The voice was low and aimed like a blow to the gut.

Matt felt the breath catch in his lungs. He froze, turned slowly to face the man, anger rising. Roy said it to get that reaction, but Matt couldn't stop himself.

Roy met his gaze, didn't flinch or look away.

Matt knew exactly what he was getting at and he wasn't going to let the man get away with a vague remark. He'd have to come right out and say it to his face. "Because of Jeffrey, you mean?"

"Figured he must have taught you a few things."

A hell of a lot and not all of it bad. "Yeah." Matt raised a brow, keeping his hands open and loose at his sides. "He did. Like how to spot it when someone else is trying to —"

"Lie?" No flinch, no tightening of the mouth.

Still. "You're hiding something."

"Guilt. My sister died on her way to my front door."

But that wasn't it. "All the more reason to figure out what actually happened."

Roy stared back. "You're not going to figure that out in here, I can tell you that much." He gestured for Matt to move, to follow him.

But Matt held his ground, scanned the small room. A wood-framed loveseat, loaded up with throw pillows, probably to make it more comfortable. A glass-topped coffee table with a metal frame, the top cleared except for a couple celebrity magazines, the fall Cottage Association newsletter — although he hadn't figured Laura for a member — and a cordless phone. Dead now, from the looks of it. A slow beep from the phone stand still plugged in somewhere in the house, too much like the beep of a heart monitor in a hospital.

There was one thing in that room that didn't match the rest of the decor: the newspaper sailboat framed in gold and hung directly over the TV across from the sofa, in full view of whoever sat there.

"Interesting choice," Matt said with a casual nod as he moved closer. Roy straightened, tensed. But why?

Roy shifted but didn't make a move to block him. "You never could tell what Laura would take a liking to."

But this was the one thing in the house you couldn't slap a price ticket on, that had no resale value.

But it had worth to Roy, that much was obvious.

Matt said, "It looks old." The newspaper was creased and weathered. The bottom of the boat was watermarked. The design was clever, detailed. A long cry from an origami speedboat, but carefully thought through. The edges sharp. Although flattened under glass, the base looked like it would open out, maybe even float. The warping and stains were evidence that it probably had. "Nice craftsmanship."

"More heart than skill," Roy said, a guttural note to the words, like they'd been dragged up from somewhere deep inside.

"Looks impressive to me."

Whoever made it loved boats, and from what Matt saw of that video, Laura had grown into that for the sheer hell of trying to prove a point. It didn't seem like she'd been the kind of kid to fold paper boats.

Unlike her brother.

A move from Roy cast a shadow on the glass, cut the glare, and Matt saw the print. Careful crayon letters on the side of the boat. A younger version of the block printing he'd seen on the sign in Roy's garage door. If he read the text, what date would he find on the article? "Is this your work?"

"Not that frame." Evasive.

"The boat though."

"I had some help."

He'd have to fight silence with silence. Matt waited for Roy to fill the gap.

It didn't take long.

Roy said, "The recycling bin was as good a toy box as any. Mom could get creative, find inspiration anywhere, when she needed an hour to herself."

This was the sore spot. This was what Roy hadn't wanted him to see. A newspaper sailboat that was hanging in Laura's house, not his. "Laura captured your ship?"

"Lost in battle?" A grin worked itself over the creases of his weathered face. "And you think that I, what, followed the pirate code? 'If any man rob another, he'll have his ears slit, and be put ashore to encounter hardships.'" A gravelly lilt to the syllables that could have made a buccaneer proud. He sobered. "But this was a case of Finders Keepers. I left it behind when I was sent to live with my dad."

It could have meant the boat, or the memory itself.

If one kid got sent away, the other one was kept — was worth keeping? "It must have been tough, being handed off like that."

"I wouldn't have stood up to the task." Roy shrugged it off. But Matt noticed his gaze roving over the boat. "Mom picked the stronger of the two."

Had Roy decided to prove his strength? The boat might not have been lost in battle, but Laura had displayed it like the spoils of war. "You planning to keep it?" The man's blank stare had Matt gesturing at the frame. "The boat."

"She staked her claim on it a long time ago." Roy turned his back on the frame, sparkling like treasure. "I thought you wanted to see the kitchen?"

The beep somewhere in the distance that Matt had almost

drowned out now gave him an idea. "Should we put that phone back on the charging station?"

Roy shrugged. "Why bother?"

Because plug it in and they'd be able to check the call log. Alex had probably thought of it, but Matt wanted to take a look for himself. "Might as well. You never know if Beverley might try to call while you're here. And a landline's a lot more reliable than cell reception."

"I'll take it." Roy held out his hand for the phone.

And get rid of it? Matt picked up the phone from on top of the newsletter, paused as a handwritten number caught his eye, carefully recorded on the paper, like she'd phoned someone or was about to.

Matt kept his face neutral as he handed over the phone. Roy left the room like he couldn't get out of there fast enough.

Matt gave him one more second. Then picked up the newsletter. The area code was local, the first few digits too.

He flipped the rest of the pages, scanning for more notes in the margins. Nothing else. It might not mean anything. But Laura had taken the time to write that number down.

He dug out his cellphone. Two bars. Enough to use data.

Reverse search through Canada 411 Yellow Pages should do it. Or at least narrow down the possibilities.

Matt shot a glance toward the doorway, pulse kicking up. Roy was out of view, probably already in the kitchen, though he might circle back any second, see what was taking him so long.

The search results loaded. A name flashed on the screen.

The Blast from the Past Boutique.

Damn. A store wasn't much of a lead, but right now it was all he had. That and a framed paper boat.

Matt folded the newsletter and slid it in his back pocket. It might be worth finding out why Laura had phoned the boutique.

TWENTY-NINE

THE FEATHER MASK was gone.

Charley moved closer to the boutique's window. The street threw reflections across the glass, hers and Cocoa's overlaid like ghosts.

The punk-haired mannequin turned her white, featureless face to passersby, the oval shape stark and naked beneath the black wig. The carnival mask had given her more definition. She now looked like a forgotten sculpture, surrounded by cobwebs. She wore a diaphanous silk dress and black Chelsea boots. A gory deep red stain concentrated on her abdomen, splashed out over the right sleeve.

Not so much a wound as the kind of splatter you'd get from a stabbing.

Where had Eric managed to track down so much red paint?

A silver bracelet, etched with repeating crosses, hugged the mannequin's bony wrist.

No, not crosses. Charley studied it. Hieroglyphics. An Egyptian ankh. But what did it mean? The art history lectures she'd taken on symbolism were a long time ago now.

She closed her eyes, picturing her notes, the symbol she'd doodled in the margins.

Life, wasn't it? That was it. The realization hit with an electric charge. The symbol was found in the Egyptian words for *life* and *nourish*. Different from the cross in Christianity that stood for the ultimate sacrifice and salvation.

But the ankh was also a classic Goth symbol that highlighted the appreciation for light within darkness. The good that comes with the bad.

It was too easy to read more into it. The blood, the ankh.

Cold dread rose in Charley's throat. Was it a subtle celebration of the good that came from murder? Could it be the equivalent of a victory lap? There was a reason why motive was essential to cracking a case. That was what Alex had said. People only killed when they stood to gain something.

Cocoa stood on the sidewalk, shifting her weight on her paws, uneasy in a way she never was when they visited the boutique. But today, Meghan wasn't with them. And Charley felt just as worried.

She pushed into the shop. In the dim light, she paused to orient herself. The musty scent of worn fabric and aged leather hung heavy in the air. Racks of clothing loomed, high as the corn stalks in the maze.

Charley walked past a spinner rack filled with cat-eye sunglasses. The convex lenses were like scaled-down versions of carnival mirrors, distorting the boutique and turning Cocoa into a three-headed hell-hound capable of guarding the underworld.

There. Eric stood near a display table. On the surface rested a shallow wooden crate filled with wallets. *Raw cane sugar* was stamped on the side. The imperfect lettering and geometric frame of the stamped logo had a retro vibe that hinted at the '50s.

Nearby was a small pile of what looked like shredded paper. He slid a piece into the bills section of a teal-coloured wallet.

"A hidden message?" Charley asked.

Eric fastened the clasp. "A note to guard against the curse of the empty purse."

She picked up one of the slips of paper. It felt thick, more like computer printer paper than the tissue-thin fortunes baked into cookies. A single line of text typed across it. *It's better to be looked over than overlooked. — Mae West.* "Hollywood style advice?"

An arch expression shifted his features. "Why not?"

Charley read another. *Until you're known as a monster, you're not a star. — Bette Davis.*

The quote snaked through her mind, working its way into the corners. A starring role as lake monster? She held up the note, heart pounding. "This one might not go over as well."

Eric glanced at it, skimmed it, then flinched. "Ah, the monster." He plucked the note from her fingers, too fast for her to snatch it back. "A bit tasteless now, isn't it?"

More than that. "Don't —"

Too late. He crumpled the text into a ball in his hand, pocketed it. "Those notes are supposed to bring luck and inspiration, not remind people of murder."

And yet the mannequin posed to attract customers to the shop looked like a stabbing victim. "You changed your window display," Charley said, as casually as she could.

Eric plucked another wallet from the crate, the pleather scaled and shimmering like faux reptile skin. "From a vintage carnival of horrors to imitation McQueen. Minus the locks of human hair. A 1992 *Jack the Ripper Stalks His Victims* vibe at a thrift store price. All it took was a splash of red paint." He shot a knowing look her way. "I was going to ask if you came for the style or the gossip, but I think I've already got my answer."

If only it was that simple. She twisted Cocoa's leash around her hand. "Good thing you only charge for one."

"Darling," he said, "it's a bartering system. You just haven't realized it yet."

Charley raised a brow. "Intel for intel?"

Eric shrugged, blue eyes too innocent. "A fair exchange, in my opinion."

The bell above the door chimed as a customer entered. Even though there were blind spots and hidden corners, sound carried through the shop, bouncing off the high ceilings and wood floors. They couldn't have the conversation here. "Could we talk somewhere in private?"

A beat went by. A moment when she thought he might say no. Flat-out refuse. But then he shrugged. "In terms of soundproofing, I can offer velvet or concrete. Above ground or subterranean. Your choice."

Not the basement. All those black bags of clothes hung from clanking pipes, like cadaver pouches. "Velvet," she said.

"The basement would have been the better pick." Eric leaned closer and whispered, "Scream down there, and no one will hear you."

It was a joke, but still her stomach twisted. He could have been speaking from experience. Maybe he was.

Eric grinned, blue eyes brightening. "But unless you're planning on shouting, upstairs will do just fine." He led the way up creaking steps.

Cocoa raced head, climbing the stairs to unexplored territory she couldn't wait to sniff her way through. Normally, Charley would have felt just as eager, just as curious. But she'd come for a reason and it wasn't vintage clothing.

Charley followed Eric into a narrow room. The space was barely big enough for the two of them and a chocolate Lab, wagging her tail.

Eric shut the door and the space became that much smaller. The air was thick with dust and a blend of floral perfume that could have been recent or a century old. The ceiling was low here, beneath the sloped rafters. Low enough to border on claustrophobic. Eric's perfect runway posture bowed an inch away from slouching. Clothing racks lined the walls, draped with plush fabric. The sounds from below, the footsteps and the conversation, deadened to an underwater murmur of muffled noise.

Charley touched the sleeve of a minidress. Velvet, the colour of crushed cranberries. "Nice."

"No." A glint of mischief in his eyes. "Barely respectable. Why are we cloistered away?"

No more chance to stall. She'd have to say it. "The black mask in your old window display. Did you sell it?"

He blinked. A startle of pure shock. "That's what the cloak and dagger tactics are about? A costume?"

Fabric whispered as Cocoa nosed under trailing hems, sniffing at party shoes and lethal heels.

A costume? It was true she was here about a costume, but a different kind entirely. One that was both a disguise and a weapon. "It's more about the feathers than the mask," she hedged.

Eric crossed his arms. "And they'll ruin the Bacall look you were going for. That's not happening. Not on my watch."

The red dress he'd found for her that fit like a glove. The structured shape, the broad shoulders, and the siren shade a perfect dupe for the gown Lauren Bacall wore in the 1945 photo by John Engstead. That dress now was hanging in her cottage closet, as out of place as a superhero's cape. "I don't want to wear the mask. I want to know if the feathers came from your boutique." She unlocked her phone. It took only seconds to find the image of the witch's ladder. She turned the screen to face him.

Eric studied the photo. "That's not a necklace or an earring." He narrowed his eyes. "It's very Comme des Garçons. The 2016 Blue Witch collection."

The casual reference so close to the truth, Charley wondered if it was an intentional hint. "I must have missed that show."

A grin flashed across his face. "Flower rosettes and feathers spiralling around the body. Knots and twisted shapes. Cord magic on the runway."

Adrenaline shot through her. A fight or flight response that had her fingers tingling. He knew, had admitted it. "That's what this is."

He tipped his head to the side. "For good luck?"

"The opposite." Her heart thudded, loud in the room that seemed to swallow sound.

Eric leaned over the phone and looked at the picture again. Looming over her. Intentionally? "They could be goose feathers. I sell them in packs of six. Ten dollars each."

It felt like a feather ran along the back of her neck. "For costume design?"

"Millinery." Eric gestured at the fedora hanging on a hook above the dresses, like a prop from the set of a film noir, tossed there and forgotten. "But most people here buy them for fly tying. The beginner kits sold at the marina only include the tools, not the materials. Roy sends anglers here, to stock up on thread, metallic braid, and chenille."

And feathers. An item Eric knew was popular. He also had the skill to tie those small, even knots. She'd seen the anger on his face in the photo, the way he'd looked at Laura with the kind of fury that couldn't be faked. "You told me that Laura only came into the boutique her first week in Oakcrest. But that wasn't true."

"A lot of people come in the store," Eric said dryly. "They don't all sign the guest book."

"That's because you don't have one," Charley said, aware of the tension in her voice she couldn't hide if she wanted to.

Cocoa came to stand beside her, brown eyes wary.

Eric feigned surprise. "No?" He snapped his fingers. "I knew I forgot something. Did that answer your question?"

"Not quite." She had to push. Charley moved to lean against the door, blocking the exit. As if walking away was the worst he could do. "You were caught on camera. Arguing. The day before she died."

A shift to his stance, shoulders tensing. "Whose camera?"

"That doesn't matter. What matters is that we have the evidence."

"Evidence?" Disbelief in his voice that would have been louder in a room that wasn't soundproofed by evening gowns. "Are you accusing me of murder? And" — Eric glanced at the phone in her hand — "witchcraft?" The inflection of his laughter was as forced and false as the tangle of gemstone necklaces glinting on the shelf.

Could Eric have killed Laura? Her stomach tightened. "I just want to know why you lied."

"I didn't." He paced the floor, a few feet forward and back. "I said she never spent a dime and that's true. She placed one special order that, in the end, she didn't want."

Why didn't he say so at the gallery? "What did you two argue about?"

"Fashion." He straightened the line of dresses, raking the metal hangers closer together. "What else? She had me order the dress, destroy it with paint, then refused to pay for it."

The dress displayed in the window. Despite Laura's death. Or maybe because of it? But in Kayla's photo, it looked like their discussion had been about more than a return. "If I can see through that cover story, so can the police."

He faced her, suddenly still. Pale. "You mean, I could run and hide? Or face the party, head held high, like a nineteen-year-old Kate Moss, caught in the sheer?"

It worked out all right for her. "That part's up to you."

Eric raised a brow. "I don't think my dirty laundry will dazzle the world."

"Come on." Charley grinned. "I'll bet it's silk."

"Not when this story takes place." He wrapped a hand around the VOGUE tattoo on his forearm. As though it was burned on, not inked. "This goes back to when I still had a twenty-three-inch waist and my mother dressed me in Old Navy."

And that was hard to imagine. "Those are dirty secrets," Charley said. "Go on."

Eric crossed his arms, took a breath that stretched his black T-shirt. "I saw the lake monster." No eloquent lines this time. Just five words.

Five words that ran right through her. "Recently?"

He shook his head. "At age seven."

It felt like he'd just projected the monster onto the wall, into the room. Charley straightened, heart galloping. "The boy who first saw the monster? It was you?"

"I took my dog for a walk by the boat launch." He glanced at Cocoa. "It was dark, misty. Hard to see. I heard a groaning sound that chilled my bones. Like something from a ghost story. A shape rose from the water. A green-black thing splashed toward the shore, right at me. Slimy weeds dangling from its clawed hands. I still remember the dog barking. I screamed my lungs out and ran."

She knew what a panicked dog sounded like, could imagine that fear echoing off the lake. "What kind of a shape? How big was it?" How tall?

"Huge." Eric shrugged. As if it was that simple. "Over time, it grew fangs. My imagination filled in the details. Seeing something like that, as a kid, it haunts you." He smiled, a bitter twist and nothing like his usual headshot-ready grin. "Take a Rorschach test and I would have seen those clawed hands, the green weeds."

Ink blot talons. "Who did you tell?"

"I would have shouted it from the rooftops, if my parents had let me." A muscle clenched in his jaw. "My dad went looking for proof. When he didn't find any, they wrote it off as another trigger for an emotionally sensitive kid. One who had a habit of finding things 'too scary,' 'too hurtful,' and 'too risky.' Who had a meltdown if pushed to do something out of his comfort zone. I got tired of hearing people whisper over my head, 'But he can't be upset over that. What's wrong with him?'" The sneer, so casual, so cruel, sent a chill through her. "Would you have believed that seven-year-old boy if he'd told you a lake monster attacked him?"

She hadn't believed Laura, and she'd been standing right in front of her, soaked to the bone. Her blood-stained hand more proof she'd ignored. "No." Guilt twisted inside her.

"They didn't either. My mother suggested that I keep what I'd seen to myself, to not tell people."

But there was defiance there. She'd gotten to know Eric over the past few months, had heard enough stories from Meghan to guess what he'd done. "You told as many people as you could."

There was no anger, just a far-off look. A gaze turned inward. "I cast a net, to catch the truth. If someone else saw that monster, I'd hear about it and I'd know I hadn't made it up."

"So that's how the legend started." With hope. The need to find someone else who had seen it, who had experienced the same thing.

"It didn't lead to anything." His tone was as abrupt as a door slammed shut. "There weren't any other sightings. No other victims. It was a prank. A one-off."

"When did you find out?" But she could guess.

"At the last potluck. When Laura threw it in Roy's face. They were arguing about the dam. She said she had insurance. A ghost from the past." Eric's eyes gleamed, bright with gossip. "And all she had to do was whisper, 'He's alive.'" The words slithered through the room.

Did she mean the lake monster? "Did it sound like she was threatening him?"

"More like boasting." He tucked his hands in his jeans' pockets, his pose more relaxed now. "She said she already had a lasting effect on Oakcrest and listed all the details of the prank."

The revelation a lifetime too late to save Eric from his nightmares. "You must have been angry." She watched him closely.

"Relieved, actually." Candid as a confession. "I'd spent too many years putting together cause and effects to explain the inexplicable. I'd either witnessed a supernatural event or the monster was a form of cognitive externalization. A perceptual issue." He took a breath, one long inhale. "When I found out it was just a prank, I could finally stop doubting my sanity."

And warding off evil with superstitions. He gave away the knotted handkerchief he'd worn to protect himself against dark forces because he no longer needed it. But, still, he could have killed to get that relief. "It would be understandable if you'd blamed Laura for what she did. For making you feel like an outsider."

Eric laughed. "Trust me, a teenage boy who daydreamed about dressing girls and stripping guys was always going to feel out of place in Oakcrest, even without the lake monster. Instincts and monsters." He shrugged. "Those are two things that can't be tamed or controlled. That live inside us, for better or worse, and make us who we are. And I'm proud enough of who I am today to not sacrifice that for murder. I wouldn't give her that power." He straightened. "Cathartic as this tête-à-tête has been, I think it's time to come out of the closet — literally. I need to get back to work."

And she had to find another suspect. Because if it wasn't Eric, the murderer was still out there. "So do I." Charley moved aside. Cocoa leaned against her leg, angling for an ear rub.

Eric paused, his hand on the door handle. "Since I'm baring my soul, I have one more confession."

Charley froze, her hand on Cocoa's head. "What's that?"

"I have aquaphobia."

She blinked. "A fear of the water?"

"Paralyzing, heart-stopping terror. I'd say, whoever attacked Laura loves the water." He strode out of the room without a backwards glance.

THIRTY

THE SMELL OF paint hit Matt as soon as he stepped inside the gallery, but still the red on Charley's fingers, staining the knitted fingerless gloves she wore, flared dark spots across his vision.

It took one breath before it clicked. Two before the adrenaline surge faded.

Paint. Not blood.

The sponge she held was saturated with a deep brown-red that had turned somehow, magically, into leaves on the wall but looked like dried blood on her hands.

Matt stepped in front of the projector beam. The shadow vanished, then reappeared, diving, filling the space. Six feet wide. The sinuous movement so natural, so close to being alive and real, it sent a shudder running through him. Which was probably the point.

Cocoa scrambled to her feet, tail wagging. Charley turned at the sound. And grinned when she saw him.

Covered in war paint, cheeks flushed with success and a take-no-prisoners gleam in her eye, it was a wonder anyone even considered picking her as an adversary. But someone had. And that thought ratcheted up the fear he'd been battling since Laura had gotten attacked by a so-called lake monster.

No one else might see it, but he knew the past week had gotten to Charley. Same way it had gotten to him.

Charley dropped her sponge on the ceramic plate at her feet. "What do you think?"

"Scary as all hell." And that was an understatement. She'd captured the stuff of nightmares and painted them on the walls. Then made it impossible for anyone to look away. The details were clever and subtle. A twist of an expression that turned a gaze sinister. The shadows hollowing out a face. And all he wanted to do was walk along the wall and take in the details. But that wasn't why he was here.

Charley grinned. "Thanks." The monster's shadow flickered over her face.

"The projector works well." She'd spent days figuring out which one to rent. Who knew there were so many options?

"I think I could have gone for the cheaper one. This one's powerful enough to cast a convincing full-colour illusion on a shower curtain hung in the middle of a lit room. It's even got a vertical display mode."

To send the lake monster swimming to the surface.

Charley planted her hands on her hips. Behind her, painted villains leered over her shoulder. "The killer's getting nervous."

As if she knew for sure. But how? But the lift to her chin, the thrown-back shoulders, and feet planted as though braced for an attack told him all he needed to know. "You got threatened."

"With a witch's ladder."

Whatever he'd expected, it wasn't that. A picture of a rope ladder hanging outside the gallery, dangling from the second-storey window, filled his mind. Snipped off at the ends, too short to reach the ground. "A what?"

"A cord magic spell." Charley wiped her hands on a rag and dug her phone out of her purse. She scrolled to an image and turned the screen to him.

A photo of string and feathers? Not spotted like the owl he'd seen perched in the branches of the trees on Charley's Fire Route some mornings. But black. The object had a sinister quality to it that went beyond knots and colour. "Where was it?"

"Hanging from the fence at the cottage."

His stomach dropped. "That close?"

She nodded. "But that means it might not have been aimed at me. It could have been meant for Alex."

Sure, but Charley was asking the questions. "You found it." Thread knotted with hatred. Meant to hurt, in some way.

"And I bagged it." She grinned.

But it didn't seem like sealing it in plastic would trap the evil radiating from this thing. He wanted to pace, but if he stepped somewhere he shouldn't, he'd never hear the end of it. Instead, Matt picked up her sketchpad from the folding chair and sat. He rubbed a hand over the back of his neck. "You know what the spell's supposed to do?"

"Nothing good."

Was the threat physical? Or a warning that nowhere was safe? Hell, he didn't have to be told that. It should have been hung here. This place that had already seen death, and now monsters, too. The illusion was complete, except for the break where the door leading upstairs stood ajar. The flash of the deadbolt he'd installed for Charley to stop visitors from wandering up was more unnerving than anything else. If he was in the gallery more, he'd want to keep that door sealed all the time. Probably the same way Roy wanted to keep his sister's house locked. "I went to Laura's house with Roy."

Charley, about to slide her phone back into her purse, paused. Straightened. "You what?"

Pure shock that had guilt rocketing through him. "The opportunity came up."

She crossed her arms. Her expression was not angry but guarded. "That's not what I call teamwork."

But he was here now, sharing what he'd found. "It took some convincing to get Roy out there in the first place. Asking him to wait might have killed the whole thing entirely."

"So, you went on your own."

In hindsight, it wasn't his smartest move. "I could have used your help."

She tilted her head back to look down at him. And grinned. "Yup. While you were touring Laura's house, I crossed Eric off the suspect list."

Matt went still. He thought of the phone number, scrawled on the newsletter crinkling in his jacket pocket. "Was he ever on it?"

"Right at the top for a couple of hours today."

And it didn't sound like she'd asked Alex for help. "You said you weren't going to do anymore sleuthing on your own."

Her eyes narrowed. "You can, but I can't?"

Christ, this was going downhill, fast. "How about you show me yours, and I'll show you mine?"

"You first," they said at the same time. In tune again, at least about one thing.

"Fine." Charley scrolled through her phone for another image. She passed the phone over to him.

Giant green hands. That was all he saw at first. Framing the couple in the front. Kayla and David. But that wasn't it. It took him a second but then he saw what Charley meant. The image in the background. The one that would have caught her eye and made her wonder. And worry.

She moved closer to look at the screen, her arm brushing his. "I came across this photo of David and Kayla on the shop's social media page. In the background, Eric's arguing with Laura." She filled him in on the details, down to the conversation in the boutique. "But anyone could have bought those black goose feathers."

"Including David."

"And Roy."

Marine knots. The thought hummed like a thread pulled too tight. He shook it off and zoomed in on the expression on Eric's face. The anger. "You sure Eric is off the list?"

A flicker of emotion crossed her face, too fast for him to read. "The only thing he was guilty of was talking her out of a fashion faux pas."

Matt shifted, pulled the newsletter from his pocket. "I found this in Laura's house." She moved to take the stapled sheets from him, but he shook his head, then laid it flat on the sketchbook. "No staining the evidence. Alex might think it's blood."

"It's acrylic. It's dried by now." She rolled her eyes. "Fine." She took one glance at the margin and said, "The Blast from the Past Boutique's phone number."

Of course she'd recognize those digits, no need to look them up. "So, it wasn't just coincidence that Laura came by the shop. They talked on the phone. Then argued."

"She ordered a dress from him. That's why —" Charley trailed off. Her eyes widened.

"What?" He knew that look, had seen that flash of insight before.

"The date."

Same level of enthusiasm as if she'd found a fired bullet. And he had no idea why. "What about it?"

"It's early." She tapped the date typed in the right-hand corner. "The Cottage Association newsletter is published quarterly. This is the fall issue. But it shouldn't be published until November."

Time travel? It was about as likely as monsters and witches. "Are you sure?"

"I submitted a sketch to go along with a follow-up piece on the exhibit. It's only going to be published in November. It's missing from this copy." She reached for her sketchbook, flipping through the pages. "I'll show you."

"You think the newsletter's a fake?"

"But why?" Charley turned the pages, thick with paint and pencil. Landscapes, creatures, faces flashed by.

One sketch caught Matt's eye, and the breath went out of his lungs. For a moment, he wondered if she'd read his mind. Slipped into his thoughts and put his — not hers — on paper. "You wanna tell me something?"

Charley blinked. "About what?"

She'd seen the photo. That was the only explanation. That had to be it.

He took the sketchbook from her, turned the pages one at a time, back to the one that had caught his eye.

He couldn't blame Charley for working through emotions in art. He did it — or used to — when he put food on a plate, carefully composed so each ingredient held meaning. But this drawing felt like a stab in the back.

Or an intentional conversation starter. To get him to spill his guts. "Did you want me to find this?"

She blinked, a flush heating her skin. "What are you talking about?"

Even unfinished, it could have been a carbon copy of the photograph he still had tucked in his wallet. The one of Jeffrey. The roughness of the charcoal, the ghostly traces of worked and reworked lines sketching out the contours of the man's face. The smudging only helped mimic the blur and grain of the time-worn photo. The only thing she hadn't gotten around to yet was the hair. So far, it was just a few strokes, showing the start of the hairline, a general contour that faded into nothing.

Matt pulled out his wallet, took out the photo he'd been carrying around with him. "It's a damned good drawing of this photo."

She tensed, deer-in-the-headlights still. "That's not Jeffrey."

There was no doubt about it. "The picture's probably thirty years old, but yeah, it is."

The flush deepened. "I meant my sketch." It looked like she was fighting the urge to yank the sketchbook from his hands. "That's you."

As far as lies went, that one was new. "I know my own face. That isn't it."

"Look, the pose in the photo is different. The angle of the head." She paused, looked at him in a way that made him nervous. "I just ... caught a likeness."

Matt laughed, but it caught in his throat. The subtext there, the way she said it, had him dropping the book on the chair, backing up a step from the drawing, the photo. How often did he look at his own face? Besides checking the level of scruff, he didn't spend time staring at himself, didn't pick up on those details Charley noticed. Only half aware of what he did, he scraped his palm over his jaw, felt the same familiar rasp of stubble. "The likeness between the two of us?" Mannerisms, sure, maybe. But not like this.

"Jeffrey and your mom were close," she said in a cautious tone.

Fear grew inside him. "Friends."

She hesitated, then let out a long breath. "Do you think it's possible they were more than that?"

He knew what she was getting at. Anger mixed with fear and left a bitter taste at the back of his mouth. The sympathy in her eyes was too much to handle. "Just because you think you see something, doesn't mean it's true."

She glanced at the wall, watched the monster dive, seemed to steel herself. "A realistic portrait is built on bone structure." Like all they were talking about was art. "The relations between features. The eyes, the bridge of the nose, the mouth. Sometimes a sketch can pick up a" — she paused, flicked a glance at him — "family likeness, more than a photograph."

There was too much certainty there for this to be some kind of guess she'd put together on the fly. And she was rubbing at the paint on her knuckles the way she did when she felt guilty about something. Matt fought the urge to pace. It felt like the painted walls were closing in, crowding him. "When did you find out?" He fought to keep the snap out of his voice. The panic.

He saw the war on her face, between compassion and honesty. "It was just a rumour."

Gut punch. Or maybe a blow to the heart. A rumour got spread around. This must be what it felt like, to be the last man standing. "One you didn't feel like sharing?"

She kept her gaze level, didn't flinch or move away. Didn't reach out to him, either, though comfort was the furthest from what he wanted or needed right now. "It was a guess."

"Made by who?" He fought to keep his own voice calm, to ask the questions that would matter later, when anger wasn't curdling in his stomach.

"Sarah Felles."

Of course. The woman watched and listened. Played matchmaker and saw the connections between people. Hell, if it had been anyone else, he might have been able to write this off as gossip. Before he could stop himself, he said, "I'm surprised it wasn't Meghan."

"What's that supposed to mean?" The sharper, defensive tone in Charley's voice was somehow easier to handle than sympathy.

Yeah, he was pushing buttons and he'd gotten a reaction all right. "Come on." He knew it was stupid, even as he said it. But he couldn't stop himself. "Your sister's made a profession out of printing rumours."

"Facts," Charley snapped. Her annoyance was tightly leashed, under better control than his.

And that irritated him. "What story did Sarah tell you?" Story. Not facts.

She swallowed hard. "She thinks Jeffrey and your mom were —"

"Having an affair?" The words left a sour taste in his mouth.

Charley looked back at him, didn't say a word.

"That's bullshit." He paced. "When did Sarah tell you this?"

She looked away now. "A while ago."

Weeks? Months? He knew better than to ask. Matt dragged his hands through his hair. "Why didn't you tell me?"

Guilt there, and a hell of a lot of it. "How would you have reacted if I'd told you that Jeffrey might be your dad?"

The scent of chocolate rose in his mind, overpowering even the tang of turpentine. Bittersweet and roasted. "Hard to say now, isn't it?"

"I'm sorry." Sorrow, raw and easy to read as an oil painting.

From nearby, Cocoa whined, but didn't move closer.

Matt nearly caved. Fought the urge to gather Charley close. Breathe in the scent of her hair, her skin. But he couldn't let this go. He'd heard *I'm sorry* before. It didn't mean much. "Yeah, well, secrets normally lead to scenes like this." His heart thudded. Some distant part of himself was aware of the fact that he was making the biggest mistake of his life. He kept talking. "You know what? I'm tired of them."

She blinked. "What does that mean?" Slow, carefully, like it cost her to say the words.

What did he mean? Christ, he couldn't think. Except that it was easier to be alone. Counting on other people never led to anything good. "It means we're done here."

"Just like that?" Voice strained, tight. Skin pale now. "You're going to throw it all away?"

Panic skittered through him. He dug his nails in his palm. There were no tears in her eyes. Hurt and strength, but he chose to ignore both, held on to one thought. She wouldn't cry over him. Same as the femme fatales she had painted. "That's what you do when a recipe goes wrong. And, the way I see it, there aren't any ingredients worth saving here."

"Fine." Charley strode to the door and flung it open. An autumn breeze rushed into the gallery, laced with traces of smoke and ashes. "Leave, then." She stood there and waited, daring him to go.

He stepped past her and walked out the door. Digging his hands in his pockets, Matt crossed the wooden deck and didn't look back. Not that he needed to. Her stunned expression was imprinted on his mind. Probably carved into his heart.

The irony of it was that a few years ago, this revelation — the idea alone that Jeffrey might be his father — would have come close to wish-fulfillment. Now, it was like looking down a road-map, marking out a trail of bad decisions, false starts, and missed chances.

THIRTY-ONE

MAYBE HER IMAGINATION really did have a life of its own. It seemed to be setting in motion things she had no control over.

She let the tears blur the paint on the walls into smudges of colour. Charley blinked them away until she saw the profiles clearly again. The tough, out-for-themselves villains she'd painted into the shadows of trees.

The lemon oil scent of potential overshadowed by the thick tang of paint that caught in her throat.

Cocoa scratched at the door Matt had closed behind him when he walked out. A familiar sound that scraped straight through Charley.

She said, "He's not coming back." He'd made that clear. And they weren't going to chase after him.

Cocoa flicked an ear, stayed where she was. Scratched again. Stared up at the door handle, waiting for it to turn.

The open sketchbook lay on the chair. The photo marked the page. Matt had seen the similarities, but he'd missed the love.

The images weren't the same. *When people look at a work of art, they see what the artist wants them to see.* She'd told Matt that, standing right here, when the walls had been covered in heroines, not monsters. Her heart tightened painfully.

She'd wanted to tell Matt the truth a long time ago and now

a piece of charcoal and a sheet of watercolour paper had done it for her.

A dark haze on the photograph, the size of a fingerprint, smudged Jeffrey's laugh, dimming that joy with a dark shroud.

First Laura. Now this.

She reached for the newsletter. At least they — she swallowed hard. *She* had that. A clue to focus on.

The handwritten phone number, printed carefully and neatly.

The date that couldn't possibly be right. The date that felt, right now, like an anchor.

Hard copies of the newsletter were only distributed quarterly. Not mailed through Canada Post, but hand delivered by road reps. The memory flashed through Charley's mind. Bicycle wheel spokes flashing in the sun. The smell of fresh-cut grass and hot earth. The rusty creak of mailbox doors opening as she helped Grandma Reilly deliver the stack of newsletters to neighbours.

As far as Charley knew, the newsletters were still distributed by volunteers.

If it ain't broke, don't fix it. Grandpa's voice echoed in her mind.

The date wasn't a printing error. Not on one copy.

But the articles looked new, like a sampling of the actual newsletter coming out in November. A call for calendar photos. Cottage fire safety tips, winter soup recipes, and instructions on how to self-rescue when falling through ice. Advertisements from local shops. Black-and-white photos submitted by members and the letter from the president. Another request for volunteers to join the board of directors. Nondescript. The minutes from the cottage road maintenance meeting about ensuring winter access to waterfront cottages and homes.

And four pages in — Charley gripped the newsletter. Blood roared in her ears. An article on the dam.

An appeal to protest the upgrade?

No. It was a notice for a Dam Safety Review. A DSR. *A systematic review and evaluation of all aspects of the design, construction, maintenance, and operation affecting the health of the dam.* The health. As though the dam had a lifespan that could be cut short.

The registered Professional Review Engineer will be free of any conflict of interest, independent from the dam owner, and impartial in the findings.

Laura read this. How could she see it as anything but a direct threat?

The DSR report will include conclusions and recommendations for the dam owner to fulfill their responsibility for ensuring safety. Detailing deficiencies in the structure; non-compliance with policies, guidelines, or standards and any other issues that might require follow-up; priorities for safety improvement and additional investigations.

Current standards might be different from the acceptable standards at the time the dam was built and could lead to a change in the classification of the hazard potential of the dam. From Low to Moderate or even High.

The report could have stopped Laura's proposal in its tracks, maybe even led to repairs, instead of an upgrade.

Loss instead of profit.

Charley glanced up. Met the gaze of the woman she'd brought back to life with paint and brushes. Felt the stare like a current in the air, tangible as ripples.

The paper crinkled in Charley's fingers. The site inspection to observe the condition of the dam system had been scheduled for two thirty on Saturday afternoon. The day Laura had died.

There was no byline. But then again, the articles in the newsletters were often anonymous. Pieced together from information submitted to the volunteer newsletter director. Finalized by the president.

By Shannon. Charley's heart pounded.

The layout was spot-on, down to the Cottage Association's life raft logo in the upper right-hand corner. The font was the same as it always had been. Even the paper felt and looked the same, that off-white shade of recycled paper preferred by the association.

Cocoa whined and lay down in front of the door.

Charley forced herself to concentrate on the typography, on the black marks. On this one next step.

Someone could have done a clever job of photographing, cropping, and embedding the logo. All it would take was an old newsletter or a copy of the Cottage Association cookbook, which was easy enough to get. But the copy wasn't just a physical cut and paste.

Charley took a breath. Focused. The print wasn't mocked up from an old newsletter. No matter how well done with whiteout and a black-and-white photocopier, the overlap would leave shadows at the edges of the paper that even heightened contrast or increased brightness couldn't hide.

The font unsettled her though. It looked the same as the one used by the Cottage Association, and that would be hard to dupe without knowing exactly which one was used. A best guess would never be a perfect match.

Charley paced the floor. "There are two ways the document could have been forged."

Cocoa raised her chin from her paws, cocked her head, curiosity brightening her eyes.

Charley squatted down in front of her. "Either," she told her, "the original document was imitated, or the original document was modified." A warm canine tongue licked her cheek. Yup. Cocoa agreed.

Which meant someone had to have the file or at least a template of the newsletter they could alter. Trying to fake the newsletter without access to the real thing would be hard and time-consuming.

"There's no way that date for the Dam Safety Review would have been published in the November newsletter." She stood, adrenaline rushing through her.

But Laura wouldn't have known that. She was new to the Cottage Association and to Oakcrest. This would have been her first issue of the newsletter.

With all the talk about the upcoming changes to the dam, there hadn't been so much as a whisper about a review.

Charley grabbed Cocoa's leash from where it lay, coiled on the floor. Hooked it onto Cocoa's collar and rubbed the dog's ears. "Someone used the newsletter, the threat of an inspection, to lure Laura to the dam." To her death.

Charley was sure of it. And she could get the proof Alex needed.

Shannon would know what was meant to be printed in the newsletter.

And she might know how the document could have been faked.

THIRTY-TWO

"SOMETHING TELLS ME," Shannon said when she opened the door, "you aren't here for dinner." She braced a palm on the door jamb. "Take a casting call for the role of Sherlock Holmes right now, and you'd score the part, honey, even without the deerstalker."

Charley touched the folded newsletter hidden in the pocket of her cardigan. "I could use a Watson." The entranceway was small and narrow, not much larger than the doormat itself. Steep, mud-caked linoleum stairs led up.

"I thought you already had one." Shannon smiled down at Cocoa.

"Actually, this is more your area of expertise."

"Well, I do love an appreciative audience." Shannon stepped back. "Come on in."

Charley turned to close the door behind her and came face to face with herself.

A reflection. Pale and determined and shocking.

Charley's heart pounded. A floor-length mirror. Fastened to the back of the door.

Shannon would be able to check her outfit on the way out. But she'd also walk down the stairs toward a figure waiting at the bottom of the steps.

Charley turned her back on her own face, followed the trail of perfume wafting behind Shannon. Something spicy and too intense for the small space. The stairs tapered off at a boot mat that marked the transition from entrance to living room. The area was open-plan and part kitchen.

Natural light flooded the space. The kind that made her artist's heart beat faster. The bay window overlooked Main Street on one side, and on the other, sliding doors opened onto a wooden deck. It must be the top of the back-alley carport and fire escape. Venetian blinds covered the sliding doors but the bay window — the one she'd seen Shannon standing at — was bare.

The beam of sunlight hit the sewing machine centred on the pine work table. Steel shears glinted on a pile of patterned cotton and silk Charley's fingers itched to paint. On the bookcase nearby, between bobbins and cushions spiked with pins, a face peered. Plastic. A fashion window display head, dressed in a bobbed wig.

Beside the workspace waited a stuffed mannequin draped in a black kaftan. Cocoa sniffed along the tasselled carpet, keeping a wary eye on the motionless figure.

Shannon adjusted the fold of the kaftan's sleeve. "I'm dressing as Clare West for Halloween. One of the greatest enigmas of silent film–era costume design. Clare achieved celebrity status, threw hellacious cocktail parties, and then vanished." She dropped the fabric, let it waft into place, like an arm lowering. "Much as I love an old-fashioned, I have the feeling that your visit is more a pop than whiskey event." She crossed the space, moving to the fridge. "Root beer?"

"Sure." The last time she had root beer was probably on the side of an A&W drive-thru burger.

Shannon held out a can. "I can even make it a float, if you're interested."

The can felt cold and clammy in her hand. "I'll stick with this for now." The way this week had gone, she needed a whole tub of ice cream to herself. One scoop wouldn't cut it.

Shannon shrugged and cracked the top on hers. "Suit yourself."

Charley glanced at the terracotta vase on the kitchen counter, filled with cornflowers and orange gerbera daisies. Light-struck petals. The watercolour study flashed through her mind. "Where did you find wildflowers at this time of year?"

Shannon raised a brow. "Magic."

Or artifice. Charley touched a petal. Silk. They wouldn't need watering.

Shannon sipped at her root beer as she led the way to the sofa. She sank onto the cushions, crossed one leg over the other.

Charley sat in the faded armchair. The vanilla licorice scent of the pop laced the air. She reached over to put her can down on the coaster on the end table. And paused. Nearly hidden behind a stack of DVDs — blockbusters and a couple classics — was a thick slab of rustic cherry wood, the engraving just visible. *Mr and Mrs.* Covering the flourish was a stone urn.

Filled with human ashes? A shiver ran through her.

Shannon watched, gauging her reaction. "Believe it or not, my husband was the romantic one."

But she kept his ashes nearby, close enough to where Charley was sitting now to make her wonder if she was in his seat. "Is that how he swept you off your feet?" Taking the conversation slow, even though impatience fizzed inside her like the bubbles in the can.

"It was more the other way around." Shannon shrugged. "I wasn't a safe choice. A little too wild." She grinned. "But he liked that. He never took the safe route in his life, if he could avoid it. Always testing the limits." Casual, she said, "That's what got him killed."

Shock jolted through her. She leaned forward. "Murder?"

"Car crash." Shards of emotion sliced through the words, although her expression stayed cool. "He swerved around a vehicle, lost control, and rolled the car." Her words came faster, speeding. "A quick adrenaline high led to cuts from shattered glass, internal bleeding." She paused. Took a breath. "And then a flatline in a hospital bed."

The images flashed through Charley's mind, graphic and detailed. Twisted metal. Sliced skin. "Were you able to see him before —"

"I was with him at the end." Shannon smoothed one manicured hand down her trouser leg. "You know what would have bothered him the most? Getting blood on the front seat of that BMW." Lingering resentment and grief, thick as a layer of primer under a still life painting. "The car was a mangled mess, but the blood on the leather, that's what he would have fixated on. I hope."

Charley blinked. "You —"

"Better that, than on the pain." Shannon smiled. "That's what I like to imagine anyway."

She said this as though she had thought about it often. Charley shifted in the worn chair cushion. "Anger is a powerful emotion." Though probably not strong enough to distract from broken bones and a fatal injury.

"Anger is potent, but it's love that we piece together in scraps to turn into Technicolor Dreamcoats." Shannon glanced at her work table by the window. Fabric shone. "Clothes represent the choices we've made. Of who we've been, who we are today, and all the" — she arched a brow — "crud we've gathered along the way. That's why escaping to the lake is so important. In places like these, we can wash the hem clean again and let those colours shine bright and true."

The lake. That was the transition she needed. Why she was here. Charley took out the newsletter, laid it on the coffee table.

Shannon flicked a glance at the title, surprise winging her eyeliner higher. "What's that?"

But the logo was easy to read. "You told me you were going to use my sketch in the winter newsletter."

She nodded. "That's the plan."

Charley turned the page, angling it toward Shannon. "But, according to this, I missed the cut-off date for publication."

Shannon studied the page. Same careful distance a hiker might use with a rattlesnake. "This is one of ours?"

"You tell me."

"Sure looks like it. That's strange though," she murmured. "The date's wrong." She straightened, gaze lifting to settle on Charley with the same intent scrutiny she'd just aimed at the typography. "But you noticed that already, otherwise you wouldn't be here. Where did you find this?" Casual interest. Not nearly the same urgency Charley felt.

"Somewhere" — she paused — "unexpected. Is this an early version of the November newsletter?"

"Zapped into the past? No. Just a couple pages, maybe. Like that article on ice safety. We're running that next. But some of the ads have been taken from older issues and cobbled in."

"What about this article?" Charley flipped the pages, to the notice about the Dam Safety Review.

Shannon read slowly, taking her time about it, long enough for Charley's teeth to clench. "I've never seen that text before." She reached for her root beer, sipped. Like it didn't matter.

"Was there a site inspection scheduled for that day?"

"Not that I'm aware of."

This was it. The lure. It had to be. Charley fought to keep her expression neutral, even as her heart raced. Cocoa shot a glance her way, as though sensing the change. "Is that something you or the Cottage Association would be told about?"

"Possibly. If the dam owner decided it was worth it to maintain good relations and let cottagers know what was happening."

Shannon stretched an arm along the back of the sofa. "Cottagers are very territorial, you know. They see the lake as an extension of their own property, even though the water belongs to the Crown."

"But not the dam."

"No, that's privately owned."

"But affects everyone."

Shannon slid the newsletter closer to herself, touching the edge, studying the article again. "Didn't David mention this in his speech? That the dam needed to be reviewed?"

Cold, sick dread settled in Charley's stomach. David taught a water unit every year. He had the knowledge to be convincing. "Did you give anyone a draft of the November newsletter?"

"I sent Kayla a digital copy — just a threadbare mocked-up version, nowhere close to finished. She was going to add the events announcements and proofread for any mistakes in dates. She could have printed this copy off on her computer." Shannon frowned. "But why change the date and add a phony article about a dam review?"

"Kayla wouldn't."

Shannon studied her. "Oh." One syllable, punch-heavy with pity. "But David would?"

Maybe. Charley stood. "Thanks for the info."

"You think David did it."

The casual statement ran through her, sharp as a pin through fabric. "I hope not."

Shannon curled one leg under her and leaned into the cushions. "Drama, drama." She tossed her head back. "Just goes to show, you're a fool if you trust anyone besides yourself."

Kayla trusted David. And he'd taken advantage of that.

All he'd needed was access to her computer.

THIRTY-THREE

IT WAS SAFER these days to get the answers himself before they got buried under more lies, Matt reminded himself as he let himself into Jeffrey's house. He hesitated one second over the scratches already worn into the surface of the side table, then dropped his keys in the same spot, leaving one more mark in the wood finish.

It should feel strange, standing here in the dark and empty house. But it didn't. It felt the same way his own place did, after he came back from putting in a full day at Chocoholic's. Too much like home. Probably because he noticed his own habits spread through the space.

And that thought hit like a gut punch.

Matt had walked around the outside of the house once, early on. Checked the windows were closed, and that was it. He hadn't come in.

The entrance felt cold. This time of year, people had a fire going at night or the thermostat on high, but Jeffrey had shut the door on this place on summer heat. Now, it was barely past five and shadows were starting to burrow into the corners.

Matt reached for the wall, hit the switch. The lights came on, the same way any of the other appliances would, because everything was still plugged in. What did they call it?

Energy vampires. That was it. Draining power and racking up electricity costs. He rubbed a hand over the back of his neck. Worse would be if a power surge had taken out the fridge.

Matt walked through to the kitchen. He should be grateful Jeffrey hadn't gone in for chrome in the kitchen. He didn't need any more reflective surfaces.

Prickles of unease crawled up his spine. It took him a second to realize why.

In the silence of the empty house, there was a sound. Like static noise. But where was it coming from?

But it was the stench that caught Matt at the back of the throat.

He yanked open the cabinet under the sink. "Shit."

The trash bin was full. The blue plastic box, too, piled high with recycled packages, empty cans still sticky with ginger ale.

Matt tied the plastic handles in a knot, yanked the heavy bag out, the acrid smell of rotting meat rising. He carted the bag to the front door. He'd take it with him when he left and do a dump run tomorrow to get rid of the trash.

At least the sink was clean. No stacked dishes. Just the Captain Morgan glass still upside down in the drying rack. Matt wiped it and put it in the cupboard, turning the grin to face the wall.

He took out a fresh garbage bag and held his breath as he opened the fridge. He grabbed items, ditched them one after the other, clearing the shelves. Coffee creamer, eggs. Not much fruit, luckily. Philadelphia cream cheese, the secret ingredient to Jeffrey's scrambled eggs. That and everything bagel seasoning.

Matt took out the bottle of maple syrup, set that on the counter. Open, but no mould. It would probably last a year in the fridge, no problem.

The bar from Chocoholic's didn't surprise him. Orange and green splatter on milk chocolate — it had to be his blood orange and rosemary. Unopened. Matt grabbed the Cellophane package. He didn't bother reading the label before he tossed it.

The glass canning jar at the back though, in the coldest section of the fridge, had him pausing. Sourdough starter. The storage date was scrawled on the label. But from the layer of brown hooch on the surface, just tinging black, the starter wasn't dead yet.

Matt pulled the jar out — sealed and airtight. He popped the lid and caught a barroom whiff of alcohol and yeast fermentation. No mould.

He heard Charley's voice in his head. *You're going to throw it all away?*

He could take the jar home, feed the starter for a couple days, and see if he could bring it back to life. Prove he didn't just throw things away. Although he had a whole bag on the floor at his feet that said differently.

Matt closed the fridge, yanked the plug out. Without that hum, the kitchen was quiet.

But not as quiet as it should have been.

He followed the static hiss of sound to the basement door.

Matt got a grip on the cold handle, wishing Charley hadn't spent so much time talking about monsters.

He yanked the door open. The hissing sound got louder, like a bed of snakes.

Along with a quiet trickling. A steady *drip, drip, drip.*

A vision of the lake monster rose in his mind. Of scales, streaming charcoal streaks of water.

Matt shook his head. Whatever the hell this was, it wasn't good. But it wasn't a giant serpent.

Matt's shoes hit the wooden stairs.

The light downstairs was bright. Only one bulb burned out. Still enough wattage to glint off the water spouting from the copper pipe.

Thin, pressurized streams shot from pinholes riddling the pipe. Old non-water soluble soldering flux probably bored its way through the copper piping, although the damage looked like the result of a scaled-down gun fight.

The puddle spread to the foot of the stairs. The concrete floor glistened with water, all the way to the carefully stacked cord of wood. The ceiling was low, the space mostly used for storage. Exposed beams, pink fibreglass insulation, and piping, mostly copper. The furnace clanked.

The cans of fruit would be fine but the cardboard packaging on the extra rolls of parchment paper were soaked through. Dark speckles of mould stained the bottom of the sturdy maple bookshelves, chock full of well-worn cookbooks.

Matt raked his hands through his hair. He had to stop the water. No point just sealing off the one pipe. Might as well shut it off entirely.

He ducked under the stream. Water hit the back of his neck, ran cold under his collar, as he dodged past, heading to the pump. The toe of his boot connected with something hard. A crate of potatoes, soft and shrivelled and soaked.

Cursing, he blinked water from his eyes and shoved the box out of his way and looked up at a photo of a boat, masking-taped to the wall.

Why bother with a frame down here? The colours were good, but the paper the kind of quality you'd get from a multi-purpose ink-jet pack. Like Jeffrey had scanned the photo himself, printed it off on legal-sized paper, and taped all four sides to the wall.

A lot of effort for a boat. Then Matt saw the tail end of a hairline crack in the concrete and grinned.

Special? Nah, Jeffrey just needed something the right size to hide that crack. Vertical shrinkage, cosmetic and not worth fixing, but it would have pissed him off every time he came to get more logs to throw on the fire.

At the pump, Matt turned the handle of the main valve sideways, stopping the water flow to the house. He'd have to get some towels down here, mop up what he could. Run a dehumidifier, if there was one in the house. Cut and solder the pipe, though he'd never been good at that.

Or just leave it as it was. The water was off now.

Matt made his way back to the pipe, ripples spreading around his boots. He meant to check the damage, but his gaze kept going back to that photo. The old boat.

Maybe because he'd looked at a framed newspaper sailboat with Roy just days ago.

The dock in the photo was different than the one on Jeffrey's property. Probably replaced over the years with something newer. The pine tree was smaller. The lake was not as populated, not as many cottages visible in the background. But the view of the bay was recognizable.

The boat — a vintage Duke Playmate — looked familiar. Like he'd seen it before, not just here on the wall, but out on the water.

Green leather seats. A wooden steering wheel that matched the boat hull so perfectly, it had custom job written all over it.

Hang on. Matt moved in closer, looked again. That steering wheel. It was the same one as in the photo he had found. The one Jeffrey had his arm slung over. That had been his boat.

You need a rescue? The shouted greeting. A wooden boat, towing theirs back to shore. The memory clicked into place, the part he'd forgotten.

The day he and his dad got stranded on that rock, Jeffrey towed them back to shore. Not a stranger. How had he blocked that out? His mom must have phoned Jeffrey, asked him to come look for them. Of course she would have.

And Jeffrey had done it, for her, even though Lizzie put family first and strung him along. Jeffrey let himself get trapped in a half-life. For sex.

There were easier, simpler ways to scratch that itch. Love, though — that was harder to shake. It hooked you right through the heart. And hurt like hell, Matt thought with a pang.

Jeffrey had to have guessed. Wondered, at least. After she died, maybe before. It wasn't just kindness when he'd taken Matt under his wing. Jeffrey had stepped in to save the day, more than once, when his dad had gotten them stranded high and dry on a rock he couldn't get them off of.

Damn it, that fishing trip was the best memory Matt had of his dad.

No. The truth of it sunk in. Not his dad. The man who had raised him.

But that had been Jeffrey, too.

Thomas's words came back to him, about the fox. *If someone threatens their young, they'll attack. Steal one more chance.*

Sacrifices? Yeah, there'd been a few. But it didn't mean Matt owed Jeffrey anything.

"Not even a second chance," he said out loud. His voice echoed off the water, sounding too much like Jeffrey's in that room, although he'd never heard the man say those words. Not to him.

Learn from your mistakes. That was what he would have said. *Try again and make it right.*

But sourdough starter was a hell of a lot easier to revive than trust.

THIRTY-FOUR

"YOU CAN'T CATCH a murderer with art," Meghan said, although her voice came out muffled. Hangers clattered as she rummaged in her cupboard.

Charley paced to the window. Meghan and Alex's bedroom faced the Fire Route. She twitched aside the lace curtains Grandma Reilly had hung there years ago, the faintest scent of honeysuckle and vanilla still clinging to the fabric. Red-tinged light hit the top of the Styrofoam tombstone, carving it into marble. "Can't I?"

Art led to Laura's death. It was time to use it for good.

Meghan glanced over her shoulder. "Alex might argue."

"And that's why we're not going to tell him." The Exquisite Corpse game was meant to be a conversation. A dialogue. And there was a reason police use conversation to expose secrets.

Charley turned around, crossed her arms. "Crime and Surrealism have been linked since André Breton suggested that the simplest Surrealist act was to fire a pistol randomly into a crowd." Then there was Dalí's technique of bulletism, shooting ink at paper to bring the real into doubt. "Questions raised by criminal activity were central to Surrealism." But not only that. "The unconscious mind is a reservoir of thoughts and desires normally repressed, which is why Surrealist artists borrowed techniques from psychoanalysis to bring to the surface subconscious thoughts."

Not that anyone needed special techniques to read Cocoa's desires. She stared up at the Ikea floating shelf Alex had installed above the framed pictures, brown eyes full of longing for the signed baseball he kept there, already pockmarked with her teeth.

Meghan sat on the floor and yanked one brown leather boot on. "Subconscious thoughts such as ..."

"Feelings of conflict, pain." Same way her sketch that looked like an old photograph had. Her heart tightened. "Anxiety and violence." Secrets.

Meghan laced the boot. "Murderous instincts?"

Hopefully. "Everyone censors their own thoughts, deciding how much to reveal to others, but these Surrealist techniques were meant to tear down those walls." To reveal psychological truths.

Meghan grinned. "A bit like a stiff drink."

"An older version of the Exquisite Corpse game was called Consequences. And someone's going to have to deal with them." Sooner, rather than later.

"Doesn't it unsettle you?" Meghan reached for the second boot. "That you might draw things without being aware of it? Of your subconscious taking over?"

More now than ever before. The slow, creeping fear spread further through her. Charley walked to the sky-blue dresser so Meghan wouldn't see her expression. The mirror frame was free of Post-it notes for once. The ragged yellow notes scrunched and stuck to the wood surface of the dresser, beside Meghan's perfume bottle. "I've never drawn a dismembered body."

"Yet."

Charley shot her sister a glance in the mirror. "Thanks."

"Speaking of murder, do I have to take a hit out on Matt?" Meghan stood, jammed her fists on her hips. "I'm happy to be your date tonight but I'm just as happy to bust a kneecap. No one breaks my sister's heart and gets away with it."

"It's bruised, not broken." She'd be able to tell the difference.

"Mmm-hmm. Keep telling yourself that."

The ache would fade. "Can we just concentrate on the art tonight?"

"Okay, I'll drop it. For now." Meghan came to stand beside her. "You need more lipstick."

"I'm already wearing some." A Turner Classic Movies poster shade of red, perfect for a 1940s-inspired parlour game.

Meghan arched a brow. "Oh, so now you're holding back on the red?" She reached for the wooden jewellery box and opened the lid on a tangle of beaded bracelets. "I figured it out." Tone too casual.

"The tiger's eye bracelet?"

"What? No. The clue." Meghan glanced up at her and sighed. "The clue in the paper."

Just like Alex had been worried about. "Are you sure about that?"

"Positive." Meghan reached into her jeans pocket and pulled out a square of folded newspaper. She held up the ad and flicked the image against her palm. "Maple syrup."

"If that was a headline, you'd demand a rewrite." The sunlight flowing into the room was as thick and coppery now as first-run sap. "Can we go?"

Meghan put the bracelet on with a twang of elastic and stones. "'Maple Syrup Meet-Cute.' How's that?"

"I thought you two met while you were working a case. You chased the same lead, right into each other's arms?"

"That's Alex's version and he exaggerated, but yeah, we did." She tapped the newspaper again. "This was it."

"A maple syrup heist?" Charley could all but see the wheels spinning as Meghan worked the column over in her mind, already drafting copy.

"That would be a good story. The perfect way to hype the Maple Syrup Festival. But no. The police —"

"A.k.a. Alex."

"Right, but I didn't know that then. The police found a strange 'unknown, sticky liquid'" — Meghan sketched air quotes with her fingers — "covering a four-foot area of sidewalk."

"It was maple syrup?"

"Allegedly."

"There was one way you could have found that out."

"Taste it? No, thank you. And the mischief charge didn't warrant a lab test."

She recognized the news reporter gleam in Meghan's eye. She'd have to hurry her along, before this turned into a three-column tale. She grabbed Meghan's red fountain pen from the vase on the dresser. "Where's your purse?"

"The kitchen, probably. Anyway, a city road crew had to be called in to clean the —"

"Crime scene?"

Meghan shot her a look. "I feel like you're not taking this seriously."

"Sorry. Go on." But hopefully she'd talk and walk. "What was the motive?"

"Edible marijuana and a dare. But that's not the point. The point is that we met —"

"Over a pool of maple syrup." Charley nudged her toward the door.

"Outside the mom-and-pop diner."

Charley paused at that. "In Oakcrest?"

"Matt took over the space, when they closed down."

And the clue would take her right to Chocoholic's. Her heart tightened. "Did that diner serve breakfast all day? I feel like this story should end with a stack of pancakes."

"It ended with Alex giving me his phone number," Meghan took the pen from Charley, tucked it in her pocket, "for follow-up questions. And I'm thinking this scavenger hunt is a lead-up to a question."

Don't react. Just grin or, better yet, shrug. "Like, what's for dinner?"

"Like a life-changing question. A forever question." Meghan looked pale.

That wasn't a good sign. "Maybe you should just wait and see what happens?"

"As if." Meghan glanced at the pictures hanging on the walls. The one of the two of them, holding hands as they jumped off the dock, caught mid-air. In the second between flying and sinking. "What if I'm not ready for a forever question?"

"You're normally pretty good with questions."

"Asking them," she admitted. "Not answering them."

Charley turned on a lamp for Cocoa. "Maybe you should listen to your heart on this one."

"Do a Q & A with myself?"

"You have twenty-four hours to do some soul searching."

"Oh, sure. Tons of time." Meghan shrugged into her coat. "Cue the countdown timer that ends with a black screen and two ominous numbers. Actually, I'd love to stretch my next twenty-four hours into twenty-four episodes."

In the entrance, Charley dug the keys to her Jeep out of her bag hanging on the wall hook. "You're not dealing with counter-terrorist attacks and sleeper cells."

"Just one cop."

"Your cop." But if Meghan decided she didn't want forever with Alex, it would just be the two of them again. The thought felt like an act of betrayal; she pushed it aside, fast. "Don't write the story before you have all the facts. This could just be an elaborate breakfast invite."

"Mmm-hmm. I think this is about more than pancakes, but I'll let myself be surprised."

"Good plan." Charley patted Cocoa goodbye and tried not to let the brown-eyed gaze of reproach cut too deep.

Meghan slung her arm over Charley's shoulder as they headed outside. "Want me to take on the role of designated sleuth and driver? Nothing numbs the pain like a chocolate martini." Meghan winced. "On second thought, hold the chocolate."

She'd never be able to taste it again without thinking of him. Charley took a breath. Skeletal shadows stretched long fingers over the ground, reaching toward the imitation corpse — the picket fence someone had tied a witch's ladder to. "Get plastered at a public event I'm supposed to lead? No, thanks."

"I can draw a mean stick figure." Meghan paused beside the Jeep. "I could take over."

Charley grinned. Now that would be an art event. "I do like that you always give them ears."

Meghan shrugged. "How else are they going to eavesdrop?"

"Stick to that tonight. I'll be fine." She would. Couples broke up all the time, though that thought didn't help as much as it should have.

"Just thought I'd offer." Meghan climbed into the passenger side. "But don't go changing your mind later, because after we get David to crack, I'm planning to have a celebratory cocktail or two. You can have a sip of mine."

"Then you'd better order something that I like." Charley started the engine.

"There's just one thing." Meghan glanced her way.

"Yeah?" Charley checked over her shoulder and backed out onto the Fire Route.

"If these drawings are supposed to circulate around the room, how are you going to look at David's?" Meghan fiddled with the radio, hitting static with a sharp hiss of white noise. "You can't gather the suspects and have them show you their unconscious thoughts, then point to the murderer and say, 'Gotcha!' This isn't an Agatha Christie."

Close enough to it. "We'll do a gallery walk at the end." The headlights flashed on eyes. A feline slant to them. A bobcat? A flash-flicker glimpse that vanished just as fast and left her wondering if she'd seen anything at all. "I guarantee that the art will tell us something." It always did.

Meghan settled back in her seat. "Reveal a killer?"

Charley nodded. "Let's hope so."

THIRTY-FIVE

SARAH CHIMED A knife on the edge of her glass, the crystal-clear tone ringing out. Slicing through the chatter and silencing it. "Welcome to the Blue Heron Lounge's Exquisite Corpse parlour game, one of many special experiences our event manager has organized around town." Sarah raised her martini in Kayla's direction. "This event tonight is an example of the unfettered power of cause and effect. Every action has a consequence. And, at the end of the game, it will be up to each one of you to decide what to do with your Exquisite Corpse."

Charley felt the tension increase, taut as a red wire strung between trees and just as dangerous.

Sarah paused there, let the beat linger on that second too long. "Allow me to turn the stage over to Charley Scott." Her lips curved, a satisfied expression on her face, as though she was about to move a chess piece into place that could fell the king. "An artist who has personal experience with reanimating monsters."

Charley stood. All eyes were focused on her, some friendlier than others, but all eager, waiting to hear what she had to say about an exhibit that had killed.

She pulled the cue card out of her pocket. She should have used India ink to jot down her notes. Her palms, clammy now, smeared the letters. "Inspired by Shudder Pulp dime magazines and the legend of our very own lake monster, the exhibit will challenge you to face your fears." She'd expected murmurs, or attention to shift away, but instead, all eyes were on her, waiting for scraps of gossip — anything to do with the lake monster or murder. "You'll walk through the piece, touch it, cast water reflections, and approach the monster. Proceeds will go toward raising money to renovate the building in the Mews in order to reopen as a permanent gallery showcasing Canadian artwork. We'd appreciate it if you'd spread the word."

"Far and wide," Sarah added. A command, not a request.

Charley looked at the text she'd written out on the card. Sitting at the kitchen table at the cottage, the words had felt right. But standing here, in the B&B, she wasn't so sure. The ink was fresh, the B&B crowded. The trap was set. And her only tools were an easel and fine-tip markers scattered across the tables.

She glanced up, ignoring the carefully composed speech. "For this exhibit, I had to consider what a monster is, and I discovered one simple truth: It's something that is created." Her fault. She ignored the thought, pushed it aside. "But it can be trapped, contained within four walls." At the bar, ice cubes crashed into a glass. Liquid splashed, poured from a height. "So, let's trap some monsters, right here, right now, with paper and pen."

A piercing whistle sounded — one better suited to a rock concert or gig than the B&B's dining room. Meghan grinned at her from their table and shot her a thumbs-up.

At each place setting, skull-shaped drinking glasses glinted. The eye socket, the hollowed cheek the right size and shape for thumb and fingers. On the bar at the back of the room, the chalkboard sign encouraged patrons to name their poison. Trays of canapés circled the room. Bacon-wrapped cheese and figs were arranged in neat rows like severed fingers.

Sarah surveyed her parlour like a chess master eyeing the playing board. "We've got four tables. Four guests seated at each.

Head, torso, legs, and feet."

"No horns?" Charley murmured.

Sarah swirled her olive in her drink, cloudy with brine. "If someone feels the desire to go beyond the limits of the page, they may use Scotch tape."

People mingled, talking and drinking. It would only take fluid brush strokes and flickered light to turn the scene into a painting of a party. The canvas was filled with activity to the very edges, but Renoir would have had a hard time capturing a joyful atmosphere here. The conversations rippled with an undercurrent of fear. Sidelong glances not flirtatious but dagger sharp, suspicious. Then again, Renoir's fused, patchy effect of dappled colours showing the artifice behind the painting would be exactly right. There was artifice here, even though no one had shown up in costume.

From the brittle smile on Jenny's face, to the loud, wicked laugh that could only belong to Shannon. A glittery charm to Kayla that almost rang true. But David — seated at their table — was the only one who looked uncomfortable. Normally at ease in a crowd, he looked like he'd rather be anywhere but here.

Distracted by his thoughts or his conscience?

"Where's Matt?" Sarah asked.

Charley felt a twinge in her chest. Eventually, she'd get used to answering that question. "He couldn't make it."

Sarah's gaze was knowing. As though she saw straight through the lie to the heart. "That's a shame."

"But Meghan came instead."

Vermouth dripped off the garnish as Sarah ate the olive off the skewer. "I hope she'll be taking notes."

"Oh, she's always working." Since Meghan right now was eyeing the cocktail menu, Charley added, "Even when it doesn't look like it."

"Hmm." Sarah sounded skeptical. "It doesn't look like she listened to the rules. No couples seated at the same table."

Charley blinked. "You're kidding." They'd decided on the rule to cut down on the temptation to share the sketches before the final round. And it was also the perfect way to split up Kayla and David, get him on his own. But Meghan was supposed to be her backup, not stuck at a corner table at the other end of the room. "Shouldn't we try to keep the press happy?"

Sarah slanted a look at her and pressed her lips together. "Fine. But remember that you two are at the head of the corpse."

And Kayla was at the feet. "No cheating." Just an improvised interrogation. "Yeah, we got it." Except she would do her best to catch a glimpse of David's drawing. It was the only way she knew how to read his mind.

Sarah picked up the call bell from the hostess stand and handed it to her. "You're in charge now."

And the pressure was on. Charley slid into her seat.

Meghan raised a brow. "Problem?"

"Not anymore." Sparkling water fizzed in her glass. The bell was nickel plated and polished to a high shine. She hit the button, the sound pealing out, loud and clear.

The game was afoot.

At the table closest to theirs, Thomas didn't look happy. Felt tip barbed lines crossed his white paper napkin and fig seeds scattered his plate.

Jenny returned from the washroom, rubbing lotion into her hands. Heading their way and looking much more relaxed than Thomas did. Maybe even relieved. She sat beside Charley and shot a glance over her shoulder, toward her father. He had his head down and missed it. "This is nice. I don't get many nights out and I plan to enjoy myself." It sounded defiant. Like she could have added a *no matter what* at the end.

"Nothing like creating a corpse to lighten the mood." David's tone was casual. His head was bowed, and his drawing was hidden behind the crook of his arm. Like an A student writing an exam. Pens scratched over paper. "Any leads in the investigation?"

"Some." Charley was aware of the people moving around them, the laughter — too loud, too bright.

She uncapped the pen, set the tip to the paper. Black ink bled on the fibres, staining. But she didn't draw the lake monster's head. She couldn't. Instead, she drew a skull with flaming eyes, peering out of a cape. The type of hooded malefactor who might have graced the cover of fifteen-cent *Terror Tales* magazines. More of a vigilante than a villain. "Alex has been looking into the deaths."

That got David's attention. "Plural?"

"The ones that happened at the dam in the past." She reached to sound the bell.

Meghan leaned over. "Can I?"

"Sure."

She slammed her palm on the bell, fast and loud, three times. Papers rustled, passed from one to the next.

"Aha." David reached for his pen lid, forced the lid back on with a snap. "The faceless numbers."

"Victims," Meghan said.

Jenny frowned. "How many were there?"

Charley drew arms, long and insect-like. She glanced up. "Six."

A flicker, nearly a wince, flashed over David's face. Impossible to miss, even if she hadn't been watching so closely. "Not enough, apparently." Face gone white, not red. Like the anger was burning somewhere deep inside. "Even when a child loses his life."

His life. David had looked into the facts, based his speech on them, but the pronoun had a familiarity to it. More than just a name sourced from an old newspaper article. "Did you know him?"

Jaw tightening, shoulders stiffening, like he'd braced for that question. "The kid?"

A chair back creaked. She felt Meghan shift beside her, lean forward.

Charley said, "Chris."

At the name, David flinched. He took a breath, composure shaken. "Yeah, well, he's nothing but a ghost now."

Jenny rubbed her arms, like the air had dropped several degrees. "How did the accident happen?"

"He swam near the dam," Meghan said in the impartial tone of a news reporter at a crime scene. "And got caught in the back current."

David rubbed a hand over the back of his neck, dropping his gaze.

A hand on her shoulder, the light touch, had Charley jumping. Sarah whispered in her ear, "The bell, dear."

Again. Hastily, she shaded fur. Hit the bell. The sound was not musical but piercing. Sharp as a warning.

Jenny jolted as someone passed their drawing to her. She didn't unfold the paper. Fear — of a mother's worst nightmare come true — easy to read in her eyes. "Was no one with him?"

David's hand curled into a fist. "No one who could help."

Like he'd witnessed it himself. Charley leaned forward. "You were there."

His head reared back. For a second, she thought he was going to bolt to his feet. "I was ten," he hissed.

Charley's heart thudded. His motive. This was it. "But you think you should have saved him."

"I didn't." David's voice was flat.

Meghan struck at paper with her pen, dashing off the legs of her corpse. Probably a few steps away from exquisite. "Better than losing two lives that day."

"Watch a friend drown and try saying that again." David's voice was loud enough to catch Shannon's attention three tables over. A sharp, curious gaze. Probably stitching together information in her mind until the seams were sewn up tight.

In a lower tone, David said, "I wouldn't wish that on anyone."

The upgrade to the dam, the risk it posed was personal. No wonder David felt the need to protect kids, the same age as the friend he'd lost. But had he killed, to stop the same thing from happening again?

The hairs on the back of her neck prickled. She realized eyes were on them. Too many people turned to watch.

"It's time," Meghan said.

"What?"

"The bell." Meghan nudged it closer to her.

"Last one," David said, like he couldn't wait to get out of here.

And she'd lose her chance to find out the rest, to trap the murderer with art. Charley pressed the button, the metal biting into her palm. "It's no wonder they called this game Exquisite Corpse. It's just like a murder case."

Meghan choked on her gin fizz, spluttered, eyes tearing. Charley ignored her sister's pointed stare.

David's pen lifted off the sheet, hovering. "How's that?"

"Only the murderer knows the bigger picture."

Meghan caught her breath. "Everyone trying to hide dark deeds from others."

Nicely served back. Charley said, "Makes you think about the kinds of things we try to hide from others. And how."

"Locks," Meghan said.

Now they were getting somewhere. "Lies." Attention only half on what she was drawing, Charley sketched a werewolf's paws. Splayed toes and claws. "Passwords."

David raised a brow. "Passwords?"

Meghan added pinpoint details to the drawing she shielded with her hand. "Computer passwords. My laptop at home is password protected. It's not like I'm keeping state secrets —"

David laughed. "Just local ones."

Charley grinned. "Meghan's got a suspicious mind."

"As if I'm the only one."

A universal element? That was perfect. She could work with that. "My first sketchbook was a diary with a lock and key. Not because I thought some burglar was going to steal it, but to keep my nosy sister out."

Jenny chuckled.

"No respect for privacy?" David asked, his expression more wary than amused.

"Are you kidding? Meghan?" Charley teased. "Her horoscope once said she was attracted to secrets and best suited to clandestine ways."

"All true," Meghan admitted. Though there was a lot of pride there. "And I found that key, by the way. You didn't hide it well enough."

"The point is," Charley reeled the conversation in, "there are things we try to hide from the people closest to us. I can't imagine sharing a computer with someone."

Meghan nodded. "I flat-out refuse to let Alex use mine. Not after that one dodgy work-related search in my browser history."

And that was a story she needed to get out of her sister later. "How does Kayla feel about it when you use her laptop?" Charley asked.

David shrugged, looking baffled at the turn the conversation had taken. "She likes to hand it off when something isn't working. Not that I've had much luck fixing computers. I've only got one magic trick up my sleeve. Turn it off and back on again. Luckily, that works more often than not." A frank grin and not a hint of a lie.

This would be easier, if he wasn't so likeable. "You're not tech savvy?"

He lifted a shoulder in a sheepish shrug. "I'm tech literate when it comes to working the remote control and streaming movies. Luckily in grade two, we're still focusing on typing skills and not coding. God help me if that ever changes."

If Kayla had handed her laptop off to him, that meant she had left him alone with it. He could have had access to her files.

Meghan said, "If Alex tried to fix anything, I'd watch him like a hawk, to make sure nothing goes wrong."

The lights went out. No warning, no time to brace. For one breathless second the room went black. Charley's heart lurched. Someone gasped.

Fast as a blink, the lights turned back on. Silence all around.

Sarah had her hand on the switch by the door. She shot a meaningful glance Charley's way. "The game," she announced, "is over."

And she'd forgotten to press the bell, had lost track of time. Charley stood. "Please put your pens down. As promised, your Exquisite Corpse will find its way back to you. In the meantime, drink the wine, enjoy the food and the conversation." Though theirs had been cut short.

David pushed back his chair. "I'm going to go find Kayla."

So close. Damn.

Meghan murmured, "I liked the segue."

"I tried my best."

Paper crinkled as the folded sheets were passed out. Laughter and groans echoed through the room as people saw the creatures they'd created.

Jenny grinned when she saw hers. "This wouldn't have ended up on the fridge. It's hideous." She beamed at the creased drawing. "I love it."

Charley watched David walk up to Kayla, the expanse of his back hiding her reaction. Did her face brighten? Or did she tense?

The waitress handed Charley her drawing. Keeping an eye on David and Kayla, she reached for it.

Charley unfolded the sketch. The black ink blended the sections together. The composite corpse was misshapen and funny until — shock ran through her. The fourth quarter. The last section was detailed. Delicate and precise.

Feet, planted on a dock. Webbed and scaled. Charley's pulse pounded in her throat.

The setting was carefully rendered, too. Light and dark shading created nooks and crannies along the shoreline. Soft, smooth planes and hard lines contoured the sharper angles where rock changed and broke. The branches of the white pine had been outlined first. The needles were roughed in with loose, scribbled strokes. Less stylized, but all the more realistic for it.

There was a fragment of wrought-iron bench and a Petro-Canada sign in the bottom right corner of the page.

The scene of the crime. Charley's breath rasped. She glanced around the room, filled with a laughing crowd. No one was watching her, but still, someone must have been waiting for her reaction.

She couldn't let the shock show. She looked at the white edge where water met land. The details showed constraint and skill. Experience.

The long dock faded into the distance. Short, parallel lines captured the reflection in still water.

Pen hatchings. Darker and denser than those used for the wooden dock, adding depth. Objects in the water in pen and ink drawings were always darker than the object being reflected, but that wasn't it. That wasn't why.

Charley bit her lip.

Woven into the mesh of overlaid pen hatchings were letters. No, numbers.

A time. 12 *a.m.*

The marina at midnight. Tonight?

Charley folded the sheet. She glanced over to where Kayla sat. She was talking to David, laughing at something he'd said.

There wouldn't be a gallery walk. Not now.

This was drawn in the fourth section of the paper. This came from Kayla's table. The drawing was less precise than her work usually was, but of course, she had to pull it off fast and not be seen. The drawing was as delicate and detailed as her illustrations, the techniques the same as if she'd been working in pencil.

Kayla might as well have signed her name to the piece.

She'd buried a code in art. In the Exquisite Corpse. On a page she knew would be returned to Charley.

Mouth gone dry, Charley took a sip of her water. She had to make an announcement. She couldn't avoid it or put it off to anyone else. Already, people were shifting restlessly, waiting for her to say something. She cleared her throat. "Thank you everyone for coming." Thank God, her voice sounded calm and confident. She lifted her chin. "The Shudder Pulp exhibit will open on Halloween." All Hallow's Eve. Like a whisper, the medieval name hissed through her mind. "Tickets can be purchased at the door or here at the B&B."

Applause broke out through the room, muffled as though from a great distance or heard underwater.

Meghan raised a brow. "What about the gallery walk?"

"You were right." Charley tucked the drawing into her pocket, not her purse. "We can't catch a murderer with art." But you could use it to pass a message. A signal for help, clear as an SOS.

THIRTY-SIX

ELEVEN TWENTY AT night and she was tiptoeing through the cottage to the front door. Charley knew it was a bad idea — dangerous, even — to meet at the marina in the middle of the night. But what else could she do?

She grabbed her sketchbook from her bag and tore out a fresh sheet. With a soft BB pencil, she scribbled in large letters: *Chasing inspiration. Be back soon.* Close enough to the truth anyway.

Using masking tape, she taped the note to the back of the front door. She'd have to deal with Meghan later. Charley grabbed her corduroy jacket off the hook and the leash. Cocoa wagged her tail sleepily, looking like she'd rather stay in bed.

Charley pulled the inner door closed, then the screen door more slowly, more carefully. Even that quiet clatter of wood in the frame seemed loud.

The darkness felt like a force at her back, thick with the dank smell of rotting leaves. Something rustled through the leaf rot. A twig snapped.

There was nothing she could do about the creaky hinge on the Jeep door as she loaded Cocoa into the back seat and snapped on her harness.

Fog coated the Fire Route, thick and heavy. "Great," she murmured.

She climbed in the driver's seat, took a breath, and turned the key in the ignition. The engine roared to life, a growl that could wake the dead.

Charley reversed, headlights off, heart thumping a mile a minute. She inched the Jeep between fence and boulders. Then touched the gas pedal, straining to see the ghostly grey line of the road ahead.

At the bend, she switched on the headlights. She turned up the radio on the late-night banter of a hyped-up DJ and breathed a sigh of relief. But she hadn't yet faced the biggest challenge of the night: The marina closed at ten p.m. It wouldn't be lit, not now. And, technically, she was trespassing. If she got caught, she'd have to explain everything to Roy and Beverley.

Why did Kayla want to meet there, at the scene of Laura's death? There had to be some sort of evidence, some sort of proof. Or a docked boat that Kayla had access to. But a midnight boat ride wasn't a comforting thought right now, even with the powerful penlight Charley kept in the glove compartment.

Would David hurt Kayla? It was hard to know what someone was capable of under the right circumstances. What mistakes they'd make.

The fact that Kayla had chosen the marina, not her house, set warning bells off in her head. If Kayla was protecting David before, something had changed. Something had scared her so much that she had to set up this meeting, at a location David wouldn't track them to.

Charley's fingers tightened on the steering wheel. She glanced at Cocoa in the rear-view mirror. "No big deal. We'll be fine." They'd handled worse before.

At least she had Cocoa with her. Kayla would be making the way on her own.

The marina's worn sign appeared ahead. Charley hit the turn signal. The road here was narrow, but not as narrow as their Fire

Route. She could risk cutting the lights again. She had to.

Take away one sense and you had to rely on the other. She might not be able to see but she could hear.

Charley slowed the car to a crawl and rolled down both front windows, all the way. Night air seeped into the car, heavy and damp. The tires cut into gravel as the car inched closer.

Her arm was so close to the open window, the darkness and the shapes moving, shifting beyond. Her skin crawled.

She pulled up at the side of the road, under a tree, shielded from view of the marina.

The parking lot ahead was nearly empty. Just Roy's truck.

Charley closed the Jeep's windows. A second ago, the car hadn't felt safe at all. Now it felt like the safest place in the world, behind locked doors.

Where was Kayla?

Charley reached for her cellphone in the cup holder. No messages. She typed a text to Kayla.

I'm here. Where are you?

Hit send. The icon spun.

No reception? Of course. Not here, under the trees, so close to the lake. The cellphone was useless.

The drawing had been of the dock. Maybe that was it. Maybe Kayla was already there, waiting for her.

Charley grabbed the leash off the seat beside her. "Let's go investigate."

Cocoa panted and didn't need coaxing to hop out of the car.

Charley locked the Jeep. The single flash of headlights blinded her to the darkness for one second and had her heart leaping into her throat. The shapes unfamiliar. In the distance, hulls bumped against pylons.

She wrapped her jacket closer around herself. At least, she'd worn a warm sweater too, had thought to layer. Still, the dampness seeped through her, the temperature hovering around seven degrees Celsius.

Near the railing lining the waterway, a human shape peeled from the shadows.

Charley blinked. Focused. The darkness swam, pulsed.

There was nothing there. Just her mind creating faces where there were none. A trick of perception, that was all.

Why here? The question circled through her mind as Charley walked over ground that police — that Alex — had already scoured. What else could there be to find here? They must have missed something.

At the end of that long driveway, the Callahans' house was dark. Not even the glow of a night light shined through a window.

Nylon ropes strained and creaked against the wooden dock, reminding her of what she imagined a hangman's noose sounded like when carrying a weight. Water lapped and splashed. White boat fenders lining the skiffs bobbed like heads in the water. The fog was thicker here. Dense white clouds rolled in.

Panic crept up her throat. Her breath shallowed. All those things in the dark. One wrong step and she could be in the lake. Bottomless and full of unseen things that circled around an unsuspecting swimmer, like the Creature from the Black Lagoon.

In his element as he watched, moving closer, stretching out a hand to touch.

A shiver ran through her. Charley checked her watch. The metal hands shone ghostly, catching just enough light for her to read the time. Two minutes to twelve. She was early.

Something hit the water, a heavy splash. Down at the end of the dock, where the fog gathered.

"Kayla?" Charley whispered. Voices carried over the water. Any louder and others might hear.

The boats blocked her view. A tarp snapped. Charley walked down the dock, slow, the boards creaking under her shoes. Inside her, a voice told her to run.

Not a chance.

Everything around her was black as India ink. The fog was like a metal pen nib loaded with white ink, etching the contours of shapes. A tonal composition. Nothing more than that.

Cocoa didn't show any signs of fear. None of her usual warning signs that a stranger was nearby, or a threat.

The dock dropped away in front of them. Charley stopped short. She was at the end now. But where was Kayla?

Maybe she'd gotten the message wrong, after all.

A board creaked behind her. Exhaled breath echoed loudly over the splash and lap of water.

Finally. Relief flooding through her, Charley turned.

She faced the monster.

THIRTY-SEVEN

IT WOULD BE just his luck if Matt burned himself making sponge toffee in the middle of the night. Especially since he hadn't bothered to grab socks or shoes. Working barefoot in front of the stove, if he splashed molten sugar on his toes, it would be his own fault. But Matt hadn't felt this sizzle of inspiration for a long time. Ignore it and it might cool off or worse, burn out completely.

Matt opened the bottle of maple syrup he'd taken from Jeffrey's fridge and breathed in the caramelized scent of the dark amber syrup. From the local sugar bush. He poured it into the deep pot, working on sight rather than using a cup measurement. Going on gut instinct and confidence, again. That elusive feeling he'd been chasing for months.

He stirred the mixture as it simmered and bubbled over a medium-high heat. Round about ten minutes to turn it into maple sponge toffee. Also known as seafoam.

Matt watched the sugar thicken. In the summer, warm, humid weather turned this recipe into a race against water. Moisture in the air could be disastrous as the sponge cooled before it was coated in its water-resistant chocolate coating. The walls of the air bubbles were so delicately thin and made of nothing but hygroscopic sugar. Humidity wasted no time turning the crisp, air-filled confection into sticky syrup. Make this in July and he'd know, as soon as the top started to get a little tacky, his minutes were numbered. But now, he had time to think.

The newsletter was at the top of his mind. Sure, the release date was early, but a mystery involving a lake monster was bound to have some red herrings. Maybe the newsletter didn't have anything to do with the murder at all. Maybe it was coincidence.

Roy had been more concerned about the call log and the framed boat than the newsletter.

Matt inserted the candy thermometer, checked the temperature. At the hard-crack stage now, just shy of caramel.

He dipped a pastry brush in water and wiped down the sides of the pot, washing away those grains of sugar clinging to the sides to stop them from burning. He poured in the baking soda and watched it froth. One moment, the toffee was a pot of molten sugar at the hard-crack stage, and the next, it was an expanding mass of foaming magic.

Science and alchemy, all in one. As a kid, he'd loved it.

Laura might have envied Roy's childhood, but she'd been kept. She hadn't been given away to live somewhere else. That had to hurt. And, judging from Roy's reaction to that sailboat, the wound had left a scar. No way it couldn't have. If Roy thought Laura was the stronger one — who came to Oakcrest to destroy his business, destroy his life — maybe he wanted to prove his strength by fighting back. He had more to protect, to hold on to, now.

Roy could have lured Laura to the water without forging any documents. He could have phoned her without raising suspicion or even getting flagged by the cops in the investigation. Asked her to meet him somewhere along the shore.

The one thing he hadn't wanted Matt to look at was Laura's phone.

Matt poured the aerated mixture into a parchment-lined baking pan. It would take about three hours for the toffee to cool. Then he'd smash the sponge and enrobe the pieces in tempered milk chocolate.

Turning it into the kind of candy a lake monster would feed on. Lake foam.

THIRTY-EIGHT

PARTIALLY SCALED CHEEKS. Gill cover. Rubber flesh — not one tone but dark vertical bands on spotted grey, fading to white at the lower jaw. Like the underbelly of a fish.

The monster's eyes were human.

A blur of motion came at Charley.

She stepped back. Nothing but air behind her.

It hit her shoulder, a solid blunt edge. Pain radiated down her arm, up into her collarbone. Cocoa pulled, jolting that same arm with the leash, snarling and barking. Snapping at the weapon that whistled through the air again, past the dog's nose.

A paddle. Letters stencilled on wood. REDTAIL. A hawk in flight, wings spread.

Cocoa danced back and away.

The monster was a blur, a shape wielding the weapon in a two-handed grip.

"What?" Charley gasped, dodged another blow. Fear tightened her muscles.

Her heel landed on air. Nothing but water below. Trapped at the end of the dock.

She ducked. The paddle slashed over her head.

Get hit, get injured, and she'd drown.

Or take the leap herself. She glanced over her shoulder, swallowed hard. No choice left. "Jump!" Charley shouted to Cocoa.

She leapt into the dark. The paddle grazed her back.

Water closed over Charley's head, swallowed her in. She sunk down.

Black, everywhere. Water in her ears, her nose, her eyes. So cold, it shocked her lungs. The only sound the rush of her own blood, the beat of her heart.

Charley fought the urge to gasp. To inhale.

She broke the surface, dragged in air. One ragged gasp wasn't nearly enough.

A splash. Cocoa landed in the water. Thank God.

She had to move. Swim to safety. Charley's teeth clenched together, her chin barely above the water.

The figure stood on the dock, the paddle the only thing bright enough to see, gleaming in the dark.

They couldn't go back on shore. Not here. There weren't enough options for getting back onto ground. They'd be trapped, too easily. She couldn't face down the attacker. Not without a weapon.

The water was cold. Bone numbing. Her clothes soaked through, dragged her down.

How long could she stay in the water at that temperature? Five, maybe ten minutes?

And she couldn't see. Not through that blanket of fog, the dark. Which way?

She turned, treading water. Tentacles brushed her legs. Yellow lights ringed the lake, small and impossibly far away, each way she turned.

Get disoriented, start off in the wrong direction, and she would never make it back to shore before hypothermia kicked in.

It was suddenly too quiet, the sound of paddling paws fading, heading the opposite way. Would Cocoa swim back toward the marina or to shore?

"Cocoa," she whispered.

A boat engine sprang to life. The growl of the motor jolted adrenaline through her.

The so-called lake monster that walked on land and needed a boat to chase them in the water.

The boat trolled. How far away?

There was no time left. Gut instinct was all she had.

Each stroke of Charley's arms set off a dull ache, numbed by the cold water. Any second, the muscles might seize up.

She had to keep moving. She gritted her teeth and swam. Pain radiated through her bruised shoulder and her right arm.

She stretched her feet down, testing for the bottom. Water closed over her head. The lake was still too deep here for her to find footing. Her heart raced — from adrenaline, and from the cold.

Her energy started to drain. She could float. Rest here, just for a second.

Something twisted around her legs, wound tight. A slimy limb. A scream pressed at her throat.

She fought free. Forced back the panic. It was just waterweed. Flexible and buoyant and long. Not a tentacle or a webbed claw. A habitat for fish. The thought cut through the grogginess.

The weeds needed sunlight. And shallow water.

Charley swam forward. Her hand brushed a head. A muzzle. She flailed, lost the rhythm. *A giant snake. A huge tail that swished when it moved. A great, shaggy head like a dog.* The description rang through her mind, echoing.

She swam backward, straining away.

A familiar whine cut through the fear.

Ripples flowed around her as Cocoa nosed her way under Charley's arm.

Charley held on to her, pressed her face into the dog's fur. "Good girl."

Cocoa swam, towing her through the water. With one hand Charley held on to the nylon collar; with the other, she kept herself afloat.

Soon, her feet hit sand, sunk in silt. Long, flat, spongy leaves brushed her arms. Cattails broke the surface.

Land.

On her knees, Charley reached out, felt rock. Caught hold of it to lever herself up.

Her palm pressed against something sharp. The tip folded, crumpled under her weight.

It took her a second to focus. To see the black print on grey.

Newspaper. Wedged in between the rocks.

A sailboat.

A paper shipwreck.

This was what Laura felt like before she drowned on land.

Charley waded behind Cocoa over rocks. Her sock slipped on algae, caught on something sharp. Her shoe was somewhere in the bottom of the lake. Dry branches caught at her. The breeze sent shivers through her. Her clothes, wet, clung to her skin. Her teeth chattered.

Anger coursed through Charley, a hot surge that got her moving again.

A thick swatch of birch trees and oak tangled here. Cocoa broke through first. Charley lifted her arm to shield her eyes, pushing through behind her.

Stones jabbed into her sock, cutting into her toes, her heel. Gravel. They were on a road. But which one?

Charley held the leash and scanned for a clue, a sign. A stretch with trees, no houses or lights.

She had no way of calling for help. Her cellphone was in her car but, without reception, it would have been useless anyway. She and Cocoa were on their own. In the dark.

Did she have her car keys? Charley touched her left jeans pocket. The key fob pressed against denim. Even if the battery-operated button was waterlogged, she'd be able to use the key to open the door manually. They just had to get to her Jeep and they'd be safe. And she'd turn the heat up high.

Thinking about hot air blowing from the vents only made the cold seem worse.

How far away were they from the marina? They were on a fire route somewhere along the shoreline. As if that helped narrow it down.

She listened, heard the rush of water from the left. That meant the road must be to the right.

She limped on, stepping gingerly to protect her foot as best she could.

Something glinted up ahead, the gleam of metal, swinging high above the road. Behind the trees, she saw the blue flicker of a TV screen reflected in a window. She sped up.

Closer, the metal took on human form. Arms, dangling legs, a corrugated torso. Tin Men. The recycled figurines were the signpost she needed.

She knew where she was.

David must have intercepted Kayla. Stopped her from coming. Met her himself. But how would he have taken a boat?

Or — an icy stream of fear ran through her — Kayla came to meet her and got attacked. By someone who had access to the boats.

Maybe the attacker hadn't known they'd be at the marina. Wasn't it more likely to think he'd seen Kayla arrive? Because he lived at the marina.

The realization stole her breath.

Roy killed Laura, murdered his own half-sister because of his love for the water.

He could have easily taken a boat docked at the skiff, attacked Kayla, then her. An image rose in Charley's mind: Kayla's body washed up on shore.

Cocoa prowled along the road, ears pinned back, her gaze roving for threats.

Charley walked along the side of the road, close to the ditch, where the leaf covering was thicker, buffering the gravel. Even limping, she hurried. If she stepped on something sharp, she'd just have to suck it up. Keep going.

And hope the attacker was still trolling the water, searching for her on the lake. Not on land.

THIRTY-NINE

METAPHORICAL BAIT MADE from local ingredients. Matt washed the dishes in the sink, filled with scalding hot, soapy water. It felt like reclaiming chocolate for himself and, yeah, like a slap in the murderer's face.

A taunt.

Had Roy used Laura's lake monster prank against her? He had more than enough choice of boats at the marina. He knew the waters like the back of his hand. After Laura had survived the attack, she had come back to the marina, to him.

She really had been the stronger one. She hadn't drowned. She'd turned around and come back to confront him.

He rinsed the pot, set it in the drying rack.

If that was how it all played out, it must have been a hell of a shock for Roy when Beverley found the body at the marina.

Shit. Dread slithered down Matt's spine.

Roy murdered his sister. His own flesh and blood.

How would he react to his wife digging up secrets he wanted to keep buried? Asking questions while he deflected the investigation with fox skulls and black magic and wore his salt-of-the-earth honesty as a mask.

Soap floated on the surface of water, now syrupy. He drained the sink, left the sugar-crusted spoon lying on the countertop, and headed for the door, his jaw clenched tight.

You could only provoke a monster so long before it lashed out at the person closest to it.

FORTY

THE OLD RED Jeep never looked so good. Charley's legs trembled with the after-effects of shock, the strain of the swim. Nothing at all like the pleasant muscle ache from hours splashing in the water in the summer.

A snap in the distance nearly had her tripping. A tarp, probably, but her imagination twisted the sound into a larger, more menacing shape. She scanned the marina, her eyes by now adjusted to the dark. Enough to see forms, nearly human shapes everywhere she glanced.

The dock was too far away to tell how many skiffs were empty.

Heart pounding, Charley hurried the last few steps to the driver's side door. Nearly safe.

Cocoa shook her head, sending her ears flapping, droplets spraying. The metal tags on her collar clattered.

"Shh," Charley whispered. Fingers trembling, aware of all that open space behind her, she pulled her car keys out of her pocket. Water ran out of the cracks in the fob, dripping.

With clumsy fingers, numb from the cold, she fumbled the key against the lock, scratching red car paint. Faster. Hurry.

Shoes crunched on gravel. Cocoa whipped around to face the sound, ears on alert.

The killer? Or Kayla. Torn between fear and hope, Charley

froze. A wind rustled through the branches overhead, whirling leaves to the ground. Shadows shifted.

Charley forced the key into the lock and opened the door. The hinges screamed.

A beam of bright light hit the Jeep, tossing her silhouette across the dash. Heart in her throat, Charley turned. She threw up a hand to shield her eyes from the blinding glare.

Cocoa growled, straining at the leash Charley gripped tightly.

"You look half drowned." There was a gravelly timber to the voice. Roy.

She'd never get the key in the ignition, never get both her and Cocoa into the car and behind locked doors in time. She raised her chin. The ends of her hair dripped down the back of her neck. Her waterlogged jeans sagged at the hem. Just like Laura's. "Not exactly what you were hoping for, is it?"

Cocoa snarled.

The light dropped away, shot toward the dog, snagging on bared teeth.

Charley saw Roy's face now. The lines were carved by the wind, the moustache bristling over his mouth. Was this what the monster looked like behind the mask? He wore a thick navy blue Aran sweater and jeans, the wool dark enough to blend with the night.

But where was his mask? Maybe floating on the lake, rubber gills turned up and drifting.

His brows knit in a frown. "What are you talking about?" Slow and careful, voice pitched low the way it might be if he was out on the lake, afraid to startle the fish.

Adrenaline sang through Charley's veins, heating her through. A cold fire, burning through the wet, the cold. She had to block out that she was talking to Beverley's husband. "What did you do to Kayla?" The question clarified the image in her mind: a blood-stained paddle, floating on the water.

Roy didn't answer right away. He seemed to turn the words over in his mind, a man brooding over a puzzle. "The better question is, what do you think I did?"

"You killed Laura."

A strangled sound escaped his throat. "Now hold on —"

She kept talking, raising her voice. "You attacked Kayla." Her wet jacket clung to her, heavy and cold. The shivers were harder to control now. "And me."

The light swung away from Cocoa, circling around them in a wide arc, flashing over the faded ice cream sign, glinting on the windows of the dock store and the white letters. *Callahan's*. "You were attacked?" Roy's voice had gone wary.

Nervous because she'd hit on the mark, accusing him the way Laura couldn't. "By the so-called lake monster."

"Let's talk about this inside." Roy reached out for her arm.

"No." Charley backed away. The Jeep's running board dug into her calf. Cocoa barked a warning.

Roy held up a hand, palm out. A gesture of goodwill, or just a visual cue that he wasn't holding a weapon? "Bev is inside, asleep. I can wake her, have her sit with us." He glanced over his shoulder again, an edgy move that had to be for show. "But we need to get into the house."

Where it would be harder for her to escape. "Won't Beverley wonder why you're dressed to search the marina?"

Surprise flickered over his face. "I heard a motor start. I came to check that someone wasn't stealing a boat."

He was better at lying than she'd thought. The tone was so simple and straightforward, she might have believed it, if her clothes weren't drying on her skin and one of her shoes wasn't at the bottom of the lake. "Why didn't you call the cops?"

"On someone's kid or grandkid?" Somewhere, a boat hull bumped against a pylon, the sound loud. The flashlight beam wavered. "I'm done debating this. Let's go. Move."

She didn't have a choice. She had to go in the house. Only Kayla knew where she was. No way to send a message or a signal.

Although ... There was cell reception at the house. And her phone still lay on the driver's seat. Adrenaline surging, Charley said in a voice as close to calm as she could get it, "Let me at least close the car door."

"Hurry up."

Back turned, heart thundering, she palmed the phone and worked it into her jeans pocket, the denim tight, the fabric soaked. But it fit. She took a breath and slammed the door, twisted the key in the lock, and fisted the key so the jagged metal teeth jutted through her fingers. A potential weapon and the only one she had.

"Go ahead." Roy gestured for her to lead the way, keeping distance between them.

The flashlight aimed at her back felt like a gun.

ROY PAUSED ON the threshold, holding the door open. Inside, the house was dark. "I'm not a violent man." A muscle jumped in his jaw. "I want you to know that."

She wound Cocoa's leash more securely around her hand, felt the dog lean against her leg. Not a violent man? The bruises on his knuckles told another story. "You punched a man at the marina."

"That was different." Roy stepped inside, waited for her to follow.

She kept a hold on Cocoa's leash. Inside, the house smelled of lemon Pledge furniture polish and faintly of vinegar. An attempt to clean grief away. And yet the source of it all was standing right here, trying to argue his humanity. "You kill the fish you catch." With lures made of feathers and string. "It's more humane that way, isn't it? A quick blow to the head with a rock, right behind the eyes." She watched for his reaction. "A spike to the brain."

He flinched. "I prefer live release."

She almost laughed. "That's obvious." Her sweater clung clammy to her skin. She could feel the knotted texture of the rug through her sock.

There was movement on her left.

She tensed, turned toward it, and saw a ghost in the mirror.

A simple square frame hung beside a coat rack, revealing not a ghost, but her own reflection. Pale face, tangled curls clinging to her cheeks. Clothes drenched and muddy. Scraped fingers. Not cut, just grazed and starting to sting.

This was what Laura had looked like when she had come to the gallery.

A strangled gasp sounded from the hallway. Charley turned. Beverley stood there in a terry cloth bathrobe, hastily tied at the waist, slippers on her feet. Ghastly pale, hands pressed to her mouth. She took a breath, and said in a voice carefully controlled, "What happened to you?" Dread more than shock in the woman's voice.

Could Beverley guess what she was about to say? "The same thing that happened to Laura." She would give him the chance to say it. "Roy can explain, better than I can."

Roy closed the door with a click of the latch that ratcheted up Charley's heartbeat. "She thinks I murdered Laura." Abrupt and strained, all that emotion taut as a sail in full wind.

Beverley shook her head. She clasped her hands together, squeezing her fingers around her wedding band. "You can't be serious."

A trickle of water ran down Charley's neck. The hem of her jeans dripped wet splotches onto the worn rug. "I know it's not what you wanted to hear —"

"You're wrong." Conviction in her voice, unshakable. Beverley didn't glance at her husband for confirmation. Simply stated it as fact.

Gentler, Charley said, "I'm not. There's evidence that proves it."

Roy snorted. "Is that so? Where's Alex, then?"

Good question. "He'll be here." It couldn't hurt to bluff a little.

"Any second now, am I right?" Roy said, dryly.

Cocoa glanced up at the tone, then sat on Charley's feet, tense and probably curious why she hadn't been let off the leash. Charley put her hand on the dog's head.

Beverley crossed her arms. A force to be reckoned with. "I think you'd better tell us what that evidence is. Now."

But she needed a bartering piece. "First, tell me where Kayla is."

There wasn't a trace of guilt in Roy's eyes. Just the slow build of frustration. "At home, I would assume."

It was warmer in the house, but it didn't feel nearly warm enough. Not with midnight veiling the windows. The cold seeped straight through her. Along with the panic. "Stop trying to cover your tracks. It's too late. But you can still do one good deed. Save a life." Hope still there, that Kayla was somewhere to be saved.

Roy rubbed the back of his neck. Turned and shot a glance out the narrow pane of glass beside the door. He shrugged, a jerk of one shoulder. "I wish I could. What the hell were you two —"

A bubbly tune cut him off, sent her heart leaping. In Charley's pocket, her phone vibrated with an incoming call. She reached for it.

"Don't —" Roy said.

"Leave her be," Beverley snapped, patience finally breaking. "You answer that, honey." She bundled her bathrobe around her and sat on the bench by the shoe rack. "We'll wait."

Charley fumbled with the screen, hit the button. "Hello?"

"Did you mean to send me that message?"

Kayla. Relief rushed through Charley. Kayla's voice sounded groggy and rough but not panic-stricken. "Are you okay?"

"No." Static crackled through the phone. "I have a killer headache."

Charley's pulse scrambled. She watched Roy walk to Beverley. He rubbed his hands over his wife's shoulders, murmuring something to her that Charley couldn't catch. Into the phone, she said, "Where are you?"

"At home." Kayla laughed. "That bartender at the B&B makes a seriously potent Negroni. This haunted carnival is going to be the death of —"

At home? "You were supposed to meet me at the marina."

A beat went by. Long enough for Charley to start to wonder.

"What are you talking about?" Kayla asked.

Charley's heart drummed against her ribs. "The message you gave me at the B&B."

"I didn't give you a message."

Charley had a sinking feeling that maybe she'd gotten everything wrong. "The Exquisite Corpse." She couldn't get her thoughts straight. "The last section of the drawing. What did you sketch?"

Again, that pause. A beat full of confusion.

"*Inukpasugjuit.*" An Inuit giant. Kayla's voice was soft. "Stepping over a mountain with a polar bear at his feet, the size of a fox. It was good, too. What's going on?"

If only she knew. It didn't make any sense. No one else could have drawn that picture. It took skill to add that much realism without sacrificing speed. That sketch was the work of an artist. But Thomas hadn't been sitting at Kayla's table. "I'll fill you in later." Still, the threat of danger crackled in the air. The bruise on her shoulder ached. Someone had attacked her. "Kayla, if you don't hear from me in fifteen minutes, call —"

Roy stepped forward, snatched the phone from her, his face livid. He hung up the call. "That's enough."

Beverley paled. "Roy, that was a mistake."

He slid the phone in his own pocket. The swirling pattern of her phone case, the art nouveau border of the Mucha chocolate ad, just visible above the edge of denim. "We need to clear things up before she tells the police anything. Before *she* makes a mistake."

FORTY-ONE

MATT'S FINGERS TENSED on the steering wheel. The truck's tires juddered over the gravel road as the headlights caught on wraiths of fog floating in the darkness.

If he was wrong about all this, he'd scare the living daylights out of Roy and Beverley. But that was better than doing nothing and regretting it forever.

He turned off at the sign for the marina. A bass-heavy song pounded from the radio and set his teeth on edge, so he flicked it off. The silence was worse. It reminded him too much of the moment right before Beverley screamed.

Then he saw the Jeep and he realized what he'd felt before hadn't come close to fear.

What the hell was Charley doing here?

He hit the brakes, not even bothering to pull to the side. He was out of the truck in seconds.

He registered it even as he walked to the Jeep: Her car was empty. Still, he peered through the window, then tried the door. The Jeep was locked. Of course it was.

He stood there, neck prickling. Where was Charley?

If he'd put the clues together, gotten this far, so had she. And she was probably one step ahead of him, too.

This was what happened when you got attached to a stubborn artist — Matt gritted his teeth — who went off chasing murderers on her own. You found yourself staring at dark water, at a marina at midnight, hoping she wasn't dead.

Did she think she was as invincible as the heroines she painted? She wouldn't bleed paint.

The image had Matt balling his hands into fists. Blocking the thought out, he dragged in a breath.

Laura died right here when she came to confront Roy.

The thought lingered, soaking through him like ice water.

Every instinct had him wanting to race up to the door and pound on it. But he took his time, scanning the ground, the leaves, hoping she wasn't in the water somewhere. Drowning.

With every step, dread worked its way deeper into him until it lodged there.

At the door now, he lifted his fist to bang on the wood, then paused one second. The ship bell would be louder. He grabbed the cord and struck the clapper to brass. The sound peeled, sonorous and mournful. A signal and a warning.

He rang again. A familiar bark echoed back at him. Matt's heart stood still. Cocoa was inside the house.

He grabbed the cord, rang the bell a third time. *Come on.* A fourth.

The door opened.

FORTY-TWO

COCOA LEAPT FORWARD, yanking the leash from Charley's fingers as she raced to the open door. The dog pounced at Matt's legs, licked at his fingers. But Matt's eyes locked on Charley's.

Before she had time to register how she felt, he'd wrapped her in his arms. She breathed in the familiar scent of chocolate and lemon shower gel.

"Are you okay?" His voice was muffled against her hair.

Her hands tightened on his back. "Just wet." Soaked to the bone, actually.

He loosened his hold, scanning her from head to toe. "What happened?"

From behind them, Roy said, "She fought off a monster."

A vision of rubber gills flashed through her mind. "Fled from it, more like. I wish I had fought."

Matt tilted Charley's chin up so he could see her face. He cursed, turned to Roy. "You'd better get your confession ready. And don't bother trying anything. Alex is on his way, and he's bringing the cavalry."

Roy blanched. "What happened to innocent until proven guilty?"

Matt shot a glance at Beverley. Gentler, as though speaking to her and not to Roy, he said, "The proof is adding up."

But they'd miscalculated somewhere along the way. "Actually," Charley said. "I'm not so sure about that."

Beverley huffed out a breath. "Finally, someone's talking some sense around here. Matt, take those muddy shoes off before you spread dirt through my house."

He hesitated one second. "But —" He sighed and unlaced his boots. "We need to talk about this."

Roy crossed his arms. "I'd like to know why you both turned up on our doorstep tonight."

Charley was starting to wonder that, too. Why was Matt here? "I got a message at the B&B. Hidden in a drawing. I thought it was from Kayla, that she had evidence she wanted to show me." The clues had all been there. What had she missed? "Then the lake monster attacked me."

Matt straightened and stared at Charley, concern on his face. "Did you hit your head?" He cupped her face, looking in her eyes, searching for signs of a concussion. He was worried about her now, even though just the other day he'd equated their relationship to soured cream and expired butter.

She brushed his hands away. "It was a mask. A good one. With gills and scales. The same colour and markings as a muskie." Charley took a breath. "The mask was probably rubber, but it looked real in the dark. The rest of the outfit was hard to see. But the 'monster'" — she sketched air quotes around the word — "was definitely human. I thought Roy saw Kayla and got to her first."

Roy shook his head. "I didn't. You can search the house for that mask." Beverley murmured a protest, but Roy held up his hand. "I've got nothing to hide. Alex won't need a warrant. I'll give him my permission to look around, soon as he gets here."

That didn't sound like a killer trying to cover his tracks. Sure, the mask might not be in the house — he could have gotten rid of it along the shoreline or in a boat — but it was a gutsy move to give the police free rein. Charley said, "Whoever swung that paddle at my head knew I would be here." And came prepared. "Unless that mask was stashed somewhere at the marina, the disguise had to be planned ahead."

Matt tensed, anger tightening his mouth into a hard line. "Back up a second. Someone swung a paddle at you?"

She saw it again — the otter tail–shaped gleam of polished aspen and strips of black cherry rushing at her in the dark. "It was either get hit or jump."

Matt shrugged out of his jacket and wrapped it around her shoulders. Kept his hands on the collar a second longer than necessary. "You jumped."

"We both did." And thank God Cocoa had. "When we were in the water, I heard a boat engine start up."

Roy startled. "From our dock?"

So close it had to be. "It sounded like a motorboat. When I first got to the marina, I walked all the way to the end of the dock and didn't see anyone." Except for the shadow at the railing. An imagined monster or the killer? "A docked boat would be the perfect spot to hide and wait." The drawing though, she still had it. She pulled the soggy paper out of her pocket, still folded in half. Physical proof she'd been tricked. Lured, the same way Laura had been.

Beverley snorted. "Roy can't draw to save his life."

He shot his wife a look. "Not to mention, I wasn't at the B&B."

It was true. There was no way he had anything to do with the message she'd gotten.

"You think the evidence survived the lake?" Matt asked.

"There's a chance." Not that far-fetched. "We used waterproof pigment liners." Charley peeled the corners apart, slowly. The lines had bled, smudged a little, but the drawing was still clear. The details on the water, the rocks, the scales. Precise and repetitive. More like a pattern on fabric than what a landscape artist would add to create the illusion of depth.

The thought teased at the back of her mind. Could that be? But there were too many questions. The link to Laura's death as impossible as a — as a ship in a bottle.

Which wasn't impossible at all.

Beverley said, "It won't do much good squinting at those squiggly lines in the dark here. Let's look at it in the kitchen. The light's better."

They followed her. Beverley spread paper towels on the kitchen table.

Charley smoothed the drawing flat. The overhead light beat down, bright white, on sodden lines of black ink.

Matt looked over her shoulder. "That's what had you coming out here?"

Roy planted his palms on the table and leaned forward. "That's our bench. The sign on the gas dock."

Charley tilted the image, so that the light raked over the surface. "A trap I walked right into."

"You're sure someone didn't copy Kayla's style?" Matt asked.

Not unless they had practice in forgery. "An art style is personal, hard to mimic." The artist's personality bled through. "Even Thomas would have difficulties imitating Kayla's delicate lines." But this wasn't a replica.

She'd seen what the artist wanted her to see, and she hadn't looked past it. Even though she hadn't felt that prickle of recognition she normally felt when she looked at one of Kayla's works, that sense of familiarity like spotting an old friend in a crowd — even when the piece was unsigned and leaning against a wall surrounded by other framed illustrations. Her brain had filled in the gaps and created a false perception.

Matt rubbed a hand over the back of his neck. "So, we're back to square one."

But they'd been collecting evidence along the way. "Not quite," Charley said. "This was the last sketch in the game. It had to have come from Kayla's table." Facts. They had to focus on those.

Matt glanced at her. "What is it?"

Who else had the skill to draw those patterns? Capture the texture of scales? Only one other person sitting at Kayla's table. "Shannon could have drawn this." All of the pieces could fit together so easily, except for one. She'd seen Shannon the day Laura had been attacked. In her apartment, far away from the scene of the crime.

Beverley frowned. "But Shannon was so concerned after Laura died. She dropped off food. Checked in on us."

Matt studied the drawing. "You're sure about this?"

As sure as she could be. "She's used to working in ink to draw costume sketches. I didn't notice it before." Didn't even think to question whose work this was. She'd jumped to a conclusion. But art detectives divorced art from its aesthetic, from inspiration. Reduced the composition to pure matter, made up of individual particles. "The sketch Shannon drew for me of the Creature from the Black Lagoon. The scales were the same." It was a small detail, but here was a common element. "I've got the sketchbook in my Jeep." Tucked safely in her purse, where it always was. "We can compare the two."

Beverley said, "If Shannon really drew this, gave you this message, we have to assume —"

"That she attacked Charley." Matt's voice was grim.

"But why?" Beverley asked.

The most important question of all. Charley said, "That's what we have to find out."

A thud on the front door. A hard pounding of knuckles on wood that had them straightening, shooting startled glances at each other.

Matt said, "That'll be Alex."

Charley glanced at Roy. Alex was here for him. "I'm sorry I doubted you."

He brushed that aside. "Let's catch the real killer."

They followed Beverley to the door, but it wasn't Alex who stood on the threshold.

Meghan pushed her way inside and headed straight for Charley. "Any broken bones?"

She braced herself for one of Meghan's cobra-constrictor hugs. "No."

"Good." Meghan cracked her knuckles, then balled her fingers into a fist. "Because otherwise, this would really hurt."

Charley narrowed her eyes. "Try it and see what —"

Alex stepped in and grabbed hold of Meghan's arm. "Don't hit your sister."

Finally, a show of solidarity. "Thank you, Alex."

He closed the door behind him and grinned. "Not until we get her statement."

"Good point." Meghan nodded. "I'll wait."

Matt laced his fingers through Charley's. "She's joking, right?" he murmured.

"I doubt it," she said. And gave his fingers a squeeze. "But I can take her."

FORTY-THREE

"NO BOATS ARE missing," Alex said.

Take a Rorschach test and I would have seen those clawed hands, the green weeds. Eric's voice drifted through Charley's mind. But she'd looked into the monster's eyes and they were human. Human and ruthless.

Meghan handed her a bag of frozen peas. Charley sat on the Callahans' sofa in their living room and held the cold veg to her shoulder. She'd borrowed a sweatshirt from Beverley and a pair of jeans, oversized and cinched with a belt. Her wet clothes had become evidence and were stored in a black garbage bag in Alex's car. The Jeep's key fob was slowly draining water onto a wad of paper towel.

Cocoa lay on the floor at her feet. A canine bodyguard.

Roy scraped a hand up the back of his neck. "Everything's in its place."

"So that means," Charley said, "the attacker had their own boat."

"But Shannon doesn't own a boat, does she?" Meghan leaned over the back of the sofa, studying the sketchbook lying on the cushion, open to the page Shannon had drawn the Creature from the Black Lagoon.

Matt paced the rug, tension radiating off of him. "She doesn't have waterfront property, that's for sure."

Roy went to the hearth, opened the fireplace door with a shriek of metal hinges. Logs hit the wrought-iron grate with a thud.

Charley looked at the sketch. The Creature from the Black Lagoon. The scaly, webbed claw. Shannon's voice ghosted through her mind. *Reaching out to the audience from a black-and-white underwater world. The Gill-Man costume was the real star of the show. Julia Adams's stark-white bathing suit was designed simply to draw attention to the alien nature of the creature.* The same way the witch's ladder and the fox skull drew attention to the alien nature of the lake monster. Creating the perfect illusion. A living, breathing monster that haunted imaginations.

Charley sat up straight. Cocoa perked her ears at the sudden move. The boat house. The leather ring, jangling with keys of different shapes and sizes. That had to be it. "Shannon has access to a boat."

Roy glanced up. "Where?"

"She takes care of the Taylor's cottage." Charley's heart pounded. "She has a key."

Roy scrubbed a hand over his jaw. "They own a Crestliner. A Fish Hawk or a Vision, if my memory serves me right. A deep-V hull to slice through rough waters. They take the boat out regularly in the summer. Keep it nicely maintained. It'd run, no problem. And with them being snowbirds, the Taylors are already off living it up in hotter climates."

Leaving Shannon with easy access. "She could have taken the boat."

"Can you check that?" Matt asked Alex. Shot at him, more like.

Alex raised a brow at the tone but said, "With a warrant, yeah."

"The paddle had a logo on it." Charley reached for the pen lying on the coffee table on top of a book of word search puzzles. Pain shot through her bruised shoulder. She flexed her fingers. "A hawk, with broad, rounded wings and a short, wide tail."

Roy lit a match with the sharp tang of sulphur and held the flame to the newspaper kindling until the corners curled and burned, flaring hot. "Red?"

The feathers had been. "Yeah."

The fire hissed and crackled. He turned around, poker still gripped in one hand. "If the logo was a red-tailed hawk, then it's a local make. A Northumberland-based paddle company."

Alex scrubbed a hand over his jaw. "It's something to go on anyway."

Charley said, "As a costume designer, Shannon would know how to transform someone." To stage a performance.

"How about pulling off a magic trick?" Alex asked, his expression grim. "She's got an alibi. You."

"Because I saw her." Firelight cast flickering shadows on the wall. Roy's silhouette stretched long, reaching toward the window casing. What if Shannon had pulled off a magic trick? An illusion, the same way Charley had in the gallery? She'd sent a monster swimming across a painted shore. A video loop, projected. "What if —" It caught in her throat. There were times when perception couldn't be trusted. "There's a fire escape in her apartment that leads down to the alley behind the shop." Where Shannon parked her car.

Charley had seen the woman moving in her apartment, her face as she came closer and stared down. But what if what she'd seen was a projection?

"That'd be some escape stunt," Matt said.

But suddenly everything fell into place. "It could work, though," Charley said. Adrenaline sang through her veins. "Laura was attacked in the lake —"

Alex leaned forward, on the edge of the armchair. "When, according to you, Shannon was at home."

And that had been her mistake all along. "Maybe I didn't see what I thought I saw," Charley murmured. "Projectors aren't expensive. People buy them to create digital decorations. Animations can be projected onto sheer fabric and turned into holograms on front lawns. Or moving window decorations. All Shannon would have needed was a similar projector, some sheer fabric — bridal gauze or a vinyl shower curtain. And a video loop recording of herself." It wasn't far-fetched to think that if her exhibit had inspired Shannon's murder method, maybe it had inspired her alibi, too.

High enough lumens and the projection would look like the real thing, especially seen from the street. What better way to fake an alibi? Even similar movements, repeated, no one would question. Not when they'd seen Shannon follow the same routine before, while sewing.

Alex looked like he was turning the possibility over in his mind, studying it for flaws. "What about the fox skull on the beach?"

Charley said, "Thomas found the carcass on Sugarbush Road. The same road the Taylor's cottage is on." Near the dam. And Shannon had tried to convince Charley to spread the news about the lake monster sighting. Fan the rumours until they spread like wildfire. "The witch's ladder was made from materials used for making costumes." Thread, the colour of dried blood. Goose feathers for millinery. Charley thought of the fedora hanging in the Blast from the Past Boutique, like a prop from a film set. "She could have drafted the article warning about the Dam Safety Review, printed off an early version of the November newsletter, and lured Laura to the point of attack." All without needing to forge anything. She could edit the document already saved on her computer.

Meghan leaned her elbows on the sofa back. "But what's her motive?"

Beverley frowned. "I simply can't see Shannon doing something like this."

Because she was kind, creative, and business savvy? Passionate about the lake. But with the right costume, "let's pretend that" became real. Shannon had said it herself. "She spent years creating costumes to enhance a character's personality," Charley said, "to hide an actor's real identity. Why couldn't she do the same thing for herself?"

"What exactly do we know about her?" Meghan asked.

Alex said, "She moved from Toronto to Oakcrest after her husband died in a car crash."

And started over by building a life for herself here. Charley had admired her for it. "Shannon told me he died of internal bleeding after his BMW rolled. Aggressive driving. He lost control of the car."

"A car crash?" Beverley frowned. "I thought it was an aneurysm."

A small discrepancy. Maybe just a mistake, a slip of Beverley's memory. But weren't inconsistencies what sleuths looked for? They were the hinge that could close a case.

"I'll look up the details of the accident," Alex said. "I just need a name to work with."

Charley opened her mouth. Shannon had talked about her husband. But had she mentioned his name? "I — don't know what it is."

Beverley said, "I'm not sure she ever mentioned it."

Meghan frowned. "We might be able to find a wedding announcement online."

Matt looked thoughtful. "Shannon was the one person in a position to put up a fight against the proposal. And she didn't. Laura pressured Thomas to side with her. Maybe she tried the same thing with Shannon."

"David thought she'd been bribed," Charley said. But a cheque made out to the Aquatic Invasive Species Prevention Fund didn't seem like reason enough. Not with the way Shannon talked about Blue Heron Lake. For her, it was a slice of heaven. A fantasy.

Home.

"Laura always fought until she got the upper hand," Roy said. He glanced at the framed poster of a seascape hanging above the TV. His tone, flat and hard. "Called it insurance."

The familiar word triggered a memory. An echo in Eric's voice, in the Blast from the Past Boutique. Laura threw it in Roy's face. They were arguing about the dam. She said she had insurance. Charley straightened. "She told you what it was."

Roy startled. "What?"

"Eric overheard you talking at the potluck. She boasted about her insurance. Said it was a ghost from the past." Eric's eyes had gleamed, bright with gossip. "All she had to do was whisper, 'He's alive.'"

"A zombie?" Meghan laughed. "You're kidding."

Alex raised a brow. "Sounds more like Frankenstein to me."

Charley looked at the drawing that had lured her to the dock. "Or a reanimated corpse. Do you know what she meant?"

Roy frowned. "She'd just confessed to starting the legend of the lake monster. I was more focused on that. You think she was talking about Shannon's husband?"

Matt said, "I doubt Shannon was worried her husband would crawl his way up out of his grave."

Meghan grinned. "On Halloween, the dead walk among the living. At this point, I'll believe anything."

Alex shot a glance at Charley. "We need proof, not another horror story. And a sketch isn't going to cut it."

Roy reached for Beverley's hand. "Bring Shannon in for questioning."

"I will," Alex said. "For assault, at least. But she has the right to silence. And, as far as murder goes, right now, we can't even place her at the crime scene."

Because she'd given Shannon an alibi. Guilt tightened in Charley's chest. "She's going to try something again." She could feel it in her bones.

"How do you know?" Alex asked.

"Because it's Halloween." And because she'd looked the monster in the eyes. "Think about it. So far, the killer's strategy has been to play on the supernatural element. On Halloween, the boundaries between worlds can be breached."

"Supposedly," Matt said.

She nodded, willing to give him that. "Sure, it depends on what you believe, but it's still a fact that the natural order of life is thrown into chaos. Ghosts and monsters become visible to humankind, even if it's just kids in costumes."

Meghan glanced toward the hearth, where flames licked at seasoned bark. "Halloween originated from the Celtic Samhain — the eve before the New Year. November 1 marked the end of summer and the harvest and the beginning of the dark, cold winter." Even though her voice was low, each word carried the weight of a story in its letters. "Decline in the strength of the sun terrified people, since it brought with it death and hardship. They tried to counter this fear by lighting the Winter Fires. During the celebration, the Celts wore costumes, typically consisting of animal heads and attempted to tell each other's fortunes."

Costumes not meant to terrify but to protect and help to prophesy a brighter future. Charley said, "Shannon will see this as her last chance."

"To blame a legend for her crime?" Alex shook his head. "There's no way I can close this case before Halloween. Getting the warrant alone takes time."

Meghan smiled, a grim curve to her lips. "Forget the scavenger hunt for now."

Alex laughed, a rough sound, half frustrated, half resigned. "Seems like we'll have to. The best thing you can do, Charley, is rest that arm. Focus on the exhibit. That's it."

Turn it all over to him? "I'm fine." She reached for her car keys.

Matt raised a brow. "What do you think you're doing?"

"Driving home."

He tilted his head, eyed her feet. "You really think you can drive in those?"

Charley glanced down at the too-large boating shoes Beverley had lent her. "I can drive in socks." Well enough, anyway.

"I'll take you home," Matt said. "Meghan can bring your Jeep." A question in his eyes that tugged at her heart.

But he'd walked away, had sliced through her with a few words.

"I could," Meghan said, a warning edge to her tone. "It's up to Charley. She might not want to go with you."

Cocoa stood, stretched leisurely, and loped toward Matt. She sat on his feet and panted, a stubborn I'm-not-budging gleam in her eyes.

"Actually," Charley said dryly, "I don't think it is up to me."

So much for picking sides. Cocoa ditched her in a heartbeat to follow the guy who makes chocolate. Typical.

FORTY-FOUR

MATT FIGURED HE deserved the cold shoulder. But the silence was getting to him, anyway. If Charley still hadn't spoken to him by the time his headlights picked up the sign for the Fire Route, he'd know he didn't stand a chance of convincing her to forgive him.

Hot air blew from the vents. Some song played on the radio, turned down too low to catch all the words. Just a few lyrics, here and there. Something about music to soothe the soul. As if it was that simple.

Charley shifted, leaned her head back against the seat rest. "Last time I checked, you said we were a recipe gone wrong."

Matt's fingers tensed on the wheel. This was the make-or-break moment. The kind of moment if you let slip by, you'd never get another chance. So, he'd better not screw it up. "I came up with a few ideas about how to fix it." He felt her turn to look at him but kept his gaze on the tree-lined road unfurling like a tunnel of darkness ahead.

"Fix what?" she asked, her tone guarded and suspicious.

She'd make him say it. "Us." His heart pounded in his ears. Just talking about food, that was all, he reminded himself. "Sometimes, a recipe just needs more spice. Some wine." He slowed at the yellow intersection sign. Hit the turn signal. Easier to focus on the turn than to meet her eyes. "Chocolate."

"Are we talking sweet or savoury here?" A little bit of humour there and just enough to kindle hope in his chest.

A smile tugged at his lips. "Definitely sweet." The tires bounced onto pitted gravel. The Fire Route. He braked, slowed for the caution sign. He caught Charley's gaze with his now and held it for one second.

A flush spread under her skin, no longer that worrying shade of pale. "I am sorry I didn't tell you earlier."

"It would have been nice to have a heads-up." The truck jolted over potholes. Up ahead, the green airplane hangar loomed, deserted. Matt kept his gaze on the road. "I don't handle secrets well."

"The truth is better?" Charley angled the vent toward her, holding her fingers to the heat.

"We could try it, see what happens."

Charley shifted to look at him. "So, let's go after the truth. Let's catch the killer. Unmask the monster, once and for all."

Not the first activity he'd had in mind, but he'd take what he could get. "You think Alex would appreciate the help?"

Charley shrugged. She drummed her fingers on her knee. "Maybe not right away, but in the long run, yeah, I think he would." She glanced over at him. "Are you in or out?"

No question. "I'm in." But — "It would be easier, if I knew what I was getting myself into." Knowing Charley, it could be anything from an elaborate set-up to a full-fledged confrontation.

An electric mix of nerves and excitement crackled off Her. "Shannon will be at the gallery on opening night. If the president of the Cottage Association doesn't make an appearance at a local event to do with the lake, she'll have to answer questions. Deal with gossip." She paused. "And there's no way she'd pass up the chance to see me, after the attack. To find out what I know."

The thought of Charley getting ambushed on the end of a deserted dock did stuff to his insides. A hard knot of worry and rage that could tighten into violence, given the right incentive. "Or she'll try something again."

"That's what I'm counting on."

The strength in Charley's voice, grim and tough as a warrior, didn't do anything to ease the nerves working their way through him. "You're not bait." Even the idea of it had him seeing red.

"It's her last shot. She'll take it."

An image flashed through his mind. Of a gun fired at point-blank. Blood. The hollow ache of loss he'd long ago gotten familiar with. "Or she'll run."

"She won't." No hesitation. No doubt. "Not from here."

She said it like the word — here — carried some magical weight. Maybe it did, but not everyone felt it. And prison could strip magic from just about anything. "Not even to save herself?" Matt asked.

"She won't see it that way. Life for her is better at the lake." Charley looked out the windshield toward the pale glint of the quarter moon shining on water between cottage sidings. "We can use the public space against her. Alex might not be able to use art as evidence, but I can."

Grounds for a murder charge? "What are you going to do? Go up and ask her about it?"

"Better." Charley grinned. "I'll project Shannon's drawing of the marina from the Exquisite Corpse game onto the gallery wall. We might as well go along with Shannon's theme and use a shock effect."

Yeah, but he'd grown up with a crime writer who loved words more than people. And he'd learned enough from Nick Thorn to know that shock wasn't always a good thing. Not when you factored in the other connotations. Trauma. Fright. An explosion. And each one of those synonyms left victims behind. "This could backfire."

"We'll catch her in a lie." Not fearless. There was fear there, but courage despite of it. "Maybe even force her to confess. And get Alex the proof he needs."

All the bright determination in her eyes Matt knew he'd fallen for from day one. "There's no point in trying to talk you out of this, is there?"

She shrugged with a grin. "Don't waste your breath."

"Okay then." He parked in front of her cottage. Hopefully, this would end well. It had to. "Let's bait the monster."

FORTY-FIVE

SHOW TIME.

That was what it felt like. A stage performance, even though the only thing on show should have been her art. Nerves rocketed through Charley.

People were starting to line up outside the gallery. They'd have to let them in soon. Hold off any longer and they'd end up with rioting ghouls.

A fleshy palm pressed against the glass in the door. Eyes peered inside. The faces beyond a blur, backlit by a glare of red light. The sun sinking fast.

"Should we let in the hordes?" Meghan asked. "They're champing at the bit."

Of course, there'd be a turnout for the lake monster. "Is Alex here yet?"

Meghan's carefully applied latex scar creased as she shot Charley a side-eyed glance, full of suspicion. Her red hair intentionally matted. A yellow HB pencil tucked behind one ear, she looked the part of zombie journalist. Infected while reporting on an outbreak. "He's running late."

She'd rather he was here when they confronted Shannon. But she'd do it, with or without him. "We'll wait, two more minutes."

"Kayla isn't who I would have picked as bouncer," Meghan said.

"Cashier," Charley said. Kayla had volunteered and shown up at the gallery early. Then she'd disappeared upstairs with a black garment bag under her arm and hadn't been seen since.

Waiting to make a big entrance was one thing, but this was cutting it close.

Charley pressed a hand to her stomach. The red dress suddenly felt too tight. So much for femme fatale glamour and power. If she could channel the cool elegance of Bacall, the tough attitude of a take-no-prisoners pulp fiction gun moll, she'd be aces.

Charley sucked in a breath and hoped her crimson lipstick hadn't smeared since she applied it.

This was different than the summer pop-up gallery. She wasn't here just to talk art and guide people from painting to painting.

She'd created a set. And there was a lot more riding on this exhibit than getting the funds to repair the building. That was the least of her worries now.

The black screen was set up around the folding table David had borrowed from the school. The wooden stamp with a lakeshore design ready to mark those who paid the entry fee with blood-red ink. The black box open and ready to store cellphones. She'd given Matt the job of collecting visitors' phones, figuring he could handle it. The exhibit was meant to be immersive, to be experienced, not viewed through a screen.

She felt a shift in the air. She didn't have to glance over her shoulder to know it was Matt behind her. She turned to face him.

He stopped an arm's length away and tipped his fedora at her in a suave move Humphrey Bogart could have pulled off in *Dead End*. But it was the trench coat that turned Matt into a private eye from a film noir, down to the hole in the lapel Eric swore was from a bullet, not moths.

"You really think she'll show up?" Matt murmured.

"I'm sure she will." But it was easy to sound confident. Harder to convince herself.

She had to turn on the projector — the one thing everyone had come to see, and she hadn't sent the monster stirring yet, swimming across that back wall. It was still a blank slate.

A horror vacui.

"I'll be right back." Charley stepped around the screen that shielded the exhibit from view.

She walked over black painted floor, through what felt like a pulp fiction cover. The space was suddenly three-dimensional and looked bigger than it really was through the optical illusions she'd worked into the painting.

Thanks to the fancy lighting Sarah had installed, the room was atmospheric but not completely dark. Controlled shadows, Charley reminded herself. Shadows that made the eyes she'd painted seem to blink, the faces contort. Frown.

Charley angled the lamp aimed at the galvanized bucket filled with water. She hesitated just one second before flicking her fingers through the cold liquid, and felt the water close over her head again. She took a deep breath, filling her lungs with oxygen, and blocked out the memory.

She looked up. Silver waves rippled over the ceiling. The reflection created the illusion of being surrounded by water.

And she was wasting time, putting off hitting the power button on the projector that was aimed at the back wall. When she'd first come up with the plan, the idea just a sketch on printer paper, she'd been alive with inspiration. Never once had she thought she'd question the idea. Or regret it.

This had to work. If they could use the exhibit, her lake monster, to get at the truth, to bring a killer to justice, it would turn out all right.

Charley glanced at the portrait she'd painted of Laura on the wall, overlaid with leaf stencils. Hidden from the casual viewer, concealed in the details, she felt the woman's eyes on her, peering out from beneath sponged-on green paint.

Charley pulled the remote out of her pocket and aimed it at the projector, which was suspended from the ceiling. Her thumb hovered over the power button. It was just a looped video.

She pressed it.

The projector hummed, warming up. An image began to form on the back wall, faint at first, then strengthening until it became so clear the monster could have been alive. A convincing illusion of movement.

Charley slid the remote into the pocket of her dress. Her fingers brushed the handkerchief Eric had given her. Still knotted.

When the time was right, she'd press the button on the remote again and the lake monster would dissolve into a different image. A confrontation on the back wall.

The wall shifted and the trees pressed in, looming toward her.

The door leading upstairs opened, the one she'd covered with drop cloth and painted over to maintain the immersive illusion. A small sign swung from the door handle. NO ENTRY. The deadbolt glinted.

A ghost walked out. The pale dress, the splash of blood over the abdomen.

Laura's dress.

Kayla swished the skirt and twirled in front of painted pine trees. She'd powdered a deathly pallor on her skin, the blue lips of a corpse.

"Well, what do you think?" Kayla asked. "I convinced Eric to sell me the dress in the window. It fits like a dream."

But she was wearing a nightmare. The last woman who tried

it on died. Did Kayla know? "I didn't think Eric would part with that one."

Kayla grinned. "Everything's for sale, so long as the price is right. He was happy the dress would be worn by someone on Halloween. What else was he going to do with it come November 1? Store it in a box in the basement?" She latched her arm through Charley's.

The blood-stained sleeve touched her skin, slippery and cool, raising goosebumps. Kayla had given the dress a second life. Maybe that was the best way to think of it. But Charley wondered if Eric knew Kayla would be wearing it to the exhibit tonight.

It really was the night of the living dead.

It seemed like there was too much fake blood everywhere. Too close to the colour of the real thing, with a sheen that implied it might still be wet.

"Charley?" Meghan called from the front. "What's the holdup?"

"I'll lock the door," Kayla offered. "You go ahead."

Charley hesitated a second. But Kayla was right. They had to start letting people in. She undid the clasp on her ribbon bracelet, slid the key off, and passed it to Kayla. "Just don't forget to bring it back to me."

"Go on," Kayla said. "Fill this place with monsters."

The real and the pretend. The large shape swam on the back wall in a slow, graceful circle, then disappeared at the pine trees, only to reappear on the other side. Circling them. "Ready or not, here we go," Charley murmured.

They were in control. They'd limit the numbers. Check everyone coming in.

Charley walked to the front door.

Behind the ticket table, Cocoa sat up, on alert. She'd be safe from the crowd on her bed, beside Meghan's chair.

Charley's fingers closed over the metal handle. She pulled the door open. A cold breeze gusted in, carrying with it the Halloween scent of caramel, fake blood, and the waxy aroma of costume makeup.

People pushed to get inside. Faces, shapes swam around Charley. Unrecognizable. Her heart pounded. Oh, the voices, she knew, but the masks, the makeup made it difficult to tell anyone apart. She searched for details, but even the shapes of bodies were hidden by capes and tentacles. The vampire could have been Thomas, but even that she wasn't sure about.

She caught her breath. It was just the first group. And in between that rumble of sound, of voices, was laughter.

But Shannon wasn't here.

Charley had overestimated her. Or maybe underestimated. Of course, she wouldn't come, not tonight. What had she been thinking? It was too obvious, too risky.

She couldn't keep standing here by the door, scanning faces. Sarah would already be rotating through the exhibit, and she expected Charley to be doing the same. To make sure the night ran smoothly.

People prowled through the exhibit like creatures unearthed from fresh graves. She'd expected there to be more talk, more whispers, than there had been even during the pop-up exhibit, but this silence was thick and eerie. The dead silence found underwater. Broken only by the occasional splash from the bucket or the creak and slide of shoes over boards. A whisper of menace and gore as someone guessed at what had caused the haunted expression in the starved man's eyes.

It was the prickle at the back of Charley's neck that did it. The feeling of being in the line of the predator's gaze.

Despite the warning tingle, she turned to face it.

Her gaze met Shannon's. The stare was the same as the one

she'd seen peering out from behind rubber gills. But this time, Shannon wasn't wearing a mask. Just makeup. Smoky and shaded to alter the shape of her features, just enough to turn the woman into someone else. Bruises under the eyes. Eyebrows no longer arched but rounded, penciled on in a vintage line. Cheeks softer, rounded, and less defined.

A wig. The auburn bob with bangs.

Her disguise was good enough to get her through the door and all the way inside before anyone noticed. Or maybe, it was the regal air that deceived. The confidence she wore like a gown. A garment she'd slipped into, the same way she put on the black kaftan.

Shannon raised blood-red fingernails to her mouth and blew a kiss. Waggled her fingers. And disappeared.

Lost in the crowd.

But not for long. Charley followed her.

MATT CRANED HIS neck, trying to catch a glimpse of Charley's red dress in the crowd. He should have been grateful for the turnout, but an empty room would have been a hell of a lot easier to manage.

Tonight was no longer about art, though it should have been. It wasn't about the building they were trying to repair. It was about catching a killer. Restoring justice.

Whatever the hell that meant these days.

And the cop wasn't here.

That set Matt on edge more than he liked to admit. But he wasn't foolish enough to think they could drag Shannon in for questioning without some kind of backup from law enforcement.

What did they have? A tough-as-nails artist. A chocolate Lab, fierce but no hell-hound. A reporter.

Courage wasn't going to cut it.

What if Shannon didn't show? Then they would have wasted time and energy when they should have been focused on raising funds.

Because, without the funds, the permanent gallery was just a wish. And Charley would leave.

And he'd have to let her go.

Standing here, in that building, Matt knew just how fast those chances came and went.

Matt wrangled another smart phone away from a visitor. "I'm going to go check on Charley."

Meghan shoved the stamp over to him, along with the wet red ink pad. "If 'check' is code for 'flirt,' you can scrap that idea and fast. Charley needs you manning the door, not distracting her while she's working. Save it for later." She tallied change. "You can't cop out on us after the first rush."

"First?" Kayla held out the debit machine for the next person. "It's not over yet."

Meghan nodded. "We need you here. Not mooning after her."

Matt frowned. "I don't moon."

"Mmm-hmm. You just stamped that man's hand twice."

Shit, he had. "Did Alex say when he'd be here?"

"Soon as he can. Why?" Meghan swivelled in her seat and eyed him, with a sharp look that made him uneasy. "First Charley asked me that, now you. What's going on?"

Matt glanced over his shoulder again, and this time, he spotted her. Charley glanced back, just once, zeroing in past the people between them, straight at him. And nodded.

Shannon was here.

He watched Charley turn and disappear into the crowd.

Matt stamped another blood-stained hand. "Can't hurt to have a cop around with all the killers on the loose." And he was pretty sure Charley had just gone off after one on her own. What the hell was he still doing here? Screw it. "Hold the fort," he told Kayla.

Meghan narrowed her eyes at him. "Walk and you'll regret it, I can promise you that."

Yeah, he probably would. But sometimes, you had to act on instinct and suffer the consequences. "I'll be back." Matt pushed his way through the crowd.

A WALL OF people blocked Charley's way, and no one was moving. They stood, turning on the spot, looking at the lake monster or up at the ceiling, which was what she'd wanted, but not what she needed right now.

A six-year-old water lily strolled past, holding a witch's hand.

Charley dodged around the next person, nearly stepping on someone else's foot. "Sorry." But she didn't pause, pushed on. Ghouls and vampires and peeling skin. A horseman cradling his own head in his arms.

A shimmer of leaves caught her eye. Sponged foliage reflected the light with a gleam of copper and gold. The door to the stairs closed on a waft of fabric.

The sleeve of a black kaftan.

But Kayla had locked the door, hadn't she?

Charley touched her wrist. Kayla still had the key.

The exhibit was supposed to be contained to one room. They'd made that clear. The bathroom at the back of the gallery was the only other space open to the public.

She'd intentionally made the painting on that side of the room less interesting to deter people from lingering so the focus would be directed toward the projection, the monster.

That mocking wave Shannon had aimed her way had been too confident. Of course she'd come with a plan. The same way they had.

There was art stored upstairs. Paintings. Her own, mostly, and some early donations to the permanent gallery.

In Charley's pocket, the remote control bumped heavily against her leg. Shannon didn't have to be in the room when she switched to the image. The commotion might be enough to catch her attention, draw her out. But if she waited, it might be too late.

Charley slid her hand in her pocket. Her fingers closed over the plastic rectangle. She ran her thumb over the buttons, searching, feeling for the triangular skip button that would move to the second file on the drive. Would it be enough to get a confession?

Shock effect. It would work.

Charley pressed the button. Held her breath.

The world went black.

Fear caught her in the back of the knees. Her head went light. People moved around her, pushing. Cursing. A senseless crush of motion.

Raw, primal fear slammed her heart against her ribs.

Broken neon lines floated in the darkness. An escape route. The glow-in-the-dark tape, marking the path to the exit. Focus on that. She took a deeper breath, slower. Don't panic. Not yet. Not now.

The lights were out. The projector too. A power outage?

No. The fuse box was behind the door she'd seen closing seconds before the lights cut out. This was Shannon's plan.

Cold sweat slithered down Charley's spine. Murky shapes floated, impossible to pick apart.

How did Shannon get the key from Kayla? Unless the door wasn't locked.

Someone shoved past Charley, bumping her bruised shoulder.

She had to control the panic. Shut it down before someone got hurt.

"Everyone, please stay calm," Charley called. But her voice

wasn't loud enough to carry through the room. She could have been shouting into a black hole, asking people to stay calm when fear snaked through her and all she wanted to do was run for the door. Get outside into a darkness that wasn't as thick as this.

Behind her, she felt the painted faces. The layers of paint. The menacing sneer of bared teeth that seemed less dangerous than these figures moving around her, growing fangs as she stared.

A hot hand clamped around her wrist, slick with sweat, fingers digging in where the red ribbon, the key, should have been.

Charley shook off the hold. Chest tight, her breath shortened into gasps. She backed against the wall. Leaned there for a second, trembling. Safe. But she couldn't stay here.

Charley forced her way forward one step at a time. She touched the wall, felt the paintbrush strokes. The texture eased the panic. She ran her fingers along the wall, using the paint to guide her through the dark.

Her fingers touched a hinge, a crack. The door.

She fumbled over the wooden panels, searching, her breath loud in her ears. People cleared out behind her, leaving.

Charley's palm brushed metal.

She caught hold of the handle and turned.

It was darker in the small space behind the door. Hazy spots flared across her vision, turning into faces, shifting shadows. Panic gripped her chest, stronger than before.

Run.

She stepped inside.

A scream cut through the dark, followed by a sharp, familiar bark.

FORTY-SIX

AT THE SCREAM, Matt's blood ran cold. Christ, it was dark. And he'd left his phone in the box on the front table, along with everyone else's.

Charley was out there, somewhere. With Shannon.

But it wasn't Charley's voice. That scream belonged to someone else. He held on to that.

People pushed past him, heading the opposite direction, following the path to the exit.

"Did you hear thunder?" a man nearby asked.

"No. Could be a derecho," a woman replied, dread in her voice. "Last time, we lost Hydro One for days. I can't go through that again."

A power outage? No. If there was a storm, it was inside the gallery.

Closing in on Charley.

It was useless. Matt paused, fighting to keep calm. He couldn't see a thing. Too many voices, too much commotion to tell one from the other.

He had to find Charley.

Or Shannon.

Matt's fists balled on a surge of anger. Hot enough, potent enough to sear away reason.

If only he had a weapon. Hell, a shotgun even.

Matt took a shaky breath. He'd wondered what it took, to make a man turn a gun on someone. Now, he knew.

He'd pull the trigger.

CHARLEY SMELLED PERFUME, the same smouldering, wild fragrance of crackling fires and spicy tonka beans she'd smelled in Shannon's apartment. "It's over."

"Not by a long shot." The voice came from above, bouncing off the walls. No more than three steps up at most, but it gave the woman an advantage Charley was only too aware of.

"I know you killed Laura." Charley lifted her hand and felt for the door frame, trying to orient herself. "There's no way out of this."

Shannon laughed, the sound full of joy. "Your acting skills need work. Improv isn't your strong suit."

Charley fought the nerves tearing at her. Swallowed. Fought to keep her voice steady. Were the walls closing in? "You mean I should have worked with the cues you gave me? It was lucky, wasn't it? That I saw your window projection."

A beat went by. Charley wished she could see the woman's face.

"I have no idea what you're talking about." Cool bravado. A line rehearsed to the bone and stripped of emotion.

"You faked your own alibi." Charley swallowed, her mouth dry. "An illusion of innocence we all believed. You used the fake newsletter to lure Laura to the lake. You disguised yourself as a lake monster and attacked her. You left her for dead" — she kept going, the words tumbling out — "but she didn't drown. She regained consciousness and came here. That must have been a shock for you, when her body was found at the marina. After, you tried your best to convince us there really was a monster, some evil force at work." The dark pooled in shades of grey and black, clotting like blood the harder she stared.

"That's a nice story." The words hissed down the stairs. "You make that up on the spot?"

As if she could. "I won't let you get away with this." The space was only a few square feet, but it seemed endless. Cavernous.

"You're a step too late." A pause fell. The beat drawn out for effect. "I already have." The whisper was loud enough to fill a dressing room.

How could she get through to her? Reach the heart of the woman who had looked with such longing at the lake. "Fantasy can be sweet as sugar, but you can only survive on it for so long."

A step creaked. "It hasn't rotted my teeth yet."

"I was thinking of your heart."

Shannon chuckled, a sudden rasp of sound that was now much closer. "It's been a long time since anyone worried about my heart."

Charley stepped back, bumping into the edge of the door frame. Rough wood snagged on the silky fabric of the dress, catching threads. Open space, the exhibit, behind her. "You're not a monster —"

"Just misunderstood?" Shannon drawled.

"You did what you had to do. Laura deserved it." Even as she said it, she saw Laura's starved eyes gazing out of the television screen and regretted it.

"Nice try." The whisper was soft and low and close enough for her to smell the mint on Shannon's breath. "But you won't trick me into confessing."

She had to get to the power switch panel. If she could flip the fuse back on, there'd be light. Her heart thudded loud in her ears. "You found the fox carcass on Sugarbush Road. Moved the skull to the beach. Left the tracks, to make it look like a monster really existed."

"Oh, sweetheart." There was pity in her tone now. "It does."

"Yeah," Charley shot back. "I'm looking at it."

"But you can't really see anything in the dark, can you?"

Panic climbed up her throat. Charley forced it back. "You got carried away. Added one too many elements to the design. The witch's ladder was a mistake."

"Are you sure?" The question plaintive in the dark. "Most people have no idea they've been cursed until it's too late."

Was that movement? A rustle of fabric? "There's no such thing as black magic."

"Just evil intentions?"

She was pretty sure Shannon had more than enough of those. "It seemed like you had those when you attacked me at the marina."

"A figment of your imagination." An arch tone, like this was nothing more than good-natured banter. "It's amazing what the mind can conjure."

"Or a costume designer."

Shannon laughed but now it sounded forced. "You'll never be able to prove it."

"You handed me the evidence. Your Exquisite Corpse." Charley inched forward, slowly moved her arm, hoping Shannon was as blind as she was. She groped along the wall for the metal door of the power switch panel. "I mean, a lake monster, really? I took a photograph of your sketch. Matt's seen it. Alex, too. Your time is almost up. There's no way you can talk your way out of this. You won't get away with murder." If she could get the power going again, the proof would be projected on the wall.

Charley fumbled with the latch, got it open. The metal hinges shrieked.

Shannon slapped a hand at the wall, slamming the panel shut. "I might as well go for a twofer, then. In for a penny, in for a pound."

The door to the gallery closed with a thud of wood. The *chink* of the deadbolt hitting home.

Shannon said, "You're not giving the costume designer enough credit." Her voice rose, tight with anger. "I create the characters. I make the roles what they are. I decide how the characters move, how they breathe. How they fight." Something glinted in the darkness. A flash of something sharp. "Who lives and who dies."

A knife? Charley's heart lurched.

Steel flashed. A curve. The shape of a handle.

Scissors.

No. Fabric shears.

It wasn't a costume, not some prop. Charley's blood ran cold.

"Thank you for following me," Shannon said.

So close, Charley felt the swish of fabric brush her skirt.

She was trapped, alone with a killer, her back to the wall.

FORTY-SEVEN

MATT GROPED FOR the door handle.

Locked. Bolted from the inside.

He slapped his hand on wood. The thud of his fist deadened by the drop cloth, the paint. "I know you're in there." But it was Charley who replied.

"Kayla has the key."

The strain in her voice, the controlled edge to it, sent terror swimming through Matt. Something dark and primal and uncontrollable.

"You're not alone." But he didn't need her to say it. He knew it down to the marrow of his bones.

He heard a hiss. A command, sharp and fast and too quiet for him to catch.

"I've got this," Charley said, stubborn and hell bent on sending him away.

"Damn it." Matt banged his fist on the door, the barrier between them. "Shannon, if you hurt her, you'll wish you'd drowned, you hear me?"

Silence. A deep, unsettling silence that raised the hairs on his arms. Matt stood there and listened, though what he thought he'd do, he had no idea. Was a witness enough to stop Shannon from doing something stupid? He couldn't bet on it. Not with these stakes.

He had to get in there. Before Shannon forced Charley up the stairs, closer to the window and that sharp, steep drop he knew could kill.

He couldn't lose her. Couldn't hear someone tell him he'd lost her in that same practiced, compassionate tone he'd heard before.

But to get the door open, he'd have to leave her. It was the only way.

Could he find Kayla in time?

Matt braced his hands on the door, fighting the urge to tell Charley he'd be back in time. To make promises he might not be able to keep.

He turned his back on the door and faced the dark with murder on his mind.

FORTY-EIGHT

CHARLEY WAS ON her own in a small, pitch-black room, with only a remote control in her pocket. Her best shot was to talk her way out of this. But she was within arm's reach of the fuse box and that gave her an advantage. "You were the only one of us strong enough to do something about Laura."

"Laura drowned." Shannon's voice echoed off the walls, hard to pinpoint. "It was bad luck. Karma. Not murder."

Is that what Shannon told herself, when she couldn't sleep at night? But there'd been a pause, long enough to make Charley think she'd hit the mark. "You and I both know there's no lake monster."

"I've seen it with my own eyes."

Her conviction had a shiver running down Charley's spine. But it wasn't Shannon's description of the lake monster that rose in her mind. It was Norval Morrisseau's horned water lynx in earth-toned acrylic and brown kraft paper she saw, imprinted clearly on the murky shadows splotched across her vision. The spirit-being that represented the dualities of good and evil. Grandpa's voice echoed loud over the beat of her heart. *The monster exists. This story really did happen.* Charley took a breath. "Inspiration for the perfect crime?"

"No. Laura has you to thank for that."

The words snaked around her, bringing back the image of accusation in Laura's eyes. *This is your fault.* Charley fought to block it out. To stop her imagination from sketching faces on the air.

But maybe those weren't Laura's eyes she saw in the dark. What if that flash of white around an iris was real? Not an illusion at all.

She focused, willing her vision to adjust.

A dim outline took form. The curve of a face.

A shift in the air, a rustle of fabric. Movement, a rush of it, coming at her.

Charley ducked and dived, tripping on the stairs.

Thud. Something hit the drywall. The scrape of a blade. Plaster rained on the floor.

Charley's stomach rolled.

"What did I tell you about playing the hero?" Shannon asked. "It doesn't end well."

Charley bit her lip and clambered to her feet, silently as she could. If anything gave her away, it would be her heart, drumming against her ribs. She backed up the steps. If she made it all the way to the top of the stairs, she'd have more space to run, more space to hide.

She carefully backed her way up, feeling around for the next step, hands braced on the wall on either side for balance. She swallowed hard.

Thunk. The blade hit again. In, then out. Dust rained on the floor.

"The actor who is dead needs to stay dead," Shannon said, a serrated edge to her tone. The letters were bitten off, ground through clenched teeth. "Solid stage advice. But some people can't take direction."

Who hadn't stayed dead? Laura came back but who else? "Like your husband?"

"Arhaan?" A startled pause fell. Then, sharper, "He's dead to me."

"To you." And maybe that was the key. "But not to the rest of the world?" She stumbled on, feeling for the truth, each word a careful step forward, even as she inched backward up the steps. "Laura knew, didn't she? She figured it out. He's alive." All Laura had to do to threaten Shannon was whisper, "He's alive." Suddenly, a reanimated corpse no longer seemed like fiction. What if her husband hadn't died? "Let's pretend that" could become an incantation. Black magic, and maybe even a curse.

For one long moment, all Charley heard was the pant of shallow breath. Like that of a trapped creature.

"Don't turn Laura into Sherlock Holmes," Shannon snapped. "She recognized him in a photo in my store because he sold her fucking house."

The real estate agent? Had he been the mystery man in the photograph of a kiss in the St. Lawrence Market? "Laura was going to use that knowledge to destroy your fantasy."

"Tear down the whole damn canvas sky I worked so hard to create."

"Once Laura figured it out," Charley guessed, "she wouldn't let it go. She used it against you, to get the support of the Cottage Association."

"She did that to a lot of people. Weaponized secrets." Shannon raised her chin. "Left psychological bombs through my shop for me to find. Images she thought could break me. I burned them."

Remains of a bonfire, mildewed from rain. Ripped magazines in the ashes she'd found at the dam. Charley remembered the smell of mouldering paper. The images of camera angles that revealed the technique behind the movie magic. Broken illusions. A threat. "But if you gave your support to Laura's proposal, you knew it could tip the scales. And change everything. Destroy that perfect life you worked so hard to create." She took one more step backward. Close to the top now.

"You start to feel safe, here." She could have been sitting on a dock, not standing in a blacked-out gallery, in an exhibit of pulp horror. "You forget that the rest of the world exists until it walks through your door."

Along with the fear. The heartache. "So, Laura had to die."

"The same way you will." Something snapped. The last shred of control, or maybe sanity. "We're well into act five. The scene is set." Drama as a shield of armour. "A good thespian always follows the words of the Bard. So, listen up. This line's yours. 'If I must die, I will encounter darkness as a bride, And hug it in mine arms.' Come closer, dear."

Yeah, right.

Almost there.

The step, old and warped, creaked beneath her heel. Charley froze.

Darkness leapt at her. A flurry of motion, a rush of movement and perfume, rich as incense.

Charley scrambled backwards, fell to the floor. The scissors struck the floorboard beside her head. Charley rolled. Her dress caught on something, tore at the hem.

Then there was light. Bright and blinding.

Charley blinked away spots. And saw the eight-inch blades, the tapered tips coming at her.

She grabbed Shannon's arm with both hands, fought to keep the shears from plunging. Her bruised shoulder rammed against the hard floor. The long, flat blades snapped shut inches away from her eyes. A brown-red thread clung to the cutting edge.

Shannon had hooked her thumb through the small handle, her other fingers through the longer one. In complete control.

Charley's muscles burned, trapped in a lethal tug-of-war.

The human hand was full of nerve endings. Where was the

pressure point? But move one second too slow and the shears would plunge.

"Have you ever stabbed anyone?" Charley gasped. "It's worse than cutting meat. Bloody."

"I'm not afraid of getting my hands dirty. I want to live my life," Shannon ground out. The shears moved an inch closer. "My life was perfect. All they ever had to do was stay dead."

Boots pounded up the steps.

"Perfect doesn't exist." Charley gritted her teeth and twisted to the side. She let go with one hand. The blades shot forward, slamming into the floor. The tip glanced off wood.

Charley grabbed Shannon's hand and dug her thumb into the valley between thumb and index finger.

Shannon sucked in a breath on a gasp of pain. Her fingers flexed, opened. The shears fell to the floor, clattering beside Charley's head.

Charley reached for them, fingers scraping over uneven floorboards. She caught hold of the handle and threw the scissors to the side just as the door opened. But it was Cocoa who pushed through first.

"No!" Shannon dragged a hand over her mouth. Her wig lay on the floor. Her hair was slicked close to her skull. An eyebrow was smudged in a streak of brown across her temple. Skin was visible through the blended contours changing the shape of her face.

She turned, searching, crawling. And stopped short.

Matt stood in the doorway, the shears in his hand. His knuckles were white as he stared down at the tapered blades.

Charley's heart thudded in her chest. She'd never seen that expression on his face before. Cold and grim. And deadly.

Matt glanced up. "It all depends on who's holding the weapon, doesn't it?"

"You wouldn't," Shannon said. But her voice was shaking.

He took a step closer and raised the shears to the base of the woman's throat.

Charley froze. This was a threat he'd never act on. She knew him. But, still, her breath came in jagged gasps.

"No." Matt lowered the shears. The blade pointed at the floor. "I wouldn't."

"Show's over." Charley stood on unsteady legs, hoped her knees would hold. "You might want to work on your confession."

Shannon lifted her chin, graceful as a performer called to take her final bow. "Innocent until proven guilty."

"Don't worry about that," Matt said. "We'll prove it."

But the power was back on. "Take a closer look in the gallery as you walk out," Charley said. "The proof is on the wall. One last projection."

"Your monster?" Shannon scoffed.

"Not mine. Yours. You'd better face it." Charley gestured toward the stairs. "After you."

"That's just typical," Shannon sneered. "The need to wrap things up, find a reason for things that can't be explained."

Charley stood in the room she'd once filled with art and would again. Matt at her side. "You're right," she said. "The 'shudder pulp' formula of horror stories had one rule: All supernatural events had to be explained away in the end as nothing more than tricks played by the villain to cover her tracks. And that's exactly what they were. Tricks. Played by you. The force behind it all. But you forgot one thing." She waited until Shannon looked at her. "If you play the role of killer, you have to see it through to the end. Right up to the moment the handcuffs snap on."

"Through to the trial," Matt added.

"And then to prison," Charley said. "Maximum security

doesn't go in for mint tea."

Shannon adjusted her kaftan, smoothing the dusty fabric with fingers that trembled. "The two-bit act is cute, but it's not going to convince anyone." She turned and sailed down the steps.

Charley followed, Matt close behind her. There was no way Shannon could escape. Not now.

Shannon crossed the threshold into the exhibit and stopped short. She choked on a laugh, on strangled shock. "This is it? Your proof?" She walked forward until she rested her hands on the galvanized metal bucket and looked up at her own drawing. The Creature from the Black Lagoon. The webbed feet of the lake monster — her Exquisite Corpse — projected on the gallery wall. "A sketch?"

"You were wrong, Shannon," Charley said. The projector hummed. Shannon's expression reflected in the surface of the water. Lake water. "There's always a seam. Why did you lie, tell everyone your husband died?"

"What was I supposed to do? Admit he was sleeping with a twenty-two-year-old?" Her fingers tightened on the steel rim, sending ripples shuddering through the water. "That he left me because I wasn't good enough? Better a grieving widow than a fool." She raised her chin. "I sent him to hell. Eternal purgatory every time I closed my eyes." Her features softened. "And I was happy again," she whispered.

Movement on the other side of the room caught Charley's eye. Alex. She shook her head, hoped he'd pick up on her meaning and wait. Just give her one more minute. "Happy living a lie."

Shannon glanced at her. "A fantasy," she said simply. "I had my life back. A better life. One that was my own. I created it. And erased what he did."

"Lie once," Matt said, his voice grim, "and you have to do it again."

"We all play pretend." Shannon straightened. "I can tell at a glance what your secret desires are just from the costumes you chose to wear tonight. Who you wish you were. Look at you." She raked her gaze over them.

Charley fought the urge to cross her arms over the red dress. "What is that supposed to mean?"

"The red dress." Shannon gestured at her. "It's one of the most reliable cards in a costumer's hands, for a reason. It's a weapon. A red dress is worn for one purpose only." She stepped forward, closer. Powerful again. "To seduce and destroy. Put one on and you're drawing on tropes. The colour, the fit, says *look at me*." As though standing at a sewing table, scissors in her hand. Snipping threads. "It's as flashy as a warning sign. The woman in the red dress has her own agenda. And she'll betray those closest to her to achieve it. Beware, Matt." Shannon glanced at him. "She'll sacrifice you in a heartbeat to chase a dream."

Guilt pierced Charley's skin, sharp as a sewing needle. "I've got all I want right here."

"Keep telling yourself that, honey." Shannon smiled. "A costume is more revealing than you think."

Charley's pulse quickened, her heart beating against her ribs. She fought the urge to glance at Matt. "And you chose to hide behind a mask. Of a monster."

Shannon shrugged. "We all transform ourselves every day. Buy a dream, not an outfit. Wear red lipstick, buy a new shirt, all to get a new and improved you for the low, low price of —"

"Your soul?" Charley cut in. "You killed, Shannon, and you were going to do it again today."

"To protect my life."

Matt shook his head. "A life that doesn't exist."

"It was real to me." Shannon spread her hands wide. "And to everyone else."

It was true. She hadn't seen through it. "I used to look at you and see a creative, successful businesswoman. Someone passionate and determined who wanted to live her life on her own terms. But that was just a costume."

"All of us have armour we hide behind."

Matt stepped closer to Charley, laced his fingers through hers. Squeezed. "But the people we care about most see past those defences. Get around them."

Shannon moved to the other side of the bucket, her steps sharp and nervy. The projection flickered across her black kaftan. "And stab you in the back."

"Sometimes," Matt agreed. The truth was raw in his words. "But not always."

"You lied," Charley said, "and you killed, and for what?"

Shannon spread her arms, taking in the room. The painted shoreline. "The lake." She pointed a finger at her heart. "I saved it."

"But" — Alex stepped forward, peeling away from the wall like a portrait suddenly turned three-dimensional — "you'll be spending the rest of your life staring at prison cell walls."

"Wearing orange," Meghan added, close behind him.

Charley held Matt's hand tight. "Remembering what it sounded like to hear a loon call for its mate across the water. Wishing you hadn't used the lake monster to commit murder."

FORTY-NINE

IT WAS HARD to slouch in a wrought-iron chair, but Charley did her best. The metal was chilly and starting to numb her back through the thick sweatshirt. She slid lower and hoped the chrysanthemums were still in full enough bloom to hide her. She picked up the heavy camera resting on her open sketchbook. It was a Canon Sure Shot that had collected dust on the cottage shelf since the '90s, but she wasn't planning on developing the film. Just using the zoom lens to spy.

She peered through the viewfinder and focused on the warped boards of the dock, up the back of the white Adirondack chair — Meghan's? No, Alex's. She moved further to the right. Of course Meghan took the chair closer to land, always prepared to dash after a hot lead.

There. Charley adjusted the lens, zeroing in on the red enamel mug on the broad armrest.

A cold, wet nose jostled her elbow and the view shot to the water. To a dark, brown, sinuous shape. A forked tongue that tasted the air. Faint reddish horizontal banding marked its back, saddle shaped. The scales were rough and keeled. Broad ripples rolled out, a wake of waves.

How big? It couldn't possibly be —

She zoomed out, widening the frame to take in the shoreline. A tangled structure of mud, tree limbs, and brushwood. A beaver's bank den. Cattail.

Nothing but still water.

She fought back a shudder and lowered the camera. Just a water snake. Probably.

She bent and rubbed Cocoa's ears. "We'll play in a second," she murmured. "But you have to be patient. He's going to propose soon." Hopefully.

The whoosh of the sliding door opening jolted Charley upright. Someone was in the house.

Cocoa turned and bounded toward the door, not snarling but wagging her tail.

Matt stepped outside, munching a strip of bacon, one hand hidden behind his back. "Hey, I wondered where you'd —"

"Shh," Charley whispered. Finger to her lips, she waved him over.

Matt took the chair beside hers and slouched down, copying her pose, his expression more than a little amused. "What are you doing?" he murmured, voice pitched low.

Cocoa put her paw on his arm and stared.

"Uh-uh. This is my bacon." He held the strip higher.

"Which you stole," Charley pointed out.

He levelled a glance at her. "Whose side are you on?"

"I call it how I see it." She aimed the camera at the dock again, focusing on the cup, the still-ring-free hand. She heard the crunch of canine teeth biting into crispy bacon. "You caved fast."

"I chose to share," Matt corrected.

"And save your skin."

"That too." He nodded at the camera. "Subtle."

"Thank you." Cellophane crinkled and something snapped. Something that sounded a lot like chocolate. Charley glanced down at the bar of milk chocolate Matt held. "What's this?"

"A new flavour." A grin tugged at the corner of his mouth.

Nervous for him, her pulse quickened. What would this one be like? "I get to taste it?"

"Unless it'll distract you," he teased.

As if. "I can multi-task."

Matt broke off a piece of chocolate and passed it to her. An intensity in his expression she hadn't seen for months. The light of inspiration she'd felt often enough to recognize in someone else when she saw it.

The square melted on her tongue. Rich, earthy, single-origin chocolate followed by the kick of espresso, the warmth of cinnamon. Delicious and addictive. Her tastebuds tingled. "I'm not sure," Charley said slowly. "I might have to try another piece."

His lips twitched. "That good, huh?"

Good didn't come close to describing it. Even the lake foam toffee couldn't compare. "You're leaving that bar here, right?"

"I was thinking about it." Matt shifted in the wrought-iron chair, stretching his legs out. "It's made with the Coffee Nook's Colombian roast." The tone, too casual, caught her attention.

Charley shot him a glance. Warmth spread through her as she put together the pieces. "A latté with extra cinnamon?" The one he'd offered to buy her the day they met.

He shot her a crinkly-eyed, knee-jerking grin. "Close enough to count?"

She shook her head, heart doing a flip in her chest. "Better."

"Turns out, the best things in life are bitter and sweet."

"Like chocolate." Or love and pain.

"Can't have one without the other." He kept his gaze on hers. "I've been collecting recipes with local flavours." He hesitated. "Typing them up."

He was playing it down, but she could tell that this mattered. "A cookbook?" She felt a smile spread across her face.

"Been thinking about it. Working on it. But I'm missing one

recipe. I can't remember the ingredients and it's driving me crazy. So" — he took a breath — "I'm going to ask him for it."

No need to ask who Matt meant. She knew. "You're going to talk to Jeffrey."

"Visit him. This afternoon." Nerves there and so much more. A range of emotions she'd never be able to catch with one painting.

"He'll like that," she said.

A gust of wind riffled the pages of her sketchbook.

Matt leaned forward and held the page down. "That's Laura."

The sketches were rough. Vertical portraits captured the woman's energy — not the ragged determination of the younger girl. The facial expression wasn't quite right though, not yet. Charley wanted to do justice to the woman's sharp wit. The final composition would be active. Alive. Laura's eyes would crinkle, her gaze directed at the viewer, but this time filled with joy.

The way it should have been. "I thought I'd do a portrait of Laura for Roy and Beverley. One that shows Laura the way she would want to be remembered." She owed it to her to do that.

"They'll love it. Charley —"

A commotion on the dock caught her eye. She picked up the camera again and focused in on Meghan bending down on one knee. Alex leapt to his feet, gesturing with a coffee cup. Arguing.

Charley bit back a laugh. That figured. "Meghan beat him to it."

"What about the scavenger hunt?"

Charley brushed that aside with a wave of her hand. "Alex settled on caffeine and words. A simple 'will you marry me' written in the bottom of her coffee cup."

"Nice move." Matt nodded.

"Except Meghan jumped the gun before she finished her coffee." Meghan always was better at asking questions than answering them. Charley picked up the camera, focused in on her sister's face, as she looked up at Alex. He reached into his pocket.

"Don't drop the ring in the water," Charley muttered.

Alex slid the ring on Meghan's finger. The sunlight gleaming off gold and pearls couldn't match the dazzling joy on her face.

Maybe it was contagious, because bright bubbles of happiness fizzed inside Charley, too. "Finally."

"Congrats," Matt said. "You've got yourself a cop as a brother-in-law."

"I guess I do." That would take some getting used to. Dad would weigh the pros and cons of that like the organs of a murder victim, perform an emotional autopsy with his usual scientific precision. But Alex would have to handle that on his own.

When the kissing started on the dock, Charley lowered the camera, fast.

Cocoa bounded toward the leaf-lined shore, turning excited loops around the couple.

"So," Matt said. "On a scale of one to ten, how would you rate opening night?"

She thought about that. "You know, all things considered, I'd chalk the Shudder Pulp exhibit up to a success. Good turnout." She ticked the points off on her fingers. "Didn't die. Caught a murderer."

"You shaved a couple years off my life at the gallery." Matt watched the dock, where Alex lifted Meghan in his arms and spun her in dizzying circles. Laughter echoed, bouncing off the water. "I figure you owe me an apology for that."

Hold on. "Me?" Charley raised her eyebrows, annoyance simmering. "You were ready to give up on us."

"Biggest mistake I've ever made," Matt admitted. "But I already paid my dues. I followed you to hell and back. And let you take on a murderer on your own."

"Let me?" Charley felt her blood start to boil. "I hate to break it to you, but you didn't have much of a choice."

He shifted, cupped her face in his hands. "And that almost killed me." He brushed a thumb over her cheekbone, his touch impossibly gentle. "I had to stand on the other side of a locked door and hope you made it back out to me alive." His thumb skimmed across her skin, dissolving irritation like fog.

She'd never forget the panic she heard in his voice. "Well, you were an okay Bogie to my Bacall."

He grinned. "Best one you're going to find around here."

As if she'd even wish for anyone else. "There's just one thing."

"What's that?"

Charley stood, slid onto his lap, wrapped her arms around him. "You don't have to act with me." The lines came as naturally as the Bacall look — a better fit than the red dress. Chin down, eyes glancing up. Husky voiced, she quoted, "You don't have to say or do anything. All you have to do is trust me."

Matt's arms tightened around her. "Took me a while to figure that one out, didn't it?"

She smiled. "You got there in the end." Which gave her the perfect cue. "If you need me, all you have to do is whistle. You know how to whistle, don't you?"

He whistled, long and low.

Matt slid his hand up the back of her neck, tangling his fingers in her hair. "From now on, let's do the sleuthing together."

So long as the only mystery they had to solve was how to stay warm through the long, cold winter.

ACKNOWLEDGEMENTS

This book is about the power of stories or, more precisely, about the power imagination has to make something from nothing. Imagination can fill a lake with monsters, turn a building into a work of art, and transform raw ingredients into a bar of chocolate.

I have to thank chocolatier Angela Roest for explaining to me the magic and the risk involved in making sponge toffee. Thank you to my fellow crime writers Tessa Wegert and Mindy Quigley for reading this manuscript and championing Charley and co. And thank you to my family for valuing creativity.

In *Shudder Pulp*, Charley wants to create a multi-sensory exhibit that enables visitors to walk through a pulp novel. When art is shown in a gallery, a piece takes on a life of its own. An immersive art installation takes this to another extreme, requiring people to interact with the display. It's through this interaction that paint becomes art.

A story is something made from nothing, but it's only brought to life by you, the reader. I'm so lucky that, thanks to the team at Cormorant Books, I get to share my vision of cottage country with you. I hope you've enjoyed your escape to the lake.

We acknowledge the sacred land on which Cormorant Books operates. It has been a site of human activity for 15,000 years. This land is the territory of the Huron-Wendat and Petun First Nations, the Seneca, and most recently, the Mississaugas of the Credit River. The territory was the subject of the Dish With One Spoon Wampum Belt Covenant, an agreement between the Iroquois Confederacy and Confederacy of the Ojibway and allied nations to peaceably share and steward the resources around the Great Lakes. Today, the meeting place of Toronto is still home to many Indigenous people from across Turtle Island. We are grateful to have the opportunity to work in the community, on this territory.

We are also mindful of broken covenants and the need to strive to make right with all our relations.